ON THE EIFFEL TOWER

Dark anger burned in Mustafa Salem el-Nouty's face as he aimed at the American's head and kicked. White-hot bolts of pain shot through Nat's head as it smacked onto the concrete platform of the tower.

"Stop! Police!" an old policeman yelled as he pulled out his revolver.

El-Nouty whirled away from Nat and squeezed off three quick rounds into the gendarme. The platform reverberated with the terror of people screaming and diving for cover.

Nat saw his shoulder bag—and the MAC-11 inside it—some 10 yards away. Too far. He sprang at el-Nouty, and landed a solid kick that catapulted the handgun from the Libyan's hand and sent it flying over the guardrail. By this time they heard whistles from below; other policemen had been summoned by the gunshots.

Nat kicked, but el-Nouty had anticipated the thrust, and responded with a block that caught Nat's leg and threw him on the pavement. With Nat down, el-Nouty gave him a swift kick to the head, and this time Nat remained motionless.

Time was critical: the police were coming. El-Nouty restrained himself from finishing off Nat. He'd leave that to the police.

Also by Lewis Perdue:

THE DELPHI BETRAYAL

LEWIS PERDUE

QUEENS GATE RECKONING

PINNACLE BOOKS   NEW YORK

QUEENS GATE RECKONING

Copyright © 1982 by W. Lewis Perdue

An original Pinnacle Books edition, published for the first time anywhere.

First printing, July 1982

ISBN: 0-523-41436-6

Cover photo by Cosimo

Printed in the United States of America

PINNACLE BOOKS, INC.
1430 Broadway
New York, New York 10018

To Mama, who would never let me use the language that the characters in this book do, and who should not be held responsible for my strange sense of imagination.

QUEENS GATE RECKONING

Chapter One

||||||||||||||||||||||||||||||||||||||||||||||||||||||||||||||||||||||||||||||||||||||||

He walked along in deep thought, concentrating on two things: how to avoid the dog shit on the Amsterdam sidewalks and how to stay alive. The first was convenient; the second was vital. He'd be a little better than half successful that day.

Threading a path through throngs of Amsterdammers grateful for this crackling warm spring Saturday, Nat Worthington pushed on to his rendezvous, oblivious to the noises of trams and traffic and to the gentle lapping of water spoken by a canal boat as it hauled a load of tourists. He was weary.

One more pickup, they'd told him. One more—just a little errand—and you can rest. He pressed on toward a rough red brick building. It reminded him of the ones in Boston and of a time of his innocence when he wasn't so afraid he feared life itself, when he wasn't so tired.

He reached up to scratch his nose and was surprised to find perspiration on his upper lip. A case of nerves: it was unusual for a pro like him.

1

Nat slipped his right hand into the pocket of his tan poplin windbreaker to reassure himself. The model 39 Smith & Wesson with its ultrasilent sound suppressor tugged at the bottom of the pocket. He'd carried this one since his days as a SEAL in Vietnam. They called it the "Hushpuppy" because it was so effective at dispatching the VC's guard dogs.

He walked though a little-used alley to check for tails, and then descended the steps to a public restroom just off the Damrak. For the millionth time, he asked himself why he was doing this, and for the millionth time came up with no answer.

He fished out a handful of loose change and gave it to the attendant. The man smiled and informed him there was someone else in the restroom. The attendant, Nat knew, was paid by the CIA to provide a spot where agents could exchange documents. A restroom provided the privacy.

Waiting for the other man to leave, Nat walked into the toilet area to relieve himself. As he approached a urinal, he caught sight of himself in the mirror. Fatigue oozed through his clothes and shone from his face.

The craggy features, with the tiny scar from an adolescent fight on his right cheek, stared back at him. The bags under his turquoise eyes looked like bruises, and added another ten years onto the thirty-four he actually had lived. Hair spilled over the back of his collar—hair too long for the CIA to be happy with. Just one more thing about him that got under their skin. A Stewart tartan plaid shirt peeked out through the unzipped front of his windbreaker. He wore faded jeans and Adidas running shoes. The shoes, he saw, were clean. No dog shit.

He looked like an American tourist, a bit shorter than most at five-eight, but trim and broadshouldered. The shapelessness of the windbreaker hid from view the results of a lifetime of sports that included football, weight lifting, running, karate, war, and quiet killing.

2

He craned his head back to relieve the stiff muscles in his neck, and massaged them with his left hand as he urinated. His neck cracked and popped as he rolled his head, releasing the tension that threatened a major headache.

He was staring at the ceramic tile wall when a shuffling reached his ears. It would be the room's other occupant departing.

Looking down to finish his business, he felt sudden pressure just above and to the inside of his right kidney, and as he looked down he was amazed to see the point of a long knife tug at the waist of his shirt, and then emerge red with what he did not immediately recognize as his own blood.

Chapter Two

||||||||||||||||||||||||||||||||||||||||||||||||||||||||||||||||||||||||||||||||||||||||||||||||||||||

"But you must understand that ballet is not just visual pleasure. It's not just about movement. It's more, *more*! Do you understand?" The lithe man's voice rose as he leaned across the table waving his hands and flooding the atmosphere with crescêndoing Russian. It was a fine language to be emotional in.

Washington Post critic Richard Snyder straightened up at the dancer's latest outburst, surprised at his intensity. Snyder had tagged along with a group of Kirov dancers that night when they slipped away from the official reception at the Soviet Embassy to listen to the music at this very small, very hot, very smoky jazz club just off an alley near M Street in Georgetown.

This, he had thought, would be his big coup. Rumors were rampant that several of the company's principal dancers were getting ready to defect, particularly Sergei Illych, who had remained behind at the embassy.

"Are you listening? Do you understand me? Do you grasp the fact that ballet is not just a dance, but a com-

5

munication, one that is more expressive and universal than words? That it reaches across cultures by speaking directly to emotions?"

Jesus, Snyder muttered to himself. Here he was, sitting in the middle of what could be his big story, listening to a half-drunk Nikolai Valente rant about artistic freedom, watching Valente's wife Tania shoot her husband killing glances every time one of the girls in the corps de ballet came over and tried to kiss him, and desperately trying to get Valente to answer questions about Illych. He had to do it quickly, before they were interrupted by the return of the dancers' "escort": an all-too-obvious KGB functionary who was getting soused and talking to a trio of attractive American women two tables over.

Snyder drained his Jack Daniels and signaled the waiter for a refill.

"Yes, yes, I *do* understand," Synder answered. "But I don't understand why that would be a reason to defect. Why would someone like Illych who has everything he could possibly want decide to defect? Certainly not your 'artistic freedom.' "

"Your very response indicates your ignorance, Mr. Snyder," Valente commenced brusquely. "For if you understood ballet as a form of pure expression then you would recognize Soviet ballet as . . . how do you say . . . censored dance. For they try to control all forms of expression.

"Why do you think Soviet ballet is so reknowned for its technical perfection? Because the whole idea is to imitate and perfect roles played by the past masters—Pavlova or Nijinsky. A role is to be learned by rote, but not to be changed, improved, altered to fit your own style of dancing. It is perfection, but it is not *art!* Art cannot exist, it is a threat to the party. *That* is why Illych wants to leave and *that* is why I have been listening to his arguments for . . ."

"Niki! Watch what you say!" Tania Valente interrupted him. "There are people here, people who would like nothing better than to hang you with that. Say that again and this could be your last trip abroad. Do you want to spend the rest of your career dancing for border guards in the provinces?"

Her knuckles were white and her clenched fists trembled as she held them near her breasts.

Snyder avoided her eyes, eyes that looked ready to assassinate in an instant. This *was* a surprise. Valente, who was nearly as big a star as Illych, was also considering defection. God has thrown me a bone to make up for missing the Illych story, the newsman thought, as he carefully reached into his inside jacket pocket to start his miniature tape recorder. The bulky jacket concealed the recorder, hanging as it did off his Ichabod Crane physique. He wanted all of this for the record.

The newspaper reporter cast a furtive glance at the KGB agent—he looked like a sack of potatoes dressed in a dark serge suit. They all looked the same: the dark suits, white shirts, and ties that were fit only for a funeral. They might as well tattoo "Secret Police" across their foreheads.

Satisfied that the agent was occupied with something better looking than he'd ever seen in Moscow, Snyder leaned across the table toward Niki Valente and asked conspiratorially, "Tell me about it."

"I don't think you should, Niki," Tania said. "I really don't think you should talk to strangers about this ... this idle speculation of yours."

"It wouldn't be the first thing you disapproved of, my dear," Valente said sarcastically, as he reached behind him and grabbed from the next table a ballerina whose eyes were still large and dark from the stage makeup. He made a show of kissing her deeply and passionately, and then drew her to his lap, where she sat under the disapproving glare of Valente's wife.

"So you see, dear wife," Valente said. "Shut up!"

7

Tania Valente shoved her chair away from the table, spilling Snyder's fresh glass of bourbon, and stalked away from the table. The KGB agent took no notice of her, so occupied was he with the ample bosom of a blonde wearing a Danskin top.

"So there, my little toy," Valente said to the ballerina as he watched his wife disappear through the haze of tobacco smoke, "back to your friends. We'll get together later, no?"

The breathless creature—no more than eighteen or nineteen years old—agreed quickly and returned to the chatter of five other dancers just like her at the table. All had, at one time or another, been a toy for Valente's pleasure.

"Just what do you want to know?" Valente asked the reporter.

"Oh, come on! You *know* what I'm talking about. A defection! Yours, Illych's. When, where, why?" The reporter leaned halfway across the round table, supported on his elbows, straining to hear the dancer, whose voice was now drowned by the strains of a jazz guitar solo.

"Here," Valente patted the seat of the chair his wife had just vacated. "Sit and we will talk."

When Snyder had settled down into the chair, confident that his machine was recording through the fabric of his coat, Valente began.

"First of all, forget Illych. He's a has-been, an old man. The Kirov will be the better for his absence—" Valente stopped and looked at the reporter. "Aren't you going to take notes or something?"

"I have a great memory," Snyder replied and groaned inwardly at the dancer's arrogance. An alarm bell went off in the writer's head: why was Valente being so reckless, so open?

"Okay. So," Valente resumed, "Illych's great contribution has been to start me to thinking about this, to finding out how to make this defection."

8

"And your decision?"

"That I must do it," Valente said. "I have choreographed a magnificent ballet—the entire ballet—but they will not even consider letting it be performed because it does not meet the ideological standards of the bureau of cultural affairs.

"Do you understand what that means?" he asked the reporter. "It means that a committee of people like him," he pointed at the KGB agent, now sitting next to the blonde, whose nipples were standing at attention in the chill of the air conditioning, "who know more about wrestling and beating in people's heads, must approve every ballet. And they say mine does not serve the cause of the party sufficiently to be staged!

"Shits," he cursed, "They are all shits! It is no better now than it was when the Kirov danced for the czar—"

"But when do you plan to . . . to defect?" Snyder asked.

"That," Valente responded, "is something I thought we could work out."

"We?"

"We—you and me," Valente replied.

Snyder took a long pull from what was left of his drink.

"We?" The newsman said weakly. "I mean . . . why *me*?"

"Of course, that is easy," Valente said. "We know that all American newsmen work for your CIA. No?"

"Uh, no."

"Yes, but you are supposed to say that. Is that not true?"

"That is *not* true," Snyder said, but at least he now knew why Valente was being so open. "There's a lot of propaganda about that, and the CIA has used reporters as cover, but newsmen don't work for the CIA—we think that impression hurts us."

"That is not what we learn," Valente responded.

9

"You are sure?" The dancer's face reflected his confusion and disappointment.

"Yes, I'm sure that—"

"Certainly, certainly you must know how to get in touch with them," Valente implored as he grabbed Synder's arm.

Snyder flinched as the dancer grabbed him, and slowly disengaged his arm from the grip. The newsman looked nervously to see if the KGB agent was looking. The stolid Russian was now cracking a rare smile in response to the blonde's conversation, but did not seem to be looking their way.

"Look, I . . ." Snyder turned to his drink and swallowed the remainder. Christ! he thought. He was a *dance* critic, not a cloak and dagger type, that was for investigative reporters. And they sometimes got hurt, he remembered.

His heart skipped. What was he going to do?

"Look, Nikolai," he began. "I am not a CIA agent and I don't know anybody who is. But I promise that tomorrow I will make some phone calls to see what can be done."

"What does that mean?"

"I don't know," he replied. "It means I'll try. I can't promise to do any more than that.

"But why use me?" The newsman continued. "Illych has his own ways—why don't you talk to him and use them? Why don't you make a run for it right now? I can give you directions, and that clod over there won't notice anything, he's got tits in his eyes."

"I can't just leave," Valente said. "There's Tania, for one thing, she—"

"Do you really think she'd mind?"

"I don't know . . . True, she is a silly woman, she fails to grasp my vision, but still . . . I wouldn't want the authorities to do anything to harm her. No—I think she must be part of this."

"Do you think she will?"

10

"Yes, but she does not like talking about it," Valente said, unusually somber. "She does not like having to suck up to the toads in the party in order to get good parts—that is one reason why she is almost back in the corps by now. Yes, I think she would if someone would convince her she could dance here. She certainly wouldn't come along just because I was leaving. And she hates Illych. That's why I can't use his methods. Besides, he talks too much, and I'm afraid the wrong people would overhear him."

"You don't seem too shy in talking."

"But to the right person."

"How do you tell?"

"You get a sense."

"And you sense that I am the right person to help you defect?"

The Russian nodded his head.

Brother! the newsman thought. Maybe he *should* have gone to medical school instead. He looked past the dancer's shoulders, and watched as Tania Valente made her way back toward their table. As she sat down, he thought her eyes looked red, but in the dim light he couldn't tell if it was from the cigarette smoke, or from crying.

"I'd like to go now, Niki," she said.

"So go," he replied. "No one is stopping you."

"I mean I want you to come with me. There is too much talk of deceit and defection. I am tired, and I am tired of all this. Please come with me?" Her voice was pleading, as she put her right hand on his forearm.

"Go, woman!" Valente snapped, and snatched his arm away. "Go and have your rest. I am not yet ready; do you comprehend?"

"Yes," she responded, icily now, "better than you seem to know." And, turning to Snyder, "Please don't misread him, Mr. Snyder. He is really a decent person somewhere in there."

11

Tania rose slowly, nodded toward the newsman, and turned toward the women's restroom.

She had walked no more than a handful of steps before a frowsy middle-aged woman shoved her way past the doorman and lunged, screaming, toward the tables where the Kirov members sat.

"Help! Outside, come quickly, they have beaten him!" It was Anna Illych, the dancer's wife. "Please help! Niki! Come quickly, it's *horrible*, horrible!" She ran into Tania's arms and sobbed. "Hooligans! His knees—they beat his knees with pipes! They've ruined him!"

Snyder and Valente leaped from their chairs and pushed their way through the crowd toward the door. But as they ran, Snyder could see only the image of the KGB agent. Instinctively, the newsman had looked at him when Anna Illych came in screaming, and the KGB agent's reaction was a chilling sight he would never forget: as she screamed, he grinned broadly at Snyder, and nodded his head toward Valente.

Chapter Three

||||||||||||||||||||||||||||||||||||||||||||||||||||||||||||||||||||||||||||||||||||||

The sun burned his eyes. Nat Worthington loved it. He'd always loved it, even when his father, who had named him Nathaniel Everett Lowell Worthington IV, took him sailing as a toddler on their fifty-four foot ketch on trips out of Narragansett to Block Island and up and down the sound.

He'd loved it as a teenager when his father would let him skipper the boat, and he loved it now, when he was simply Nat Worthington, tacking north by northwest along the eastern shore of the Chesapeake Bay.

A twenty-knot wind beat steadily north of northeast, and he was close hauled into the wind, setting a course to clear the bow of a tanker oozing its sluggish path southward from Baltimore.

Chesapeake water foamed over the leeward gunwale as Worthington fought to stay on the razor's edge between maximum speed and capsizing. His left hand caressed the tiller as he tugged on the main sheet of

13

the fourteen-foot sloop, adjusting sails and course, using the last ounces of his skill to squeeze the last ounces of thrill from the ride.

He was hiked out over the windward rail, leaning as far out as possible to counterbalance the wind; the sloop was heeled over so far he was literally standing on the top of the centerboard trunk, holding the main sheet like the reins of a wind-driven mount. A mount that would throw him over in a second, into the path of the oncoming tanker, should he make the wrong move: an overcorrection on the tiller, hauling in the main sheet too far.

It was the edge of danger that he liked—no, that he needed—that set this course for him across the bow of a tanker whose very unmaneuverability would prevent it from stopping or turning should Nat take a spill.

He needed the danger because it fed on total concentration. It was only during such intense times that Nathaniel Everett Lowell Worthington IV could forget that he was no longer himself. And during the concentration, he could ignore the steady pain that sometimes racked his gut, the screams of nerves severed and never healed. And he could also forget the darkness, and the stench of death, his handmaidens who had left him only after months of hell.

The morning sun was still low on the horizon and painted long shadows across the water. The rush of the Chesapeake's water over his own gunwales was joined by the sound of another: the crashing of water as the tanker's bow divided the water. The tanker's bow grew larger and the sound intensified. Worthington looked as the hulk loomed larger and larger just off his starboard bow until it seemed to fill the sky.

He could see the individual rivets and welds on the tanker now, and the scrapes and dents received in its intercourse with docks and tugs and harbor life in general. Someone on the prow was waving frantically at

14

him. Worthington waved back in a cordial manner and smiled. Nat noticed that the man wasn't smiling.

No matter, Worthington thought, as his sloop crossed the centerline of the tanker's path and glided into the cool morning shadow cast by the tanker's bulk. August sunshine was hot, even this early in the day, and the shade was welcome.

But safely crossing the path of the tanker brought another problem, albeit a temporary one—it created a wind shadow, and robbed his tiny boat's sails of wind. He was suddenly becalmed. With sails luffing, Worthington tried desperately to catch what little wind he had to take his craft away from the wake of the tanker; the whirlpools left behind had been known to swallow smaller craft.

But as the danger diminished, so did Worthington's concentration. He set the main and jib sheets in their cleats, and holding the tiller with one hand, used a cut-off bleach bottle to bail out the water he'd taken on in his mad flight across the tanker's bow.

The mechanical rhythm started his mind off on the same train of thoughts that had rumbled through his head for the past seven months and the unanswered questions always concluded with more questions: Who was he now? And if he wasn't himself anymore, who *could* he be? And always the darkness of pain.

He did not immediately recognize the blood on the knife as his own until someone started to twist the blade as it penetrated his abdomen. The pain whirled him face to face with his assailant, who was shocked by his speed. An amateur, Worthington remembered thinking, the knife still in his body. He should have remembered to immobilize me as he thrust in the knife. And the thrust was much too low. The man was heavy and Slavic in appearance with thinning gray hair plastered to his head with grease. One of the last things Worthington remembered before he lost consciousness

15

was the odd way the blood spread across the man's yellow knit shirt as Nat pumped a ragged pattern of shots across his chest.

Shivers raced up Worthington's spine, chills not from the shadow of the tanker, but from a much larger shadow that hung over him.

He remembered waking up in a hospital near Nuremberg in West Germany. The male nurse by his bed refused to speak to him, but the doctor who came said he had been unconscious for nearly a week.

The knife, according to the doctor, had neatly skewered his kidney, nicked the aorta, sliced a nice gash in his stomach, and chopped up a handful of nerves.

"What about their agent?" was Worthington's first question. He'd been satisfied when the doctor remarked that the man was probably dead before he hit the floor.

The wounds would have healed cleanly, said the doctor, but an infectious serum placed on the blade had inflamed his insides with the dreaded and potent peritonitis. For weeks he was on the verge of death, and drifted in and out of consciousness. Doctors packed his fever-racked body in ice to cool it as they fed him massive doses of antibiotics. When it was over, his clean wounds were ragged and nerves that might have healed now screamed a blaring reminder of the episode.

A series of operations followed to give him some relief by severing nonvital nerves at the spinal cord, and to repair scar tissue that had healed poorly. The lapses of consciousness left over from the high fever could not be treated, said the doctors. It was mild brain damage that might or might not go away after the brain rearranged its patterns and circuits.

Tests showed that his intelligence and memory had not been impaired, just his ability to remain conscious all day long.

Worthington leaned against the transom of his tiny

16

rented sloop, and gazed over his right shoulder at the refinery-like structure of the tanker as its mammoth bulk lumbered on, moving great shadows like the sun as it sets.

He squinted at the brightening sky above the tanker's deck, and the marshmallow clouds that glowed in the sun's rays. A contrail pointed like an arrow to a minute silver speck just ahead of it, and Nat seethed quietly as he followed it with his eyes. He had been a qualified pilot before, now his blackouts had grounded him. Despite the fact that he'd not had a blackout in the past three months, the doctors still refused to certify him as fit to fly.

Christ! He thumped the fiberglass hull of the sloop with his fist. He was grounded, discharged from the Company on full disability, blacklisted from the foreign service because of his intelligence work, and psychologically unequipped to deal with workaday life.

Specialists told him that strain could rip loose the scar tissue inside his belly and kill him, that he might black out at any time—even years later—that he shouldn't fly, scuba dive, box, climb mountains, or jump out of airplanes again.

Yet in the three months since his discharge he had done most of those things. Worthington had ignored his doctors, and started a conditioning program. He was running more than five miles per day, and working out with weights. When he'd regained his wind, he rented scuba gear and went diving off Cape Hatteras; he made two parachute jumps with a northern Virginia skydiving club; and soon regained his coordination rappelling down the sheer rock faces at Great Falls along the Potomac. He made peace with his injuries by conquering them.

He knew a blackout of a second or two, or the sudden tearing loose of a scar during any of those activities

17

could mean instant death, but that, Nat told himself, was better than slowly rotting behind a desk.

But where those made him feel like his old self, something was missing that disturbed Nat Worthington more than anything else: he no longer wanted to kill. Not, he thought, that he'd ever really liked the kill so much as the challenge of outwitting another human being for the ultimate in stakes, but now he wanted to *avoid* killing, and he was uncomfortable with that.

That challenge had made him—Boston Brahmin and Phi Beta Kappa Harvard class of '68—join the Marines during the height of the Vietnam War, a hitch that was served as a member of the elite SEALS. He had been weary of competing and excelling for insignificant stakes—money, status, a job. His family had always had plenty of those, and they were no challenge at all.

But staying alive by outwitting the best that the enemy could toss at you: *that* was a challenge, and that challenge was his life.

Now . . . Worthington pondered, looking up at the mainsail as it started to luff; he tugged on the mainsheet and the luffs vanished; now he wasn't sure what sort of challenge he could find, or if he could find one that was worth living for.

The tanker slid slowly south and exposed the sloop to the full force of the wind sweeping across the open water of the bay. Worthington quickly headed the boat into the wind to avoid capsizing, and hiked out over the gunwale as the little sloop picked up speed and skipped once again across the water.

As he leaned over the edge, Nat scanned the horizon for traffic, and saw only a respectable-sized motorsailer as it motored out of some hidden cove toward the middle of the bay. Boats under sail have the right of way, Nat reminded himself, but he decided to keep a close eye on the boat, since some powerboat sailors didn't always follow the rules.

18

The wind was coming in gusts now, and Nat strained to keep the small craft from capsizing. Each sudden gust tested the ability of his reflexes to compensate quickly enough, but he was determined to keep the boat on the edge of speed. Conservative sailing was for a bunch of pussies.

So busy was Nat with staying afloat, that he failed to keep careful watch on the motorsailer coming from the west, hidden as it was by the expanse of sail. He had just hauled in the jib sheet, and was leaning down to chock it in the cleat when the sound of throbbing diesels drew his attention. Looking under the boom, Nat saw the motorsailer heading on a collision course.

He heaved on the tiller, jerked the jib sheet out of its cleat, and slacked off on the main sheet. The new tack brought him about on a course parallel to the motorsailer. As Nat wondered whether or not to curse at the boat's pilot for his disregard of the rules of the water, the motorsailer made a sudden turn to starboard, again blocking the path of Worthington's sailboat.

"Hey, you stupid motherfucker," Worthington yelled as he frantically came about to avoid a collision. "What the fuck do you think you're doing, asshole!" He played out the main and jib sheets to begin running with the wind. He looked for something to throw at the boat's pilot, silhouetted against the sky on the flying bridge less than fifteen yards away. Worthington leaned over to grab for an empty Coors can when a ragtag line of holes tore through the fiberglass seats on the port side. He spun around in time to see a sniper on the boat's deck taking aim at him with a silenced H & K machine pistol.

Oh great! He thought. They messed up the job in Amsterdam and they're coming back to finish it.

Accidental jibes are the fear of every inexperienced sailor when running with the wind. At best they are frightening, as the boom unexpectedly swings across the cockpit. At worst, they knock people overboard and capsize the boat.

Nat Worthington reacted to the gunman by hauling in the mainsail from its position over the port gunwale and shoving the tiller to starboard. The wind from astern caught the sail, snapped the boom across the cockpit, and neatly capsized the fourteen-foot sloop in a textbook example of what not to do.

Worthington ducked as the boom swept across the cockpit and, as the sloop leaned over, dove into the water. Underwater, he swam along the mast, grabbing it near the top, and dove deeper. The boat quickly turned turtle, centerboard pointing skyward, trapping a pocket of air under an inverted hull.

The throbbing of the larger craft's diesels slowed, and then reversed. Worthington could hear shouting, but could not comprehend any words. Soon he heard the twin props of the boat stop, followed by more shouts and a loud splash.

They had launched their dinghy, he surmised, and were coming to look for him. He hoped that the jibe looked enough like an accident caused by a startled sailor, and that they would think he was still weak from his injuries—an easy kill.

He had little time. The voices grew more distinguishable, but as the dinghy drew closer to the capsized sailboat, the men spoke more quietly. Worthington was unarmed. He moved silently toward the bow of the boat, and searched among the items stored there for his rucksack and the Swiss Army knife stored in the outer pocket. He hoped the pack hadn't been lost in the capsizing.

The interior was pitch black. The jib covered the bow, and its sheets lay in a tangled mass, floating on the surface of the water.

The dinghy struck the sailboat's hull. Worthington

froze, listening to the thumps of hands and feet, trying to decipher from their movements how many there were and what they would try to do.

It didn't take long. There were two men, he gathered, and from the sounds, it seemed as if they were attaching a rope to the centerboard to try and right the sailboat.

Hoping their sounds would mask his own, Worthington tore at the jib with his hands, searching for the rucksack, and the only weapon he had on board.

But he was too late. He heard the whir of the dinghy's outboard churning the water, then felt the sailboat's hull lurch and tilt.

Electricity tingled through Worthington's body as daylight peeked under the edge of the hull. He stared in horror as his refuge began to disappear. He could hear the little outboard laboring now. The sodden sails would make righting tough, perhaps impossible to do completely. But staying there, he knew, would only delay the inevitable. He would soon be exposed to their view—and, he knew, another barrage of machine gun fire.

Heart booming, he gingerly touched the scar on his belly. Something hurt. He wondered if it was just a reaction to the sudden dive into the cold water or if he had pulled something.

Part of Nathaniel Worthington reveled in this challenge to outwit humans once again, to have a shot at those who had tried to destroy his body and who had destroyed his life instead.

But another part wondered if he was up to the challenge. And even if he was, would his body hold together?

He quickly shoved the thoughts aside, and decided to take the only action he could—when attacked, go on the offensive.

Bracing his feet on the portion of the hull still under

21

water, Worthington took a deep breath, and dove, deep and toward the dinghy.

He had to exhale to maintain enough depth to remain concealed by the water, and his lungs felt as if they would burst. He homed in on the dinghy by the sound of the outboard. After swimming no more than ten yards, the prop sounds were behind him, and moving sluggishly.

Heart pounding and lungs on fire, Worthington swam for the surface slowly. He looked up and opened his eyes, and could make out the shadow of the dinghy's hull. From its shape, he recognized it as an inflatable four-man raft commonly carried aboard larger yachts.

Cautiously, Nat made his way toward the bow, placing the dinghy's hull between him and the yacht. He prayed that the raft's occupants would be preoccupied with raising the sailboat, and would not be facing the bow.

His prayers were answered. Nat surfaced alongside the starboard bow of the dinghy, relieved to hear both men muttering over the outboard and its weak performance. His diaphragm quivered as he stifled a gasp and slowly filled his oxygen-starved lungs. He was light-headed from the exertion, and the scar on his belly throbbed with every heartbeat.

He still had no weapon, and no plan. The maneuver had bought him a few more minutes, and he tried to ignore the pain he felt as he clung to the dinghy's painter, to catch his breath and plot his next move.

His wind slowly returned, and the throb from the scar tissue diminished. Nat convinced himself the pain came not from a serious internal injury, but from battered nerve endings.

The raft made very little progress in righting the overturned sailboat, and the two men argued loudly over who was at fault. Nat briefly considered taking the two of them as they quarreled, but quickly dismissed it as a dead end. Where would he go after dispatching them? And what chance would he have in a raft pursued by gunmen on the faster yacht?

It was no good.

The yacht, which was now almost dead in the water, was trying to maintain position with the raft as it struggled with the sailboat. From his waterline vantage point near the raft's bow, Worthington could see a sliver of the yacht's bowsprit.

There was only one way out of the bay, Worthington decided, and it was aboard that yacht.

His pulse had returned to normal, and Worthington decided it was as good a time now as any. So he took another deep breath and dove again.

His last dive had given him confidence, and he suffered from none of the panic he'd felt moments before. The pain in his belly subsided.

Eyes closed against the murky water, Worthington found the yacht when he swam headlong into its slick, clean hull. To his relief, the boat moved sluggishly. Cautiously, he surfaced, careful not to splash when he broke through the water. Voices from the deck drifted downward, but he could not see the speakers; the curvature of the hull concealed them. Nat turned and watched the two men in the raft some twenty yards away. They had halfway succeeded in righting the sailboat so the mast was now parallel with the water.

The yacht's diesels reversed as the men on the raft stopped to inspect the capsized vessel. The yacht was dead in the water now, with the raft and sailboat just off its starboard bow.

The voices on the yacht gathered above Worthington on the bow, and as he stealthily swam toward the stern, he estimated the boat's length at fifty to sixty feet. The white fiberglass hull glistened with the gloss of expert care.

At the stern, he found the ladder used by the men to gain access to the dinghy, and he grabbed the bottom rung and scanned the transom. *Go for Baroque* was the yacht's name, Annapolis its home port.

Feeling naked without a weapon, Worthington eased himself up the ladder, pausing with his feet in the bay to allow the water to drain quietly off him. As he paused he listened: for the creak of the deck, for breathing, coughs—anything that would give him a clue of what awaited him over the transom.

Hearing nothing but the voices coming from the bow, Nat took the steps slowly until he could see over the top. He surveyed the rear deck and saw nothing unusual for a boat this size: a stairway leading to cabins below, a sheltered cockpit, and stairs leading upward toward the flying bridge. It was, he thought, a typical power boat, a stink pot.

Cautiously, Nat pulled himself onto the boat, and padded into the cockpit. Through the hatch above him, he could make out one khaki-clad leg of the boat's pilot. Below, there was only darkness. But maybe he would find a weapon there.

He took the steep steps quickly, then stood in a shadow beneath the steps for a few seconds to allow his eyes to adjust to the dim light in the passageway. He could see a bulkhead amidships, its watertight door open. Four doors lined each side of the passageway, each with a dim light burning next to it. Behind him a doorway led aft, probably to the engine room.

For an instant, he considered setting fire to the engine room, and escaping in the confusion, but he discarded that as a long shot. Once he took care of the others, he still had to get to shore. Still, the engine room as a diversion was a tantalizing idea.

He tried the unlocked door and climbed down a short flight of steps. The oily odor of diesel fuel and lubricating grease drifted up warm and moist. The clunking of the idling engine filled the tight space with a soothing pulse. It felt like a womb.

Closing the door, Nat fumbled for the light switch and marveled at the spotlessly maintained area. The owner must be some perfectionist.

Rummaging through a mechanic's tool case beside the engine block, Nat pulled out a ratchet wrench handle that fit handily in his fist, a package of single-edged razor blades, and a length of fine steel wire. He cut about half a yard of the steel wire, and wrapped each end around spare manifold bolts.

Thus armed, he climbed the stairs and doused the overhead lights. When his eyes had adjusted, he opened the door and stepped into the passageway. He had just started for the first cabin door when he heard loud footsteps on the deck above him.

Nat flattened himself against the wall under the steps and waited. It sounded like only one person. Then Nat's shoulder muscles gave an involuntary shudder as he saw first one huge foot and then the other descend the steps. In these close quarters, the man's size would be a disadvantage. Nat took the steel wire, one bolt in each hand, and waited as the large man descended.

Twisting to one side to clear the opening, the man—who looked at least six-foot-four—continued down cautiously. A silenced H & K MP5 hung casually over his shoulder. When the man reached the bottom of the steps, Worthington sprang. He passed the loop of steel wire over the man's head and jerked it tight.

The big man's hands flew to his neck as he tried to twist and gain a look at his assailant. But Worthington jumped back to the second step and heaved up with all his might.

The H & K clattered as the man's body collapsed against the stairs, the head tenuously attached. Blood from the man's severed carotid arteries soaked the stairs and dripped down the front of Nat's shirt as he lowered the body to the deck.

Nat pulled the body into the engine room and shut the door. He took the three extra clips for the H & K and returned to the passageway, where he carefully unscrewed the light bulbs from their fixtures to help conceal the blood on the deck. He worked coldly and methodically now, all emotions vanished.

He searched the four cabins on the aft side of the bulkhead, when he realized he had an easier way out—he'd close the watertight door and dog it shut so it couldn't be opened from the other side. He'd have his rear secured, while he concentrated on the attack.

He moved toward the bulkhead.

"Jesse?" a voice from the cockpit called down below. "Jess, are you down there? Get the line, we're gonna have to tow the sailboat ourselves."

Too late to hide under the stairs, Worthington ducked through the bulkhead, and flattened himself against the wall. He heard the man grumble and then start down the steps.

"Shit, can't rely on anybody any—" the man's voice caught; despite Nat's precautions, he had probably spotted the blood. Preceded by the muzzle of the H & K, Nat spun into the middle of the passageway and fired at the stairwell.

The burst from Nat's weapon caught the man across the knees, and he yelled as the slugs ripped into his legs. Worthington followed the man's fall with the gun's muzzle, and emptied the clip into his head and shoulders as he hit the deck and stayed there.

The sounds of footsteps clomped toward the stern of the boat. Worthington slapped a fresh clip into the H & K and stepped through the watertight door and started to close it when a volley of shots rang out above, their slugs tearing into the blood-soaked carpeting beneath the steps. Nat checked the empty corridor behind him, and decided to run for the forward set of steps.

First, he turned toward the stern to loose a covering volley. He set a dozen slugs clattering up the metal steps and started to turn when he heard a door open on his left.

"I think that's enough, Mr. Worthington," a voice behind him said. "If you value your life, you'll make no further moves." Nat's back muscles knotted up, waiting for the slugs to rip through them.

Chapter Four

‖‖‖

This is a very nice room they have given us, Tania Valente thought; probably the KGB's attempt to persuade Niki not to defect. First the threat, and then the sugar. Illych had been taken to Georgetown Medical Center after his beating, and then sent straight to Moscow. There was no talk of him ever being able to dance again, only of whether he'd walk without crutches.

No one could prove anything, but the KGB had been skillful in planting the rumors that Illych was beaten because he planned to defect after the final performance at the Kennedy Center. Oh, Illych and his big mouth! And now Niki was ready to defy even the KGB threats to defect for his artistic freedom.

Artistic freedom indeed, she said to herself as her eyes followed a settling crack across the ceiling of their room on the tenth floor of the Plaza Hotel in New York City. *He* wanted more freedom to screw pretty ballerinas, though God knows he'd had plenty from the corps.

The crack looked like a lightning bolt, running in

jagged fractures from its origin just to the left of the ceiling light, across the ceiling to the corner by the bathroom. They *really* ought to fix that, she thought, but then felt guilty and ungrateful for even thinking that their accommodations were not satisfactory. She'd been taught all her life to be grateful, not to complain, to comply with authority. She'd never forget the morning just after her sixth birthday, when she complained that their drafty communal apartment in Gorky was cold, and her father cursed her for being ungrateful.

"Suppose, just suppose," he yelled at her, a big barrel of a man whose chest hair was matted like a dog's coat. "Suppose that we let you sleep outside tonight when you come home? See how you like that. You sound like a damned princess with your talk. Now shut up and eat your breakfast!"

And she would never forget the way the knuckles on the back of his hands felt as they crushed her jaw when she complained of the roaches crawling across the breakfast table that same morning.

There was still a lump on her jaw just below her chin where the bone had healed wrong. Fortunately it failed to mar her face, with its high cheekbones sitting below sparkling green eyes. She'd always hated her eyes —her father was convinced she was illegitimate since no one in their family had ever had green eyes. And few of the children at school had green eyes, and that made her an oddity.

No, it didn't pay to be different, and it didn't pay to be a complainer, Tania thought as she lay on the queen-sized bed with its clean sheets in the luxurious hotel with her legs spread, staring at the crack in the ceiling while her husband Niki—principal Kirov dancer and soloist known for his breath-taking leaps from the Corsaire *pas de deux*—mindlessly thrust himself in and out, telling her all the while how grateful she should be to have such a lover.

She thought about the crack in the ceiling and tried

to forget that she was dry and he was rubbing her raw. She tried to concentrate on the cool clean sheets, the luxurious room, the freedom from hunger; she tried to be grateful, but somehow her mind kept returning to a time when they were in love, when he'd cover her breasts with kisses, and tell her how beautiful she was naked, and reassure her that her breasts made her beautiful *because* they were bigger than any other ballerina's in the corps, and she remembered how he used to kill her between her thighs and how he could make her wet just by looking at her.

And she wondered where it all had gone, and why she was such an ungrateful bitch.

It was like a hundred other mornings in a hundred other hotel rooms, and, as always, the lump on her jaw-bone throbbed and reminded her that she did, after all, have all these creature comforts, and a beautiful apartment overlooking the Neva River in Leningrad, and didn't have to dance for illiterate factory workers in Gorky, mainly because she was married to the great Valente.

As he pounded and thrust, she recalled their first meeting at the reception following her performance in *Giselle* at the competition for regional companies in Leningrad. The competition was the Cultural Affairs Ministry's way of assuaging provincial party officials who felt neglected.

True, it gave all of the party free trips to Leningrad, but it incidentally served a useful purpose: it gave the ballet masters at the Kirov a chance to view what was being groomed in the outer reaches of the republic, and a chance to select the best for their own use.

Gorky's company was one of the strongest of the regional groups, and Tania outshone all of her companions.

After the performance, she shyly joined the crowds at the official reception, and was stunned when she entered to find herself the center of the judges' attention,

31

and snared by the dark brooding eyes of Nikolai Valente. The room grew quiet as she crossed the floor, walking with the semi-waddle which comes from turning out the legs too much. And she was overcome first by being informed by the Minister of Cultural Affairs that she had been chosen to study at the Kirov's school, and second when Valente himself took her into tow and refused to let go until the next morning when he walked her back to her hotel room.

A month after moving to Leningrad from Gorky, she and Valente were married.

Her monumental infatuation shielded her for months from the company gossip until the evening when she stumbled over two copulating bodies in the costuming department. One of them was Valente.

The shock drove her into the only thing she was still sure of: her dancing. But even that was a compulsion not of her own choice.

Though she had never told anyone—for she had never known anyone she thought would understand—she hated ballet. She had always been better at math and sciences in school and loved art and history, but her mother had decided that her daughter was to become a ballerina. To Tania's dismay, she was *good* at ballet, and excelled in classes her mother forced her into. She continued to excel, and was selected by the Gorky regional ballet theatre, where she quickly worked her way to soloist and principal dancer at age nineteen.

Though she detested the drill, and the endless hours of practice and rehearsal, she grew to love the sensuality of dance. Where else was it acceptable for men—mostly half-naked, muscular men—to run their hands over her body in public, fingers brushing her breasts, hands massaging her inner thighs on lifts, encircling her waist during pirouettes and arabesques?

Slowly, as she tingled with the sexuality of the dance and basked in the respect and applause her proficiency

32

brought her, she fooled herself into believing that one should do something merely because one was good at it.

Her obsession with dance drove her relentlessly and her standing with the Kirov soared even without the patronage of her husband. She thrived on the competition as long as she was good. Then, eight months ago, an Achilles tendon injury effectively ended her dancing career. The inactivity, the inability to practice, cast her into the deepest of depressions as she watched her parts danced by other ballerinas. Without the relentless drill and rehearsal to distract her, she drifted further and further away from dance, and back toward books.

She loved to study more than she ever had loved dancing, but to the Kirov she was now useless. She was only an appendage to Niki, the cuckolded wife with nowhere to go. Kirov management was pushing her to teach young students, but she had not the patience.

Now she read, avoided the other dancers because she no longer had anything in common with them, and served occasionally to satisfy Niki's lust.

Yet what she wanted most was for Niki to love her. And so, as always now, she clutched him tightly to her breast as he thrust in and out, so that when the tears came, they rolled quietly into his hair to mingle softly with the sweat that already matted it. And he always thought she was having an orgasm when she cried out, and it made him feel like a man for having satisfied her.

Chapter Five

‖‖

Behind him someone screwed in the light bulbs, and Worthington's eyes were stunned by the brightness. As he stood in the narrow passageway in the belly of the *Go For Baroque*, Nat wondered briefly why the man hadn't shot. His mouth was dry and filled with cotton and his tongue tasted like brass. Nat's mind focused on the alternative to being shot immediately: death in little bites, torture.

He heard the latch of another cabin click, and the hinge squealed as the door opened. The pungent stink of stale tobacco smoke diffused throughout the corridor, and Nat heard the labored breathing of someone who was either overweight or had emphysema. Or both.

Nat listened. Then he recognized the breathing, and remembered an image to go with it.

He saw the man's outline. Did he know his killer? And suddenly it came to him: Everett Lowell, assistant director of the CIA for covert operations, a Yale man, class of '52 and a notorious glutton.

"Lowell?" Nat asked.

"Your memory never ceases to astonish me," the voice behind Nat replied. The breathing got closer, and as it did, the air reeked with garlic. "Yes, Nat, you're right. Now, listen closely to me and I think we can do business. Would you like that?"

"Do I have a choice?"

"No, Nat. No you don't, not in a realistic sense. In a philosophical one, you do—you can do what I say, or you can die."

"Thanks for the options."

"They're yours."

Nat could visualize the man behind him. Food stains on his vest, a Phi Beta Kappa key dangling from a gold chain that draped over his huge belly, and a brilliant mind that would be worth admiring if it weren't so corrupt.

"Spread your legs, slowly," said Lowell's voice. "Now hold your arms straight and away from your body." Nat obeyed.

"Okay," Lowell murmured to someone else, and Nat was frisked roughly by another pair of hands. The wrench handle and the razor blades were removed from Nat's pockets.

"He's clean," a voice told Lowell.

"Nat, my boy, you can turn around now—but do it slowly."

Worthington lowered his arms, and turned to face his attackers. Two men stood in the corridor next to Lowell, and both trained their H & K machine pistols at him. Lowell smiled unctuously at him, revealing flecks of food lodged in his front teeth.

"I know what you're thinking, Nathaniel," Lowell began. "You'd like to try to escape. Wait. I'll give you plenty of time to try that in a minute. But first I'd like

36

you to listen to what I have to say. Will you grant me that?"

"What makes you think I've got any interest in what you have to say?"

"Listen."

Nat shrugged his shoulders. "Go on."

"You see," Lowell said. "We're not here to kill you at all. We merely wanted to find out if what we'd heard was true."

"If what was true?" Nat was perplexed now. He had worked indirectly for Lowell during the Amsterdam operation, and the rumors—which he believed—said that Lowell had set him up to make him an example for other rogue agents. It would be logical, Nat thought, for Lowell to finish him off.

"If it were true that you'd gotten yourself back into shape despite the best predictions of the medical and psychological professions."

"You mean . . . this was a . . ."

"Qualifying exam," Lowell completed the sentence for him.

Rage rose in Nat's throat. "A qualifying exam?" he repeated incredulously. "You let me kill those men because you wanted to see if I was in shape? The extent of your corruption surprises even me, Lowell."

The other man merely smiled.

"And just *what* is so fucking important for me to do that I have to kill people to qualify? Can you answer that question for me?"

"No," said Lowell.

"No?" Worthington frowned. "No? Just like that? Then who can?"

"In there." Lowell cocked his head toward a nearby cabin. "The man in there will tell you."

"Do you know?"

"No. He's the only one who does."

Worthington started for the cabin.

37

"Hold on," Lowell said, and Nat stopped as the two men raised the barrels of their guns. "Does this mean we're in business?"

Nat glared at him. "Not with you, lard ass," Nat said as he continued to walk toward the door. "With whoever is in that cabin . . . maybe. But definitely not with you."

Lowell moved aside to let Worthington enter the cabin. Nat opened the door partially, and turned to face Lowell.

"You know," Nat said to the fat man. "I've always owed you something."

Lowell tilted his head inquiringly. "I don't understand," he said.

"You'll understand this, I think." And Worthington brought his right fist from the doorknob and smashed it into the fat man's nose. He could feel the cartilage twist, and the thin bone between the nostrils crack. Turning toward the door, Nat slashed backward with his left fist. It landed, amid the flab, squarely on Lowell's testicles, and as the man bent over in pain, his teeth met squarely with Nat's elbow. He noted with satisfaction, as he entered the cabin and closed the door, that he had heard at least one tooth snap. And the jaw would definitely have to be wired back together.

As Nat slammed the door and leaned against it, relieved at being out of the gunsights of the thugs in the corridor, he heard Lowell's soft body slam against the wall and slide to the floor.

In the dimly lit stateroom, a man sat behind a dark wooden desk illuminated by a circle of yellow light that fell from a single-bulb desk lamp. The man's face was lost in the shadows that surrounded the light.

As his eyes adjusted, Nat found he was once again in the sights of a machine gun. The man holding the gun was an enormous hulk, shapeless in the shadows and nearly as big. He was grinning broadly.

38

"Sit down, Mr. Worthington, please," said a voice from behind the lamp, and a pinstriped arm gestured through the lamplight toward a chair beside the desk. "Come, come, there's nothing to worry about—Ivan, please lower that monstrous weapon and quit that silly grin. Ivan," said the man, turning again to Nat, "has had several nasty run-ins with Mr. Lowell, and I'm afraid he has taken severe pleasure in your treatment of him."

Nat could no longer see the huge man's toothy grin in the darkness, but relaxed when he noted that the machine gun was now casually cradled in the crook of his arm.

"It has been quite a while since I've seen you, Nathaniel—may I call you Nat?" he asked and then continued without waiting for an answer. "Your father and I had many business dealings and continue to maintain our . . . lines of communication."

For the second time that afternoon, Nat's memory searched for a match. Mentally he ran down the list of his father's earliest business associates, and tried to correlate that with someone who would have access to information about a super-secret CIA operation. The mental exercise was like a meditation for Nat, helping to calm his screaming nerves, soothe the ragged breathing. He was only faintly aware that the abdominal scar throbbed.

Rinehart! It came to him clearly now. Richard B. Rinehart, former assistant secretary of state in the Kennedy Administration, a warhorse recalled to duty in the current administration to serve as National Security Adviser. A multi-millionaire conglomerate builder, oil magnate and architect of American trade policy with both the Soviet Union and China, accused of structuring trade policies with those countries to allow his companies the best shot at profiting—some said profiteering—from the trade . . .

39

"Please, Nat," Rinehart interrupted his thoughts. "Come have a seat and let's chat a while."

Stepping toward the chair, Nat cast a cautious glance at Ivan, who remained stolid as a statue. The blood rushed back into Nat's face, and he flushed, angry at what had happened, but still in some awe at the man he now confronted.

"My goodness, you are a *mess*," said Rinehart as the light illuminated the still glistening blood that soaked Nat's clothing, and trickles down his throat and arms, mingled with the sweat of fear and exertion. Nat sank into the leather upholstered chair and stared through the gloom at Rinehart.

He was rarely at a loss for a thought or an action, but now Nat sat wordlessly, waiting for the older man to take the initiative.

Nat's eyes scanned the room, and then came to rest on Rinehart's face, now partially lit by the lamp. Though the face and the body were definitely those of an old man, Nat was startled by the clarity of Rinehart's gray eyes, eyes that seemed to shine from their own internal illumination. The skin of his neck sagged a bit over the careful knot of the club tie, and his abdomen tugged at the belly of his vest, but Rinehart's eyes dismissed any illusion of weakness or frailty. Rinehart spoke first.

"You look fit," he began, "and I gather from the past hour or so that you are. Though regretfully brutal, this has been—"

"A test," Nat interrupted, his anger rising again. "A fucking test! What right have—"

"Calm down, please Nat." Rinehart placed a hand on Worthington's shoulder. "I know you're upset and you have a right to be, but please hear me out. It's of the gravest import for you and for all of America. Please? Hear me out?" Nat stared at the glowing eyes and nodded, slouching back in the chair.

40

Silence reverberated through the shadowy room. Nat heard Ivan's heavy breathing, waves lapping against the hull of the boat, air rushing through a vent in the ceiling.

"Ivan, the earphones please," Rinehart ordered, and Nat turned in the chair in time to see the guard placing heavy black earphones on his head.

"It's to assure that our conversation is heard by only you and me. This cabin has been thoroughly swept for eavesdropping devices and," he nodded toward Ivan, who slid a heavy accordian-like panel in front of the cabin door, "it is very much soundproof now. What I have to tell you, Nat, will go no further than you and I. Of course, pieces of the intelligence you will hear are known to a select few with the highest of security clearances, but only I have a complete picture, and only I know of the operation you will perform."

"What if I don't want to perform this operation?" Nat inquired, full knowing the answer.

"That would be most unfortunate—for us as well as you," Rinehart replied evenly. "For you would not leave this room, and we would be forced to find an alternate agent, and I'm afraid there is simply no one else in our employ whose skills and background are as suitable for this as yours."

"Unfortunate," Nat agreed wryly. "Certainly most unfortunate. I like living, so continue."

Rinehart smiled diplomatically, and spoke again.

"As you are no doubt well aware, the increasing age of the members of the Russian Politburo, along with the failing health of the current premier, have sparked massive speculation about the future of the Soviet leadership." At this point Rinehart paused to pull some papers from a buff folder on his desk. Toward Nat he pushed a newspaper clipping, with a photo in which Nat recognized the Russian leadership standing atop Lenin's tomb reviewing the May Day Parade. It was clipped from a recent *Pravda*.

41

"Flanking the current premier," a well-manicured hand stabbed at a face, "is Valery Kokh, the head of the KGB and probably the most powerful single personage in the Soviet Union. And here," the hand indicated another face, "is Andrei Pugachev, the head of the Defense Ministry, and a real political comer.

"And look at this." Rinehart placed a yellowed newspaper clipping beside the first one. It was an identical pose from *Pravda*, dated May Day, 1967. "You see that Kokh is in the picture separated from the premier by three people. Pugachev is not in the picture at all.

"Now in this one, from 1969," Rinehart went on. "we find Kokh next to the premier, and Pugachev separated from the premier by only two people."

That was remarkable, Worthington knew, since proximity to the premier at these events was a direct indication of a person's standing in the politburo. It was doubly significant since normally it took decades to progress within the Politburo from one position to another, providing that the perodic purges were survived.

Nat was most familiar with Pugachev as the head of the Red Army that masterminded the 1968 invasion of Czechoslovakia. But as a field operative, Nat had lost sight of him when Pugachev was elevated to the politiburo. He had not been aware of his spectacular advancement within it.

"Most Kremlinologists, including all of our best people, say the internal struggle is divided up between supporters of Pugachev and Kokh . . ."

"And who are they putting money on?" Nat asked.

"Pugachev," said Rinehart with a frown, as he leaned back in his chair, plunging his head into the shadows. He reached into his side coat pocket and withdrew a pipe. "Do you mind?" Worthington shook his head, and watched as Rinehart meticulously scraped the pipe, filled, tamped, and lit it.

"Pugachev," Rinehart began, leaning forward again, smoke curling through the penumbra of the light, "is a dangerous man. He's a hawk in international affairs. His brilliant strategy in Czechoslovakia won him many powerful allies within the government, and his beefed-up GRU intelligence forces have begun to match in power—but not in sheer numbers—that of the KGB.

"Even though his blunders in Afghanistan have cost him a little support, he's been able to convince his allies that the operations there were botched by meddling from Kokh and others. He is a neo-Stalinist," Rinehart continued, "and a Russian to the core. He is the ideological leader of a growing number of Russians—powerful Russians—who are alarmed at the increasing numbers of ethnic minorities—Lithuanians, Tartars and the like—in the Soviet Union, and at their nation's diminishing world influence, particularly in the Third World."

Rinehart paused and looked directly into Nat's eyes. "The Neo-Stalinists," he said somberly, "will accept nothing less than Russian domination over all ethnic minorities in the Soviet Union, and Soviet domination of the world. If Pugachev becomes the next premier, we will see persecution of Soviet minorities and dissidents on a scale that will make Stalin's gulags look like a Caribbean holiday. And we will have war."

"War?" Nat said. "Can you be *that* sure?"

"Yes.

"Now," Rinehart continued, sweeping up the newspaper clippings and returning them to the folder, "Let's take a look at this." He pushed a green folder into the light. "Oh, by the way, that folder will be yours. There is more information—much much more—for you to read. But for now, pay attention to this."

Worthington frowned, confused.

"Just hold your questions," Rinehart said, reading Nat's thoughts. "Things will be much clearer in a few moments.

"Here is a picture," Rinehart continued, handing Worthington a glossy photograph that looked like a standard publicity shot, "of Nikolai Valente. You're familiar with him, I presume?" the older man looked at Nat inquiringly.

"Certainly. Principal dancer with the Kirov for the past five years or so; parents of Czech descent, also dancers, mostly folk ballet; temperamental, a womanizer, married to a dancer also with the Kirov," Nat recited. "That's about all I know. I haven't followed dance that intensely since I left Harvard. I don't suppose I know any more about the current scene than the casual viewer."

"Well, there's more in here," Rinehart tapped the green folder with the mouthpiece of his pipe, "that you can go over later. But for the purpose of our discussion now, the following will suffice: Valente is a brilliant dancer—some say he is the reincarnation of Nijinsky. He is a nonconformist in the Soviet sense, and the bureaucracy is beginning to resent what he considers his artistic freedom. He's also a spoiled brat, having nearly every wish granted, and even the most mundane chores taken care of by either the company's flunkies or his wife Tania." With this, Rinehart slid another publicity shot out of the folder and handed it to Nat.

The face that stared out at him made him sit up in his chair. Tania Valente was simply the most captivating woman he'd ever seen.

"Funny, I don't remember her from my studies," Nat said. "Is she a recent addition?"

"Very," Rinehart said. "She was an unknown dancer with the Gorky troupe when she was spotted at a competition—both by the party and by Valente who is always looking for virgin territory—and selected to dance for the Kirov. She hasn't danced for some eight months now. But more about her in the other folder— that's not germane to our present briefing," said Rinehart as he returned his attention to the contents of the green folder.

"Valente, though a spoiled artist and a scoundrel, is a brilliant performer, certainly in the same field as many of the other Kirov and Bolshoi defectors now dancing in the West." Rinehart drew heavily on his pipe.

"The Soviets put up with his hijinks and unorthodox ways because he is good. But even that is not enough in Soviet ballet," Rinehart said. "What really keeps Valente on top are his high-ranking political contacts, plus the fact that he's screwing the wife of a top political figure and she pulls the strings for her stud."

"Pugachev?" Nat asked.

"We'll get to that," Rinehart promised, with a wave of his hand. Nat nodded.

"Valente is really on top now, with the beating of Illych in Washington last week," Rinehart continued. "The ballet troupe thinks it was KGB retribution for Illych's plans to defect. Our intelligence confirms that beyond a doubt. Although set up to look like another D.C. mugging, it was intended to stifle any further such moves by other members.

"But the ploy backfired. The Soviets—as unsubtle as usual—miscalculated the dancers' reactions. Word now has it that half the troupe is ready to storm off the stage after the conclusion of the New York performance and ask for asylum."

"And Valente is one of them, right?" asked Nat. He leaned forward in his chair, elbows on his knees. The story had begun to intrigue him.

Rinehart nodded. "Valente spoke with a dance critic for the *Washington Post* one evening after a Kennedy Center performance, and the reporter contacted the State Department the next day. It was going to be handled in the usual way for prominent defectors—though God knows we don't need any more Russian

45

dancers—until the boys at the CIA ran the usual background check on him. That check confirmed a lot we already knew or suspected, but revealed a key fact that has resulted in our little meeting here today."

Suddenly Nat's head began to swim. A defecting ballet dancer. Schism in the Politburo. KGB thugs ruining one of their own dancers. And on top of it, his vision was blurring. Oh God, not now. This was an opportunity to return to living, and now his vision was going, just as it did every other time he'd blacked out.

He couldn't let Rinehart see. He couldn't black out now.

"Nat? Is something wrong?" Rinehart's voice was concerned, suspicious.

"No," Nat lied. "No, I'm just thinking . . . trying to absorb all these facts . . . that's all." He needed some silence. He needed to concentrate, to block the darkness that was seeping into his head. "May I see those again?" Nat asked, stalling for time. Rinehart handed him the pictures of the two Valentes to him. He stared at them as if committing them to memory, and Rinehart didn't interrupt.

Nat stifled a sigh of relief as his vision started to return to normal, and his heart rate slowed to a calmer pace. He had defeated the darkness this time.

"Go on please, Mr. Rinehart," Nat said, handing the photos back.

"You're obviously searching for a way to tie things together, Nat, so I won't keep you in suspense any longer. As you guessed, Valente's biggest patron is Pugachev. Despite his belligerent nature, Pugachev has long been a lover of the arts and ballet in particular. Pugachev's power, and the shield of his GRU agents, have kept Valente's enemies at bay."

Rinehart leaned toward Nat. "Kokh and his KGB would love nothing better than to get rid of Pugachev," he said somberly. "Pugachev's GRU, though, has him so tightly guarded that even the omnipresent KGB can't get next to him, can't get into any sort of position to carry off a sanction."

"And?" Nat asked.

"We want you to kill him."

Chapter Six

||||||||||||||||||||||||||||||||||||||||||||||||||||||||||||||||||||||||||||||||||||||||||||

The fragrance was sweat. Stale sweat from rehearsals past, fresh sweat dripping from the glistening bodies of forty dancers straining through their paces. Sweat embedded in the walls and ceiling, sweat staining the barre and darkening the backs and armpits of the dancers' tops, and hanging in the woolen leg warmers and matted towels flung over the wooden barre that ran around the circumference of the room. It was raw sweat, refined sweat, vintage sweat, the lifeblood of ballet.

For Nathaniel Worthington, there was also the sweat of anxiety and embarrassment.

"All right now, we do routine, eh?" The wrinkled crone at the front of the cavernous room issued her orders, and Nat tried to concentrate on them. "Now diagonal. You do *coupé, glissade, cabriole,* and *arabesque.*"

How in hell did I get into *this,* Nat thought, as he searched his memory for the right movements. By the time he had things worked out, the class had started to move, and he was off by a beat.

Three days ago—was it only three days?—when he'd met with Rinehart, he had thought the task was impossible, suicidal. And it quite possibly was. But it was the only chance he had.

"Number thirty-three," a voice penetrated his thoughts. "Number thirty-three, are you listening?" Nat realized the old woman was looking at him.

"Uh, yes . . . yes, ma'am . . . sorry, please excuse me." Nat stammered.

"Well, if you are going to remain in this audition, you take it seriously. Now, children . . ."

The woman continued, and as she did, Nat brought his attention back to the room. Morning light poured into the whitewashed industrial loft and painted long shadows, anchored to the floor by eighty slipper-clad feet, and reflected in the mirrors that covered three walls.

The other ballet students ranged in age from a young boy of about twelve to a woman Nat figured must have been pushing forty. All had come to audition for Madame Vazem, one of the few surviving ballerinas from the era of Imperial Russian Ballet. She had first danced with the Maryinsky Theatre in St. Petersburg as a member of the corps de ballet in 1910, and here she was, more than ninety years old, still living—living ballet and teaching it to youngsters who knew the Maryinsky only as the Kirov, and St. Petersburg as Leningrad. But they came because they wanted instruction from a woman whose tradition extended in an unbroken line from Nijinsky and Pavlova to the present.

"Numbers thirty-four, thirty-seven," the woman's assistant called. "You may leave. Also numbers seventeen, nineteen, and twenty-three."

A teenage girl with knock knees, another one with the figure of a beer keg, and a spindly acne-faced boy

50

of indeterminate age all slouched dejectedly from the floor. A woman in her twenties in front of Nat who had been performing her routines well, but who was barely five feet tall, hesitated, and then stalked across the floor.

"Number twenty-three," Varem's assistant repeated herself. "Number twenty-three, did you hear me? You may leave." It was the older woman, and she glared at Varem and her assistant, and then imperially strode from the studio. That left thirty-five dancers. Nat knew the only reason he hadn't been cut by now was the relative scarcity of male dancers.

Not that he was that bad, he reassured himself during this short break. The three days of intensive practice Rinehart had arranged for him had freshened his abilities, unused since his days at Harvard.

Instead of taking up better-known sports, Nat had defied his father's more conventional wishes of crew and rugby and had studied karate and ballet, two activities whose movements he found almost identical, but whose purposes were diametrically opposed.

The study of karate and other martial arts over the years had kept his body facile, and he had been surprised at how well his muscles recalled the ballet movements. No, the boss' strategy had been faultless in this regard.

Rinehart's people had outfitted Nat with the typical accoutrements of the ballet student, and had taken care that the materials looked appropriately used: his slippers were taped together, the tights mended, the tank top frayed, and the canvas practice bag suitably scuffed and beaten. It lay in a corner of the room, surrounded by other bags, containing more tights, leotards, tops, dance belts, slippers, toe shoes, towels, needles and threads, colognes and more. The practice bag lent as much to the stereotypical appearance of dancers as their erect carriage, scrubbed complexions, and the turned-out way they walked.

51

For Nat's part, only a thin line of flab around his waist might suggest that he was not a dancer—perhaps a slightly clumsy one, as evidenced by his performance today—but nothing to raise an alarm.

Damn Niki! Damn the Kirov! Damn them all, those sycophantic little assholes. And damn the KGB who always had enough people to follow her everywhere.

Tania looked to her left as she strode across Forty-fifth Street against the light. Her escort quickened her pace as a barrage of yellow taxis bore down on them. The KGB escort—who lived in New York and functioned as combined guide and keeper for visiting Russians—shot her an angry glance, as if Tania's crossing had been a deliberate attempt to injure them both.

"You really should be careful," the guide said. "This is a very dangerous city. Capitalists care little for the safety of citizens."

Tania gave her a withering look and walked on without replying.

They walked uptown on Second Avenue, threading their way among the throngs of pedestrians who clogged the sidewalk.

Once, when Tania stopped to gaze at a display of jazz albums, her guide berated her. "That's the height of Western decadence," the woman said. "I am surprised you would be attracted by that sort of hooligan music."

All Tania wanted was just to be left alone for a while. But no. Niki was after her to continue to dance. The Kirov director was still trying to force her to teach ballet—and had set up the appointment to which she was presently going. And the KGB dogged her every step.

They're all tearing at my body, she thought. They won't give me time to think, time to figure out what I want to do.

Maybe they were doing it on purpose. Maybe they

knew that, given her own way, she'd do something they didn't find acceptable. Suddenly Tania knew that was right, and the guilt of the ungrateful child swept over her. Even the brilliant sun now failed to penetrate her gloom as she continued to march toward the ballet studio and her guide prattled on and on with the timeworn clichés of the Soviet ideologue.

"You are so fortunate to live in the Soviet motherland," the woman said. "I fear the corruption of the American capitalist system, and take special care to assure it does not affect me." She looked up at Tania for a reaction and, receiving none, changed the subject.

"Madame Varem is a glorious teacher, a well-known opponent of the czars and other oppressors of the Russian people. It is widely known that she would return to her native Leningrad if only the Americans would allow her. But it is also widely known that she is held under virtual house arrest, and the imperialist Americans force her to give them all her students' tuition and in return give her only a poverty wage to sustain herself."

As they reached the mammoth brick building with its domino-stack of dirty windows and peeling white paint, Tania had already fantasized half a dozen ways of killing her escort, two of which involved torture. Why were people like this necessary? Why the self-deception? Why was it all necessary, Tania wondered. Why did Russians have to lie to themselves and everyone else, and why were they the only people who actually believed their own lies?

In fact, Varem remained in the United States voluntarily, and though she hated communism as much as she had the czars, she kept her mouth shut, for only by doing so did she remain an acceptable person for Kirov and Bolshoi personnel to visit. And those visits were second in her life only to her teaching.

So it was to Madame Varem that the Kirov director

53

had sent Tania, in hopes that the old woman's lifelong love of dance and teaching would somehow inspire her.

She had really wanted to visit the Museum of Modern Art, and the Whitney museum and the Guggenheim and the other famous New York museums, but those were labeled "hotbeds of artistic perversion and decadence" by the party officials who accompanied the tour. They forbade her to visit them.

So this was it. But at least this gave Tania a chance to get away from the company and the incessant atmosphere of the performance for a little while. A chance to walk and to enjoy people who weren't dancers. Normal, Tania reflected, that's what she'd like to be—like all the people she saw around her that afternoon, normal.

The hallway was painted in dusty shadows, and the stairs were steep, and complained in squeaky voices as Tania and her companion climbed them. From the head of the stairs, strains of piano music drifted downward, and she found herself humming a familiar strain of Stravinsky as she reached the landing. She liked the music. Perhaps I'd like the dance too, she told herself, if only I weren't forced to do it.

A knot of expectant mothers, anxious friends and rejected auditioners who wanted to watch the rest of the audition clotted the corner of the studio and bled onto the landing. Tania and her KGB escort pushed their way slowly to the front to watch the proceedings.

"No, no number twelve," Varem's voice was strong yet conveyed the frailty of age. "You are jumping like a cow. You go thud, thud, thud, thud. Land softly, don't try to break my floor! Now try it once again the series of four leaps."

The piano resumed its melody, and as it did, the studio reverberated with four window-rattling booms.

"Thank you, number twelve, you may leave."

Varem and her assistant had winnowed the original

number down to twenty-three, of which only ten would be accepted.

Worthington's heart skipped when he spied Tania Valente pushing her way through the throng in the corner. Rinehart's intelligence had been right on the nose. Nat looked up at the clock on the wall, and noted that the Kirov ballerina, accompanied by a lumpy woman who looked like a jailer from San Quentin, were exactly on time. It was 11 A.M. precisely. He tried not to stare or show them any undue attention as they settled themselves at the edge of the crowd, leaning back against the barre.

She looked even more beautiful than in the publicity shots, Nat thought as the audition continued. Her hair now fell around her shoulders, and her breasts tugged at the fabric of her plainly cut silk blouse. Beneath the hem of a simple navy blue skirt her slender legs showed the muscular beauty of a dancer.

The music resumed. Pirouettes and more pirouettes. Nat was breathing hard, and he felt tiny drops of sweat pelt his skin as they whirled off nearby dancers' bodies. His mind was no longer on the audition, as he tried to figure out what to say first. His inattention achieved a natural reaction.

"Number thirty-three," Nat looked down to make sure it was his number, "Thank you. You may go now."

Feigning deep disappointment, Nat walked to his practice bag, and headed toward the crowd by the door.

Chapter Seven

||||||||||||||||||||||||||||||||||||||||||||||||||||||||||||||||||||||||||||||||||||||||

"How do you think he will do?"

"Brilliantly, of course." Rinehart placed his cut-crystal tumbler carefully on the table and turned toward the leaded glass window that overlooked the rear grounds of his Foxhall Road estate. "He has always been brilliant and I detect no change—"

"But the . . . accident . . ."

"The 'accident,' if indeed it was one, seems to have left young . . . well, he's getting older . . . Worthington in excellent shape. He seems as fit and acute as the day I recruited him."

"You're sure?"

"Of course I'm sure." Rinehart turned from the pastoral scene, its manicured grass and docile geese and the little pond in which they lolled, and confronted the man with just a hint of irritation. To those who knew Rinehart, that little hint was all that ever showed, and when it did it signified an underlying fury. "I'm positive . . . not that it makes any difference, does it? You don't seem to have come up with any alternatives on your own."

The man was silent. He glanced uneasily at the older man's piercing eyes, and then anxiously shifted his eyes to an antique china cabinet beside the window. The silence bore into him. "Well . . . he, uh . . ." Silence must be broken, even if by nonsense. "He *is* the best choice," the man said. "After all, he's the only agent we've got who ever took ballet. And he speaks Russian," the man was warming to his task.

"Don't forget the Spanish," Rinehart said coldly. "Nor the French, the German and the working fluency in Portuguese and a dozen dialects of Chinese and Southeast Asian."

Silence returned and it was chillier than before.

Rinehart walked to the liquor tray and freshened his Chivas. He didn't offer to freshen the uncomfortable man's drink.

Rinehart approached the man as he stood awkwardly by the dining room table, looking out the window as if he could regain his composure by imitating Rinehart.

He looked at Rinehart, and could not fix the gaze. He looked about the room in skitterish jerks of his head: at Rinehart, at the window, at Rinehart's drink, at the liquor tray wondering if he dare pour another, at the china in the cabinet and finally at his own shoe laces.

"It's all right," Rinehart said, satisfied he had wrung his vengence, noting that the man's upper lip looked like the frosted side of his freshened drink. "I suppose I shouldn't be so hard on you. But I want to be sure that you have put any personal grudges aside. Put Amsterdam and all that led up to it in the past. This is *the* big play, and I don't want your petty jealousies to foul it up. Is that clear?"

"Yes . . . sir," the man's voice cracked; it was

nearly a high-pitched squeak. He cleared his throat and tried again. "Yes, sir." This time he succeeded.

"Good," Rinehart continued. "Because the success depends on each person doing his assigned task to perfection. It's of the utmost importance that you do exactly as instructed, even if it seems irrational. Understand?" He looked for recognition and obedience in the man's eyes and, finding both, continued. "Because I am the only person who has the entire plan, you and the other key personnel must not try to second-guess the action. Creativity is not called for, just precision and execution. Agreed?" Rinehart frowned at the man's flicker of hesitation as he nodded. Rinehart attributed it to the man's crushed vanity. After all, he mused, the director of the CIA is used to knowing the entire game plan.

As he walked from the audition area, Nat had a pang of disappointment that made his act for Tania Valente not altogether an act. For several moments there, he had been back in the studios at Harvard, trying to perfect his leaps, trying to do the endless pirouettes that brought crowds to their feet. Funny, he thought, how our minds play games with themselves. For the last five or ten minutes, he'd been dancing like he was really trying to make the final cut.

He could see himself, the meaty freshman arriving at the stuffy, decrepit space that Harvard allotted to dancing. But there he was, overconfident after a stellar four years in prep athletics, eager to conquer this new sport. Now as he walked through a studio in New York some seventeen years later, he could still recall the hungry look on the college instructor's face, as she surveyed the only new male dancer that year.

Nat smiled faintly as he remembered the look on another face—his father's—when Nat informed him that he was not only refusing to try out for football or crew, but also intended to try ballet dancing instead. The

59

mask of abject horror that spread across his father's face that day, and the way he spilled his scotch on the new cream-colored cut-pile carpeting in his study, was enough to convince Nat he had made the correct decision.

His best images of his father—indeed his whole damn blue-blooded family—was one of club ties and pin stripes and cotillions and noblesse oblige and forever, forever doing the proper thing for a member of the Worthington family to do.

It was pre-Baryshnikov, pre-*Turning Point*, pre-Nureyev-as-Valentino. It was the era of "All ballet dancers are homosexuals." Nat liked the way the word *homosexual* rolled off his father's tongue, and the distasteful way he had of wrinkling up his face when he said it. It was not "queer" or "homo"—his father was too formal for those colloquialisms (Everything has a name, Nathaniel, remember that. Everything on this earth has a name, and as long as you can describe them properly, you will never suffer the slings of the inarticulate, nor the arrows of confusion and miscommunication.") and the term "gay" still described the sort of apparel that most people donned at Christmastime.

Soon after he began studying ballet, Nat wandered by the gymnasium and, attracted by the thuds and grunts from one of the exercise rooms, peered through a crack and saw roundhouse kicks that looked like arabesques, and precise movements that covered the gamut of every movement in ballet.

Karate was a different form of expression of movement. Where ballet was literature to be read for its intrinsic beauty, karate was a how-to manual, valued more for its results than for its own style. The one made him better at the other.

Nat realized that he might have attempted a career in dance had it not been for the intervention of a visiting professor who lectured in a course on defense poli-

60

cies and arms control and who wound up teaching Nat more than a lesson.

The visiting professor had been Richard B. Rinehart, part of the Kennedy brain trust. Seventeen years ago, Rinehart had taken a lithe, strong, mentally facile but essentially naive Nathaniel Worthington who was wedged between rebelling from his family and finding out who he was, and propelled him into a maelstrom which everyone—including Nat—thought had ended in Amsterdam.

Nudged on both sides by the mob of spectators, and from behind by her "companion," Tania Valente felt claustrophobic, crushed by the moist essence of strangers' bodies: musky, fragrant, rancid, clean, dirty, like the odor of freshly plowed humus, and the dank smell of dark wet places. The scents of those around her enveloped her; it made her uncomfortable, and she began to perspire, and add her own contribution to the stew.

"This is only a preliminary weeding out," her companion interrupted her, jabbing a finger into Tania's back to get her attention. Tania winced and twisted away from the woman.

"Yes," Tania replied curtly. "Yes, that's apparent." She returned her attention to the floor routines, puzzled at her inability to assert herself any further. Silently she watched as Madame Varem went about her skillful discharge of the less-talented dancers, feeling, as she instinctively judged each one's form and technique, a pang of guilt. The old, familiar guilt. After all, who was *she* to judge?

Rubbing her temples to ward off a headache she knew was coming, Tania cringed imperceptibly as a boy thrashed and clomped through a series of leaps, and was dismissed, followed by an older male dancer who looked to her practiced eye like someone trying to make a comeback.

61

The young boy dashed for the shelter of the crowd, crimson with embarrassment, and the older dancer walked slowly to the barre and angrily jerked his practice bag from the floor. The swift movement surprised Tania, and she found herself following him with her eyes as he made his way around the studio. She hoped he wouldn't leave right away. To her pleasure, he stopped several feet away from her and stood stolidly watching the remainder of the audition.

Out of the corner of her eye, Tania saw the man's easy breathing and the relative lack of perspiration on his face, indicating that he was in very good condition. But for the tanned-away, thin lines about his eyes, and the slight bulge at the waist of his tights, she'd have thought him to be twenty-four or twenty-five years old. But she figured his age more correctly closer to thirty. She admired his muscular legs, and noted how tight his ass was when he bent down to pick up his bag. But she liked most the easy air about him, and the character of his face. She liked the way the lines ran from his eyes—smile lines, as if he laughed a great deal—and the angular masculinity of his cheekbones.

An image of going to bed with him, feeling those muscular legs wrapped around hers, flashed through her mind, followed by guilt. This time she angrily chased the guilt away. If Niki can play around, there's nothing wrong with my looking, she told herself, directing her eyes back to the audition.

The next time she looked toward Nat, he was standing next to her, and she felt her heart beating faster. She was trying to look at him without seeming to do so, when he suddenly turned his head and smiled at her.

A hot embarrassed flush spread over face and she snapped her eyes back to the dancers in front of her. Her entire body was hot, as if she had walked into an overheated room with a fur coat on.

Stupid child! Tania cursed herself. Now you've been

caught eyeing the forbidden fruit, disgraced yourself, and what will the KGB say if he talks to you, and American men are like that, likely to talk to you for no reason at all, but the KGB would think it was more and . . .

"Hello."

The simple greeting sounded like a blast and Tania stiffened under its shock wave. The back of her neck tingled as she stared wide-eyed at the audition, seeing nothing and wondering what to do.

Nat saw her stiffen, and for an instant was angry at a system that could make people so afraid of other people. As he looked at Tania Valente's profile in the crowd, he caught a deepening in the perpetual frown worn by the San Quentin prison guard behind her. He'd have to play this one naively, or it would be all over.

He watched as she stared rigidly ahead, moving only her right forefinger as she caressed a tiny scar on her jaw. Without the scar, Nat reflected, the face would have been almost chilling in its classic beauty. But the scar gave her humanity. He wondered how she had gotten it.

"Pardon me," Nat said. "But maybe you could give me some insight on why I was cut? You look as if you know ballet well."

It was only a professional question. Tania relaxed a little, and returned Nat's smile, half disappointed that he wasn't trying to make a play for her after all.

However, her smile quickly faded as her companion jostled her in an effort to come between them.

"Excuse me," the San Quentin prison guard barked at Nat, "But this is a very special visitor and you should not bother her with such requests."

Nat played the wounded waif. "I . . . uh, it's just . . . I'm sorry if I acted . . . ah, what I mean is that I don't want to bother anyone," he said dejectedly, his voice aching with the disappointment of someone twice rejected.

"It's all right," Tania told him sympathetically.

"No," said the guard shoving her way forward, "I think—"

"I *said* it's all *right!*" Tania said with such ferocity that she surprised herself. The guard backed down, but continued to glower at them.

"It's all right," Tania repeated herself softly. "But what makes you think I would know something about ballet?" She gave him a coy smile, vaguely conscious that she was flirting with this American stranger.

"You look like a dancer," the young man was saying to her.

"I guess it's the . . . the *knowing* look on your face," Nat continued, "as if you knew exactly what was going on. Do you understand?" He looked into a pair of startling beautiful green eyes. *Colleen had green eyes.* Damn it, he admonished himself. Colleen was another life. This is business; don't mix them, or you've had it.

"I hadn't realized that one could look as if she knew ballet," Tania said.

"Well . . . you do. Don't you?" Nat said uncertainly. Perhaps, he thought, he should have been an actor.

"Yes," Tania smiled broadly, "I do know something about dance."

Nat's shoulders relaxed, and he wore a gratified face of relief.

"Well, then," he said.

"Well then, what?" Tania replied.

"My dancing," he said. "Why did Madame Varem cut me?"

"Because you weren't good enough," Tania replied and then regretted her bluntness as she saw the smile vanish from the young man's face.

64

"Yes," Nat mumbled. "I know that. But what wasn't good enough?"

"You're a good dancer," Tania replied, trying to repair the damage she had done. "Your technique is excellent, but you're out of practice. Yes, I'd say you were—"

"Now," the scowling KGB companion had come to life. "Madame Varem wants to introduce you."

Tania looked toward the aging prima ballerina, and noted that, indeed, she was being summoned. She started to move toward the old woman, and then stopped to look at Nat. She nearly stumbled as the guard thumped into her back.

"Wait!" she called to Nat. "Don't go away. I'll be right back." She smiled at him, and the smile he flashed her in return convinced her that it would be worth the hassle the KGB would later give her.

The city lay before his eyes, submerged in the frenetic scrambling of its occupants to survive yet another day. And by the reckoning of the ultra-thin Piaget watch on Mustafa Salem el-Nouty's dark slim wrist, they had so far made it past half of their working day—it was nearly noon. He yawned his greetings to the new day, and stretched languidly before his plate glass window overlooking the sprawling megalopolis. He thought of the people below and what they might be doing this day: cringing under the criticism of a superior, screaming at shopkeepers over real or imagined frauds, dodging taxicabs and the other projectiles of fate that made a city more of a jungle than Darwin's and the game of survival possible only by the fittest of the fit.

Complacent in his judgment that he was the fittest of all, el-Nouty turned from the window and padded barefoot across the deep cut-pile carpeting to the telephone and ordered breakfast sent up.

His voice was rich like a bite of cheesecake, and his manners impeccable. The front desk always gave him

65

this suite when he stayed here; they *liked* the elegant and gracious Mr. el-Nouty. Though he spoke little, and never repeated himself, he was courteous to doormen and chambermaids, considerate of the bellhops who carried his hand-stitched leather luggage to his suite, and a handsome tipper to all. Despite his obvious wealth, he was *with* them, never belittled them, always remembered their names, and was careful to listen to their little tales of common life and woe. He *understood*. Here was a rich man who truly deserved his wealth.

And so it was that he was almost worshipped by them all. El-Nouty pushed away from the king-sized bed—he needed its length to comfortably accommodate his six-foot-seven-inch frame—and walked to the anteroom to the bathroom, where he flicked on the light and squinted briefly as the flourescents blinked on. He let his velour robe fall open and drop to the floor, leaving his smooth olive skin framed in the mirror.

He was lean but muscular at 210 pounds. Veins throbbed on his arms, his legs and the washboard ripples of his stomach. There had been a time when he was emaciated, left to die, his body feeding on itself like a snake eating its own tail.

But that was for a history book, el-Nouty told himself, a biography that could rock and topple world governments, and one he would never write. He would never write it, he thought, as he leaned close to the mirrors to look at his black piercing eyes, because to do so would end his wealth and, quite possibly, his life.

Satisfied that no new wrinkles had creased his face during his sleep, el-Nouty straightened up and stared nose to nose with his reflection, so convinced of his own superiority that he believed his reflection would blink before he did.

He chuckled at the thought, as he entered the bathroom and turned on the shower. Steam curled up

66

from the tub, and flowed like tiny cumulus through the air-conditioned suite.

He let the water beat on his back as he let every muscle relax: concentration on every cell, one by one, would neutralize the toxins, drive them out, let them flee from the power of his will, leave him strong, afraid of none but Allah. He shampooed and soaped quickly, rinsed, and then shut off the hot water entirely. The water moved through gray temperatures, and then cascaded cold, frigid. When the last of the heat was swept away from his body, el-Nouty shut off the water, and stepped out to towel off.

There were twice as many towels in here as there should be, he noted. The chambermaids were always trying to do something extra for him.

He never wondered about why the little people loved him. They always had, and he'd come to expect it. The generals feared him, but the spear carriers worshipped him.

As he dried his full but neatly trimmed mustache, he wondered what the chambermaids who left him extra towels would think if they knew he was due in two hours to meet with the director of the American CIA's covert operations division. And he wondered how they would view him if they knew that he lived in this world for only one thing: to kill.

"This is ill-advised," Tania's companion admonished her. "I have received no instructions about this sort of . . . of . . . deviation from the schedule. I am to direct you back to your room in time for the midday meal with company members. This is definitely not—"

"Shut up," Tania snapped. "Will you just shut up! There is nothing in the world wrong with attending a theater production, and besides this one is filled with dance." Tania paused, enjoying her new-found anger. "And it's for *children* . . . can you understand that?

What possible harm, what possible damage to my ideology can a children's play cause? *What*?"

For the first time since they had begun to walk from Madame Varem's ballet studio, the KGB escort was silent. Perhaps she was tired of arguing, and would instead settle for a condemnatory report on Tania's rebellious conduct that would absolve *her* of any responsibility for it.

Nat had no way of knowing, and actually didn't care. What was important was that he was walking to a theatre with Tania Valente where he would get a chance to talk with her about a defection: hers and her husband's.

After the introductions at the studio, where Madame Varem had presented Tania to the assembled crowd of aspiring or rejected dancers and other assorted hangers-on, fawned over her, and called her to stand with her and her instructors, Nat had invited Tania to go with him to a friend's noontime production of a Winnie the Pooh tale adapted to the stage.

He'd produced two tickets from his rehearsal bag, and that was when the KGB escort really began to squawk: it was not on the schedule, the play might not be approved, there were only two tickets, suppose this man were an agent provocateur for the American CIA and wanted to get her in trouble, and so on and so on in a steady stream.

Nat allayed one fear: his friend was at the box office and would have another ticket for the escort. No, he couldn't guarantee that the seat would be next to his and Tania's but he promised to try—knowing that the theatre would be full and the only available seat well out of earshot and nearly out of sight.

It had been surprisingly easy to talk Tania Valente into attending the performance. Nat had expected a great deal more paranoia. Though Tania was still definitely suspicious, she'd agreed quickly to come along. It was a good sign, Nat reflected, as they turned the corner and sighted the theater marquee. A sinuous line of toddlers and adults worked its way along the sidewalk halfway down the block.

"Now look at that," Tania said to her escort. "Do they look like they're dangerous? They're just children."

The escort said nothing, though Tania thought she could imagine what the woman must be thinking. And perhaps the woman was right. What *did* she think she was doing? It was wrong, incorrect, deviant . . . ungrateful to those who had planned her day.

And yet . . . for once, it was what Tania *wanted* to do. Wasn't that enough reason? True this man might be dangerous. But wasn't he attractive? It was all rather delicious.

"Yes," she had said aloud, and startled herself as she did so. She'd meant to tell him no thank you.

The yes drove her heart relentlessly. She felt lightheaded and—what was it, she wondered, as she strolled along between this Nat Worthington and her escort—alive? Yes, came the triumphant thought. *Alive.* And colors seemed brighter, there was contrast where she was used to seeing blurred margins to life. *Alive!*

And as quickly as it had materialized, the euphoria dissolved. Reality; what could she *really* do? She was breaking the Kirov rules, bossing about a KGB escort, placing herself in jeopardy for . . . for . . . a fantasy about a stranger.

They stopped at the box office, and she looked at him: faded jeans over his tights and a blue chambray work shirt. She felt her cheeks burn with embarrassment . . . and the passion of her fantasy as her eyes enjoyed the look of his body.

She walked through a daze of conversation. Somewhere her KGB escort protested the location of her seat, and Tania heard herself telling her to shut up and sit down. A kaleidoscope of emotions was spinning around her, prisms of blinding exhilaration and life shining against dark facets of guilt and fear serving only to show her how good it felt to be alive if for only a short while, to show her how satisfying it felt to do what *you* wanted to do, and to be away from those who only wanted you to do what they commanded.

Her elbow burned from the touch of Nat's hand as he guided her to their seats. She sat down and slowly tested the elbow with her hand to see if it really was as warm as it felt. She wanted to take his arm and lean her head against it, run her hand along the inside of his thigh. . . .

That's enough! She thought and straightened up in her seat.

The house lights dimmed and the curtain rose. Small talk faded, but the soft chatter of small children unaccustomed to being quieted mingled with the rustling of tiny bodies squirming in their seats. Unaccountably, Tania was reminded of rare times of happiness in her childhood, summer vacations in the Baltic. There, even on the quietest of evenings, the forest still lived and breathed, but out of direct human sight or hearing. She relaxed. Yes, this was vacation and she never wanted it to end.

Was this how Niki felt when he defied the Kirov management? Did he feel this alive? She wondered. And if he did, was that why he did all those things? Was his rebellion against authority a way for him to capture this brilliant feeling?

And a darker thought crept across her mind: Was she his wife, his officially sanctioned female marriage partner—a part of the authority he wanted to—had to—flout in order to stay alive. And for just an instant, Tania understood his adultery, and it was all right. And she wondered if the brilliant feeling of being alive could be prolonged by defecting to the West. Or was that, too, just a fantasy? She was losing her head.

She looked sideways at Nat, who seemed to be concentrating on the play, his sparkling blue-green eyes fixed straight ahead.

The first act passed quickly, and when the lights came on for intermission, they watched a frantic exodus of parents and toddlers streaming to void filled bladders.

"Well, what do you think of the play?" Nat asked by way of small talk as they stood up to stretch their legs. In the rear, the KGB escort was trying futilely to push her way toward them against the rip tide of bodies. Nat smiled inwardly, knowing intermission would be nearly over by the time the woman got to them.

"It's . . . well, we have nothing like it in Russia," Tania replied. "Most children's theatre is not for fun. All the plays must have an ideological theme that supports the motherland, or the Ministry of Culture will not allow it to be staged."

Nat knew all about that. But he professed ignorance.

"Really," he said in a surprised voice. "I didn't know that. You mean people can't just stage anything they like?"

And the conversation continued in that vein until the escort arrived, and denounced the play as a "bourgeoisie capitalist distraction to divert the minds of the young from the horrors of the oppressive American system."

Nat smiled politely, then watched smugly as the tide reversed itself, and the thuggish woman elbowed her way back to her seat.

"I'm so sorry that she—"

"Sh-h-h-h, it's all right," Nat said.

"But she was so rude!"

"A performer gets used to rude people, no?"

"Yes," she said slowly, realizing the truth of his statement. And it dawned on her that she liked this even-tempered stranger a lot. "Of course," she mur-

71

mured. And they sat down as the house lights dimmed for the second and last time that performance.

The play started, unnoticed by Tania, absorbed as she was in her own passion play. She was so engrossed that she hardly noted Nat when he leaned over and whispered in her ear. In fact she caught only the last syllable.

". . . ect."

"What? I'm sorry, I wasn't paying attention," she whispered back, checking behind her to make sure her escort couldn't see them talking. What he said when he repeated himself loosened a hurricane inside her.

"I said, would you like to defect?"

Chapter Eight

|||||||||||||||||||||||||||||||||||||||||||||||||||||||||||||||||||||||||||||||||||

"Tania?"

She sat unmoving, insensate. She could not feel the chair seat under her, nor see the play on the brilliantly lit stage, and she could barely hear the young man as he spoke to her in quiet, measured tones. This could not be happening to her.

Tania Valente closed her eyes and wished for once she could wake up from life into a dream.

"Tania?" the stranger repeated. Reluctantly, she opened her eyes. Color and sound rushed back into her consciousness. This *was* what she had been wishing for, wasn't it? Well, wasn't it?

"I don't know," she told Nat.

"The offer is good for you and for your husband," Nat added.

The mention of Niki angered her.

"Who are you?" she whispered viciously in his ear. "Whom do you work for? Why have you come to me in this . . . this . . . underhanded manner?"

"Sh-h-h-h, calm down," Nat said soothingly as he

leaned toward her. Tania had turned in her seat to face Nat and was clutching a handful of his shirt sleeve in a tiny fist.

"I'll explain everything," Nat continued. "And you don't have to do a single thing you don't want to—nothing. All I ask is that you listen to me." He looked at the stage lights reflecting in her eyes, and without thinking brought his hand up to cover the hand gripping his arm. He watched some of the fear drain from her face, scowl lines smooth, and the pupils of her eyes relax from their pinpoint stare.

Her hand was warm, soft. Heat rose to his face.

Colleen's hands were warm and soft, they exuded love, when. . . .

Goddamnit! Stop it! This is not Colleen. This is a defector. You are an agent. This is not allowed. You're going to get somebody hurt if you get emotional.

Slowly Nat returned his hand to his own lap.

Tania sighed. However was she going to be able to sort this all out? No matter how badly Niki had treated her, she wasn't going to do anything that could hurt him. And there was definitely danger here. This seductive stranger—whoever he was—could get them into the same sort of trouble as Illych.

She heard the screams of Illych's wife that night in Washington, and shuddered involuntarily at the thought of KGB thugs pounding those beautiful legs.

"Are you cold?" Nat persisted. "I have a sweat shirt in my practice bag if you need it."

"No, no. I'm all right really," she replied. She liked looking at his face. She liked the faint scar under his right eye, and reminded herself to ask him how he got it, when they got a chance to. . . .

To do what? Just what do you think is going to happen here? You're not rehearsing for a production, you know.

But he still had a nice face, and she did like the scar.

"Listen," she began. "I don't really know what I should be doing. I somehow feel that I shouldn't be talking to you, that what I really ought to do is get my KGB guardian and leave here. . . ."

"But?" he asked.

"But I'm not, and I don't know why."

"I'm glad, because I want you to hear me out," Nat started. "It is something that will change your life drastically—for the better." He looked at her, and saw her not just looking *at* him, but into him, searching. She was falling for *him*, not for the defection or anything else. In fact, Nat realized guiltily, but with a sense of professional satisfaction, if she hadn't been attracted to him, she would probably be gone by now.

Careful, he cautioned himself. The attraction is okay just as long as you can use it. Play her for all it takes to get the job done. Just don't *you* get sucked into it.

But it didn't feel right, and that worried Nat, because he knew that sooner or later affection for this woman would get him into more trouble than he could handle.

"But we can't talk here," Nat said, looking around at the people nearby.

"Where?" Tania asked.

Nat relaxed. She was hooked. She'd meet him to talk further.

"If my information is right, the KGB people at the Kirov mostly watch your husband," Nat said, wondering briefly why he hadn't used the man's name.

"That's right," Tania said. "They assume I wouldn't do anything without him, and so they don't watch me as closely . . . except like today when I spend an entire day away from the company."

"So they only watch your hotel room. . . ."

"When Niki is there," she responded. "The guard outside the door follows him whenever he leaves me."

"And leaves you unguarded?"

She nodded.

"Good. Here's what we do."

Mustafa Salem el-Nouty winced as Everett Lowell spoke. The CIA executive sprayed the table and his Libyan guest with a shower of moist crumbs as he delivered a muffled oratory with a mouth stuffed with bread.

But el-Nouty kept his temper. After all, it was Colonel Muammar Qaddafi himself who stressed the importance of gaining the favor of the U.S. intelligence agencies.

"It will provide us with an edge," the colonel had told him years ago. "It gives us knowledge of how they work, where and who their people are. And knowledge, my old friend, is the armorer of God! For the faithful shall know, and in knowing shall surely slay their enemies!"

Mustafa smiled to himself. How well he thought he knew his old schoolmate sometimes, but just when he thought the colonel was transparent, he did the unexpected. And usually it was brilliant.

People called him a madman, insane. Yes, el-Nouty thought, by some standards he was crazy. But those standards were the standards of people who could not understand brilliance: brilliance and a sense of mission.

When they were cadets together at the military academy el-Nouty first thought the only thing about Qaddafi crazier than his fanatic adherence to Islam was his notion of leading a military coup. That some crazy Muslim who was a green cadet in a military academy could lead a coup to topple the throne was a running laugh.

But as time passed, some people stopped laughing and eventually started running. Many hadn't run far enough when September 1, 1969 arrived and Qaddafi's forces took control of the country.

El-Nouty's thoughts returned to the business at

hand, and the contract the American CIA covert operations chief was offering.

"We . . . have our own reasons for wanting this man terminated," Lowell said over a mouthful of roast beef. Simpsons-on-the-Strand always prepared the best roast beef. Mustafa liked it for its atmosphere, its elegance in an almost extinct British tradition. He also liked it because the maitre d' knew him, and gave him exceptional service. Like today when he wanted a private table, not so much because what they were discussing was classified, but because this man's table manners were so atrocious Mustafa wanted Lowell placed where no one could see him eat.

"What are your reasons?" Mustafa said, as he sipped at an excellent St. Emilion.

"You know policy is set above my level," Lowell replied.

"Certainly you have your guesses," Mustafa pushed. He was curious. Both the Russians *and* the Americans had approached him about this sanction. He'd talked it over with Qaddafi before meeting with Lowell, and Qaddafi approved accepting the contract. The colonel had his own reasons to see this man killed. And so much the better that it didn't cost him anything. Didn't cost him anything, but could be blamed on the Americans if anything went wrong.

"Yes, I have my guesses," Lowell replied, and then returned to his frontal assault on his lunch. Obviously, Mustafa thought, eating lunch is going to take priority over revealing his guesses.

"You know that you need to tell me what those guesses are if you expect me to take this assignment," Mustafa pushed.

"Look here, el-Nouty," Lowell said harshly, letting the heavy silver fork crash to his plate. Several nearby diners paused and tried, in a restrained British manner, to snoop. "Get this straight. *We* are offering *you* a contract. We are calling the shots and it doesn't make any

77

difference *why* we want the sanction. Get that? You aren't the only hired assassin in the world."

Mustafa stifled a smile. Here was this toadlike man who sounded like the gangsters in the old black-and-white American films. Edward G. Robinson; this man sounded like a horrid imitation of the tough gangster.

"You *could* give someone else the contract," Mustafa said evenly, smoothly. "And you *would* end up with your typical CIA foul-up. You know that, don't you, Mr. Lowell?" Mustafa looked at him and saw the anger sparkle in the fat man's eyes.

"You are aware of that?" Mustafa repeated, and in the silence continued. "Because you know that this assignment requires the highest level of skill and experience *and* both an acceptance by the host government and a working knowledge of Soviet intelligence."

"We have . . ." Lowell stammered.

"You *don't* have others, and you don't have a choice," Mustafa said authoritatively. Lowell nodded, defeated.

"So why don't you just share your educated guesses with me so we can get on with things?" Mustafa smiled charmingly. Personally, he didn't care about reasons; those were for the colonel. Qaddafi wanted every scrap of information about both the CIA and the KGB, and kept a complete file on their activities. A file full of information that could be used to neutralize either superpower's intelligence network if desired, or to blackmail its leaders into doing their bidding when the right time came.

Qaddafi believed there was one right time for every act. That was why he had postponed his coup a half dozen times between March and September 1969, and that was why it worked so smoothly when it did. No, Mustafa knew that when the right time came, Qaddafi would use those files and his other talents to make the entire Middle East his power base. And the national leaders there who were laughing at him like those at

78

the academy laughed at a raw cadet, would find their heads buried in the same soil.

"Because . . ." Lowell hesitated.

"Because what?"

"We want him out of the way because the man's intractable. He refuses to listen to reason; his army is threatening Iran and we believe he plans to invade that country. In a word, he is a threat to long-term stability in the Middle East."

"And because you feel you have a pretty good chance of installing your own people in a countercoup, is that correct?" Mustafa asked the obvious. Lowell nodded.

El-Nouty smiled and poured both of them more wine.

"Well, then," Mustafa raised his glass. "Here's to success."

"Here, here," Lowell seconded.

But it will be *our* success, you porcine bastard, el-Nouty thought. Because if you know what the Russians were going to do, you'd go hide under your mother's skirt. El-Nouty knew what the Russians were going to do because they had told him. Under much the same conditions, Lowell's Soviet counterpart had asked him to sanction the same man. And what they planned had nothing to do with stability in the Middle East.

Shoulders hunched, hands in his pockets, Nathaniel Worthington observed the tops of his shoes as they passed over the cracks in the sidewalk and around the mounds of dog shit on Forty-second Street on the way to his hotel. He should have been pleased, he knew. Things were going better than he could possibly have hoped. Yet something was not right.

He stopped for a moment at Broadway and then joined the pedestrian stream crossing, against the light. A phalanx of yellow taxis rattled down on them, lurching from one pothole to another. He paid the cabs no attention and gained the safety of the curb as they clattered through the intersection.

Point one, Nat thought for the twentieth time as he walked back from the theatre, Point one in trying to allay this nagging anxiety: Tania Valente would meet him as planned. That was the most important point. All else was secondary. Point two: they had allayed the suspicions of Tania's KGB escort and were fairly sure that the report that would cover Tania's "deviation" would not be too condemnatory.

Point three: Tania had been much more compliant than he had a right to expect. And point four—

Suddenly Nat bent forward, as a shaft of pain impaled his belly. He pressed his right hand to the scar and pressed on it. Odd, he thought, there was no pain—no feeling at all—along the sixteen-inch scar that ran across his abdomen like the Trans-Siberian Railroad.

He walked on, barely losing stride. His vision didn't blur, and he knew the pain was just another aftershock of the damaged nerves, nerves the doctor had not been able to sever.

The Trans-Siberian Railroad. That's what he'd named the pain in the hospital, because it felt like a freight train highballing it through his guts. But it was no longer knocking him flat like it used to.

Now if my insides will just stay glued together, I'm gonna make it, he thought.

Point four, he reiterated, and the pain returned in a grayed hue. Point four: Tania's infatuation with him would make it easier to manipulate her. He'd done it before and it worked. He never liked it but it was part of the job. She was an assignment, and he'd damned well have to remember it. With Colleen, he'd forgotten. And he knew the consequences of that, goddamnit.

That was it, he realized. The inability to put the second thoughts about manipulating Tania behind him was eating him. He knew that the success of the mission hinged on not getting involved with this woman. It would cloud his judgment, it would impair his efficiency, it would . . .

"Watch where the fuck yer walkin', mister," cursed an old crone with a fat frazzled shopping bag in each hand.

Mumbling an apology, Nat quickly tried to pull himself together. I'd better keep my mind on business, he told himself, and set off with a more determined pace toward his hotel.

He had always stayed at the Tudor when he came to New York, even when his father gave him enough money to stay at the Waldorf-Astoria. Nat preferred the time-crusted patina of the Tudor to the haughtier service at the Waldorf, where even the time was washed from the cracks and crannies. The Tudor was a block away from the United Nations building, and the lobby was always filled with the cacophony of foreign languages competing for his ear—a sound that made him hunger to learn more.

Colleen had stayed with him there once. . . .

At the next corner, Nat narrowly missed bumping into the rear of a gray-pinstriped businessman who had stopped for the light at Lexington Avenue.

Wandering, my mind is wandering, Nat thought. This is just what I need to get killed for good this time. It had been months since he'd been forced to be this wary, months since his life had depended on it. But it was something one never forgot how to do.

As he walked, Nat now scanned the crowd for the tip-off to surveillance: someone a bit too aware of what he was doing, someone who looked a bit too aimless, someone caught in the act of staring at him. There would be nods to partners, blinks, and body language that painted "tail" on all but the very best. Only the best could master the technique of truly blending in.

Nat took in the scene, first as a whole, trying to spot an errant particle in the crowd, and then piece by piece. He saw nothing alarming: office workers returning to work after too many martinis, shoppers winding up the afternoon laden with packages, taxis disgorging and accepting fares, a derelict curled up against a rubbish can.

Normally, he'd take some assurance while he was in a streetside crowd, but in New York a hit man could walk up to you, gun you down in the middle of a crowd and walk away without having a hand laid on him, and with no one left behind who'd claim to have seen the shooting.

Nothing alarming here, though, and only two more blocks now to the hotel. He looked up the slight incline past the Daily News Building on the right, and spotted the flags flying from the Tudor's entrance.

At Third Avenue Nat crossed to the south side of Forty-second Street so he could gaze through the big plate glass windows of the Daily News as he passed.

As he stepped up on the curb in front of the old Horn and Hardart automat, he spotted them: a woman carrying a dress box, with her other hand on the forearm of a man. His left arm was in a cast, suspended from his neck with a sling. Husband and wife, Nat supposed, yet there was something odd about both of them that he couldn't put his finger on.

They were maybe fifty yards away, walking toward him along 42nd Street. Nat continued without breaking stride. Nerves? Nat asked himself. Overly cautious after your daydreams?

No. There was something about the way they moved that raised an alarm. They didn't walk together the way people who know each other well do, adjusting to each other's stride, smoothing the motion. And the way they looked at each other as they talked—it appeared they were strangers, or slight acquaintances. Yet she held her hand on his arm, indicating a closer tie. They could have just had an argument, Nat considered. That might account for their out-of-sync movements.

82

There was more, though Nat couldn't articulate it at the moment. If he had, he'd have realized that the woman was cradling the dress box like a weapon, rather than like a cardboard container filled with cloth. And the man's cast was jerking around slightly, indicating greater mobility to the arm than one normally associates with a limb in a cast. And they never took their eyes off him, even when they spoke to each other, except when they looked past him at someone behind him.

But these observations never reached Nat's conscious thoughts. What did, however, was the urge to run. But they were no more than thirty yards away now. Where to run? There were no office entrances in front of him, and the homicidal rush of Forty-second Street traffic had not yet been clogged by afternoon rush hour.

Nat turned to run, and as soon as he did, he saw them: three swarthy men dressed in dark suits running toward him.

They were at the corner, pushing their way through the crowd, thirty feet away maybe? They had timed things well; there was nowhere to run.

Time ran in freeze-frame slowness, and with each split second Nat devised and discarded a plan. His heart thundered like an old two-cylinder farm tractor as he decided he could do only one thing: attack. When the enemy has you outnumbered, they're prepared for you to run, not to attack. That element of surprise can be the margin of victory.

"Nat, Nat old friend," it was the man calling him from behind. "Nat, it is you, old chap, isn't it?" Nat started to turn and stopped. It was the classic crowded street snatch ploy. It was so damned obvious, Nat thought, why didn't I see it before?

No matter. Nothing mattered but concentration. A battle is won or lost before the first blow is struck, Nathaniel's first martial arts instructor had said. It's in your mind.

Like a parachutist poised at the jump door of an airplane, Nat felt the adrenalin shoot through him. He hesitated. There was a precise moment: timing was all, concentration was all. His muscles felt so tight they would snap, and then tighter, tauter, he waited, timing, concentrating; they were 10 feet away now, two feet closer with every step, a step a second. The man on the right started to move his right hand inside his coat.

Now!

"Yah-h-h-h-h-h-ei-i-i!" Nat lunged through the crowd at the man, screaming at the top of his lungs, the sound a battle cry that shocked the three men, and every other person in the afternoon street. It was bewilderment for them, and a bloody mantra of violence for Nat, a savage meditation that had to end in death.

Faces in the crowd focused on the corner of Forty-second and Third, but of the two people in the crowd that afternoon who would admit to having seen the incident, neither was clear on who had been involved, what they had looked like, or who had started it all.

The split-second of hesitation was all Nat needed. In one flying leap, he covered the remaining ground between him and the other three men. The man who was reaching into his coat stood on the end of the phalanx—to Nat's left—and was going for his gun with his right hand. Nat slammed his own right hand into the man's bent elbow, shoving the elbow upward across the man's shoulder, neutralizing it for an instant. And in that instant, Nat battered first the man's right kidney, and then his genitals. As the man went down, Nat pivoted on his right leg and delivered a roundhouse kick with his left that struck the middle assailant in his solar plexus. Nat heard but took no note of the man's desperate gasp, for by this time the remaining man had withdrawn his handgun and was bringing it to bear on Nat.

84

Nat stepped directly in front of the man, battering the gun hand outward and upward with his left forearm. The pistol discharged impotently into the granite of the office building, causing a shower of fragments onto the sidewalk. As he deflected the man's shooting arm, Nat reached into his assailant's shirt pocket and withdrew a plain yellow no. 2 pencil with a fair point and an eraser in excellent shape. As he plunged the pencil through the bottom of the man's jaw, shoving the point through the tongue, the soft pallet, it made the faint sounds of tearing flesh.

Nat held the surprised man's neck in the crook of his left arm to support the final thrust, hoping the pencil wouldn't break. And in one final shove with the base of his hand, Nat rammed the fair point of the plain, yellow no. 2 pencil with the excellent eraser into the soft gray gelatin of the man's brain. Nat felt him stiffen, and then let him slide limply to the pavement, the shiny brass eraser mount with its green band and excellent eraser protruding obscenely from his throat.

The shrieks of sirens penetrated Nat's concentration, as through a mist. His breath came in swift, even draughts; the exertion had not winded him. Now Nat had to run. There would be no protection from Rinehart. The National Security Adviser had made it clear that as far as the CIA was concerned, Nat had ceased to work for the government after his "accident" in Amsterdam.

Nat looked around. It had been but a few seconds and there was as yet no crowd. He looked one bystander in the eyes, and the man scurried quickly away.

"Police officers!" a voice behind Nat commanded loudly. "Up with your hands." Nat's even breathing was ripped to shreds when his heart bounded into his throat and beat like a berserk tympany. Obediently, he turned with his hands over his head. It was the couple. Gone were the dress box and the cast, and in their places were police-issue Smith & Wesson .385.

85

The woman shoved the muzzle of her .38 into his belly just below the belt, and the man produced a pair of handcuffs and reached for Nat's wrists. Nat watched, his heart sinking, as a plain sedan pulled up to the curb. You were daydreaming, he cursed himself, and you walked right into their hands.

The man's pistol prodded Nat's back toward the car. "Get in," he barked. "Hurry!" Nat moved toward the car, stumbled, and caught his balance. It was awkward walking with your hands secured behind you.

It doesn't pay to get smug, Nat thought grimly as he slid into the rear seat of the sedan after the woman. Just as you get gutsy enough to look around and think that life is going well, just as you cautiously begin to hope that you might have things under control, life short-sheets you.

The man bounced into the seat beside him and slammed the door, leaning into Nat's ribs as he did. A flush of anger spread through Nat and he wanted to act, but he also felt the doughnut-shaped cold spot in his ribs where the woman's pistol pressed into his flesh.

He was not about to give up. Not yet.

As the car sped down Forty-second Street and then shot down Second Avenue, Nat grew suspicious: This car—though it resembled an unmarked car—was in much better shape than the city could afford: it smelled new, there were no scratches, no police equipment inside, he remembered it having whitewall tires, and besides there was a tiny Hertz decal on the lower corner of the windshield by the driver. These weren't police.

He turned to look at his captors. If not police, who were they? And why hadn't they killed him? They obviously wanted him alive, but why?

The woman, seated on his left, was in her mid-thirties, stocky, on her way toward matronly. She had dark hair—he couldn't tell if it was black or dark brown in the light—pulled back severely and fastened into a bun. Her face was grooved with frown lines.

The man, by comparison, was a portrait in serenity. He sat relaxed, the pistol resting easily in the crook of his left arm. Nat judged him to be about five-nine, average build, with dark curly hair that frizzed above an age-lined olive face. He looked like a middle-aged businessman in a dark blue Brooks Brothers suit. His "wife" too, was dressed in traditional East Coast garb: khaki skirt and button-down shirt. Nat looked at him and got a "we've-got-you-by-the-balls" smirk in return.

At Thirty-fifth Street, they pulled into a parking structure. There, Nat and his two escorts were hustled into the back of a waiting panel truck. When the truck emerged from the garage, it made straight for the West side.

None of his captors had said a word during the ride or the vehicle swap. The light was shallow in the rear of the van, and reflected dimly off the polished metal of their weapons.

Nat had regained his composure. They would have acted by now if he was to be killed. Though the alternative might be death after torture.

But who were they, Nat wondered. They didn't look like Soviet agents, nor did they act like them. And why did they want him? Was it the Valente case? Or was it for some previous case; was this revenge?

The *who* would determine the *why*.

The van swayed from side to side, slamming Nat into the back of his seat every time they hit a pothole, which was almost continuously. And each time that happened, the handcuffs bit into the thin flesh at his wrist.

"Uh, I was wondering if you could loosen the handcuffs?" Nat grimaced. "They're cutting my wrists up."

The man looked inquiringly at the woman. She shook her head.

"Please," Nat persisted. "Look, I'm bleeding. You obviously want me in good condition and this isn't going to help things."

The woman glared at him. The light reflecting off her eyes made them glow evilly.

"All right," she said sharply. "But this first." She produced a small case from a compartment in the panel truck's seat. "David," she barked at the man, "hold him."

Silhouetted in the faint light, the woman plunged a hypodermic needle into an ampoule, carefully squeezing out any air bubbles. Then just as quickly, she whipped the needle from the rubber seal, and sat beside Nat and jerked off his right shoe and sock.

"Hurt him if he moves," she ordered, then sank the needle into the large vein on top of his foot and emptied the hypodermic's contents. Moments later Nat felt warm and happy as the drug spread through his body.

He relaxed, and gazed euphorically at a small red drop of blood as it oozed from the hole left by the needle.

Chapter Nine

‖‖

The veil of drugs grew thicker. Nat's head spun as he shrank and fell toward the drop of blood on his feet, a drop that had grown into a lake, a lake that wanted to swallow him, drown him.

The falling was forever, but the terror was second by second. Nat swallowed and felt his parched throat drag across itself, and when he opened his mouth to scream, nothing came out. Over and over he tumbled, downward, closer. He saw Colleen's face in the blood, and he cried as he plunged through the surface.

And below there was Harvard, and Colleen.

"Would you like to continue this *pas de deux* after class, *mademoiselle*?" he'd asked her. It was the same spring day in April when the air was light and she'd just joined the class. She had some connection with the instructor, Nat surmised, since she was thrust directly into the routines without any transition. She was a good dancer, and the instructor had known it. At the end of the session, they danced together, they danced with each other, they *were* each other in the movement. They were like missing pieces that had become one.

"Of course," she answered. "But only if you tell me your name." They laughed. Nat heard the laugh. He'd heard the laugh over and over throughout the years. Time hadn't erased the sound. They laughed as they walked through the gate, past the Coop, elbowing their way through sidewalk traffic and the crowd that jammed the Rathskeller. He remembered the daisies he bought from a sidewalk vendor, and how she shortened one of the stems and tucked it behind her ear, and he remembered how it looked, all bright white petals against the raven hair so dark it shined with rainbows in the sun. And how pale her complexion was and how bright her eyes shone: a yellow-green that looked like a cat's.

With her lithe dancer's body, she was as tall as he, and a good five inches taller *en pointe*, and she weighed a bare one hundred pounds. A willow, he used to tell her; if she ever came back as a tree, she'd be a willow but not a weeping one. And they laughed when she said that he'd undoubtedly come back as something bearing nuts.

He saw her now, but he couldn't touch her, speak to her. He shouted at her, once, twice, and the cry transported them to New York. It was two years after that first magical day. He was walking through the arches at Washington Square in Greenwich Villages. Tables were set with petitions opposing the draft, volunteering for duty for a peace march. Johnson was getting them deeper and deeper into war, and the self-styled urban guerillas were making headlines.

Nat detested the war, had marched in his share of protests. But he hated the violence of groups like the Weathermen, felt they were destroying his rights as much as Johnson and his fascist regime. Rinehart played on this. Years later, Nat would realize bitterly just how far his idealism had been manipulated by Rinehart, but on that day in Greenwich Village, Nat was on a holy mission.

He was a senior at Harvard, and this was the spring of his last semester. Nat was in New York ostensibly to help organize a protest, and in reality on a mission for Rinehart.

They had located the approximate location of an armory for a group calling themselves "the Revolutionary Urban Brigade" and Nat was to find its exact location so federal authorities could raid it.

They thought the armory was located in a rowhouse in the village near Washington Square and so Nat, accompanied by Colleen, was going door-to-door with petitions against the war and asking for donations for the rally. It was a perfect cover. The Village streets were filling with fog . . .

. . . fog that now seemed to wrap itself around him, him and Colleen. He felt her arm around his waist, her fingers hooked through a belt loop of his jeans. He felt the warmth of her body through their coats as they walked along, arm in arm. He stuck his tongue in her ear. She squealed and dropped the clipboard with her petitions, but the laugh came to him now as through water, garbled and thin, and it set his soul on edge.

The afternoon passed into evening, and the streets had started to clear of people. Their feet hurt. Twelve hours of walking gained them a clipboard of names for their petition and no Urban Brigade. The brittle edge of tension that started the day had passed into relaxed conversation. One more house on the block, a brownstone like scores of others they had visited already.

(Stop it! No, don't!)

(It's a dream.)

Nat screamed at the self strolling arm in arm with Colleen. But the self walked on, legs unheeding, the mind helpless. Why was he kissing her on the steps? How could he hold her warm body in his arms with death doors away, steps away?

Her lips were so moist, so soft. Nat could hear himself say: "It's the last one, then we can eat."

"I'm starved," she answered.

"Then let's split up," he said. "So we can save time."

"You start here," Colleen suggested. "I'll run up to the top and work down."

They kissed deeply on the landing.

"That's enough," Colleen laughed as she pushed herself away. "Save it for later. No public displays of affection." Something inside Nat's chest collapsed as he watched her take the first step of the stairs—

(Stop her!) But his feet wouldn't move.

—and then the next step, and soon disappeared.

(Run after her! At least you can die together.)

But Nat saw himself turn and raise his fist to rap on the first door.

The fog had followed him inside. The door opened and he saw an older woman cautiously peek out through a trebly chained door. He saw her mouth move, but he heard nothing, the fog ate the sound, he saw himself pass the petition clipboard through the crack in the door, and he saw the lady smile as she asked for a pen.

He saw himself reach for the mangled Bic he carried in his side pocket.

From somewhere, he thought he heard Colleen knocking at a door somewhere, and he heard himself think that she was just about the best person he had ever met in his life, and he felt himself grow warm at the thought.

The little old lady smiled as she passed his clipboard to him and closed the door.

But when the door closed, it wasn't the gentle clatching of latches swallowing hardware: it was seismic and it was fire and the sound pierced the fog and threw him to the floor, and he heard Colleen scream.

"Thank you for finding the time to see me, Mr. President." The old man walked painfully but erect into the Oval Office. He was damned if he was going to let his arthritis turn him into a slouching old coot.

"Richard, it is I who should be grateful." The President pushed out of his leather upholstered chair and walked around the desk to greet his National Security Adviser. "Why don't we sit over here," the President gestured with his hand, "on the sofa."

"Fine with me, Mr. President, fine with me," Rinehart said as he laid his manila folder stamped "For the President's eyes only" on the mahogany butler's table, and slowly lowered himself to the sofa. He saw the President's look of concern.

"Just a bit too much handball is all," Rinehart offered, retrieving the folder and settling into a comfortable position. "Getting too old for this sort of thing." The President's face relaxed, and he sat in a wingback chair just to Rinehart's left.

"Would you like something?" the President offered. "Some coffee—"

"Tea would be delightful," Rinehart accepted and waited while the President ordered tea, coffee, and croissants. Rinehart smiled: the President always tried to please him. Croissants were a Rinehart passion, and the President had them made specially for him. It was an insecurity, Rinehart understood. He'd seen it all his life. People like the President needed—craved—the approval of people like him: establishment, old money, old family, respectability. Of course the President had studied at Columbia, and obtained his law degree from Yale—there were few as good and none better—and the education brought this un-Eastern chap in contact with the real establishment. Yet, though he'd bested the lot intellectually, there still remained a social insecurity that made him putty in the right hands—*his* hands, Rinehart reflected complacently.

So desperate was the President for that clubby familiarity with the Eastern establishment that he would do almost anything to get it—*anything*. But he never would achieve it. Rinehart would never address him as anything but "Mr. President," regardless of the President's frequent use of his first name.

"Well, what's on the agenda this morning?" The President asked eagerly.

Rinehard cleared his throat. "Mr. President, I have here a project of the utmost importance, and have taken the liberty of setting preliminary actions into motion—of course nothing is committed, nor would it be without your support." Rinehart paused. The President looked first at him and then at the folder. Rinehart opened the folder, and presented it to him. "Please give this summary consideration, and then we can discuss it fully."

The President was reading the folder, hunched over, elbows on his knees, when the coffee, tea, and croissants arrived. Rinehart was pleased to find his special blend of tea—mixed for him by Twinings of London—sitting next to the hot croissants.

As the President sipped at his coffee and read the report, Rinehart opened the inlaid teak box and carefully measured the tea blend into a sterling tea ball. He poured scalding water into the porcelain teapot, swirled it about, and emptied the contents into a small silver urn. He then filled the pot and immersed the tea ball and its contents. By the time Rinehart had finished his ritual, the President was through with the report and was waiting for him to speak.

"Well, what's your opinion?" Rinehart asked as he filled his antique Limoges cup.

"Well it's . . . quite, ah . . . daring," the President ventured.

"It's definitely that," Rinehart agreed, sipping from the cup.

Silence filled the Oval Office.

"Is it . . . I mean, do you think it's necessary to take such a . . . a Draconian action?"

"I submit that it is our best course of action to insure a continued flow of oil from the Middle East," Rinehart replied.

"But assassination?" the President asked. "I understand that Congress has given the intelligence community more leash, and of course this plan fits within the charter, but are we really against the wall?"

"Not yet," Rinehart said. "But we will be."

"Please explain."

"Certainly." Rinehart leaned back against the velvet of the sofa and continued. "Since the death of Nasser in 1970, the Arab world has been without a unifying leader. The routs of Arab forces in every skirmish against Israel has been due as much to the disarray of the Arabs as it has to the courage of Israel.

"The Shah's rule in Iran was a stabilizing factor, but with that gone, and with the increasing instability of the sheiks in Saudi Arabia, the region has grown so unstable that it cries for either all-out war, or an Arab strongman." Rinehart paused a moment to sip again at his tea. "Two rulers have emerged to fill the leadership role: Qaddafi in Libya, and Saddam Hussein in Iraq," he began again.

"Qaddafi's a crazy man," the President interjected.

Rinehart smiled indulgently. "Perhaps. Yet, despite his financial support of some of the most outrageous terrorists, he has devoutly maintained a nonaligned foreign policy. He hates the Soviets as much as he does us."

"Yes, yes, I'm familiar with his 'Third Circle' theories," said the President quickly.

"Of course. His Islamic alternative to capitalism and communism. But that's not really the big issue at this point. The real issue is the massive shipment recently of arms to Iraq by the Soviet Union. As I've been able to interpret it, the arms buildup by the present regime

95

is a prelude to massive war in the Middle East during which Iraq will attempt to assert superiority over the region. Such a war centered around the Persian Gulf will inevitably cause a shut down of tanker activity through the Hormuz Straits, and most likely cause the destruction of oil production and refining capacity. The result, regardless of whether or not Iraq is successful, will be a shutoff of Arabian oil, and a global depression. Remember that all our allies—Japan, West Germany, all of Western Europe for that matter—depend on Arabian oil more than we do."

The President nodded grimly. "But what will the assassination of Hussein gain us?"

"Time," Rinehart replied. "Time and more oil." He picked up a flaky croissant between two carefully manicured fingers and began to eat it.

The President took the opportunity to return to the folder before him.

"Yes, Richard," the President said pensively after a moment, "I see your point. With Hussein gone, the internal confusion over who will take his place will definitely scotch immediate plans for war. There is one thing, though, that worries me about it."

"Which is?"

"This vacuum at the head of the Iraqi government seems like an open invitation to a Soviet coup. Russian advisers are already crawling over Baghdad. And besides, the understanding I have is that the Soviets are getting desperate for petroleum. Have you considered those factors, Richard?"

Rinehart nodded impatiently. "Of course. First, let's take the oil question. New intelligence—which we want to keep classified, naturally—indicates that new Soviet oil finds in Siberia and in the regions adjacent to Iran and Iraq have relieved some of the pressure.

"And secondly, the Afganistan and Polish situations have pretty well tied up whatever ambitions the Soviets may have for further conquest. Pugachev, as you know, is no fool. Although many members of the politburo disagree with him and are pushing for an invasion of both Iran and Iraq, Pugachev, as a military man, knows the necessity to consolidate other areas before taking on another armed conflict. In a word, the Russians are spread too thin to invade Iraq; as long as Pugachev is head of the Red Army and on the politburo, there will be no invasion. Besides, he's likely to be the next premier, and I don't think people want to cross him. He already blames his opposition for pushing him against his better judgment into Afghanistan, and he's not going to be forced into another battle not of his own choosing."

"Yes," the President said pensively. "Well," he took a deep breath and let it out slowly. "Let's go ahead with it." ·

"Shall I explain our plans?"

"Of course not."

Rinehart smiled wryly, and the President returned a broader one of his own. So, Rinehart mused, the man was catching on quickly.

Mustafa rolled his head on the pillow and focused his eyes on the dial of his watch: 4:37, or 16:37 by the British. He let his left arm float back to the coolness of the soft, clean sheets that formed themselves around his body, draping and folding and looking, to an eye that was mildly glazed with opium, like a thousand dunes of the desert.

The British. Fuck the British. A broad smile crept across his mouth as he remembered that he *was* fucking the British. Literally. He raised his head and propped himself up on his elbows. Margaret Somethingorother curled on her side, her auburn hair splayed across her back and down over her shoulder and between her breasts, incredibly white breasts, and remarkably pink nipples. Poetry ran through his mind, a hundred stanzas of a score of verses. He loved Arabic, the rich flowing depth, the beauty and expressiveness. The British language was a series of grunts and snorts beside it.

Margaret Somethingorother's feet were tangled with another pair of feet, smaller, daintier but every bit as British. Mary. He could never remember the last names. Didn't matter, el-Nouty thought as he gazed at her face. It was a beautiful face, an erotic face peeking out behind a shock of blond hair. Not natural, and that excited him. Only whores bleached their hair.

Mustafa watched his penis swell and stir as he remembered his first sight of her, as he thought of this woman who, to him, was only for fucking. He looked at her face, buried in his own pubic hair, his hardening cock gliding past her cheek, past the delicate strand of drying semen that led from the corner of those full lips. The glans of his penis nudged her ear, and Mustafa felt his loins burn as she smiled and slowly cracked her eyes. She had had more opium than he and her eyes were glazed, but at least she hadn't passed out like her friend Margaret.

"Suck it," Mustafa ordered.

She ran her tongue under the bottom of the glans, and el-Nouty arched his back but made no sound. It wouldn't be proper for the woman to think she was controlling him.

"Fuck me," she said dreamily, "fuck me, please."

"No, just suck until I come."

"I want you to fuck me," she persisted, "you fucked Margaret."

Mustafa leaned forward and slapped her.

"You're here to please me; forget that and you go home poor."

Mustafa liked the way she pouted as she folded her lips around his cock once more.

Whore. They have to be beaten to understand. Women are like that, he thought, and momentarily forgot his thoughts as he felt something at the base of his

98

penis release and then shot warmly, wetly into Mary's mouth. He felt her swallow and then dreamily lean her head back into narcotic dreams. The arms of Morpheus, Mustafa thought.

He would never understand it. How the British—and the Americans for that matter—could allow their women to be such whores, even the ones who didn't ask for money afterward.

They were somebody's daughters, and their conduct was dishonorable. In the Bedawi tribes where he grew up and became a man, it would be the dishonored father's right and duty to kill such a whoring daughter, and then to kill him for prompting the bloodshed of a family member. Blood demands blood.

But Mustafa Salem el-Nouty felt warm inside—he was dishonoring the British, the people who had blackened the face of his father and his tribe. His wajh would be redeemed, his face whitened as he blackened the wajh of the British; Badawi blood avenged as he shed the blood of the British, and their allies and companions in the enslavement of the Arabic race.

"I and my brothers against my cousin, I and my cousins against the world," he said quietly. The old proverb brought purpose to his life.

It was a good life now; he had been spared the shame of working with his hands. No Badawi could retain his honor if he had to work with his hands, for they were the children of Cain, destined to wander the desert, nomads always in search of what they never found beyond the next rise.

He was like that, Mustafa reflected proudly. He wandered the world just as his grandfather now wandered the Libyan desert. He survived as his tribe had survived for centuries. They had survived the French, the British, the Italians, the Americans; every colonizer who had tried to subdue the Bedawi had failed to master their proud spirit. They had even survived those tenets of Islam that tried to overrule the traditions of

99

the Bedawi that had ruled them long before Prophet was born.

No, he could never understand people who submitted and forgot. He could never understand, but he was glad they were around, he thought as he looked at the two still, sleeping women on his bed, they had a use: his use.

White light diffused through the curtains, and lit the room in shadowless matte. Mustafa liked the light, craved it. He leaned over to the bedside table and languidly grabbed the telephone receiver.

"Front desk, may I be of service?"

"Yes, this is el-Nouty in Room 773. Please wake me when the sun sets."

"Of course, sir."

"Thank you," el-Nouty said and replaced the receiver. That was what he liked about the Dorchester: no unnecessary questions. They assumed the guest knew what he wanted and conducted themselves accordingly.

"Up!" he yelled at the two prostitutes. "Up, both of you. Get dressed and get out!" Only the one called Mary stirred. Mustafa sat up and slapped her face.

"Get your friend up and depart," he told her. "Quickly, I want to sleep."

Slipping between the sheets, el-Nouty closed his eyes, after they left and drifted as the afternoon light filtered red through his eyelids. Red: anger. Red: hate. Red: rage. Red: blood. Red: revenge. Red: comfort.

Comfort, light.

El-Nouty fell asleep immediately.

"Where do you live, you thieving little bastard!" And the soldier slapped him again with the back of his hand. "Tell me or we'll cut your thieving little Arab cock off, we will!"

Mustafa spoke no English. Few Bedawi spoke more

100

than their Arabic dialect, and eight-year-old Mustafa Salem el-Nouty was no exception.

"Tell me, you bleeding wog, or else!"

Mustafa cried and screamed. The soldiers seemed like giants to him and they were shaking him and yelling at him in grunts and groans and squeals that made no sense to him. The tears streamed from his eyes and he felt ashamed, for a Bedawi should fear no man, should cower before no one, especially strangers. His father would be angry at him now for conducting himself in such an unmanly way.

But still he cried, and his nose ran and he wanted to wipe it but one soldier held his arms while the other yelled at him.

Then the worst! The soldier lifted Mustafa's robes and pulled from his pocket a folding knife.

"Look what we have here," the soldier said to his companion. "He's not even circumcised like a civilized person. What do you say we give him a proper cut for his own sake?"

Mustafa's sobs rose into a piercing squeal. He couldn't understand what they were saying, but the intent was clear.

Tobruk. Why had his father brought the tribe so close to Tobruk. Food, Mustafa remembered, they were starving. The men of the tribe wanted to barter, or to steal from the British. They'd left at dawn that morning and Mustafa had followed their prints at a distance. The men forbade him to come with them, but he was a *man* now, he was not going to remain among the women while the other men provided for their tribe.

So he had crept into Tobruk determined to bring back food to prove that he was worthy of being included with the men the next time.

And there at his feet were the loaves of bread he had grabbed from a shop. He ran to the street with the Arab shopkeeper in close pursuit, and crashed headlong into the two soldiers who now held him.

"No, no, lad, that's not what these people do to thieves here." Another soldier had approached the scene which had now attracted a hundred onlookers. Mustafa looked around for sympathy, for help, for his *father,* but in his breathless fear, he found only blank stares. It would be suicide for one of the villagers to interfere with the British. One wrong move and the British authorities would throw them all in jail.

"The punishment for a thief under Islamic law," the new arrival said, "is to cut off the right hand."

"Jesus!" said the soldier with the knife, "that's barbaric! No wonder these people are so bloody primitive."

"But you *do* understand that it is their law?" the new man said.

"Sure," said the man with the knife as he dropped Mustafa's robes. "Sure."

"Look, why don't we just let the kid go and forget this whole thing?" said the soldier who held Mustafa's arms. Mustafa felt the grasp relax a bit.

"No, no," the shopkeeper protested now in broken English. Much of his trade came from the wives of the British officers stationed here.

"No," demanded the shopkeeper as he approached the new arrival. The shopkeeper saw that the new arrival was a sergeant and outranked the other two soldiers. "Begging your kindest pardon, Mr. Sergeant, sir," the shopkeeper said in his most obsequious tone, "but this boy is a thief. All Bedawi are thieves and do much harm to my business. Do not, I appeal to your honor and justice, let this boy go free, he will merely return to steal another day. Please give him to me for punishment."

The man with the knife had folded it and returned it to his pocket. Mustafa saw this as his only chance, and twisted from his captor's loosened grip. He lunged at the soldier who had threatened him with the knife and shoved his fist into the man's groin. Mustafa heard a bellow of pain as he plowed his way through the crowd and ran for safety. His bare feet plopped against the broken pavement, and behind him he could hear the wooden thuds of the soldiers' boots in hot pursuit.

Mustafa groaned in his sleep. The nightmare was always this way. Always just the way it happened.

Young Mustafa crashed through the bazaar shoppers, twisted among their bodies and dashed in and among the peddlers' booths. He heard angry shouts behind him as the larger, less agile soldiers slammed into people and upset carts and tables set with goods.

His breath raced until his lungs burned. Mustafa was lost. Even if he evaded the men, could he find his way out of this city? Could he ever find his tribe again? He wanted to cry, he wanted his father. Oh, why did he disobey his father's admonition to remain at the camp?

He ran on; surely he had outrun them, but every time he slowed to check, they still pursued. The crowds had thinned now, he was leaving the marketplace area. There was nothing to do but press on. Residents of the narrow grimy shadowed street took little notice of the small boy sprinting down the middle of the rough stone pavement.

They took a little more notice of the three furious British soldiers with red faces and contorted features. But there was blood in the men's eyes, and it would do no good to cross any of them, particularly one tall one who brandished a folding knife as he ran.

Mustafa saw them look at him as he passed their homes, and quickly dismissed the thought of asking them to hide him. His father told him that people who lived in cities were devils.

Mustafa ran looking at his feet, watching the pavement for glass that could cut his bare feet, irregular stones that could trip him. He knew only sand, not stones such as these, not this many.

On and on he ran. His chest burned now, the taste in his mouth pasty and foul. One foot bled from a

103

jagged cut and both legs felt like lead. But he could hear the soldiers behind him, and so he ran. He looked up and saw the narrow twisting street had come to a T. He ran left, careening off the wall, and suddenly he stopped: it was a dead end. Mustafa heard the soldiers' footstrikes on the stone pavement. He spun around, but the soldiers were nearly on top of him. He ran toward the blind alleyway and started screaming upward for help, but of the faces that appeared at the glassless windows, none moved.

Mustafa looked at the alley's end: There were no doors, no steps, only windows whose ledges were beyond the reach of an eight-year-old boy's arms.

Panting, gasping, Mustafa turned to see the three men approaching. They had slowed their pace now that they were certain he couldn't escape.

"Help me, won't you help me," Mustafa cried to the people who stood at their windows, and as he cried, they sank deeper into the darkness within the rooms until Mustafa could no longer be certain that anyone was watching.

"All right, you fucking little piece of camel shit," said the man with the knife, "I've had it with you."

Mustafa's eyes were riveted on the knife's blade, now glinting brightly in the gloom of the alley. He backed up till he could move no farther. The soldier approached, rage in his eyes. His wet, sweating face was flushed and his ragged, furious breathing burned with hatred.

"You're not going to get away from me this time," the man said. But Mustafa could understand none of his words.

"Don't do anything you'll be sorry for," the sergeant cautioned.

"Court martial me if you want, sergeant, sir," the man replied. "But I'll never let it be said that some bloody wog kicked me in the balls and got away with it."

With that he lunged for Mustafa, and caught him by the arm.

"Here, help me with this," the man with the knife called, and the other enlisted man stepped forward.

"I'll be around the corner, gentlemen," the sergeant said, and walked silently out of sight.

"You're not gonna cut his—"

"No, I'm not going to cut his little pisser off," said the man with the knife. "I'm just going to give him a taste of his own law. Here, hold this out." The man with the knife turned Mustafa face down and sat astride his back.

Briefly relieved that they weren't going to castrate him, Mustafa's calm turned to horror as he felt the men stretching out his right hand. He was still shrieking with pain and disbelief when the man with the knife finally got up and handed Mustafa his own hand.

For years, Mustafa would wonder why the stump suddenly stopped hurting, why the pain disappeared as he stared at the ragged bloody pulp that had been his wrist, at the way the bone stuck through when he tried to make a fist.

He screamed again when the man lifted the cover of the cistern and threw him in, and threw the hand in after him. Mustafa always remembered the soft plop the hand made when it splashed into the muck at the bottom of the cistern, and he remembered how the rats felt in the dark when they'd replaced the cistern cover so that no light entered and he remembered the things he couldn't see that slithered about in the slime at the bottom of the blackness.

Mustafa Salem el-Nouty awoke with a low groan, covered with sweat that soaked the fine linen sheets at the Dorchester Hotel. He wiped the sweat from his face with his handless right forearm, and thanked Allah it was still daylight.

Nat felt the coolness on his cheek and shoulder first. The light came moments later. And then the smell of cool, damp spaces that never see sunlight, mingled with the acrid odor of stale urine: the last smell he remembered in a toilet in Amsterdam. His eyelids seemed glued together, and his mouth tasted like someone had filled it with rubber cement and cotton balls.

Heart pounding, Nat jerked his head up and tried to prop himself up on the filthy concrete floor. Quickly the hangover of the drugs exploded in his head, and he sank back into his fetal sleeping position, satisfied at the very least that this was not Amsterdam.

But where was it? He tried to remember. Times Square, Forty-second Street, men. He'd killed one. The man and woman, a panel truck, the handcuffs cutting his wrist, a needle prick, and darkness.

Slowly rolling over on his back, Nat gingerly ran his right hand over his left wrist. There was a scab there, not a big one. He felt tender, bruised.

I'm all right, he told himself. I'm all right for now. But his head cried out for rest, for time to recover.

Summoning more strength than he consciously felt, Nat tentatively raised himself on his right elbow. Blinding bolts of light shot through his brain, and echoed through his entire body. "Jesus," he muttered to himself, and then raised himself to a full sitting position. The express was roaring through his entire body now, aimed at his head. The silence rushed at him like crashing waves; vertigo spun his head.

Nat drew up his knees and rested his head on them, waiting for the room to stop spinning, hoping he wouldn't faint.

He sat there for what might have been hours; he didn't know how long, they'd taken his watch. Finally he raised his head and took in his surroundings: a cubicle about six feet on a side. The floor was cement, two walls cinder block, the other two wooden. The boards, he noted, looked new. The ceiling was covered with a mass of pipes. There were only ends of the copper pipe left: someone had probably stolen the rest to sell for scrap.

A single domino-shaped window at the top of one of the cinderblock walls let in the fading rays of daylight. The glass had long been missing; left were two iron reinforcing bars.

He was in a basement.

But where?

Not in a very good neighborhood, judging from the condition of the plumbing and the stench of urine, which grew more oppressive as he regained consciousness. This part of the building had probably been used by vagrants as a pissing place. He was in a slum somewhere.

It was still daylight outside, so they couldn't have taken him far. Unless—his leart skipped—unless he had missed a day and this was more than twenty-four hours later. If it was, he was soon going to miss his rendezvous with Tania.

Despair swept over Nat briefly but he shook it off. He couldn't afford to give in to it now.

Methodically, he scanned the walls of his cell. He walked the perimeter, tried to peer through the cracks, and saw nothing. The door defied his firm shove. Finally he returned to the barred window. This was no time to panic; anxiety only brought inefficiency. He concentrated on the window. It was at the very top of the wall, about eight feet off the floor. Nat crouched at the base of the wall and leaped. His right hand shot over the sill of the opening, and, as his fingers searched for a grip, he felt his palm impaled. He suppressed a cry as pain shot through his hand.

He landed on the balls of his feet with a soft thud. Slivers of filthy glass bounced about him with a muffled tinkle and a billowing cloud of dust slowly diffused through the cell.

Cursing silently, he plucked a shard of glass from his

right palm, and pressed the tail of his shirt into the wound to stem the blood. His pulse throbbed in the wound.

Like ink in a beaker of water, the pain spread, first to the freight that plied his gut and then to his head, already trembling from the drug's aftereffects. To his dismay, the room suddenly began to grow dim. No. Not now. There's no time.

Nat rocked back on his heels and sat down awkwardly as his vision blurred. He had to concentrate on the pain, concentrate on the vertigo. Center on their source. Tai Chi', slow motion, visualize yourself rising through the pain, the pain parting, yielding.

When Nat opened his eyes again, he found the room in focus and the pain subsiding. He exhaled slowly, focusing on the air flowing from his body.

The wad of his shirttail was still pressed into his left palm. Cautiously, Nat removed the pressure and examined the wound. It was about two inches long and ran parallel to his lifeline, but it was superficial. Already the shallower ends of the cut had clotted, and only the middle, from which he had plucked the glass, still oozed blood.

Nat started to rise. This time he'd grab one of the iron bars instead. Then he heard muffled voices from beyond the wooden walls.

Had they heard him? Were they coming to interrogate him?

Returning to the spot in which he had slept off the drug, Nat tried to remember the position he found himself in when he woke up.

Semi-fetal, head resting on his right arm, he curled up facing the door and feigned sleep. He wanted a confrontation with these people, but on *his* terms. He closed his eyes to minute slits, and turned his cut palm downward.

The voices grew louder, the sounds of footsteps distinct: there were two of them.

". . . think that you may have given him too much," one of the voices said. "What if something happens to him?"

"You worry too much," a female voice said. "I know what I'm doing."

"Then why is he sleeping so long?"

"It may have something to do with his previous injuries; just quit being so fainthearted."

A hinge squeaked as the cover to the Judas window opened. Through the fuzzy veil of his eyelashes, Nat saw a face, and then the Judas closed. He heard a padlock click open and the door swung open. The man who had accompanied him into the panel truck stepped through the doorway, pointing his machine gun at Nat's head. The woman who had administered the drug followed.

"See, he's still out," the man said, nudging Nat with the toe of his loafers. He still wore the same suit.

"Don't worry, I tell you," the woman said. "He's only been out for five hours, give his system time to work things out."

Nat relaxed. He had more than twenty-four hours to get free and meet with Tania.

His earlier thoughts of wrestling the gun away from the man he now rejected. He had some time to work with—another couple of hours before they'd expect him to be awake—and he wanted his body in good shape, and enough time to think of the best plan of attack.

"Is he still alive?" the man asked.

The woman sighed exasperatedly and leaned down toward him.

"Cover him. He may be faking," she directed the man, and then Nat felt her hands on his shoulder.

His heart pounded. She'd be sure to see that cut on his hand now.

When she shoved on his shoulder and turned him on his back, Nat let his left hand drag limply, palm down on his chest. Eyes closed Nat waited for her to reach for his wrist, to take his pulse, waited for the discovery of the cut and the swift kick and accusations that would surely follow.

Instead, a thumb plucked at his eyelids. He saw her gaze perfunctorily in first one, then the other eye.

"His pupils contract normally," she said. "And look at his belly, he's still breathing. Are you satisfied now?"

Nat heard the man grunt, then the gritty crunching of a dirty concrete floor under leather soles. Finally the door shut and the sounds of a padlock being secured faded away with their footsteps.

Nat did not move immediately. He remained supine, letting the chill of the concrete floor seep through his back, waiting for the tension to drain. When he was sure it was safe, he got up and relieved himself in the corner where a hundred hobos had before. And now, as always since Amsterdam, he looked over his shoulder when he took a piss. And as in every other time, the wound in his back above his kidney throbbed a reminder.

The sun had finally set and the darkness glowed pink from the sodium vapor streetlights somewhere beyond the little rectangle that was Nat's only link to the outside. He reckoned that an hour and a half had passed. His captors would probably return soon, and now was the time for action.

He hadn't spent the intervening time passive. Rather he had first hung from the bars of the basement window, mentally mapping the world outside: the space directly in front of the window looked like a bombed-out ghetto, rubble and fire charred timbers littered the landscape.

Few people passed along the street a hundred yards away, and the air was still save for the sounds of traffic in the distance. Only once did he see anyone: about

110

half an hour ago, a gang of six black teenagers crossed the rubbish strewn lot, cutting diagonally from one street to another.

It had to be the South Bronx. It looked like all those pictures that ran in the newspapers when political candidates wanted some mileage and visited some demolished neighborhood to announce some poverty program or another.

But it wasn't the charming character of the neighborhood that kept him dangling from the bars of the window until the muscles in his arms and shoulders knotted into knots tied in knots. Rather it was a sentry sitting on the front stoop.

Swarthy like the others who had attacked him earlier, he was younger than they were and dressed in beat-up jeans and a fatigue jacket. He carried a large revolver with a silencer. Nat couldn't discern the caliber in dimming light, though he ordinarily could, even at the fifty-foot distance.

Nat watched the sentry, noted every movement.

The man was edgy. Every time an erratic noise found its way around the side of the building, he crouched and pulled out his pistol with his right hand.

Nat dropped to the floor of his cell to allow his tortured muscles to recover, and then set about removing the window bars. They had been set in holes punched in the upper surface of the transom, and immobilized by concrete troweled onto the lower surface. It had been an amateur job, and the expansion and contraction of years of seasonal changes had weakened the concrete.

In less than fifteen minutes, Nat had managed to work the concrete away from the base of three of the four bars.

Two of his fingers were bleeding from his assault on the concrete, but it was worth it. Clinging to the remaining bar, Nat squirmed through the opening. Warm air hit his face.

111

Ahead, he could see a faint black on lighter black outline of the sentry, sitting on the stoop of the building—a fire-gutted brick tenement about eight stories high.

Nat rose to a crouch, and hugged the wall as he picked his way among the rubble. One clatter of precariously stacked bricks, one high-pitched tinkle of broken glass, and his night would be interrupted by gunfire.

Over the rush of blood in his ears, Nat heard the background noise of traffic in the distance, and the sounds of children, voices, and a radio. He was grateful for this faint vortex of sound in which he could hide his own.

Suddenly, the sentry shifted and turned his head toward him. Nat froze, one more immobile mass among many in the desolate yard. The man scanned the yard from Nat's position to the other corner of the building. What had aroused him? The two men were no more than thirty feet apart—point blank—when the sentry began fumbling with something metallic. The man was reaching for his flashlight, and just as quickly a beam of light shot from the end of a long, eight-battery light, the sort policemen sometimes use to subdue the people they arrest.

A wave of nausea swept through Nat's body. The man was turning the flashlight in his direction! Nat picked up a brick fragment and hurled it over the sentry's head. It clattered among the rubble near the opposite corner of the building, and the light beam followed, searching for the source of the noise.

Nat raced toward the sentry, who heard his approach and whirled to meet him. But the man had to shift the flashlight to his left hand before drawing his revolver, and by the time the gun was out of its holster, Nat was swinging one of the steel reinforcing bars from the basement window.

The end of the bar caught the tender flesh behind

the sentry's right ear, landing with a hollow thump. The pistol clattered down the steps. But the man did not go down. He was at least six inches taller than Nat and built like a fullback.

Nat jumped on the man's back and wrapped his legs about the man's waist. He then brought the steel bar across the man's throat, and heaved back on both ends with all his strength. Nat heard the cartilage in the sentry's larynx crack. The man's hands shot up to his throat and he tried to yell, but only a gurgle found its way out.

The sentry jumped and whirled, trying to shake Nat off. He spun and repeatedly slammed Nat into the wall of the building. The night spun crazily. Nat leaned as far back as he could to avoid the man's hands as they searched for Nat's eyes and would surely gouge them out. But the farther out he leaned, the easier it was for the man to slam his head into the wall.

Nat felt wet warmth on the back of his head, and knew that the last blow had drawn blood.

Die, damn you! Nat cursed silently.

But this bull refused to die.

Nat felt his grip loosen around the steel bars. He was losing consciousness, one more blow against the wall and it would all be over. Nat heaved on the ends of the bar for all he was worth. The sentry groaned a complaint that never left his chest, and then stumbled off the landing and collapsed face down on the stairs.

In ragged gasps, Nat drew in great gobs of breath as he lay atop the now-immobile sentry. He closed his eyes, trying to still the vertigo. As he lay face down, exhausted, he felt a warm trickle snaking its way from his crown, around the back of his ear, and finally he tasted the salty iron flavor of his own blood.

Rolling off the sentry's still form, Nat scrambled down the stairs on all fours, retrieved the pistol which lay among the sidewalk's debris and shoved it along with its long silencer into the back of his jeans.

113

Nat's body cried for rest, his head throbbed from the blows, and from the drug hangover. Stopping at the top of the steps he rubbed a galaxy of colored stars from his closed eyes, then focused them on the open doorway and stepped inside.

Nikolai Valente enjoyed the sight of his naked body. It was the only sight he liked better than the naked bodies of the women he took to bed.

Standing before the elegant full-length mirror in his room at the Waldorf, he struck an arabesque. When he saw the way his muscles rippled, how they stood out in perfect definition, how his penis and testicles dangled so gracefully against his left thigh, he smiled contentedly.

Across the room, Tania watched him with irritation. She knew Niki's posturing for what it was: a prelude to an assignation with some pretty young dancer. He always did this before leaving her to screw someone else.

But tonight, she felt oddly unaffected by his performance. All she could think of was Nathaniel Worthington, the American who had made her such an outrageous proposition. What if it were *he* standing nude by the foot of her bed, instead of Niki?

"I said, what do you think of this?" Niki was angry. "Do I have to repeat myself every time? Are you getting senile? Ungrateful girl, Tania. Where is your loyalty?"

"I . . . I'm sorry," she stammered. "I was . . . thinking."

"Is that what you call it?" demanded Niki. "I'd call it dimwitted. Since you've stopped dancing, Tania, you've become impossible: Flighty, absent-minded, totally unconcerned about your future—"

"I was thinking of your defection," Tania replied.

"Oh? What is there for *you* to think about?" Niki sneered. "I am the artist the Americans will want. You will come with me because you are my wife. It doesn't

114

matter what—or even if—you think about the defection."

"I can arrange it."

"I think you are going to have to relearn a lot of . . . What did you say?" Niki stopped and looked at her.

"I said I can arrange it," Tania repeated patiently.

Disbelief swept over Nikolai Valente's face, followed by a broad smile.

"This is a joke, right?" Niki laughed.

"It's no joke, Niki," Tania said, so firmly and quietly that Niki had to be silent to hear her. "I have a meeting with the Americans set up."

Niki's smile vanished. His mouth opened and closed, but no words issued. Throwing a robe over his shoulders, he sat slowly on the foot of the bed, never taking his eyes off Tania.

"Go on," he urged. Tania remained silent. "Well, *tell* me, woman! What have you done? How have you done this? Where did you? Who—I don't believe you. You could not have—I mean . . ."

"You think I'm not capable," Tania said. "That's what you mean, isn't it?"

"Well . . . ah—"

"Of course you do," Tania said. "But if you'll please shut up I'll tell you what—"

"Don't tell *me* to shut up, woman!" Nikolai thundered and sprang from his seat toward Tania. She stared at him but didn't flinch. He stopped short. There was something new in her expression, something that he couldn't fathom.

Tania's heart raced, but when she spoke her voice was steady. "Slap me, and you can go back to Leningrad, Nikolai Alexandrovich Valente," Tania said.

Now her fear turned to wonder as Niki lowered his arm to his waist, took two steps back, and sat on the edge of the bed. He did not speak.

115

He's waiting for *me*, Tania suddenly realized. A quiet exhilaration filled her.

"Nikolai," she began slowly, "if we are to do this . . . this thing right, you are going to have to listen to me very carefully and do exactly as I tell you, do you understand?"

She looked for consent, but found only a stare of amazement.

"Do you understand, Niki?"

Tilting his head to one side, Niki started to speak and then stopped.

"If . . . if what you say . . ." he spoke hesitantly. He wanted with all his heart to defect, but he couldn't show weakness to this woman. "If what you have to say is . . . of interest to me. If I . . . consider your directions sound, then I will—"

"Fine," Tania interrupted brusquely. "Then you can find your own way to America!" She pushed her way up from the bed and started for the bathroom.

"Wait," said Niki. Tania smiled to herself. Niki was pleading! She turned back to face him. He was sitting on the edge of the bed, his bathrobe untied and draping over his legs, his face devoid of its usual contempt for her. Instead, he looked confused and . . . afraid. For just an instant, she felt sorry for him.

"You're going to be late for your date," she said smartly, "if you continue to sit around like that. Or are you going like that to save the time it takes to remove your clothes?"

Heart pounding, she whisked into the bathroom and shut the door. She knew he'd be gone when she came out again. And then—yes, then, she'd be in a pickle. What on earth had possessed her to talk to her husband that way? She'd really gone and done it now. Why, oh, why hadn't she listened to her escorts? And all this because of some attractive American stranger who was just another provocateur out to corrupt her.

The sweat beads on her forehead found one another

116

and then joined to trickle into her eyebrows. She wiped them away with the back of her hand.

For a long time she stood in the bathroom, waiting for the churning in her stomach and the surf pounding in her ears to calm. Taking deep breaths, she washed her face with cold water. She was patting her cheeks dry with the thick Waldorf towels as she opened the bathroom door. What she saw made her jump.

Niki had not moved from the bed. He was looking up at her. "I will listen," he said solemnly. "I want to defect so badly—"

"Badly enough to obey me?" Tania asked.

He nodded. "But only in this matter, do you understand?"

Tania understood. Power was a high; it felt almost as good as sex.

The hallway smelled of garbage and stale urine and things decaying. Inside, Nat waited for his eyes to adjust to the darkness. A furry object scurried across his right foot, startling him. He jumped and a piece of debris rattled dully in the dark.

Nat soothed his jangled nerves and shoved the complaints of his body aside. He stood still in the darkness. Then he caught a faint whiff of tobacco smoke brought on a light breeze. Silently he followed the odor.

As the stench of cigarettes grew stronger, Nat heard voices. He padded carefully among the trash-strewn floor. Conversation drifted from a room at the end of the corridor, and Nat thought he saw a very faint light issuing from a doorway, the sort of warm light made by candles.

The voices grew louder, and Nat saw cigarette smoke in the dim light. He was no more than a dozen feet from the door. He tightened his grip on the dead sentry's pistol. The dim light outlined the shadows of the rubbish in the hallway. Nat picked a careful path to avoid making noise. He placed his foot next to a

117

rent garbage bag, its contents spilled on the floor, when with a squeal and the sounds of scurrying feet, a mammoth rat leaped from the bag accompanied by two smaller rodents. An empty tin can rattled like cannon fire in the hallway as the rats scurried toward the corridor's end past the candlelit door.

Nat leaped for the darkness of a shadowed doorway as two silenced pistol shots coughed discretely. The large rat was splattered across the wall and floor. Nat pressed himself in the doorway, breathing silently through his mouth. A man's voice laughed, and spoke in a quick language Nat thought sounded like Hebrew.

The voice got louder, and the hallway brightened with candlelight. Someone had entered the hallway bringing the candle with him. Nat pressed himself as flat as he could against the door.

A trickle of sweat ran through his eyebrows and into one eye. Steps shuffled in the hallway. Nat flinched when he heard the person kick the garbage bag, sending bottles and garbage clattering across the floor.

"Ha-ah!" the man cried. Nat heard four rapid coughs of the silenced weapon. Shooting rats! The man was shooting rats for a diversion. The light in the hallway receded with the man's footsteps, plunging the corridor once again into the dimmest of light. As he waited for his eyes to adjust again, Nat heard scratching on the other side of the corridor, reflexes of a dying rat, he thought.

He shut his eyes, almost overcome with the compulsion to go over and put the rat out of his misery.

Nat clenched his fist and wanted to pound the wall, but instead, pushed silently away from his hiding place and crept down the hall. When he reached the doorway he flattened his back against the wall and listened. He heard two voices, a man and a woman's, conversing in muted tones. Nat heard a metallic click, and the sound of empty shell casings clinking against the floor.

His gun was empty, he'd expended all the rounds firing at the rats. Now!

"Hold it, don't move or I'll blow your fucking head off!" Nat shouted as he jumped in front of the door just outside the room and aimed the pistol at the woman who was reaching for an Uzi machine gun.

"You!" The man shouted, his eyes wide, his mouth a perfect "O" of surprise, and then turned to the woman, "You told me he'd be out for hours, you incompetent bitch." He raised his hand.

"Hold it!" Nat said training the gun on him. "That's enough. I want both of you up . . . now!" Both stood up slowly. The woman fixed him with an assassinating stare whose message was unmistakable even in the dim candlelight.

"Now over to the wall behind you." After they complied, Nat spoke again. "I want your legs spread— wider," he ordered. "Now hands high over your heads and against the wall."

After they had assumed the position, Nat crouched in the doorway and stuck his head quickly in to make sure no one else was hiding out of sight. No one was.

Satisfied, Nat stepped into the room and assured himself there were no doors or closets in which another person could hide.

"All right, I want some answers," Nat told the two people. "Who are you?"

There was no answer. He hadn't really expected one.

"Who are you working for?"

Silence.

Nat walked first to the man. "Out from the wall," he said. "I want your feet farther away from the wall." The man complied moving away until he was supporting himself on his arms. "You too," he told the woman, who also sullenly obeyed.

Covering them with the gun, Nat frisked both with one hand, coming away with the man's wallet and

119

passport and a small arsenal of hidden weapons ranging from a derringer to a wrist knife from both of them.

Nat retreated to the dropcloth on which the two had been sitting. The man's papers identified him as an Israeli citizen and a dealer in heavy machine parts. The usual odd collection of credit cards, small bills, pictures and billfold clutter failed to clarify the picture.

The woman's bag, which lay half open on the dropcloth provided little more. She was also an Israeli citizen, a businesswoman with her own import-export business. But a tiny photograph—a clipped fragment from a larger snapshot—showing the woman he had captured posing with another woman in khaki fatigues struck him as familiar.

Neither of the women was familiar, but the tiny fragments of background visible in the inverted triangle where their shoulders met stirred a memory. It wasn't much: a half a square inch of photograph, containing a pattern of scrubby trees against an odd, bunker-like structure.

Nat searched his memory, trying to match this jigsaw piece with an experience. He *knew* he had seen it before. Where? Obscure fragments drifted through his head: heat, thirst, noise—not just noise but gunshots—Israel, naturally, but not a city. It was a strain remembering, like someone was dragging a chain through the very length of his body. Israel, but he had only been there twice: as a courier, and he'd never left the airport at Tel Aviv and—of course! To teach a weeklong session in Tai Chi' Chuan at one of Mossad's secret training centers in the Negev.

The realization slammed into his belly like a fist: they were Mossad, Israeli intelligence. He had always worked *with*, gave lessons to, took training from the Israelis. They were the only Western intelligence agency he had any respect for, the only one that really merited respect as a whole.

Why did they attack him? Over Pugachev? But Pugachev was a Russian, a Neo-Stalinist whose policies would make life rougher on Soviet Jews. Why would they abduct him? How did they know about Pugachev? *Did* they know about Pugachev?

The confusion and introspection combined with the pain of his recent ordeal to divert his attention from his captives. Nat was unaware of the woman, who had slowly turned her head toward him and had slowly pushed herself away from the wall.

Nat went over the possibilities in his mind: Pugachev had engineered the invasion of Afghanistan, he was a militarist who believed in war. He was a threat to Israel, so why was Mossad . . . better yet, *how* did Mossad find out about the operation? There was only Rinehart and him . . . unless Ivan had overheard, unless someone had managed to bug the most secure quarters in the country. That would mean penetration at the highest level of the national security agency . . . by an *ally*.

Of course, allies spying on each other was far from unheard of. The United States had placed agents in the services of just about every NATO country, so this wouldn't be unprecedented.

But that was only an if . . . it said nothing about the why.

Attention riveted on the photo fragment, Nat compared first one scenario with another, oblivious to the woman who was reaching inside her matronly bosom for a thin, miniature single shot pistol the size of a small cigarette lighter.

it didn't make sense, Nat thought. If they *had* penetrated the National Security Adviser's staff, they would be following him, waiting for him to move against Pugachev. Or they could contact him. There were at least a dozen Mossad agents with whom he had worked, any of whom knew him well enough to make a phone call. . . .

Whether it was a sixth sense, or whether it was a change in breathing patterns or a sensitivity to the scent that every person emits, Nat looked up abruptly and saw the tiny one-shot weapon aimed at him. From his long association with Mossad, he knew the single hollow-core .22 caliber slug would be coated with succinylcholine hydrochloride, a deadly nerve poison. A graze would be sufficient to put him away.

Nat rolled to his left. The woman's arm followed him. There was no furniture in the room, no cover. The woman dropped to the floor as Nat raised his pistol and fired, the slug scattered plaster fragments harmlessly about the room. The man pushed away from the wall, but Nat's concern was the woman. Nat rolled again, over and over.

Somewhere as he was completing his third roll, he heard the sharp report of her pistol and felt something tug at the cuff of his Levis. More plaster rained on the floor. Nat jumped up and started to fire the pistol but something restrained his finger on the trigger.

He was panting, and the cold calculation had turned to anger.

"You!" Nat shouted at the women. "Back up against the wall!" The woman glared defiantly at him as she stood still like a cornered animal on her all fours. The man still stood against the wall. "One more stunt like that and I'll—"

"Go ahead," the woman interrupted as she got up from the floor. "Go ahead and shoot. You'll gain nothing." Nat fixed the woman's face with his eyes, conscious of his pistol resting steadily in the corner of his vision. The woman turned to the wall, and assumed a stance identical to her male companion's.

"You're Mossad," Nat said as he started rummaging through the rest of the woman's bag.

"You're mistaken," the woman replied derisively.

"No," Nat said as he upended the bag and let its contents clatter upon the dropcloth. He raked through the pile of papers and mostly personal items. He uncovered the black plastic covered hypodermic kit and snapped open its fake leather-grained cover. About the size of a hardback best seller, it was filled with a number of syringes, needles and ampules of clear liquids.

"Sodium pentathol," he said looking at a partially empty vial. "That's a pretty standard choice," he mumbled. "But what have we here?" he posed rhetorically as he withdrew another vial. "Scopolamine? That's pretty crude stuff, I'm sure you've gotten a little more sophisticated in your drug interrogation tactics." Neither replied. "What was this in here for, to scare me into talking?"

As Nat finished his inspection of the kit, noting the more sophisticated drugs he knew would be in it, he realized that they were after information—after information *he* had. But all he had that they would be likely to want would concern Valente, Valente and the death of Pugachev.

"What do you know about me?" Nat asked as he left the drug kit and walked over to where the two Mossad agents stood. Neither of them replied.

"I said, what do you know about my activities?" Again there was silence. Anger rushed from his gut to his head and Nat grabbed the man by the shoulders, twisted him around and slammed him against the wall so hard it knocked him breathless.

"I *know* you're both working for Mossad," Nat began. "But I don't know why you have attacked me. Nothing I have ever done and nothing I am doing now is contrary to the interests of Israel."

"You are a fool if you believe that, Mr. Worthington," the woman said. "We have heard too much about your previous achievements to think you are so naive."

"Maybe," Nat stare at her and then at the man who fixed him with a defiant glare.

123

"Back against the wall, asshole," Nat said and stepped back as the man sullenly resumed his face-to-the-wall stance.

Nat paced the filthy room from end to end. At last he decided, there was only one choice: he was not a physician and it had been half a decade since he had sat in a tiny training classroom and watched a technician question a subject using drugs. Techniques had changed since then, new drugs invented. There was always the danger of using too much and tipping somone over into a coma from which they'd never return.

Needless killing bothered him. But, he thought as he knelt on the dropcloth and retrieved the black plastic leather grained drug kit, if he was careful, no one would die. And if they did? He'd worry about that, he decided as he removed a plastic syringe from its sterile paper covering, if it happened. No use in worrying about anything, he thought, until it happened.

Chapter Ten

||||||||||||||||||||||||||||||||||||||||||||||||||||||||||||||||||||||||||||||||||||||||||||||||||||||||

Nat had slept little the rest of that night, tossing and turning in his room at the Tudor. After placing a call to Rinehart in Washington, and another to Everett Lowell the next morning, he ate a breakfast sent up by room service and then dozed while he waited for the calls.

It was now 6:30 p.m. and neither man had called him back. Nothing was going well. He had a doomed feeling about this mission. The drug interrogation of the two Mossad agents had gone smoothly, although it had yielded more mystery than information.

The man in the tenement knew nothing. The woman, though, revealed that Mossad had an agent aboard the yacht on which Nat had met Rinehart. The only other intelligible fact that he had dragged from her was that Everett Lowell was on a mission that higher-ups at Mossad knew much about. Nat, she said, was being questioned because he had once worked with Lowell, and had met with Lowell on the yacht.

They didn't know what his mission was; Nat at least

had that much security. But what was Lowell up to that Mossad wanted so badly to stop?

As the elevator stopped at the eighth floor of the Waldorf-Astoria, Nat quickly set aside the question. This part of his mission *had* to go smoothly. The doors opened. Tentatively, Nat stepped into the carpeted corridor. He looked confused—a guest in an unfamiliar hotel trying to remember where his room was. He looked at his key, and then up and down the hallway. There was no one in sight. Either Tania had done her job well, or she had failed. He'd find out in a few seconds.

His key slid easily into the door. The lock yielded as Nat turned the key and felt the cold air-conditioned air as it whiffed through the opened door.

Tania sat in the reading chair by the window and looked at him curiously as he entered. The faint strains of fear on her face relaxed as she recognized him.

"You're on time," Tania said. "That's a good sign, I suppose."

"Yes. Well, I try to be. It's . . . very important in this line of work," Nat replied lightly. There was a wall here now that hadn't been erected two days before. Had she had time to think about it? Had she told the KGB and led him into a trap?

"Did you have any trouble?" Nat asked as he walked to the vanity, pulled out its chair, and sat down.

"Of course not," Tania replied proudly. "They are all such children. Niki was . . . overwhelmed when I informed him. He did exactly as I told him"—there was a hint of pride in her voice—"he left the room on schedule and the guards followed him down the elevator and left the corridor empty. After all, I'm just a woman," she added sarcastically. "And I took the elevator up here. There was no trouble at all."

This Russian ballerina had changed somehow, in the less than forty-eight hours since Nat had last seen her.

He tried to put his finger on what it was—a new self-assurance? Yes, or even arrogance. Or . . . the false bravado of someone frightened. Though her body still moved in the same self-deprecating manner—as if she were apologizing for some insult—her voice and her eyes said something new was firing her.

The change was attractive, though Nat feared it would make her harder to control. Her hair fell resplendent across her shoulders and glowed against the black of the leotard top, which conformed faithfully to a full, muscular body. Her legs, demurely crossed, emerged from the hem of a gray wraparound skirt, and ended with delicate ankles in modest-heeled shoes. And she wore makeup—she hadn't the previous time.

"Have I spilled something on myself?" Tania asked suddenly, looking down at her arms, breasts, and legs.

"Why? Oh, no, of course not." Nat's mind had drifted while he thought of the subtle change that had taken place in her. She had overwhelmed him.

"That is, I was thinking." Nat shifted uneasily on the straight-backed chair. "I've had a very trying time since the last time I saw you." Nat gestured with his hands. "And it's just that—"

"Your hand!" Tania interrupted him. "What is that bandage on your hand?"

Nat flushed in embarrassment. Her concern was making him uncomfortable. Or was it something more?

She was sitting in profile to him, her breasts silhouetted in the light of the dying day. With a great effort, Nat forced his eyes back to her face.

"I, ah . . . cut my hand on a piece of broken glass last night," he explained. "It looks more serious than it is," he added unconvincingly. "But we're not here to talk about my hand. Have you and Niki come to an agreement about the defection?"

"He will do what I tell him," Tania replied with a toss of her head.

"Which means what?" Nat asked, suppressing a

127

smile. Tania continued to surprise him. And keep him off-balance.

Her golden-brown eyes were fixed on his. "He wants to defect," she said thoughtfully, "more than anything else I have ever seen him set his mind to. Except dancing, of course."

"Of course," Nat agreed. "But . . . in order for this plan to work, you must promise in advance to do everything I tell you, exactly as I tell you. And you must do it precisely when you're told." He looked toward her. "Unless you consent to that, the deal is off."

"But you must tell me in advance so I'll know whether or not I can agree to it all."

"I can't do that. In explaining it, I would be giving you information about agents and methods that I could not give you if you were not going through with it. I can't risk your returning to the Soviet Union and talking—or having someone force the information from you."

"She nodded. "And if I agree," Tania said, "and you tell me as much as you can and I then change my mind . . . then what?"

Nat's face hardened. This was going to be more difficult than he had imagined. "Remember Illych?" he asked.

"You wouldn't!" Tania gasped, searching his eyes. Gradually, a mask of shock crept over her face.

"You would . . ." she said with amazement, "you really would."

"Yes," Nat said softly, "I would. I have no choice, for your betrayal could mean my life."

They stared at each other in silence.

"I suppose I have no choice," Tania said finally.

"Yes, you do. You can walk out of this room and tell Niki the deal is off."

"That is no choice at all." Tania remembered the surprise on Niki's face, the rush of power she had experienced. No, she wasn't ready to give that up. She took a deep breath.

"I suppose," she said, "I will have to trust your judgment. Trust does not come easily to a Russian. . . ."

"Nor to an American, for that matter," Nat added reassuringly.

"Yes, but we are taught all our lives not to trust," Tania continued, and then fell silent.

"Tania," Nat said quietly. "The reality of this situation is that you must trust me, and you must follow my every instruction to the letter, if the defection is to be successful. This plan has been discussed at the highest levels of the American government, and it has been agreed by men much, much higher than myself that if the defection is to occur, it must occur through me and in the manner we prescribe."

She stared silently at him, a look of fear in her eyes. He knew he had won.

"All right," she said quietly. "But you must not deal with Niki directly. You must let me deal with him."

"No conditions," Nat said, admiring her refusal to surrender completely. "There can be no conditions. Do you understand?"

Reluctantly, Tania nodded.

"We have an agreement, then?"

She nodded wordlessly.

"Good. Now," Nat said coldly, "let's get down to details." Well, you're still a hard-nosed son of a bitch, Worthington, Nat thought to himself. Yes, he added mentally. And that's why you're still alive.

"Your defection will take place in Paris," Nat began, "after the opening night performance at the opera house."

"Why Paris?" Tania said, agitated. "Why not here, why do we have to leave the United States? What happens if they send us home early before we get to Paris? What would happen if the KGB—"

129

"Hold on," Nat raised his voice to override Tania's rising alarm. "I can explain, please allow me to explain . . . all right?"

"Yes." Tania agreed curtly.

"Fine. Well, it should be in Paris because you and Niki will not be guarded as tightly as here," Nat began. "If we tried it here, we might have to fight with the KGB and if that happened—particularly on American soil—well, we'd have an international incident of the highest magnitude.

Nat saw that she accepted the logic, it was written in her eyes. But he saw more in her eyes, and it excited him and scared him.

Something was stirring inside and he wanted to laugh and cry.

Stop!

"What we must do now," Nat continued, "is to arrange a meeting in Paris. I'll have to work through you and arrange a meeting to make the final details," Nat said.

"I see," Tania said. "But one thing I don't see," she continued, "is why you keep referring to this as a 'mission.' A mission seems like a very complicated thing, a very important thing—can we be that important?"

Nat had been afraid of this. She was more suspicious than he had anticipated, and there was something else at work, she was seeing the holes in his presentation. Had he become such a poor liar? Lies were the spy's stock in trade and if they didn't work . . .

"Are you listening to me?" Tania asked, annoyed.

"Of course," Nat said. "It's just that—"

"That you haven't been telling me the whole truth and you wonder how much you can get away with now?" she interrupted.

"Look here!" Nat said angrily. "I will tell you just as much as *I* think you need to know and I'll tell you *when* you need to know it. I told you before that you have to follow my instructions to the letter, and that

130

holds whether I tell you everything now or wait until later, do you understand?"

Nat caught his breath and watched Tania's face turn from anger to calm. She had reached some decision.

"You're a cold man, Nathaniel Worthington," she said. "You do what you do because that's all you can do," Tania's voice trailed off. "Why, you're no better off than I am."

Nat looked at her quizzically.

"You know," she began as she got up from her chair and sat on the foot of the bed next to him, "just because people argue with you doesn't mean they're not on your side. People aren't machines, Nathaniel, they do things better when they know *why* they're doing them, when they know what's at stake.

"For many years—for all my life in fact—I've done things because I was told to," she continued. "First I did things because my parents told me to; then I did things because the school or the state or the ballet academy, or Niki told me to. And here I am, trying to break out of that and do what I want, and to do it, I have to take a step back to what I'm trying to escape from and let you tell me everything. Do you understand what that makes me feel like? I need to know *why* I'm doing things now."

"You . . . you have a very good point," Nat said. "In fact a lot of good points."

She took his words skeptically. "If you really mean that," Tania challenged him, "then take me into your confidence. I think you should."

Nat knew she was right, and further, he had an uncanny sense that she was reading his every thought: that he couldn't hide anything from her anyway.

"Yes, I suppose so." Nat walked to the window and stood beside her. They both looked out the window at the tiaras of bridge lights strung together in the darkness, at the rectangular blocks of office lights stacked one on top of the other for a hundred stories and more, the trails and winking of headlights and tail-lights of autos scurrying among themselves like Kafkian beetles in the night.

They stood side by side, not touching, absorbing the scene played out before them.

"Shall I start over?" Nat broke the silence.

"I'd like that, yes," Tania said.

"Good. The Kirov opens at the Paris Opera House exactly two weeks from today, Nat said as Tania nodded. "Starting nine days from now—that's five before the opening night—I will be standing on the second-level observation deck of the Eiffel Tower from 11 A.M. to 1 P.M. I'll be there for four days. See if you can get away alone."

"And if I can't?"

"Come anyway, but don't speak to me," Nat said. "I'll have to contact you directly—at your hotel."

"How?"

"To tell you the truth, I don't know right now. But I'll figure out a way.

She looked at him uneasily.

"There are a hundred different ways," Nat explained. "I'll just need a few days in Paris to figure out which one will work best. Understand?"

Relieved, she nodded.

"Now, returning to my other question—do you mind if we sit down?" and without waiting for a reply, Nat returned to the chair by the vanity. Tania remained standing by the window. "What would you like to know that I haven't already told you about?"

"The conditions," Tania said. "You said the defection would take place in Paris after some—you said preliminary conditions—were taken care of. I need to know what those are."

How long had it been since he knew someone to confide in, he thought as he looked now at Tania who waited silently, standing by the window. It had been too long since he could talk to someone, and now, he

132

thought, he'd found one if only for the duration of this mission.

He turned and looked at her; she returned the look.

"Sit down," he said flatly, "it's a long story—and not a very pretty one."

"Sit down now, will you?" Nat asked again. Tania reclined in the armchair staring at him down the end of her nose.

"You wanted to know about the preliminary condition," Nat began. "Well, if you and Niki want to defect, you first have to kill a man."

"Good God, Rinehart! What have you got him doing?"

"You know better than to ask me that, Everett," said the other man dismissively. And he leaned back in his leather-upholstered chair to read the onionskin copy Everett Lowell had just brought to him personally. Lowell sat on the edge of an uncomfortable armless chair across the desk from the elder gentleman. It contained the summary of a radio transmission intercepted and decoded by Lowell's covert operations division of the CIA.

Now Lowell's face was clouded with anger. "This little screw-up," he said, shifting his bulk in his chair, "could well sour the best working relationship we've ever had with Mossad—and I don't have to tell you how important that is."

Rinehart looked up from the paper and fixed the obese intelligence agent with a chilly, silent stare. The street chatter of Pennsylvania Avenue drifted faintly through the sealed windows of the National Security Adviser's corner office atop the new executive office building on Seventeenth Street.

"No, Everett, you *don't* have to tell me that," Rinehart said as he swiveled his chair away from Lowell and stood up facing the window. Below him he saw the patchwork of a dozen restored Federal era townhouses occupied by such venerable bodies as the National Trust for Historic Preservation, and beyond them, Lafayette Park, the park of the Presidents.

Traffic on Pennsylvania Avenue below him was blocked by police and as Rinehart watched, helmeted police on horseback and motorscooters were mopping up the stragglers of a demonstration. Some Middle Eastern group or another, he surmised, blasting the U.S. for meddling in their affairs—or else for not meddling enough. Whatever their cause, it would soon be moot. He turned slowly from the window, the onionskin held in his right hand.

"This," Rinehart said calmly, holding up the paper, "means little to me in the whole fabric of my duties." Lowell started to sit up in protest. "But," Rinehart barked, pinning Lowell once again to the back of his chair, "it is a mistake of no small import."

Rinehart returned to his chair and sat down again, slowly, deliberately. The sound of the fat man's breathing—labored, as if he had a sinus problem—irritated him.

"It is a mistake of no small import," Rinehart repeated, now facing Lowell across his desk, "and it is *your* mistake." Lowell's wheezing ceased momentarily and his eyes opened wide.

"As you . . ." Lowell swallowed to moisten his parched throat. "As you can see, the, ah interactions—"

"Fracas, Mr. Lowell. Do you people always have to talk in terms of 'interactions,' and 'sanctions'? What's wrong with 'killed' or 'stabbed'?"

"Uh . . ." Lowell chased a stray lock of hair from his forehead, "nothing . . . nothing at all, Mr. Rinehart. The . . . uh . . . fracas that took place as described in the message we intercepted, left a Mossad agent dead on a crowded Manhattan street. Further—"

"That's enough," Rinehart cut him off. "Don't get so damned tangled in your erroneous story. First of all, I

134

sent Worthington on a mission—the subject of which is not subject to review by you or any other spook that works for me," Rinehart began.

"Second, the issue is not whether the purpose of the mission is contrary to Israeli interests, or whether I sent Worthington to blow up the goddamned wailing wall, understand?"

Lowell didn't, but he nodded just the same.

"The *point is* that they know something and they found out about it too damn quick, and that means someone on that boat of yours is getting an extracurricular salary."

Lowell swallowed audibly. "I was unaware that—"

"Of course you were," Rinehart interrupted. "All you can do is take your little ciphered messages as if nothing else existed in all the world and try to kill people with your creative erector-set weapons. I'm weary of having to lead you by the hand. I want people I can rely upon. If I can't rely upon you, then I'll find someone else . . . Worthington, perhaps?"

Rinehart smiled and watched the deliberate insult play across the fat man's face, first as rage in his eyes, and last as a momentary tremor of his round face as he fought for control. Lowell, the ultimate elitist bureaucrat, had hated Worthington from first contact. Nat's unorthodox methods and his flaming disrespect for the system were a nettle that constantly smarted. Had it not been for Rinehart's sponsorship of the young agent and the fact that Worthington was so competent, Lowell knew he would have disposed of "the boy" as he called him, long ago.

Stung, not really sure whether or not Rinehart was really serious, Lowell sat stock still in his chair searching for a reply. What could he say? What did Rinehart want him to do? What was the answer that Rinehart wanted from him? If he could only figure out what Rinehart wanted him to say, he'd say it.

"Worthington called me yesterday," Rinehart stated flatly, breaking the silence.

"But that's a violation—"

"Yes, Everett, I know that's a violation of the agreement we have with him. I don't need for you to point out his transgressions. I care less that he violated the agreement than about *why* he did. You get upset because he broke a rule—that's what's wrong with you, everything by the book whether it makes sense or not."

Lowell had gotten a call also. He'd planned to trace Nat, trap him in his violation and turn over the evidence to Rinehart. But he hadn't had an opportunity to do it before the intercepted Mossad message describing the abortive attempt to kidnap Nat blew up in his face.

"Nat's call was obviously related to this attack on him," Rinehart said. "So I intend to contact him and get to the bottom of this."

"What would you like for me to do?" Lowell offered eagerly.

"Nothing," Rinehart said. "Nothing that has anything to do with Worthington. Is that clear?"

Rinehart turned his attention to the papers on his desk. Lowell waited awkwardly for a send off and when none came stood up, started to say something but thought better of it. He whirled on his heel and strode angrily from the room.

You've pushed me too far this time, you withered-up old bastard, Lowell thought to himself as he passed through the anteroom to Rinehart's office. I've been here too long to let you run over me. Lowell stabbed impatiently at the elevator call button and paced back and forth in front of the doors while the car made its erratic way to the top floor. He waited for the car to empty and then stepped inside, the car's only passenger. As he punched the button for the first floor, he realized that for the first time in years, he hated someone more than Nat Worthington.

It would assure him a place in history, Mustafa reflected contentedly as he walked up the moving escalator from the Russell Street station and emerged into a rare sunny London morning. He stopped to purchase a copy of the *Guardian* from a young hawker on the street, raised his face to the sun and momentarily let its warmth flow through the red world of his closed eyelids, and then set off resolutely down Euston Street toward the university.

At the first traffic light, he unfolded the newspaper and scanned the headlines: there was nothing surprising, only the usual death, disaster, and destruction. The mob of pedestrians surged across with the green light, and Mustafa moved with them, a head higher than most, seeing along with the usual sights of the world, a collection of bald spots, balding spots, and the tops of hats. Within blocks, the commercial district gave way to the trees and carefully preserved homes and townhouses of the university, and they in turn to the imposing edifices of the university itself.

Yes, *Inshallah,* God willing it would make history. *He* wouldn't make history unless he failed and got caught, but the assassination itself would be a first. Just imagining the headlines it would produce shot a blast of adrenalin through him. The thrill lifted his spirits even higher, and Mustafa strode with the conviction of a man just granted invulnerability.

For days he'd savor each headline, absorb each news telecast. And plunging still further into the future, he mused on the second assassination—he already had that contract too—and how it would be the beginning of a legend. Him. Mustafa Salem el-Nouty, the avenging sword of Arabia. He tossed the copy of the *Guardian* into a rubbish bin and walked on.

Chapter Eleven

||||||||||||||||||||||||||||||||||||||||||||||||||||||||||||||||||||||||||||||||||||

Tania Valente stood beside the gathered curtains, stage
left, resting her foot on the seat of a folding chair. The
final instructions delivered by the director through the
stage loudspeaker buzzed as the dancers drifted off-
stage in pairs.

". . . gaining weight and was absolutely horrible,"
one member of the corps said to another as they
walked by her.

"Definitely," said her companion, "you most definitely should have been given the role of Gamzatti—
you're much better than she."

". . . dirty brown-noser . . ."

". . . he's sleeping with her . . ."

"I was horrible . . ."

". . . stomachache, I don't know if I can . . ."

"The costumes are too heavy . . ."

"The stage is too cold . . ."

"The lighting is too warm for this . . ."

"I'm too hot . . ."

"My feet hurt . . ."

Tania nodded to several of the dancers as they passed. They were friendly to her now that she was no longer a competitor, now that they no longer need be jealous of her. After all, she didn't sleep with Niki any more—everyone knew that—and she no longer danced.

"Hello, Tania, you're looking stunning today," a bent little gray-haired man said affectionately. It was Andropov, the rehearsal pianist. "Won't you dance with us?"

Tania smiled at him. "Not this time," she joked. "They're saving me for better things, you know." Andropov had been one of the first members of the company to visit her at the hospital after she had strained her Achilles tendon, and he had been the last to give up on convincing her to return to dancing. "But how about you, grandfather, how are you faring?"

"Ah, not to complain," he said rolling his eyes comically. "But you know how it always is with me, I sit at my piano, dum-te-dum and then, pow! I'm interrupted. Once, just once, I wish I could play the piece from one end to the other, but no. I'm a rehearsal pianist, not a concert pianist—I get five, maybe six bars at a time. I—" the diminutive old man stopped suddenly and looked around, aware that an eavesdropper could interpret his harmless grousing as criticism of the company administration.

"Don't worry," Tania said and put her hands on his shoulders, "even the *stuckachi* love you." She kissed him on his forehead and sat down in the folding chair as he walked off.

On the other side of the stage, her husband spoke furiously to his Nikiya, gesturing wildly with his hands.

His Nikiya, Tania thought. Was it so long ago that *she* played Nikiya to his Solor? She loved *La Bayadère,* a true Maryinsky classic.

She watched Niki as he calmed and no longer beat the air with his arms. She tried to think of how it had

140

felt to be in his arms—he had hardly touched her since New York—but as she tried to remember, only Nat Worthington entered her thoughts. She looked at Niki, but instead saw Nat in the studio in New York City, she felt again Nat's incidental touch and the electric feeling she had experienced then.

The past two weeks had torn her apart. She fought with herself fiercely, the Russian patriot tearing at the traitorous defector, and all of her upbringing against the sybarite who wanted nothing more than to submerge herself in Nathaniel Worthington's flesh, to feel his skin, to watch him grow passionate, breathless under her touch.

She wondered what he looked like under his clothes. Did hair cover his chest? She remembered him in his leotard: yes, there was hair, just enough. She hoped his back wasn't covered. She remembered how the muscles in his legs bulged when he danced, but didn't really look like a dancer—an athlete, yes, but not a dancer. There was just too much bulk, he lacked the almost emaciated thinness seen even in male dancers.

"Are you ready?" A question penetrated her thoughts. She looked up and found Niki standing over her. Already the stage was growing dark as technicians extinguished bank after bank of lights until there was only the warm yellow of low-wattage bulbs illuminating the stage.

"Tanya," Niki repeated patiently, "are you ready to go back to the hotel?" He'd been supremely polite for the last two weeks. He wants to defect, Tania thought with amusement, and he'll even be civil to me to do it.

"Yes," Tania replied curtly and rose from the chair. "We must go. We must be ready for tonight."

The heat didn't bother him. Even the tickling from the almond-sized roaches that jittered across his ankle failed to bend his nerve. But as Mustafa Salem el-Nouty crouched in the nether space between two converging walls just below the gaudy, gilded ceiling of the Paris Opera House, what distressed him was the failing illumination from his flashlight. Sweat trickled profusely down his face and from his armpits, streaming down his ribs, soaking the cheap cotton shirt he wore under his tattered workman's overalls. The approaching darkness pulled him backward through time toward a dark cistern filled with vermin.

He cursed himself under his breath. Stupid! That's what you get for being in a hurry. He never, ever went anywhere day or night without his flashlight and fresh batteries. But in his haste this morning he had left the fresh batteries behind. With the lights burning and the curtains pulled to shut out the night, he had overslept in his room at the George V, and by the time he had awakened, pulled on the grubby clothes and cracked leather boots and slipped out the hotel's service entrance carrying his tool case, it had been too late to buy fresh batteries; he had to slip through the opera house's security among the morning flow of workers preparing for the opening of the Kirov's performance of *La Bayadère*. Ordinarily the security would not have been difficult to circumvent. But the opening night presence of a top Soviet politburo member, Comrade Pugachev, had dammed the sieve to a trickle. It would have been easier if Pugachev weren't coming; but then, Mustafa had mused, he wouldn't need to get inside.

On the pretext of scouting inadequate wiring, Mustafa had located an ideal niche inside two of the opera house's decorative walls. The structure was honeycombed with such nooks and crannies, left as space between the structural supports of the building and its decoration.

It had taken him less than half a day to locate a niche in the appropriate position—one through which the stagelight wiring ran and to which access could be made through a ventilation shaft large enough to accommodate his extraordinary frame.

142

Now, however, he was cramped. His knees ached from the immobility and the back of his head pounded from the irregular wall upon which it had been resting for nearly three hours.

As the beam from his flashlight grew more feeble, Mustafa's breath quickened. He contemplated leaving to hide in another spot until it was time for the other workmen to leave. But he knew he couldn't take a chance on being spotted by any of the personnel associated with the Kirov, who were rehearsing below him even now. There were always KGB members salted among them, and someone might recognize him.

El-Nouty tried to distract himself. Calm was what he needed. Odd, he thought, that he who feared nothing else, not even death itself, could be so immobilized by this one thing. He'd hidden it from all but one person, a woman. Only Sarah knew that Muammar Quaddafi's top assassin was afraid of the dark.

He tried to think of her, of their last night together. How long had it been? A month? No, closer to six weeks. How he missed her! Though he had all the women his body could possibly want, there were none like Sarah. She was sex for his mind as well as for his body. He visualized her face: the dark Mediterranean skin, smooth and unblemished, like fine velvet under his fingertips, and her dark eyes, set above high proud Arabian cheekbones. And her lips; he nearly forgot the darkness as he remembered her full, sensuous lips against his, against his skin, consuming his body. He saw her then, her sultry eyes staring up at him through wisps of her shiny black hair. She was beauty and ecstasy! And for just a moment, thoughts of the dark vanished and he felt his groin burn, and he could feel her. . . .

His reverie was shattered by the thundering of feet below him, the rumbling of stage scenery being rearranged. The strains of the rehearsal piano no longer sifted through the walls, and the regular pulses of the dancers working through their routines yielded to the discordant sounds of stagehands arriving.

Just a few more minutes, he told himself, just a few more and they'll be gone. Using what was left of the flashlight's illumination, Mustafa checked his connections. The splices were insulated; everything was positioned precisely.

Slowly, he started to make his way through the ventilation shaft, a long and winding vertical passage that plunged from the roof to the subterranean reaches of the opera house's basement. He had to crawl upward for nearly thirty feet before reaching the shaft's access grill above the stage. One slip and he'd be battered to death as he fell to the bottom.

But the climb was no match for his nerve. He would find the light soon, and later, there would be Sarah.

An unseasonably cool breeze whispered through the open French doors and set the curtains undulating gracefully. Nat stood pensively by the window, gazing at Notre Dame just beyond the Quai Montebello.

It was September second, but Nat saw the venerable cathedral through the eyes of the past: the leaves were gone from the trees and a light rain fell. It had been December then, and Paris is not so beautiful in the winter. But it was a fantasy land for him and Colleen and he recalled how romantic it had been to walk arm-in-arm through the rain-sodden streets of Paris until they were both soaked and their shoes made slurping sounds every time they took a step.

They laughed. Nat heard the laughter even now, for not before nor since had he ever laughed so deeply, for so long.

He remembered all that and more as he leaned darkly on the window sill wondering.

Suddenly he once again saw the trees dressed in the dusty green leaves of late summer, too old to be fresh and exhilarating, too young to turn to the warm colors

144

of fall. The grass in the park below him also looked fatigued, as if waiting to turn brown so it could have a chance at a new start.

Nat felt tired. But there was much to be done that day, and he abruptly shoved himself away from the window, grabbed his navy blazer, descended the uneven stone steps of the hotel, gave his key to the concierge and walked into the sunshine.

As Nat walked northeast beside the Seine toward the Pont Neuf bridge, he remembered the last time he came to Paris and how he'd found time to take a tour of the city's infamous catacombs, the ancient quarries that honeycombed the rock on which Paris was built. Over the centuries, residents of the city had gone underground to mine the rocks and minerals they needed to build their homes and streets and after half a millenium the earth grew fatigued by the undermining and began collapsing. Nothing was spared; private homes and public buildings—even the grand domed Cathédral of the Sacré-Coeur—were destroyed or damaged by *les consolidations*.

Portions of the catacombs were converted to burial vaults in the eighteenth century, and today more than six million Parisians were interred there.

But Nat knew the catacombs open to the public were but a fragment of the abandoned quarries and passages under Paris. Other abandoned areas were converted to communication networks by smugglers and brigands who even dug their own tunnels to better connect one quarry to another and make passage more convenient. Over the centuries, the underground spaces were used by thieves and pirates of the underground, religious fanatics, undertakers, mushroom growers and even the partisan resistance movement in World War II. Using a combination of catacombs, the massive and extensive sewer system (some of whose passages were large enough to accommodate boats the size of a bus) and parts of the métro subway tunnels, French freedom fighters could move from one area of the city to another undetected by the German occupation forces.

Nat smiled to himself as the vision of this old and grand city sitting atop a honeycomb came to mind. It was, he thought, as if the city was set above one of those glass-sided ant farms sold in novelty stores where tunnel after tunnel worm their way from top to bottom.

Nat continued his reflective walk until he came to the Rue Dauphine. There he detoured half a block south to stop at a small cafe to take a croissant and *café au lait* as a midafternoon lunch. His outdoor, corner seat gave him an excellent perspective of the sidewalk and street.

He scanned each face as it passed, finding no hint of recognition in the eyes of the sidewalk's passersby nor of the other patrons in the cafe. No one lingered at shop windows.

Nat finished the coffee and croissant quickly, then paid for them and left unexpectedly. He wanted to see if anyone moved rapidly in order to catch up with him. It never hurt to double-check for tails.

He walked briskly up Dauphine to the Pont Neuf bridge, crossed it, but didn't continue to the other side. Instead, he strolled casually down the steps that led to the waterline of the Seine, and walked along the path to the tiny park at the island's tip. No one followed, no one waited on the bridge for him.

After regaining the bridge, Nat turned left, along the Quai de la Mégisserie and sauntered toward the Louvre.

Traffic was growing heavy and had turned into intermittent snarls as he drew closer to the Louvre. He continued past it, and turned by the sphinx and entered the Jardin des Tuileries. Nat strolled past the round pool down the main walk toward the Place de la Concorde. It had been the playground of royalty, this park, Nat thought—and a slaughtering ground as well when the mobs attacked Louis XVI's mercenary Swiss Guards. But nearly two centuries since that blood-letting had restored the bucolic nature of this striking urban park. Nannies and mothers strolled with carriages, the wheels grinding and popping on the hard-packed pea gravel. Ahead near the obelisk in the place, a uniformed pack of school children followed their teacher, looking like gangly penguins in their black uniforms and white blouses.

Since his conversation with Rinehart regarding the Mossad attack, Nat had demanded some route of communication with Rinehart, and he had readily—to Nat's surprise—agreed. The contacts would be made somewhere in the Jardin des Tuileries, and each time by a different agent. Nat had only to walk down the main alley of the gardens between 3 and 5 P.M. on any day during the Paris operation, and he'd made contact.

Nat walked around the octagonal pond, and through the gate leading to the Place de la Concorde. As he did, a thirtyish man with unruly blond hair, dressed in jeans and a fatigue jacket stepped into Nat's path from his resting place.

"Pardon me sir, could you spare any change?" the man asked.

Nat took in the blue-eyed, clean-shaven man with the immaculately manicured nails and faint smell of expensive cologne and decided the CIA had found him. He looked at the statue below which the man had been standing: it was Mercury on a winged horse—a messenger. He groaned inwardly and deduced he had a Yale classics major infatuated with symbolism.

"Of course," Nat said reaching into the pocket of his gray flannel slacks. He pretended to fumble in his pocket as he moved them both out of traffic and against the garden wall.

"Well?" the man snarled. Agents meeting for the first time always reminded him of dogs sniffing at each other, Nat thought.

"You don't have to be so surly, you know," Nat said. "It's not as if I'm going to ask you to strain yourself." Then, as if the thought just flashed in his mind, "You're one of Lowell's people, aren't you?"

"Yeah, hot shit, I'm one of 'Lowell's people' as you say," he answered sarcastically. "Now what do you want? None of us particularly likes dealing with you—we've heard about you—so why don't we skip the pleasantries and get down to business."

Nat's resolve kept the rising anger from betraying him.

"This was just a test," Nat said.

Another American in a tacky polyester suit had walked through the gate and feigned interest in the statue of Strasbourg. "I just wanted to see if you people were on your toes, that's all," Nat said. "So you can go home now." Nat looked at his watch—it was 4:37 P.M.—and turned to walk away.

"Not so fast. We've got something for you," said the blond man brusquely. He thrust a used copy of *Le Monde* at Nat and whirled on his right heel and marched across the place to join his companion. Nat stared at them blankly as they disappeared together between the Hôtel de la Marine and the La Vrillière next to it.

Stunned by the hatred in the blond man's eyes, Nat stood silently for several minutes before he resumed his walk. Carrying the folded newspaper gingerly in his right hand, as if it contained a stick of dynamite, Nat strode from the Place de la Concorde and made his way through the Place Vendôme to the Rue de la Paix.

He passed the Cartier shop quickly, then stopped and returned to look at the display. He seemed to be a tourist whose eye was snared by the opulent display of jewels and precious metals. By abruptly reversing his course, he got a good look at the people behind him.

No one hesitated or seemed startled by his move, and Nat gazed at the display for several minutes, giving anyone observing him time to get nervous and make a mistake. Satisfied, Nat resumed his stroll.

Traffic had congealed around the Place de la Concorde, immobile but trembling with the anger and frustration of tired motorists who'd rather be almost any other place. A battered Fiat had rear-ended an even more battle-scarred Simca at the corner in front of Citroën, and Nat paused at the corner to watch the two Frenchmen scream maledictions at each other.

Gripping the folded copy of *Le Monde,* Nat stepped off the curb and picked his way through the stalled traffic across the Avenue de l'Opera to the Clerc store on the corner. Nat paused again, partly to check for a tail, and partly for the majesty of this store's display of jewelry: No one, not even Cartier, rivaled its sheer grandeur.

But as he scanned the display, his eyes continuously refocused on the glass reflecting the scurry of the passersby behind him. The sidewalks were full now, jammed almost as tightly as the streets.

Picking his way through the mass of cars, Nat crossed the Boulevard des Capucines and circled the opera house, staying always on the opposite side of the street. He wanted to locate the best spot to meet with Tania after the sanction, and to map out an escape route in case things went wrong.

The KGB would be effective in their security, he knew, and backed up by Pugachev's GRU, any escape routes had to be effective and unorthodox for an escape to succeed. That made the spy's first rule—always leave an exit—even more difficult.

Turning left into an alley between two chic boutiques, Nat soon found what he wanted—a loose grate on a sewer connector. In the dim twilight that filtered down into the narrow alley, Nat could see the sewer was large enough for a normal sized man to nearly stand up in. Which wasn't surprising, since the big collectors into which ones like this flowed were massive corridors the size of subway tunnels. He knew that from the tour he'd taken several years past.

149

About twenty yards from the loose grate were a set of garbage cans, filled to overflowing. As he approached them, two sleek Norway rats scampered out of a can, belligerently glared at him, and then scurried into the shadows. Nat returned to the sidewalk, and located the café on a side street to which the garbage cans belonged.

Clean, not well lit, fairly packed with after work sojourners sipping wine or espresso, it had a large interior with booths.

Perfect, Nat thought. Tania would wait for him in a booth close to the kitchen through which they could escape should their roles in the sanction be discovered.

Crossing the Rue Gluck to the opera house itself, Nat walked its perimeter, refreshing his memory, looking for clues—to what he didn't know—but he always absorbed as much information as he could, should some trivial part become the factor between life and death. It had happened more than once, Nat mused.

The margin between life and death, Nat contemplated as he made his way toward the Café de la Paix, was as often as not as slim as the chance timing at a traffic light, the serendipitous discovery of an unlocked door, or a careless word casually offered that gave warnings when none were intended.

After winding through the crowd, Nat joined a small clot of patrons waiting for tables and offered his name to the maitre d' who frowned at his request for a table for one. Nat let the excited, day's-end conversations drift into a humming murmur that washed over him like waves as he settled back into his revery.

He had been the margin between life and death for several people now: seventeen to be exact. Contrary to their portrayals in pulp novels, agents—even the contract ones who handle the government's dirty work at an arm's length—did not engage in wholesale slaughter. Neither did they relish the tasks.

Nat remembered every one of them, could replay

each one's killing on demand, recalling each minute detail down to the look of astonishment in their eyes as they died. Death was an astonishing visitor when it finally came, Nat knew; he had felt astonished when he looked at the bloody blade emerging from his belly. But, he supposed his anger had saved him.

Others had not been so lucky, at least not the ones he had astonished. He'd been too thorough for that.

"We have a table for you, *monsieur. Monsieur?*"

Nat smiled graciously as the maitre d' led him to a surprisingly good table beside the sidewalk. Nat thanked him and tipped him well. After ordering a bottle of Mâcon Lugny, some brie and a baguette, Nat settled down with his thoughts, watching the crowd as it flowed along the sidewalks like a stream of pebbles from some distant avalanche.

The wine arrived. Nat tasted it, then tipped the steward after finding it acceptable. Crisp, cold and dry, it slaked his throat, parched after his walk, and brought to his mind memories of seafood and garlic and—for some odd reason he could not place—artichokes.

Seventeen people, Nat thought. Seventeen human beings, so similar to those who swept by the window, or sipped wine at the table next to him. Sixteen men and a woman who would make interesting dinner companions, fascinating conversationalists and not altogether unpleasant business associates died by his hand because they were on the wrong side.

His ease at accepting their deaths—at his hand in killing them—never ceased to astonish him. How could he? he asked repeatedly. And he would always answer, Because. Not because *of,* just because.

The first one had been the hardest. Rinehart had read him well and used Colleen's death and his anger to manipulate him. Three weeks after she had been blown apart in that Manhattan brownstone, Nat found himself in Madison, Wisconsin, where he fired a silenced .25 caliber pistol into the skull of a man Rinehart

151

told him was responsible for setting up the bomb factory that had killed her.

In a rage, Nat had fired once, twice and until the nine-shot pistol's chambers were spent. Revenge rushed through him, a warm exhilaration that both lifted and terrorized him. His satisfaction at exacting a price— no matter how insignificant—for Colleen's death was overshadowed by a dread feeling that he had been admitted to places where human beings should not go. He felt like Dr. Faustus, terrified by his knowledge and power yet unable to extricate himself from their domination.

Traffic in the Place de l'Opéra thinned as twilight turned to night, like ink spreading through the water in a tumbler. Nat looked at his watch. It was 6:30 P.M., only two hours to go. He looked at his wine and figured he could not stretch it that long. Refilling his glass, Nat thought of the meeting in two hours, of the killing that was scheduled to take place across the street on opening night, of the woman he was to meet, and of how weary he had suddenly become of the whole game.

The scar above his kidney began to throb a basso profundo ache. Nat winced as he felt the pain shoot from his back, through his insides connect with the scar on his belly. The taut chain of agony scraped from one scar to the other, running a gauntlet of adhesions and poorly healed tissue like a rope of razor blades slashing and reaming.

Nat plunged his hand inside his blazer and grabbed the medication. He pulled the flat pillcase from his pocket and fumbled with its catch, and then stopped. The medication made him dizzy and distorted his depth perception. He'd need those. He was vulnerable now and would be for hours. No, he'd just have to ride the breakers of pain.

"Pardon, Monsieur," the waiter had returned to

152

Nat's table. "Are you ill? Do you need a doctor?" Nat looked at him questioningly. "You look pale."

"*Non, merci,*" Nat interrupted him and smiled. What sort of excuse could he give? He began to mumble something, embarrassed, about his wife.

The waiter nodded knowingly, and poured him some more wine. Nat nodded his thanks. The wine would do him good. He could control alcohol much better than the narcotics in his pain pills. Nat replaced the pillbox and tried to convince himself the pain was already subsiding.

A wife, Nat chuckled ironically. Who would have him, and who in the world could he ever get along with well enough to live with? He checked his watch again and then, slowly and deliberately, unfolded the copy of *Le Monde*.

Chapter Twelve

|||||||||||||||||||||||||||||||||||||||||||||||||||||||||||||||||||||||||||||||||||||

The evening sky had turned a fine inky color, unsullied as yet by the dust of the stars, and still blue enough to avoid reminding the sky gazer of the cold eternity that waited beyond.

Mustafa Salem el-Nouty strolled casually along the left promenade of the Champs Élysées, gazing into the display windows of shops, stopping to examine their products, casting occasional glances up at the sky and frequent ones behind him. But the after-work crowds had evaporated like wisps of human fog, leaving him an easy time at spotting any possible tails. Thus far, he'd seen nothing suspicious; that was good, for his mind needed purging. The afternoon's exhilaration at the opera house had distracted him from serious planning of his next moves. And Mustafa Salem el-Nouty knew that his survival had long depended on a passion for detail and order and discovering the significance of things other people failed to notice.

Reflecting on that now, he allowed himself the luxury of letting his mind freewheel briefly. Pausing before a display of Baltic Sea travel posters in the window of the Aeroflot office by the Rue Marignan, he recalled his first airplane flight—aboard an Aeroflot liner that took him to Moscow and led him to the life he now lived: Patrice Lammumba University, guerrilla training, Marxist political indoctrination (which he viewed as so much camel dung, but he could parrot it for his teachers with excellence), graduate work in assassination in Cuba and finally his ascendance as an assassin *par excellence* whose first allegiance was to Muammar Qaddafi. He killed for the KGB and the CIA as well as for any other organization that met his price and Qaddafi's approval.

Past the Renault showroom and Crédit Lyonnais bank, Mustafa crossed the street and gazed sadly at the shabby remnants of Iranair and the Maison de l'Iran. Madmen, he thought. This batch of Persians were slathering lunatics who had ruined their land for the sake of a set of dubious interpretations of the Koran. He was personally ashamed that people of the world, in their ignorance of the Islamic people, associated these pitiful creatures with his proud race. May Allah reward you appropriately, Mustafa muttered softly as he turned to resume his walk. And let Allah use me to bring you the reward. Mustafa smiled broadly now, and picked up his pace. He could see the madman's face in his sights already. His springy steps brought him quickly to the Avenue George V and then to the hotel of the same name. He greeted the doorman in faultless Parisian French, and stepped into the lobby. Immediately he knew something was amiss. Without breaking stride or betraying his alarm, Mustafa surveyed the lobby and its people and took the image with him as he approached the clerk at the front desk.

"Are there any messages for me?" Mustafa inquired politely. He was well known; there was no need to give his room number.

156

"Oui, Monsieur el-Nouty. One moment, please, and I will get them for you."

While he waited, el-Nouty leaned casually on his left elbow, scanning the room. Before the clerk returned, Mustafa had spotted the two men: one, standing beneath an oil hung on the far wall near the front entrance, pretended unconvincingly to read a copy of *Le Figaro*; the other, looking suspiciously like a bulldog, sat on a sofa at the far end of the lobby. Mustafa couldn't place them yet, but he knew he'd seen both before.

Were they KGB? Could they possibly know why Qaddafi had sent him to Paris? Or was it the GRU, having discovered the same thing? It had to be one or the other, Mustafa thought quickly, exerting his self-control not to panic.

The clerk returned with several slips of elegant memorandum stationery. Absentmindedly, Mustafa took the papers and tipped the man. Feigning interest in the messages, he stalled for time, trying to place the two men, weighing the possibility that the Russians might somehow have learned of his assignment. Suddenly he remembered where he had seen them before: they had accompanied his KGB control officer—albeit at a distance—when he assassinated the Saudi prince in Dubai, early in his career. Fools, Mustafa thought, to send people he could recognize. And then he grew angry; they were underestimating him. First it had been the people of the villages who treated him as if he were mentally retarded because he was a Bedawi. And then it had been the condescending British, exercising paternalism toward what they considered to be dumb animals. And then it had been the Russians, with their thinly disguised contempt for his dark skin and Arabian genes.

Damn them! *He* was Mustafa Salem el-Nouty and he could kill better and faster than any ten of those

157

hamhocked Slavic clods with the potato-bag suits and their pig manners and their—

He broke the thought and made his way toward the elevator, scanning the message slips as he did, trying to give the impression of a preoccupied man, someone unaware that he was being watched.

His ruse worked. As he waited idly for the elevator, both men abruptly rose to their feet and headed hastily toward him. No finesse, el-Nouty concluded, monitoring their progress in his peripheral vision.

Mustafa stood there waiting for the elevator to arrive, glancing from the messages in his hand to the elevator's floor indicator, pretending interest in both while he worked through the situation in his head. The two KGB agents were about ten yards to his right, walking together now and chatting in French like two businessmen engrossed in bottom lines and profit spreads.

They were too casual, he decided, to be an execution squad. There was none of the stone-faced tension that always accompanied the KGB's less talented agents—which these decidedly were. No, el-Nouty decided, they were an escort team. They would make sure he traveled straight to his room: someone was waiting for him, someone important. The two KGB agents were nearly beside him now.

Feigning surprise over a previously overlooked fact in one of his messages, Mustafa whirled on his heel and traversed the lobby, heading for the clerk. He smiled at the startled expressions on his two stalkers' faces, and the reflexes as they both reached inside their poorly cut suit coats for their guns. Imbeciles, if he were going to attack them, his speed would kill both before they could withdraw their guns from the holsters.

Mustafa leaned over the counter for a brief moment, spoke a few words to a very confused clerk, and then pushed away from the counter and strode through the front door.

Outside, springing along the Avenue George V, his long muscular legs carried him swiftly to the alleyway leading to the hotel's service entrance. Before the KGB agents gained the sidewalk, he disappeared into the alley, then slowed his pace to a fast walk. He didn't want to arouse the suspicion of the hotel's security personnel. A well-dressed guest entering the service entrance would strike them as odd, but not suspicious—perhaps an errant husband avoiding an angry wife bivouacked in the lobby. But one who ran as if pursued would be stopped, questioned.

Mustafa heard the dull thuds of the KGB operatives' feet on the sidewalk. There was but a single set. They must have split up to search both directions. Mustafa stopped beside a boarded-up doorway, and then stepped into the recess, flattening himself against the back. He felt like a piece of sculpture framed in a castle niche.

A potpourri of hotel smells wafted past him, borne on the cool night air. The chill of the day moderated the stink from overflowing refuse bins, and the result was not terribly unpleasant. Melded with the odors of decaying vegetables and fruit were the exhaust vapors from the kitchen, carrying a medley of sautee, broil, and bake fragrances that reminded him he hadn't eaten for more than eight hours.

Cautious footsteps gritting along the alley bricks chased away his hunger and grew louder until momentarily the KGB agent appeared before el-Nouty.

El-Nouty catapulted from the recessed doorway, slamming into the KGB agent's solid body, and rode him to the ground, left forearm across his Adam's apple. Mustafa cinched the chokehold and shoved his right forearm against the back of the man's head. The Russian gagged and gurgled for only a few seconds before he lost consciousness.

Tucking the body in the recessed doorway, el-Nouty positioned him like a drunk who had made it no farther. He would regain consciousness in five or ten minutes; that was enough time.

At the service entrance, the Libyan smiled an embarrassed grin at the security man, mumbled something about his wife, and walked quickly to the open door of the service elevator, where he punched the button for his floor.

The elevator smelled of stale room service coffee and dirty sheets, but Mustafa concentrated on his next steps.

There would be someone—perhaps more than one person—waiting for him in his room. He visualized the room's layout: a king-sized bed dominated, its headboard on the left wall near the door. The bathroom, too, was to the left, a closet to the right. Against the window wall stood a velvet-upholstered love seat, a cocktail table, and two armchairs.

He tried to remember the light switches. Could all the lights be extinguished with the controls by the door? Yes, he remembered, for the convenience of conscientious guests who would help the management save energy as they departed.

The service elevator grumbled to a halt on the sixth floor. Once the doors had opened, El-Nouty turned off the power to keep this elevator here in case he should need it again. He stopped to listen for people in the hallway. He heard no one. Bending to a crouch, he peered around the corner of the open door. The hallway was empty.

Straightening, el-Nouty made his way silently to the intersection with the corridor his room was on; there he once again peered around the corner in a crouch. This hall, too, was empty. If someone was waiting for him, he—or they—were counting too much on the other men to escort him. Careless, el-Nouty thought— unless they were not planning any rough stuff. Nonetheless, he did not relax his caution. Far safer to plan for the million-to-one happening.

Reaching inside his coat, Mustafa pulled from his wallet pocket a hand-tooled leather dart case. He rarely carried firearms, disdaining them as lacking finesse and sophistication.

From the case, he withdrew two darts—actually tiny hypodermics with minuscule capsules of compressed gas to discharge their contents. They were basically the same devices that the Bulgarian secret service had used on the tips of umbrellas in the late seventies during a widely publicized wave of assassinations of that country's dissidents.

Mustafa affixed tiny plastic fins—flights, they were called—to the darts—and replaced the case in his pocket. These darts would incapacitate within seconds, but would not kill a healthy adult: they were just a hand-thrown version of those tranquilizer guns the zoos used.

Arriving silently at the door of his room, Mustafa noted with satisfaction that the telltales he had left in the door had fallen to the floor. Someone *was* in there.

He willed his nerves to be calm, his reflexes to be quick. He tested the door. Still locked. With a startling fluid swiftness, Mustafa plunged his key into the lock, heaved his shoulder into the door, and shut off the lights as he dived into the room and kicked the door shut.

Two dark shapes were dimly outlined by the streetlighting that filtered through the curtains. As he dived for the secure space between the wall and the side of his bed, Mustafa hurled the darts at them. Curses of surprise from two distinctly different voices was music to him as he crouched beside the bed, listening.

The only sound was the soporific breathing of two drugged men. Still wary, Mustafa crept swiftly along the base of the wall around the corner to the bathroom. Once he gained its safety, he reached out and flipped on the room lights. Still there were no sounds.

Cautiously, Mustafa peered into the now brightly il-luminated room. He checked the closet and under the bed. The two unconscious men were alone. He bolted and chained the door to guard against the arrival of the two agents who had followed him, and then crossed the room to examine the two men more closley.

Effortlessly, he hoisted one corpulent body from its face-down position on the floor and deposited it on the bed. He recognized the man as the number-two KGB official at the embassy. As he approached the second man, he recognized the balding pate of the KGB sta-tion chief in Paris.

Stunned by this retinue of brass, Mustafa sank into the royal velvet armchair by the window and regarded his acquisitions. The station chief, Alexandr Popov, looked benign—like a provincial baker or carpenter.

Memories of Popov's rise from a functionary in the dank pits of Lubyanka Prison and the throats, literal and figurative, he had slit along the way sent chills of apprehension the length of el-Nouty's massive body. He glanced at the other drugged form, and recognized Dimitri Karsavin, an agent.

El-Nouty turned within himself and emotionlessly ticked off his options: he could leave now and run, he could wait until the men revived, question them and then run. He could kill them now or kill them after he'd talked to them.

His reverie and the silence of the hotel room was shattered by a heavy pounding on the door. It must be the other agents, arriving with their tails between their legs to report their failure to Popov.

The pounding resumed, frantic now. "Just a minute, gentlemen," el-Nouty said softly, as he leaned forward to smile at his impression in the mirror. He adjusted the Windsor knot of his tie to fit more perfectly against the v of the collar, and then started for the door. The pounding came in intermittent bursts, the silences filled

with sotto voce pleas for Popov and his assistant to respond, to open the door.

In a flash, el-Nouty reached into Karsavin's coat and
removed his pistol. Popov, he knew, never carried one,
but he checked anyway. Carrying the pistol in his left
hand, the Libyan returned to the door, slid back the
bolt, unfastened the deadbolt lock, and opened the
door.

"Good evening, gentlemen," el-Nouty said, watching
their faces transform from masks of shock to horror
and confusion. "We've been waiting for you."

Nat read and reread the message from Rinehart with
growing amazement. The words, the message just
didn't ring true.

It had been in two parts. The first telex, which was
encoded, had come from the embassy in Paris. The
other had been received in London and flown over in
the diplomatic pouch. It contained the code to decipher
the Paris message. Both had arrived in tamper-proof
containers so only Nat could put together Rinehart's
message.

But the message, once deciphered, made no sense: it
ordered him to use Niki to pick up a packet from a
Russian agent and pass it along to the CIA.

Nat sipped the last glass from his second bottle of
wine and checked his watch. He still had more than an
hour before meeting Niki and Tania. Nat stared
through the reflections of the restaurant mirror, gazing
beyond them even as his mind tried to see through the
confusion in Rinehart's message. What did the man
really mean? There had to be an ulterior meaning. Nat
was sure a hidden purpose lurked beneath the actual
words.

True, it was not unusual to use a neutral courier to
serve as a buffer between two agents, to conceal the
true sources of the information—or its true destination.

That made sense. But what didn't was the use of

Niki Valente—an amateur who was well known and, more important, under KGB surveillance. Valente, vital to the mission in Paris, should not be needlessly endangered. He was also a hot-headed egotist who might just refuse to do it, depending on his mood.

Nat swirled the remainder of his wine and held it up to the light and peered through the glass, tilting and examining it like a connoisseur scrutinizing it for clarity and body. It was as difficult as mastering the intricacies of wine, this business of *knowing* but failing to articulate to himself what was known. It would come. He knew it. It always did, but he worried that, like the incident in Amsterdam, it might fail to come to him in time.

Nat settled his tab and walked into the night.

The view from their suite at the Intercontinental was lovely. Tania loved its historic atmosphere, the elegant lobby and high ceilings. The Champs Élysées stretched to one side and then the Seine just a short distance across the Jardin des Tuileries.

The additional corps members had been flown in from Leningrad to join those who had arrived from the United States. In addition dozens of the company's own stage crews and musicians had also been imported, all because Comrade Pugachev would be the honored guest on opening night. Many of the extra dancers, musicians, and technicians would be Pugachev's GRU security people who would not take the chance of entrusting their glorious leader to the rival KGB.

Although none of it ever saw print, nearly every Russian knew that Pugachev and the chief of the KGB were mortal enemies locked in a clandestine war for the double post of premier and president of the Communist party.

Tania wondered how many other people in the entire world knew what she knew: that Pugachev wouldn't make it.

Behind her, Niki talked on the telephone to a breathless corps member whom he hadn't seen since leaving Leningrad. Though infrequent snatches of the conversation pierced her thoughts, she continued to stare out the window at the lights of Paris. Niki's escapades no longer bothered her.

That was why she knew that Pugachev wouldn't make it. She and Niki had to succeed; she would not return to that other, subservient life.

The other members of the Kirov had sensed the change in her, and in Niki's attitude toward her. Like him, they now treated her with respect. No, she could not give that up. Never again would she submit to such degradation.

Since the meeting with Nat, Tania had struggled with her decision. The idea of killing repelled her, and the notion of assisting the United States to kill the future leader of her country aroused such massive waves of guilt and anxiety that she had remained in bed, nauseous, faint, and dizzy for nearly three days. She'd dreamed nightmares of her father accusing her, cursing and screaming and waving that hideous hunting knife, accusing her of being a whore for the enemy: the worst sort of human being who would betray her country to get fucked by the CIA gigolo. The same dream always appeared, she had grown up, but she found herself in her father's apartment and he looked as he did when she was six or seven years old. Nat Worthington was there also. The room was cold, with the cold of Russian nights, and the cold of fear and desolation. The apartment smelled of stale cigarette smoke that hung in layers. Neither she nor Nat smoked, so she knew it must be because her father had recently departed. She sat at the end of a massive antique sofa upholstered in gold brocade. The sofa seemed to glow in the gray, gritting drabness of the rest of the dimly lit room, il-

165

luminated only by the flat cold grayness of light that had battled thick clouds to shine its fatigued rays through a smudged window glass.

Nat Worthington—Nathaniel Everett Lowell Worthington IV, she remembered—sat at the other end of the couch and looked at her with a strange light in his eyes, a light that seemed to overpower the room and the fear that her father would soon return. She was cold where she sat, the room seemed to suck the warmth from her body and she shivered. But Nat radiated warmth. She wanted to go to him, wrap her arms around him. The look in his eyes was . . . love? She wasn't sure what it was but she could not turn away. He smiled and without opening his mouth or moving his lips, spoke to her and invited her to sit next to him, to share his warmth. And she did.

Shivering violently, she slid across the shiny brocade to the shelter of his arms. He hugged her and she felt the chill of her body and of her mind melt.

Tania tilted her head to kiss him, and as she did her father raged into the room, brandishing the hunting knife, it's blade wet with blood. His hands were stained with red and like magic he materialized beside Nat and slit Nat's throat, smiling demonically at Tania as she screamed the silent throttled cries of nightmares, watching blood stream from the dreadfully obscene grin in Nat's throat.

Tania shook her head to clear the images from her mind, to return to a hotel room in Paris.

She worried for Nat. The lobby and every entrance crawled with KGB and GRU. She wondered how he would make his way to their rendezvous.

But he would; he was that sort of man, she reflected with admiration. And she—and here was a new thought for her—she would also. After all, hadn't she accepted her role as an assasin?

It hadn't been easy. She had wrestled with her own sense of decency, propriety, and partiotism. But it

166

came down, finally, to a concept so startlingly simple she was amazed it had not come sooner: what have they done for me? In the many hours of reflection since her meeting with Nat, she had come up with no good answer to that question that might prevent her from seeing this killing and defection to the end.

And something Nat had said to her fortified her resolve. "This is war," Nat had told her. "There is no 'fair' in war, there is just reality."

She smiled, gazing out the window at the Eiffel Tower, remembering the stern set of his jaw three days ago as he passed her the message setting up their meeting tonight.

No, Tania, there is no "fair" in war she told herself. There is just the reality that must be survived. And she thought how similar Nat's words were to the way she had lived—survived—her life. She had always done things because they were all that could be done. No, there had been no fairness. Her anger boiled, because she had *expected* fairness; and because she had expected it, she acted as if it would somehow come to her. Never in her life did she realize that fairness was something you *took*.

Nat had his war—a war between superpowers, between capitalism and communism. And now she had her war. Tania stood again, and looked out the window at the people scurrying by on the street below. Her war lacked the global importance of the one Nat had drawn her into. Hers was a civil war, a revolt. A one-person insurrection. But war sanctioned all things, for only winners may arbitrate fair from unfair, right from wrong. To the victors go not only the spoils, but also moral authority.

Niki Valente lounged on the bed, propped against the tasteful headboard. He was talking on the telephone to Natalia Alexandropova, nineteen years old.

He hadn't slept with her since the night before the company left for their tour nearly a month ago.

As the ballerina chattered unceasingly, Niki unconsciously mumbled during the pauses, but concentrated instead on Tania as she pensively gazed from their hotel window.

She was a stranger to him now and she terrorized him with that strangeness. He could not understand the change and why she wanted so badly to defect.

He understood his reasons clearly enough: *he*, Nikolai Valente, was an artist, and nothing in the world mattered more to him than his dancing. For that he would kill. It was wicked and it was mad, but Russia reveled in its history of betrayal and intrigue. From Rasputin to Stalin, killing has always been an acceptable means to Russian ends.

Yes, he understood his motivations, his artistic need. But Tania? Why was she doing this? Niki wrinkled his brow as he concentrated on her image, stark stillness framed by the window and the lights outside. The thought dawned on Niki that she gazed inside herself.

Where had this woman come from? Could two weeks so transfigure a person that even those she was closest to no longer recognized her? He had heard stories in every situation from wartime to religious conversion in which people had changed like this under stress. But Tania?

After finally concluding the call, Niki sat up on the bed and looked at her. She was as immobile as a statue, and a wave of pity swept through him. He felt sorry for what would happen to her when she arrived in the West with no money, (no talent, no job, and—he surmised—no prospects for any of them.) For a moment, he felt like comforting her, holding her in his arms. But the urge evaporated as quickly as it had arrived. Things would not be all right for her. Misery would find her. But he'd say nothing. Dancing was all—his dancing—and he would allow nothing to stand

168

in the way, not Tania, not Pugachev, nothing. The world needed his art and it must not be denied.

Although he'd first felt guilty about killing Pugachev, the guilt passed rapidly as he remembered how his patron had climbed to power over the bodies of people who had fought beside him for years.

"Remember, dear Niki," Pugachev had preached to him several years before, following the rumors of a particularly bloody purge in the Red Army, "that life lasts as long as your enemies want it to, unless you ease them to retirement first." Pugachev loved to preach to this young ballet star, and had revealed secrets to Niki that he spilled to no other. Niki had no illusions: he knew Pugachev told him these things because the general did not consider him a potential threat. That violated the general's own first axiom.

"Everyone is a threat," Pugachev had intoned drunkenly one night as they sat over a bottle of vodka at his Leningrad apartment. "Everyone is a threat, and you've got to deal with them before they deal with you.

"There are no true friends in this life," he'd continued. "No true friends. For if they would conspire against you, then they are no friends at all. Friends are a threat, and you must never let one stand in your way, never hesitate to . . . eliminate their threat . . ."

The words came back to Niki now, more than five years later, as he lay on the bed pondering the past two weeks and the changes they had wrought, and looking with anticipation at the next two days, and the joy the future would bring.

Niki had managed to conquer his feelings of guilt by quoting the general himself. Was it his fault that the general failed to follow his own philosophy?

The fear still remained, but he knew he'd do it, could do it, would do it. After all, the plan was remarkable in its simplicity, and there was no way the Soviets could pin it on him. Besides, there was destiny.

Destiny must be fulfilled, and the world was preordained to enjoy his art. Destiny, he thought as he closed his eyes, is my sword; then he dozed off, smiling, satisfied that he could coin such literary passages. Destiny.

Chapter Thirteen

|||||||||||||||||||||||||||||||||||||||||||||||||||||||||||||||||||||||||||||||||||||||

The unseasonably cool Paris night vibrated with expectancy. Nat walked with a spring in his step, down the Boulevard de la Madeleine toward the huge Greek temple architecture of the church of St. Mary Magdalen. Stars shone brilliantly in the clear night sky, its haze swept away by whatever weather had brought the chill.

Nat's heart beat lightly, as if it, too, had to tread softly. Every step brought him closer to the action, closer to the danger. And closer to Tania.

He was afraid. Afraid she would get hurt, and afraid of his own feelings. He was also still concerned over that incongruous message from Rinehart. To clear his head, Nat deeply inhaled the chilly night air. He must concentrate on the next hour. He checked his watch, satisfied, assured his pacing was correct: he'd arrive at the lobby of the Intercontinental exactly fifteen minutes before the KGB's security men there changed shifts. The timing would be perfect. Sentries, he knew, were always less observant at the end of their shifts. Physical and mental fatigue, boredom and the daydreams they inevitably spawned, wove a fabric nearly as good as a blindfold.

At twenty minutes before eight, he tipped the bellman at the Hôtel Crillon and took the briefcase and beige overcoat stored there into the men's room. In the toilet stall, Nat withdrew a mirror and propped it against the toilet paper holder. Next came a gray wig which he adjusted over his own hair, followed by a pair of heavy black-framed eyeglasses with nonprescription lenses.

People failed to realize how tiny changes in appearance rendered even their close friends unrecognizable. Large changes were just insurance.

The doorman at the Hôtel Crillon took little notice of the distinguished elderly man who stepped gingerly through the doorway. He was surprised, though, by the strength of the man's grip as he helped him into the waiting cab.

The doorman at the Intercontinental was even less observant, perceiving only the presence of a respectable tip. Once inside the hotel's lobby, the shuffling old man in the beige topcoat, bent with the weight of many years, gathered hardly a glance from hotel guests as he stepped into the elevator and disappeared.

Nat rapped the door sharply four times. Behind the door he heard a frantic whispered conference, and soon after, a woman's voice, diffused through the door.

"Goethe?" the voice inquired.

"In the beginning was the deed," Nat replied, as prearranged.

"And in the end?"

"Nothing."

The door opened and Tania stood there, her blond hair cascading down her shoulders. As Nat stepped forward, her expression of eager anticipation turned suddenly to fear: she beheld not Nat Worthington, but a wizened old man.

172

"Oh!" she exclaimed, her hand rushing to cover her mouth. "You . . . ! I—"

"It's all right," Nat said reassuringly, wiping away a bit of the makeup. "It's just a little disguise to make the KGB work a little harder."

Tania's anxiety gave way to a smile and she stood there, gazing at him. The moment lingered.

"Uh . . . may I come in?" he asked in Russian.

"Certainly," she replied, also speaking in Russian. An embarrassed smile lit up her face; her eyes continued to meet his. "Come in out of the cold."

Tania bolted the door while Nat stepped into the foyer. As per his instructions, the room was part of an adjoining suite, and the drapes were drawn.

"We can speak English for things you don't wish Niki to understand," Tania said quickly in English as Nat doffed his wig and removed the rest of his makeup. "He speaks very, very little, certainly not enough to converse."

Once again their eyes met, and Tania flushed.

Nat felt off-balance. His grown-up logic endeavored to set his limits straight, but the infatuation had intoxicated him.

Turning to make his way into the main portion of the room, Nat saw the woman's husband for the first time. On the bed, Nikolai Valente lounged amid a disheveled mass of bedspread and coverlet.

The two men weighed each other.

"Niki," Tania stood by Nat and spoke in Russian. "This is Mr. Worthington."

"Nat," Nat said to him, smiling. "Please call me Nat." He avoided looking at Tania, but he could feel the intensity of her presence near him.

"It's good of you to come, Mr. Worthington—Nat," Niki responded politely, and then was silent.

Finally, Tania spoke.

"Won't you have a seat, Nat, I've bought some

vodka—some good vodka—and I thought we could drink a toast to our common purpose."

"Yes," Nat replied, grateful the quiet had been dispelled. "That would be very nice; thank you."

Niki continued to stare silently. Nat felt a silence of calm disquiet like a hot dusty Missouri afternoon when approaching thunderstorms hide beneath the horizon, felt but not seen in the blinding sun-washed sky.

An armchair stood by the door connecting the room to the adjoining one. Nat settled into it, reassured by the nearness of the additional exit.

Niki watched Nat settle into the chair, and suddenly a wave of jealousy obliterated all the other feelings he had experienced in the first moments of Nat's arrival.

The ties between this American and his wife stretched invisibly between them: the way Nat looked at Tania as she walked away to the bathroom to retrieve the vodka and glasses that had been soaking in ice for more than an hour now—and the urgency Tania had displayed earlier that day to locate the best vodka. He hadn't thought of it then, but now he could see the extraordinary care she had devoted to that simple task.

And the silence at the door when Nat arrived. Niki shifted uneasily on the bed as he remembered how that silence had lasted, followed by an exchange in English. Now he regretted not learning more than a few words of slang—the English language seemed a private secret shared between them, its every phrase a conspiracy against him.

He'd seen that glow from Tania's green irises only twice—when she had performed in the ballet competition, and the first time they made love.

Niki burned with shame—what had they done? How many times had they seen each other? Had Tania lied to him about the meetings in New York? The vision made him queasy, and he eagerly accepted the vodka Tania proffered. Niki sat up and perched on the foot of

174

the bed, as Tania pulled up a chair and sat between the two men.

Niki watched her carefully. Did she put the chair closer to Nat than to him? No, it is closer to me, Niki realized, and decided she had deliberately done that to deceive him, which proved she was having an affair. Which way was she leaning—toward Nat? toward him? Niki slugged the vodka back with a manic determination.

"Tania has already explained to you what the procedure will be. Am I correct?" Nat sipped at his drink and waited for a reaction.

Niki shook his head, startled. He had not been paying attention to the conversation. "Sorry? I'm not sure I caught all of that. I'm afraid I was concentrating on . . . this extraordinary vodka. You certainly did well to find it, my dear. In fact, if you'd pour me another glass, I'd like to propose a toast."

Tania refilled their glasses.

"To a . . . successful conclusion," Niki began. "To the promise of America; to Mr. Worthington—Nat—and his employers, and to . . . to destiny." Simultaneously, they tossed back the tumblers of vodka.

"I hope you will excuse my poor manners," Nat began, "but I believe we ought to dispense with further toasts until we conclude things here. I have a lot to tell you, much to explain, and I'd like to do it with as clear a head as possible." Nat raised his eyebrows questioningly. Tania nodded her assent quickly, and Niki followed in a moment.

"Good," Nat began. "Though I've briefed Tania on the details, and I understand she had relayed the . . . pertinent . . . details to you, I'd like to go over them again just so there can be no misunderstanding." Nat took another sip of the glass Tania had refilled and continued, directing his remarks more toward Niki than Tania—he didn't want to brave those eyes right now.

175

"The reception for General Pugachev will begin at 7 P.M. in the foyer of the opera house. As always, the security will be as tight as any in the world. Pugachev's GRU will search every guest of the reception save those for whom such measures would be a diplomatic insult—the French prime minister, for example.

"A ridiculous situation," Niki said scornfully, "absolutely adolescent. Just because Pugachev wants to feel like he's on stage."

"Niki, I've never heard you talk about Pugachev in such a way before," Tania said. "Such disrespect."

"Things are . . . different now," he said looking at them each in turn. Yes, they all knew the situation had changed. It was time to put some emotional distance between Niki and Pugachev.

"Regardless," Nat picked up the thread of the briefing and continued. "You're not going to be searched, if for no other reason than the common knowledge that Pugachev has treated you as a son. And, even if you were searched, it's unlikely anyone would find these—" Nat reached over the arm of the chair and retrieved his briefcase. From it he withdrew two small packets whose decoration identified them as a Russian-made imitation of Alka-Seltzer in little foil packages. Nat held one for Niki to see, and tore it open. A half dozen gray-purple spheres the size of small green peas rolled into the palm of Nat's hand.

"Here." He offered a couple of the peas to Niki. "Go ahead," Nat urged, when Niki didn't move. "They're perfectly safe—right now."

"They're known as binary agents," Nat said. "Look—" he whipped a diagram from his briefcase and showed it to them both. "Each capsule is actually two hemispheres separated by a partition." On closer inspection, the peas could be seen to have a fine joint resembling the equator on a tiny plastic globe. Nat passed one to Tania, who squinted as she examined the surface.

176

"As long as the chemicals in each half remain separate," Nat continued, "they are relatively harmless. But once they combine, they form a deadly nerve gas that can be absorbed through the skin. The chemicals here are essentially the same as the Soviets use in their chemical warfare devices."

Niki looked at Nat quizzically.

"Yes, it's a Russian device," Nat said, reading Niki's thoughts. "We obtained these from an agent in place in the KGB. It gives us deniability—the KGB would love to use it on Pugachev themselves, which is why his GRU guards him so tightly. The retribution the Red Army would exact if they learned their leader had been slain by the KGB would make Stalin's bloodshed seem humanitarian by comparison."

"But this could—" Niki protested.

"Do the same thing? Yes, I suppose it could. But by that time, you'll be an American, and I'll be long gone. None of us will be suspected."

"But I . . ." Niki started and looked over at Tania, ". . . we will be suspected because we defected. . . ."

"No, you just took advantage of the confusion that reigned after Pugachev's death."

"Yes . . ." Niki's voice trailed off as he visualized the scenario. "Yes . . . I see your point."

"At any rate," Nat went on, relieved to see Niki following him so loyally. He'd lost the ballet dancer for a while, but now Niki seemed attentive and willing. "To activate these little devices, you take this—" Nat withdrew from the briefcase a stubby red cylinder the size of a chapstick, with a needle protruding from one axis "—and insert the needle here." Both Tania and Niki stiffened with apprehension as Nat pointed to a bright red dot on the pea's equator.

"You stick the needle in on the red dot and this little device," he indicated the cylinder, "will inject a drop of chemical that will begin eating away at the wall between the two halves. Two hours later, the chemicals will combine, the resulting chemical reaction will heat up the contents and cause a pressure buildup, and the capsule will explode with a tiny pop—sending a miniature cloud of nerve gas on its way to Comrade Pugachev.

"All you need to do is place two or three of these in a pocket or something close to him," Nat concluded. "The gas will do the rest. Less than half a drop on his skin will kill him instantly."

"And others around him?" Niki questioned. He was looking pale.

"Not that likely," Nat responded coolly, closing his briefcase and leaning back in the chair. "The gas is potent, but it would be diluted by the air. To be affected, a person would have to embrace his eminence, or be very, very close to him."

"I see," Niki said thoughtfully, as he handed the peas back to Nat. "And just how am I supposed to . . . to position these little peas on Comrade Pugachev?"

"It's really quite simple." Nat wiped his brow, pleased that he, Nat Worthington, had the answers. His role, not Niki's, demanded that solutions be found.

"To answer your question," Nat continued, "once you clear the GRU's security and enter the reception crowd, take the devices you've primed and slip them into Pugachev's coat pocket or any other place they will stay. You can do this when he greets you formally, with the hugging and all. With any luck, there'll be a crowd around and no one will spot you."

"With luck?" Niki asked nervously.

Nat smiled reassuringly. "Of course, we're going to help luck out a bit. You'll go late, try to time it for about the midway point of the reception, when the most people will be milling about. There's protection in a crowd, more people for the GRU to watch, fewer

178

moments to spend on watching you, after all, you are one of his most trusted associates."

While Nat continued his briefing, confusion and apprehension was building in the mind of KGB lieutenant Nikita Galaviz. Galaviz had followed Tania Valente for a day now, since he had been tipped off by a well-paid clerk at the front desk that the ballerina—former ballerina—had paid for a room on this floor.

Was the great cocksman's wife sneaking off behind his back and balling another member of the Kirov—or was there more to it than that? Regardless of why she had taken the room, it clearly violated the company's rules. That little piece of information would be a useful addition to her dossier; as the informant, his status would rise. On the other hand, perhaps if he kept it to himself, she might be induced to . . . He let the eye of his imagination roam over the image of her naked body.

No, that was impossible. The fantasy faded in the face of what he knew to be his patriotic duty. As he looked through the peephole set in his room door across the hall from Tania's room, fat frown wrinkles grew between his eyebrows. His first surprise materialized when Tania took Niki into the room with her. That was hardly a tryst—after all, they had their own room. Until then he had failed to notify anyone else about his observation—he wanted to take credit for this one himself, and he wanted to prevent his superior office from taking all the credit.

But Galaviz buried his thoughts of personal glory beneath the visions of how he would suffer at his superiors' hands if this turned out more important than a juicy tidbit for the Valente file. Reluctantly, an hour before, he'd put in a call to his superior, Captain Alexi Rostov, to inform him of developing events. He hoped his superior officer wouldn't seize all the credit for himself for turning up this information.

But Rostov had failed to get back to him, and Galaviz was growing anxious. No one had called with instructions.

He couldn't have known that Rostov had passed the message along to *his* superior, Sergei Markov, the commander of security for the Kirov performances in Paris, who had left standing orders that he wanted notification if the Valentes made any suspicious movements. Markov left this standing order because *his* superior in Moscow left standing orders with him that he'd spend the rest of his days fighting frostbite at a frozen gulag if any harm came to the two dancers. He didn't know why. But it didn't matter—orders were orders, especially when they came from Valery Kokh, head of the KGB, member of the politburo, and—said the smart money—the next premier of the Soviet Union.

But for Galaviz, whose status hovered a rung above rock-bottom in this mission, the passing of the buck all the way back to the Kremlin passed him by, leaving him with a fearsome anxiety attack, the conviction he had been abandoned, and a screaming full bladder he dare not relieve lest the Valentes decide to leave. He had no idea that Nat had entered the room while he telephoned Rostov.

Galaviz had never excelled with the KGB. It annoyed him when people classified him with the *stukachi*—the common stool pigeons, and whispered behind his back—but in tones they knew he'd hear—that the only reason he wasn't pulling security duty at a shoe factory in the provinces was an uncle who worked as an interpreter for the politburo.

As he stood on his toes peering through the peephole—for he was only five foot four and the glass was above his eye level—his mind replayed these insults until his anger blanketed both his fear of Rostov and the ache from his bladder. Damn them all! He wanted to do something to show them he had earned

180

his job, and deep down he wanted to do something to prove it to himself.

But what? Break into the room? What if they weren't doing anything? He reminded himself that the very act of hiring a room was against the Kirov rules. And where had she gotten the money? *That* could prove more substantial than the other relatively minor rule infraction. Visions of the door yielding to a powerful lunge of his shoulder brought a smile to his face.

Obstinately, Nikita Galaviz scanned the corridor, fortifying his scheme with visions of the respect he'd reap from capturing what he now believed was a black-market currency plot. What else could it be? Tania must be planning to meet people there, the people who'd supplied her with the money.

Oh! He could see their faces, when he, Nikita Galaviz, presented them with the guilty parties, tracked the ring down, and nailed its American co-conspirators. He visualized Sergei Markov's expression when he, Nikita Galaviz, jammed his finger in the KGB bigshot's face and berated him for allowing security to grow so lax that currency smugglers could operate at a whim.

He had to do it.

But there was the matter of his bladder. If he opened his door, and left the bathroom door open, he'd hear their door if it should open. Yes, he concluded, that would be the professional thing to do. He broke into a broad grin. In just a moment, he thought, reaching inside his coat to make sure his sidearm rested lethal and secure in his armpit, in just a moment he would rap on the door, demand entrance, and then confront them with the incontrovertible evidence of their guilt. They would be forced to expose their American counterparts—probably CIA—and then those people who'd made fun of him all these years would know humility. In just a moment, he repeated mentally, summoning the courage to open his door.

When the irises of Niki's eyes lost their fury, Nat decided it was time to confront Niki with the second task, the change of plans presented in Rinehart's letter. Nat couldn't decide whether he was reluctant to present the idea to Niki because he feared a firestorm of temperament, or because of his hunch that something was very wrong with the order. Fighting his own emotional inertia, he leaned toward Niki.

"Niki," Nat began, "There is one more very minor task which you must perform." At this Niki sat up straighter. Tania cast Nat a quizzical glance. Her eyes told him she didn't appreciate the surprise; that she'd expected to know all of it, and thought she had.

"I've received a message only this afternoon," Nat said more for Tania's benefit than any other, "from my government. They want you to meet with a man tomorrow, obtain a packet, and deliver it to another." Despite the alcohol, Nat watched the color of Niki's eyes grow bright and full with anger.

"A messenger! You want me to be a messenger?" Niki leaped off the bed and stalked up and back in the confined room with the frenzied pace of a wildcat trapped in a zoo.

"I am a dancer!" Niki screamed. "A dancer—an artist—and you want to use me as an errand boy? Is this a game?

"Well, if that is your idea," Niki continued without pause, "then I will be no party to this all. I will *not* be so abused, I will not be insulted, and embarrassed and humiliated." He was standing in the middle of the room now, shouting until the arteries on each side of his neck stood erect, framing the scarlet flush of his anger. "I will not! Do you understand?" He stood there, glaring at both of them, his heavy breathing the only sound.

Nat regarded Niki steadily. "No, Nikolai Valente, that is not my intention at all," he said. "While it's true that this request is a bit unusual, it is of the highest importance, of the greatest value, and my superiors have determined that only you and your special talents can accomplish the job."

Niki's face grew calmer; the flattery was working. Yet the dancer still appeared suspicious. Christ! Nat thought. What more can I say? What can I do to bring him around?

I'm too old for this nonsense, Sergei Markov muttered as he trod the service stairs upward. Ought to leave this for younger agents. But Kokh wouldn't understand. If younger men could do it, Kokh would say, then Markov should be replaced with a younger man. No, Markov resolved, he would check it out himself.

He reached the third floor landing and stopped to catch his breath before continuing. What could the Valentes be up to? he asked himself as his breath grew calmer. And how had that incompetent fool Galaviz lucked onto whatever it was? If it weren't for his uncle, Markov reflected ruefully. . . . He checked the floor number of the landing and then continued upward.

"Everything is in place for tomorrow?" asked Valery Kokh. It was more a command than a question.

"Of course," confirmed the aging voice at the other end of the scrambled, ultrasecure connection, a continent away. "He's our very best. I've never known him to fail. If any agent can do it, he can."

Kokh gazed, frowning, out the window at Dzerzhinsky Square. "I still fear for the operation. And this new complication," the KGB head added, turning his powerfully built body back to his desk, "makes it even more imperative that it proceed like clockwork. So much is riding on it . . . so very much. There are too many parts . . . too much to go wrong."

"Yes, my old friend, there are many things that could go wrong. But chance and uncertaintly accompany us constantly, and a frontal assault is not always the best way. I agree the strategy is complicated, the tactics risky, but we must not lose our nerve now."

"Yes. Of course," agreed Kokh as he stared vacantly at his desk, an antique relic preserved from the days of the czars. "Your agent knows nothing of the contents of the packet?"

"I assure you," the old man replied. "Nothing. He believes it contains faked defense documents to mislead you—us. And yours?"

"We are using a highly trusted contract agent selected by Popov."

"Why isn't Popov handling this himself?"

"He wants no chances taken that even one of his own agents would connect him to this . . . yet. You know that fear is ever present."

"Certainly," the old man said, "I've been here so long, I forget."

"That could be dangerous," Kokh admonished him. They both knew that creative paranoia was his policy—even the head of an agency could not be certain that his subordinates wouldn't spy on him and report to a higher authority. The other man kept silent, trying to recall any suspicious incidents to indicate that he might himself be under surveillance. He quickly dismissed the thought; his position was unassailable, the practice unthinkable.

"Fine," he commented after a moment. "We have the drop and we have the sanction in motion."

"Yes," said the KGB chief, "Everything is in motion. We can do no more now. Like generals, we must rest in the faith that our plans are sound and our soldiers competent in the field. So until tomorrow. . . ."

"Until tomorrow."

The scrambled connection linking the two men on opposite sides of the globe faded into the ether.

Sergei Markov wheezed as he leaned against the

stairwell wall. He tried desperately to catch his breath so he could move silently in the corridor. He mopped his forehead and cheeks with his handkerchief, blotted his neck with it, and then began the process anew as beads of sweat popped out again on his brow.

He thought of Galaviz, and the image of the short runt—stunted intellectually as well as physically— helped to clear his head. Galaviz had been a pain in the ass of every KGB case supervisor for years now, and today was no exception. Markov pushed himself away from the wall and lumbered into the hotêl hallway; he'd better reach Galaviz before he fouled up something else.

As Markov padded along the carpeted corridor scanning room numbers, his mind replayed images of the past seven years—seven years of playing nursemaid to Galaviz and his erratic and incompetent ways.

Crazy little bastard. Insecure, insane little bastard who tries so hard to be something he's not.

Markov walked on and soon spied a partially opened door on his right: Galaviz's room. Markov reached inside his coat and felt for the strap of his pistol, and unsnapped the catch. As he approached the door, he heard muffled shouting from the room across the hall; the voice could have been Nikolai Valente's. Softly, Markov pushed open the door of Galaviz's room and looked inside. There was no sign of Galaviz. Markov entered the room, and looked around. Seeing no one, he stuck his head into the darkened bathroom.

The blow didn't hurt. For years later, Markov would remark that he had felt nothing. Instead a galaxy of pinpoint colored stars suddenly filled up the darkness of the bathroom, and swept him into a deeper darkness beyond. Galaviz was a remarkably strong man for his size.

If he hadn't just voided his bladder, Galaviz would have wet his pants when he turned on the light and discovered Sergei Markov slumped on the tile floor, a

185

plum-colored bruise on the back of the man's skull. Mesmerized with horror, Galaviz stared at the swelling, which looked just like half of one of those juicy red plums you could buy on the black market in the summertime.

Panic-stricken, Galaviz tried to devise a way to handle this unbelievable situation. He thought of making up a story about intruders attacking them both. Perhaps, he could even bang himself up a bit for the sake of realism.

No, he decided, that wouldn't work. His only hope for redeeming himself lay in his original plan. He must capture the black-market currency smugglers and build his case against the Valentes. Yes, it was not only the most honorable way, it was the only way. Galaviz leaned over and grabbed Markov under the armpits, dragged him out of the bathroom, and arranged his unconscious body on the bed. He then checked to make sure the KGB official's breath coursed in and out regularly, withdrew his sidearm, and walked toward the door.

Mustafa chuckled to himself as he thought of Popov and then abruptly sucked in wind through his teeth as Sarah bit him playfully. He arched his back, forcing his swollen penis deep into her throat. Why the vision came to him now he didn't know, but it pleased him: Popov had been furious when he'd awakened and saw his two thugs trussed like sheep headed for slaughter. Once Mustafa had explained what had happened, the KGB official had transfered his anger to the two tails who had botched their assignments so badly. Finally the Russian had reluctantly congratulated el-Nouty on his professionalism.

Mustafa now recalled his relief at Popov's reaction. Things could as easily have gone the other way, and he'd now be fleeing—four dead bodies in his room and the KGB on his trail.

Instead—he arched his back as Sarah ran one fingernail lightly around his anus—instead, he enjoyed Sarah's erotic ministrations and looked forward to the next day, to the simple, quick, and profitable KGB contract. Retrieve a packet for the KGB.

Thoughts of Popov and his contract evaporated as Sarah straddled his thighs. He unleashed a low groan of pleasure, opened his eyes, and lifted his head to kiss her. They undulated up and down, rider and steed galloping to the slow motion rhythm of his hips' powerful thrusts. She smiled down at Mustafa and gracefully began to shake her full breasts. Blissfully, he gazed at her. She played his passions with a skill born of practice and the finesse of knowing his body and mind. It was difficult to believe, Mustafa thought, this woman was but a girl of fifteen years.

Sergei Markov dealt with his own disbelief: he had allowed Galaviz to get the best of him! The KGB officer opened his eyes. He nearly vomited as the walls of the room spun crazily. He rolled over and held onto the whirling bed with his arms as he threw first one leg and then the other over the side. And then, kneeling on the floor like a toddler at bedtime prayer, he closed his eyes to summon the resolve to stand.

He passed his hand inside his coat to check for his sidearm. It was gone! The shock bolstered his strength, and he pushed himself up shakily from the floor and opened his eyes carefully.

Unsteadily, Markov stood fully erect and lurched toward the room's door. He progressed two drunken steps and then stumbled to his knees over some object on the floor. On hands and knees, he fumbled for the object. It was his gun. He looked up and saw Galaviz at the door of the Valentes' room, his pistol in his hand hanging by his thigh, the clumsy standard issue silencer drooping off the muzzle like a bratwurst. It looked just

187

like the wurst they got in that smoky, hot little beer hall in Berlin before the partition. What was . . .

Galaviz turned, and now he was facing Markov, who fumbled with his super-quiet machine pistol, another product of the famous American inventor of death, Werbell. Protect the Valentes, he thought. Don't let Galaviz get to them.

Goddamn! Galaviz thought as he prepared to knock on the Valentes' door. He heard a clatter from the room behind him; Markov was crawling around on his hands and knees. His machine pistol had fallen out of its holster when Galaviz dragged him from the bathroom. Damn! Why hadn't he thought to take the pistol with him?

Markov struggled to his feet and deactivated the safety silently. He raised the pistol, but, through the mists and movement of his vertigo, could not train its muzzle on Galaviz.

Galaviz stared wide-eyed as Markov tried to take aim. He knew he must act, quickly, now!

Galaviz watched his arm, almost of its own will, bring his pistol to bear on Markov as the older man propped himself against the wall in the hotel room. He watched as Markov tried to steady his shooting arm against the wall. He sighted along the barrel of his gun, trying to decide whether to take Markov with a head shot or a torso shot. He decided on the later: he had a better chance of hitting him. Galaviz noted with satisfaction that Markov was still unsteady. Then, with a coolness that surprised him, Galaviz centered the barrel on Markov's broadening middle-aged girth and squeezed the trigger, slowly, firmly, as they had taught him in training.

With an emotion bordering on amusement, Markov

watched as Galaviz brought his pistol to bear on him. Galaviz aimed first at his head. You dummy, Markov thought, didn't you learn anything in training? And then a cold fist slammed into his gut as he saw Galaviz lower his sights and aim for his chest. That cleared his head and he brought his machine pistol to bear, but too late. Before he could, Galaviz squeezed the trigger.

Markov prepared himself for the hot burning collision of bullet against flesh.

But it never came. Markov grinned in amazement: Galaviz had forgotten to take the safety off before pulling the trigger. Your luck has run out, Markov thought, as he aimed his machine pistol and fired a three-shot burst. Galaviz spun about and landed softly on the carpeting in the middle of the stairway, his pistol still gripped in a well-manicured hand.

Hours later, back in his room, Nat slumped in an armchair, his nerves frayed by the evening's ordeal. Niki had finally relented and would serve as a courier. Egos, Nat thought: the larger they are, the easier they are to manipulate. The rest of the briefing had gone well, and now he was left alone with visions of Tania that would give him no rest. What *was* it about her? Why did she possess him? The smile, the eyes full of intelligence . . . and a hint of a secret knowledge she held. It didn't make sense. Here he was, a grown, mature man, for Christ's sake! Yet his heart played with him as if he were a teenager again. It was like he . . . like he was in love.

Love! Goddamn, Worthington, you've really gone off the deep end this time, he muttered to himself and wearily pushed himself out of the chair, reached for his briefcase and snapped open the clasps. He shuffled quickly through the jumble of papers, poison, and makeup searching for his briefing notes, when his eye caught sight of a folded piece of hotel stationery. He

189

picked it up gingerly and unfolded it. Tania's handwriting spoke to him.

"Dear Nat," the note began in English. "Though your conversation with Niki seems finished, I don't think ours is." He caught his breath, his topsy-turvy emotions struggling for control.

"I have little time to complete this," the note continued. "I'm writing it while you finish giving Niki his instructions. So I'll just say that tomorrow night, I will wait in this room from 6 P.M. until 8 P.M. If you can come, please identify yourself as you did tonight. Tania."

Stunned, Nat placed the note on the bedside table, his emotions too overloaded to let his thoughts form coherently. He cleared off the bed, turned out the lights, and fell fast asleep with his clothes on.

For the first time in a decade, he slept without the nightmare of Colleen's death.

Chapter Fourteen

The next day, a chilling rain drenched Paris and sent pedestrians scurrying about, clutching their coats and umbrellas against the snatching gusts of September wind.

Lost in thought, Nathaniel Worthington pushed through the rain, and stepped off the curb at the Place de l'Opéra into a foot-deep stream of water. Cursing himself for his inattention, he shook the water out of his shoe and made his way to the rain-slicked opera house.

Posing as a municipal employee making a check on fire code compliances, he gained entrance to the massive old theater. No one gave his faultless Parisian French a second notice.

Once inside, though, he quickly made his way lower and lower in the old structure, past makeshift plywood barriers that covered obsolete passages leading to a cavernous underground room that had been constructed to serve as a reservoir in case of fire. No longer needed due to the installation of modern firefighting systems, it remained—drained and shuttered. It took Nat only minutes to locate a number of small feeder passages that connected it with the monstrous Paris sewer system. It was the ideal escape route. He retraced his steps, mapping in his mind alternate routes to the old reservoir from a half-dozen locations within the building. He then left the way he had come, an anonymous bureaucrat.

The next night, dressed as before in the guise of an elderly gentleman, Nat stepped from the elevator at the Intercontinental Hotel and walked with a giddy lightness in his head to his encounter with Tania. He knocked on the door of the adjoining suite which led to Tania's room. It was a precaution which he always took; there had to be an avenue of escape and this was the best of them: The adjoining suite was on a corner and had its entrance on a different corridor than Tania's. They had left that way the night before to confuse anyone who might have seen them enter Tania's room directly.

Nat waited and soon he heard the sound of the chain and bolt being unfastened.

The door opened a crack and Tania's face appeared. He smiled at her and she returned it. For several moments they stood there, awkward, afraid, expectant. Neither spoke. Then Tania opened the door fully and stood to one side, fixed Nat's eyes with her own, and said, "You're right on time . . . again. That seems to be a habit with you."

Nat stepped into the room and waited as Tania shut and rebolted the door behind him. "I usually do that when things are . . . important."

Tania murmured something and they walked to the chairs by the window. Sitting on a butler's table between two armchairs was a bottle of vodka frozen into a block of ice, a tray of mixers and a plate of cheeses

192

and hors d'oeuvres. Nat sat down and noted that the hors d'oeuvres were still hot.

Tania looked at him as they exchanged the small patter that accompanies the initial meetings of people who know little about each other, but who want to know more. She liked the sound of his voice, listening not so much to the meaning of the words themselves as to the way they sounded, to the thoughts behind the words. And she liked the sound, the thoughtful way, cautious to the point of hesitancy, in which he spoke now. It calmed her, warmed her heart.

Nat rubbed away his makeup and disguise while they chatted.

As Nat talked, his brilliant turquoise eyes danced, lending emphasis to this, a lightness to that, supplementing words with meanings a dictionary could never capture. The eyes peered out from a face not handsome in a classic sense, but possessing a rugged boyish vigor.

Yes, she thought, that was it; his face spoke of experience and strength in its angles and abrupt features: the jaw that jutted from earline to an almost imperceptible cleft on his chin, high cheekbones beneath the eyes and a nose that, while not quite hawkish, came to an abrupt ending after running a crooked line from his forehead. He'd broken his nose at some point, she decided. Perhaps at the same time he got that scar under his right eye? She would ask him about that some other time.

". . . the scar?"

"Pardon?" Tania responded.

"I said where did you get the little scar on your jaw?"

Nat instantly regretted asking the question as her hand shot up, fingers tentatively touching the scar, and a look of disquiet passed over her face.

"I think it's really attractive," Nat said quickly. "Don't worry, I was just curious . . . It's . . . it's just that it gives you . . . character." He saw her face lighten. "I spotted it the first time I saw you," Nat said, emboldened to continue. "And I thought that it . . . I thought that it . . . made . . . uh, gave your face a, a certain . . . a certain—oh, hell! What I wanted to say was that you are so beautiful that without the scar, I don't think you'd be human," he blurted.

Tania surveyed Nat's face in the silence; his eyes warmed her insides.

"Thank you," she finally replied. "I never quite thought of it that way." She smiled, more confidently now. The ice had been broken.

They talked: about her childhood and parents, and about his; about her education and his.

Nat watched, entranced, as she spoke. The animated way she tilted and moved her head to lend emphasis to her words, and the life radiating from her eyes fascinated him as much as her beauty. He saw now, as he hadn't really seen before, because he had been too timid to take a long careful look. He felt intoxicated, and couldn't tell how much of his light head originated with the vodka. They talked and talked, and to most things the one said, the other replied "Me to." Their overwhelming similarities manifested themselves, crowding out earlier visions of their differences.

"But there's something I have to ask you," Tania said, sitting up and placing her empty glass on the table between them. Nat looked at her, vaguely disturbed by her suddenly businesslike manner. "Something that's been bothering me from the first time we ever met."

"Yes?" Nat said. "Go ahead, please ask."

"Promise you'll tell me the truth?" she said, fixing his eyes with an iron grip. Nat nodded.

"I want to know if you've ever done this before," she began, "if you've ever . . . ever—"

"Let someone think I was in love with them just so I could manipulate them?"

194

"Yes," Tania said.

The room echoed with its own silence. Nat swore he could hear Tania's heart beating above the sounds of the traffic beyond the closed windows.

"Well," Tania broke the silence. "Have you?"

Nat looked at her. "Yes," he said. "Yes, I have done that and I did it because . . . because I—But this is—"

"This is different?" Tania asked. She saw the alarm on his face. "Yes, I know this is different. Don't ask me why I know this—you and me—is different this time. I don't know why I believe you, and I don't have any idea why I'm allowing myself to believe you, but somehow, I know you're not lying to me. And you don't have to tell me the because, why you did it before—you told me the answer to that when we met at the Waldorf in New York. It was because you had to. You and I are a lot alike, Nathaniel. We're a lot alike, because we've done a lot of things because not to do them was worse, not because what we did was right. We—"

A rap on the door, followed by greetings in French, interrupted Tania and announced the arrival of the meal she had ordered earlier.

Tania accepted the cart from the bellman, tipped him, but wouldn't allow him to enter the room.

Damn, damn! Sergei Markov muttered to himself as he gazed through the peephole and watched the room-service cart enter the ballerina's room. From Galaviz's old vantage point he'd kept her room under constant surveillance, and she was the only person he'd observed entering the room. But the room-service cart definitely had two meals on it. Damn! Markov cursed himself.

For the hundredth time, he considered pulling a couple of his men off their other duties to keep Tania Valente under twenty-four-hour surveillance, but again he rejected it—for now. He reported to Kokh. Before he brought his subordinates in on this, he wanted to have a good idea of what was going on. They all kept tabs on each other, and he knew that one of them—he couldn't tell who—undoubtedly sent reports on him to Kokh.

Markov shifted from foot to foot, his legs like jointless granite pillars stuffed into too-small shoes. He checked his watch . . . he'd been standing there for more than four hours now.

Who was the second person? Did Galaviz know . . . had he known and was that the reason that twit had decided to surprise them?

Galaviz. The man was a pain in the ass in death as he had been in life. At least, though, he hadn't bled too much on the carpeting. But what had made Galaviz decide to enter Tania's room as he'd been about to do just before Markov came out of the bathroom? What had seemed so important that Galaviz could overcome his innate lack of courage and take independent action?

The question played in Markov's mind like a tune that one could not banish. It was just that annoying, the entire situation was. Soon he would have to report Galaviz's disappearance; perhaps they'd never find his body in the dumpster. As for Tania Valente, she was probably just getting even with her husband for his infidelities. Markov had no way of knowing that the man supping with Tania Valente was the same man he had tried to kill in Amsterdam. The man he thought was permanently disabled.

"All right," Tania said as she poured coffee for both of them, "You've heard my story. Now I want to hear yours."

Hours later, when Nat finally ran out of words, he sat silently, searching her face for some sign, praying he hadn't driven her away.

Quietly, raising her eyes again to his face, Tania spoke.

"You've told me how you operated out of a lust to . . . kill. But," Tania coughed to clear her throat, "but you don't seem to like it anymore. Your eyes have no spark in them when you talk of killing Pugachev. They grow dull when you talk of this . . . this mission of yours—ours. Why? What's happened?"

Nat sighed. "Every intelligence agency has people like me," he explained dryly. "And they do their jobs carefully and discreetly. Every agency accepts a certain level of hazard, that they will lose some of their own. Beyond this reasonable body count, they plot reprisals. I was working out of Amsterdam for several months, working with some . . . less than competent agents, on a mission to interrupt a smuggling operation engaged in selling diamonds from Russian mines under the counter to avoid the international cartel rules. The KGB directed that operation, and its chief was one Sergei Markov who—"

Tania's wide-eyed gasp interrupted him. "He's . . . he's—"

"I know," Nat said. "Remember, I told Niki about him. He's a ruthless operator. He has to be in that job."

"But you sound so non-emotional when you talk about him."

"He's only doing his job," Nat said, his voice hardening. "And I do mine. There's no room and no reason for emotion.

"In any case, wrong things kept happening. The men who worked for me kept killing Markov's agents instead of roughing them up and harassing them."

"Why?"

Nat hesitated. "Because they were inexperienced," he lied. "Because they were incompetent."

He took a sip of the cognac, and closed his eyes contemplatively as the liquid burned its icy way down his throat and spread warm and cozy in his belly. He dared not reveal what he really believed—that the

197

three agents, all selected by Everett Lowell, had intentionally killed the Soviet agents specifically to violate the acceptable level of deaths and spur Markov to take action against Nat. He didn't want to tell Tania that, for to hint that he had been set up because of his violent disagreements with Lowell would shake her confidence in him and could jeopardize the success of this mission.

"What happened?" Tania asked.

"Markov took action." Nat related the story of Amsterdam, his lengthy recovery, and the pain the wounds still caused. He didn't tell her that the company had booted him out on full disability, that he had been given no chance to resume his position, or that he had experienced blackouts and could, according to the doctors, do so at any moment.

He also failed to tell her about the incident in the Chesapeake Bay.

When he finished, Tania could think of no reply. Words eluded her. She pushed her chair back and stood up slowly. Never taking her eyes from his, she went to his chair and put her arms around his shoulders and hugged him. She couldn't figure out why she was crying, and she didn't care.

Chapter Fifteen

||||||||||||||||||||||||||||||||||||||||||||||||||||||||||||||||||||||||||||||||||||

Shafts of sunlight danced through the sheer curtains, playing with a gentle breeze. The morning came to him in perfect orange slices of time as he waked slowly, drifting in peace.

He could still sense her perfume in his mind, feel her lithe body against his, see the profound depth of her eyes and hear her voice. Had it all really happened?

Nat rolled over on his side, lingering in the wakeful dream, savoring every moment of it.

Pushing himself up on one elbow, he cupped his left hand over his eyes to shield them from the sunlight. He was alone in his bed in his hotel room. He reached for his watch on the bedside table: it was a quarter to nine. He lay back down and closed his eyes briefly, and then opened them again.

"I love you."

He heard it now; his voice, hers too. Nat's eyes gazed up at the ceiling. Yes, he'd said it, he remembered it distinctly. And yes, he'd meant it. But it was so unlike him, he could not trust it. A small persistent doubt nagged at him.

In his training at the intelligence academy, the psychiatrist had warned of the dangers of so-called love. Nat could see the thin birdlike man even now, his beaklike nose and the bobbing Adam's apple that jiggled about on his scrawny neck.

"Stress," he had said, "causes your body to react emotionally. Anger, fear, infatuation, sadness, joy—they all provoke the same physical response: rapid heartbeat, a heightened sense of awareness, changes in your perspiration, respiration, and so forth." Nat closed his eyes, felt nothing but the cool sheets and the hints of the morning breeze.

People fall "in love" much more easily when they are in danger, the instructor had explained, for their minds mistakenly tag the physical symptoms of their peril with the emotion of love, rather than its correct one of fear. This, he told the fledgling group of agents, was an occupational hazard of every intelligence agent.

He and Tania were in danger, he admitted to himself. But he'd been in danger many times before. He'd never felt anything for other women then. No, he thought, as he opened his eyes again and sat up on the edge of the bed, his love for Tania had no connection to the danger. "None," he said aloud and pushed himself up into a standing position. "None whatsoever." His voice reassured him, and he went into the bathroom to make himself ready for the day.

Nat burst out of the shadows of the hotel lobby into the bright sunshine. He glanced briefly at Notre Dame and swiftly turned his back on it.

For a brief moment, he wanted to linger a while, sightsee, but the feeling passed quickly. This morning he had no time for beauty and history—only for the unremarkable purpose of catching the métro at the Odéon station.

As he descended into the underground, he thought, for some reason, of *Les Misérables*, of Victor Hugo and of his character Jean Valjean and the harrowing escape through the Parisian sewers—the main underground of the time.

Reluctantly, Nat concentrated on the morning's tasks as he entered the metro station. Though the use of Niki as a courier continued to nag at him, Nat conceded that the operation would probably work. During a tour of the UNESCO headquarters, Niki and the other escorted members of the Kirov would be herded into the center's theater to view a UN film. Nat purchased a ticket, passed it through the turnstile, and walked through.

Standing on the platform Nat continued with his review of the morning. The Kirov members would check their shoulder bags and purses at the cloakroom. When the tour was over, the item—whatever it was—would be in Niki's practice bag, inserted among the pages of a paperback copy of the *Guide Michelin*.

Following the tour and film, the group would visit the nearby Eiffel Tower, and Niki would give the *Guide Michelin*—still bound in its shrink-wrapped plastic—to the maitre d', saying that he'd discovered it lying on his seat, apparently left by another diner. The maitre d', Nat knew, had been paid.

His train rumbled in, bound for Porte d'Auteuil. Nat boarded with a sparse crowd of mostly students and old women with shopping bags, and found a seat by the door.

The train whined its way out of the light, into the maw of darkness. And as it did, Nat leaned his head against the Plexiglas partition, and closed his eyes. His optimism, born on the rays of the bright day, disappeared into its own black tunnel, eclipsed by hunches, hunches of how this was so wrong, so wrong to use Niki like this. Nat trusted his hunches—they were a sixth sense, and he knew that agents either developed

201

and trusted this sense very quickly, or they didn't live long. But he had no grounds to delay the mission, no valid reason to communicate with Rinehart, nothing to substantiate his hunch.

Nat opened his eyes slowly, and thought for a second that a wiry man on the other side of the car peering at a map of the métro had actually been staring at him through his bushy steel-wool eyebrows instead of examining his map.

Nat feigned disinterest in the man, but continued to watch him discretely between occasional glances about the car. The man's face reflected a stalwart French ancestry—Gallic nose and cheekbones, the cheeks sunken in a faintly malnourished manner, and a heavy shock of black hair manifested most remarkably in two wooly caterpillar eyebrows that seemed knitted together from heavy black yarn and nearly joined each other in an unbroken march across his forehead. Blue eyes the color of new Levi's stared from beneath the mantle of eyebrow.

The man looked slight—like most Frenchmen—and dressed in a nondescript Parisian manner: dark coat, cream-colored slacks, a white shirt open at the collar, and black Italian shoes with pointed toes and hardware at the instep.

The man's unremarkable demeanor—he now appeared engrossed in the map—soothed Nat's fine sense of paranoia. He relaxed a bit, still suspicious, but now convinced that if the man had been looking at him, his interest had more to do with his American appearance than a spying mission: Nat's Topsider shoes, khaki pants, canvas belt, and blue oxford cloth button-down shirt made infrequent appearances in Paris.

The train decelerated for a stop at the Duroc station. Spy or not, Nat resolved to take no chances, and so stood up as the car drew to a halt, grasping an overhead bar for balance. A sideways glance at the man with the eyebrows showed him still engrossed in the métro map; he did not even seem to note that Nat had left the car.

On the platform, Nat hesitated and satisfied himself that the man was still reading the map when the train pulled out, leaving the station filled with settling dust and distant echoes.

Glancing at his watch, Nat decided to walk. He had more than an hour before the Kirov group's scheduled eleven A.M. arrival.

With the taste of too much coffee and a hangover of too little sleep lingering between his ears, Sergei Markov watched the Valentes take breakfast together.

Markov raised his cup and took yet another sip of coffee, and attacked the crumbling remains of a croissant. Continental breakfast indeed, he thought; no wonder Napoleon couldn't reach Moscow. This was breakfast for a woman.

Something was up. The room. Galaviz's surveillance, and . . . most puzzling of all, the old man exiting Tania Valente's room at 3:17 A.M. this morning. An old man Markov had never seen before, yet . . . yet the man looked familiar.

Was Tania Valente having an affair with an arthritic old man? Markov replayed in his mind the painfully slow way the man had walked. Could this be her answer to Niki's philandering? No, it rang false.

He'd watch the Valentes closely, very, very closely until the company returned to Leningrad. Quickly in his mind he ran over the roster of his agents here, and selected four to tail both of them twenty-four hours a day.

Markov didn't know why Kokh wanted them watched so closely, but he knew that if he failed, he might as well kill himself before Kokh's people got to him.

The United Nations Educational, Scientific and Cultural Organization is housed in a complex of buildings and underground grottoes at the Place de Fontenoy across the Avenue de Lowendal from the Ecole Militaire—the French Military Academy. As Nat approached the complex, he pulled a tourist map of Paris out of his plastic Pan Am shoulder bag, and pretended to study its contents.

The main building, Nat noted, was what passed for futuristic in 1958—a wishbone-shaped structure set up on pilings, like some bizarre alien spacecraft landing on struts.

Nat checked his watch—it was almost 10:30—and strolled up the ramp to join a throng of tourists milling about in the entrance hall staring at posters and exhibits. The hall had the sterile airiness of modern museums, and the distinct aroma of spaces that play host to bustling transient populations.

Feigning interest in the displays and merchandise Nat surveyed the hall, located the cloakroom counter, the auditorium where the film would be screened, and three exits along the route he could use in case things aborted.

This preliminary reconnoitering accomplished, Nat entered the men's toilet, locked himself in a stall, and once again applied the makeup to age him by decades. He took out a worn, but still bright red, cardigan sweater, which he pulled on over his shirt and buttoned; then he slipped on a shabby pair of overshoes to cover his loafers. If the morning ended in disaster, people would see a red sweater and overshoes—things he could discard in an instant.

Nat ambled from the men's room. It was 10:54.

At three minutes after eleven, the entry doors filled with chattering dancers, preceded by a phalanx of dark sack-suited KGB who barked at them in Russian. Bent over like the old man he was supposed to be, Nat turned toward the group and cocked his head to one side in a gesture half curiosity, half senility. He caught

204

sight of Tania, walking beside another female dancer, and his heart stumbled over itself.

For Sergei Markov, these outings were a security risk and a nuisance. But he complied. He rode on the lead chartered bus with the Valentes, and with the two KGB personnel assigned to watch the Valentes for this twelve-hour shift.

As the amorphous crowd poured through the doors of the UNESCO center, Markov remained at the entrance, watching his herd. Nothing appeared unusual. Perhaps his earlier fears were unfounded.

A rear-guard of KGB finally drew abreast him, and he followed them into the building.

Markov lingered behind the group of dancers, scanning the hallway; still he saw nothing. He walked more easily now as the mass arrived at the cloakroom. Over the dancers' protests, they were ordered to check their handbags, practice bags, shoulder luggage and other items. Their KGB escorts told them fire rules mandated the measure, but it was Markov's order—he wanted all of the bags searched thoroughly in the event the Valentes—or any other dancer—carried contraband.

Markov brought up the rear of the throng, the dancers milling about now, waiting for their turn to reach the counter, chattering, complaining in rapid-fire Russian. About twenty feet from the cloakroom counter, Markov noted an old man in a red sweater who had turned and now faced the clot of dancers. Although Markov couldn't see the man's face, something about him was familiar. Markov stopped and observed him as he in turn watched the commotion. Could he be the same man Markov had seen leaving Tania's room? If he were, more than coincidence was involved now. The old geezer would have a lot of explaining to do. Markov moved toward him.

205

Tania whispered furiously to Niki, who nodded but said nothing. They both looked so frightened, Nat wanted to reassure them.

Tania caught Nat's eyes for a moment, then quickly glanced away, fearful of giving Nat away to the KGB men.

"What if they find it, Tania? What if they discover the book?" Niki fretted. "I should never have listened to you and your Mr. Worthington."

Markov moved one step closer to Nat.

"Niki, get yourself under control," Tania snapped. "They're not going to find anything. Nat—Mr. Worthington—and his people are capable. They're used to this sort of thing, they'll take care of it. You must be calm or you will get us into trouble. Nat is here," she said in an undertone. "Don't look suddenly, but he's over by the exhibit to your right disguised as—" she broke off. Markov was approaching Nat.

Left silent by fear, Tania watched as a stranger with wild bushy eyebrows, dressed in a shabby dark coat, suddenly appeared and moved toward the KGB agent.

Louis Gold had seen Markov approach Nat and quickly set out to distract him. Just over an hour ago when Nat had disembarked the train at Duroc, Gold's companion in the adjoining car had followed him. By radio, Gold received Nat's route, and arrived at the UNESCO building minutes later. Gold's companion now rested outside on the building steps.

Gold had followed Nat into the building, watched him enter the restroom, and when no one exited other than an old man in a cardigan sweater, he'd checked the facilities and found them empty. For the last fifteen minutes he had admired the man's superb performance: Nat Worthington was a magnificent character actor.

"Pardon, monsieur," Gold spoke once softly, and when Markov failed to respond, he repeated himself.

206

"Yes?" Markov replied in French, annoyed at the interruption. He whirled on his heel to face the voice. "What do you want?" Markov stared irritably down at the scrawny man with the most unruly eyebrows he'd ever seen.

Unaware of the drama playing behind his back, Nat shuffled to another exhibit about ten feet farther away from the cloakroom, dragging his flight bag along the floor as he did.

Gold told Markov that he looked official and could he tell him where he could find information on native handicrafts from South America?

No, Markov replied, he wasn't connected to UNESCO. Are you positive, Gold persisted. Markov cursed at Gold, of course he was sure, if anyone ought to know what he, Markov did, it was he, no? And would the man with the ridiculous eyebrows stop bothering him?

Pretending to be insulted, Gold sulked away as the Kirov members finished checking their bags.

Markov straightened his coat, took one step toward Nat, and stopped. He looked back at the tail end of the crowd entering the auditorium, and then again at the old man. Nat chose that moment to move to yet another display, and hobbled over to it, still dragging the flight bag.

"Just a tired old man," Markov muttered to himself and, casting one last glance over his shoulder, turned to rejoin the troupe.

Relaxing, Gold loitered in the sales hall, watching the last of the dance company empty the hallway.

Louis Gold always seemed on the verge of starvation. As a child he had suffered from a gastric disorder that left him frail and thin. Books became a refuge for the sickly. unathletic boy, and words became the nourishment that compensated him for a lifetime lack of close friends. It was therefore to his profound incredu-

207

lity that a recruiter from Mossad, the Israeli intelligence service, approached him during a semester of study in Tel Aviv two years before.

Intelligence agents weren't all commandos, the recruiter told him. *Intelligence,* he said, came from . . . well, from intelligence, and that was Gold's strong suit.

The recruiter's pitch appealed not only to a repressed sense of manhood that never quite came to terms with Gold's anemic existence, but also to his Jewish roots and to the intellectual challenge that outwitting others might provide.

He'd said yes. And for the next twenty-three months, Gold had spent most of his time translating documents for Mossad to justify his regular stipend. The stipend came as an enormous boost, for at age twenty-four, Gold was still in school, now as a postdoctoral economics student at the Sorbonne.

He saw his position with Mossad as a humanitarian act to help a struggling people fight for their survival. Even though his distance from any actual violence lent an air of unreality to it all, it still made him feel like a whole person for the first time instead of a doormat. Was that what it felt like for the Jews who had survived the Holocaust and managed to make it to Israel?

He thought so.

Thirty minutes passed. Nat moved down the hallway a bit as half a dozen KGB thugs arrived from the screening room. They shoved their way behind the cloakroom counter and proceeded to ransack the items left behind by the Kirov members. Crude jokes and curses could be heard from within the room, along with an occasional cry of triumph as hard currency or a forbidden magazine or newspaper was discovered. But, to Nat's relief, nothing major was discovered. Half an hour later, when the last of the KGB filtered out of the cloakroom, stomped out the last of the cheap Russian cigarettes (they smelled like burning electrical insulation, Nat mused), and returned to the auditorium, the drop was still to be made.

Nat leaned over wearily to pick up his shoulder bag when he saw them coming down the hall. He froze: Lowell's two men from the Jardin des Tuileries! This place was crawling with spies, he thought; might as well have a convention. To keep them from getting a good look at his eyes, Nat turned as they approached and then watched in irritation as they, too, went toward the cloakroom. Were these fools going to screw up the drop? And then Nat gaped in amazement as the blond man—the same man who had snarled at him so viciously that night in the Place de la Concorde before handing him Rinehart's message—withdrew from his inside coat pocket a thin green shiny elongated book. A *Guide Michelin*. Nat stood transfixed. Rinehart's message specified that the information to be passed would flow from Russian agents to American, with Niki as the intermediary.

The possibilities, as Nat saw them, were limited: either Rinehart's message was incorrect or Lowell's two men were working for the Russians. Frantically, Nat searched for another possibility but none appeared. Something awful was taking place before his very eyes.

The blond man reappeared in the corridor and slapped his accomplice on the shoulder. Nat stared into their backs for a long time, until they walked out of his sight. It could mean many things, Nat thought, but it probably meant an answer to so many questions that had plagued him over the past five years, including the penultimate one of why he was stabbed in Amsterdam. Things began to make sense. Everett Lowell was a double agent for the Russians. It was Lowell who had tried to kill him and it was Lowell he had to kill. As soon as Pugachev was out of the way, it would be Lowell's turn.

His surveillance at an end, Nat shuffled into the men's room. There he reversed the aging process, carefully stowing the garments under a pile of soiled paper towels in the waste can. Looking neither to left nor to right, Nat strode briskly out of the UNESCO building and headed for the Eiffel Tower.

The day came as a blessing for Mustafa Salem el-Nouty. Despite Sarah's warm presence at his side, the night had been plagued with nightmares. They always came to him during those times when he tried to sleep during the night. They never bothered him when he slept in the daylight.

Now, as he watched Paris speed by the window of his taxi, he could banish the nightmares to the barren reaches of his mind, where they belonged, and concentrate on the task of the morning. He remembered Sarah's face as he kissed her goodbye at Orly for the shuttle for London. He remembered how her eyes seemed to devour him even from under her closed eyelids, and his groin stirred as he anticipated their reunion the following week in London. She was a prize, Mustafa thought, dismissing her from his mind. His sister was a prize.

The thin gold watch on Mustafa's wrist marked exactly 11:30 when he emerged from the taxi at the Place de Trocadéro.

Taking his time—ninety minutes remained before the drop was scheduled—Mustafa strolled across the terrace between the two buildings of the Chaillot Palace, and hesitated at the railing, drinking in the view of the Eiffel Tower, standing at attention astride the Champs de Mars like a sentinel surveying the Seine to one side, and the Ecole Militaire at some distance to the rear.

Mustafa brought his gaze back across the Seine. Immediately below him, several youths were skateboarding along the smooth, almost traffic-free pavement of the circular drive that surrounded a classic elongated pool. He pushed himself away from the railing, descended the steps to the circular drive, and made his way briskly across the Pont d'Iéna to the Eiffel Tower, where he bought a ticket, and strode quickly up the stairs, his powerful legs carrying him to the first platform faster than the elevator.

He found the small, overpriced restaurant on the first platform, located the maitre d's station and surveyed the platform for ambush potential. He didn't like it: with one set of stairs, and a creaking elevator, only a wild climb over the outside of the tower's superstructure offered an alternate avenue of escape.

By his watch, at least an hour remained before he was to make the pickup. His face brightened, an idea sprang into his mind. He flew down the stairs and hailed a taxi on the Quai Branly. In the distance, he saw the ballet troupe approaching with their ranks of KGB escorts.

Louis Gold and his partner played tourist, milling about on the second platform, cameras slung about their necks, snapping shots of each other with the panorama of Paris in the background.

But well-framed snapshots occupied no concern at all in Gold's mind, or in the mind of his companion, René Schwartz, for they were there to watch Nat Worthington. Like Gold, Schwartz had grown up in Paris, the son of French Jews. But there the similarity ended. Where Gold's body barely cast a shadow, Renés reflected a lifetime of bruising physical activity and stress, the embodiment of the superb athlete.

Without understanding why, this odd duo kept Nat in sight, puzzled by his initial burst of activity in striding to the tower from the UNESCO building, by his quick, almost cursory, exploration of the restaurant on the first level, and now by this waiting. They watched him attach himself to an American couple admiring the Seine when the Russian group poured out onto the platform. Two people, according to the spy's adage,

211

are less conspicuous than one, three less than two. Nat's serendipitous friendship with the couple ended, as Gold had expected, when the last Russian disappeared from the platform, summoned—Gold's rudimentary command of Russian indicated—to the restaurant to eat.

Then Louis Gold had a hunch. Later, when René Scwartz related the story to his family and to close friends in bars, he would blame himself for complying with Gold's instructions.

"Go down and wait for me at the base of the tower," Gold said to him. An odd tone in Gold's voice puzzled René, caused him to hesitate. "Go on," Gold insisted. "Take the radio, we'll remain in contact. I want to make sure that Worthington doesn't slip past us by taking the elevator or something."

In the end, Schwartz decided that Gold must have needed to prove something to himself by handling this alone.

By 12:50 the last of the Russians had crowded into the elevators or stomped down the fire escapelike stairway. Through a crack in the platform, Nat watched them leave. Despite all his efforts to force emotion from his mind, his chest ached when Tania disappeared from his sight. Security demanded they make no further contact until after the Pugachev assassination.

With Tania gone, Nat focused all his concentration on the drop. For the millionth time that day, he checked his watch; then he started down the stairs to the first platform.

Gold watched Nat emerge from the stairwell and make his way slowly to a souvenir stand by the entrance to the restaurant. Light-headed but alert, Gold lingered near the elevator; he felt sure Worthington hadn't picked him out.

For months afterward, Nat tried to figure out where el-Nouty had come from. The tall dark Libyan seemed to have summoned himself out of thin air and suddenly materialized on the Eiffel Tower platform some twenty yards from the restaurant entrance, a blue plastic shopping bag in his good hand and a determined look on his face.

Nat turned quickly to avoid being recognized. Langley training had engraved el-Nouty's face into the memories of all its recruits, along with hundreds of other prominent agents from the international intelligence fraternity.

Cautiously, Nat turned his head to catch el-Nouty in his peripheral vision. Nat knew that although el-Nouty sold his services to the highest bidder—subject to the approval of Libyan strongman Qaddafi—he worked most frequently for the KGB. If Everett Lowell was working a doublecross delivering documents to the Russians without doing business directly with the KGB, then el-Nouty filled the task admirably.

Nat clenched his fists in anger. The reason for the double blind drop was clear to him now. If Lowell worked for the Russians, he couldn't have his agents deliver anything directly; but the more layers, the more insulation for him—hence the sequence of the blond agent to a dead drop, the drop to Niki to another dead drop, to el-Nouty, to the KGB. Thus, Lowell could credibly deny almost anything.

Just wait, Everett Lowell, Nat thought. Just you wait until I get back to D.C.

But what was so damned important to merit this elaborate deception? Nat watched el-Nouty set the bulging shopping bag down by the railing and walk slowly but purposefully toward the restaurant.

Instantly, Gold knew he'd made a mistake by sending René away. Whatever happened between these two men—and he believed something would—would not be gentle. Although terrified, Gold stood his ground. Was that what courage felt like? he wondered as he stared in awe.

Mustafa el-Nouty scanned the platform with hawk-like precision, his body charged with caution. Gold thought he saw the Arab's glance rest briefly on him, then quickly move on as he turned and made his way toward the maitre d' in the emptying cafe.

Absently pawing through the vendor's collection of cast-metal Eiffel Tower replicas and grotesquely colored photographs of the Champs de Mars with twenty-five-year-old cars in the background, Nat watched el-Nouty. The maitre d' smiled unctuously at the large dark man as he retrieved the *Guide Michelin* from beneath his podium and handed it to him.

What could be so important that Lowell would arrange a blind drop? What could be so important, so important? The question seized Nat and would not cease. In slam-zoom brilliance, Nat saw Lowell's sweating face on the boat, winced briefly as he felt the pain . . .

covered with blood he didn't immediately recognize as his own

. . . and then pose after pose of Lowell—behind his desk in Langley chewing Nat out for some minor breach of the rules, in front of a safe house in Hamburg sending his agents off to be killed, crouched in a dark corner of a restaurant emitting disgusting sounds of too much food being eaten too fast, image after image in rapid fire like a slide projector gone berserk, and as subtly as the images were abrupt, he realized his duty. Whatever the *Guide Michelin* contained, no matter how important it was, he must abort the drop, take the information as evidence, and lay it on Rinehart's desk as proof of Lowell's treason.

Carrying the book in his good hand, el-Nouty walked from the retaurant. Timing, Nat thought, it was timing. . . .

Now!

Nat spun away from the souvenir stand—to the obvious displeasure of the stand's vendor—and took a step toward el-Nouty. The Libyan spotted him immediately, and froze.

Though they stared at each other for less than a second, each assessed the situation in trained micro-second increments of thought, and formulated a strategy. The wrong one—they both knew—could be fatal.

"El-Nouty," Nat said in a conversational tone, while his hand plunged into his shoulder bag in search of his Ingram MAC-11. "I want that book."

El-Nouty smiled broadly at Nat's request and stood fast as Nat walked slowly toward him. "Is that so? Well, you can piss in your mother's vulva."

"That's as articulate as you can get?" Nat asked sarcastically, still walking slowly toward the other man, and trying to extract his Ingram, which had snagged on something in the bag. As in a slow-motion frame, Nat saw el-Nouty transfer the book to the stainless-steel clip on his right hand, and slide his good hand swiftly into his coat.

There was no time to get the Ingram out of the bag. Nat did the only thing he could before el-Nouty withdrew his weapon. He threw his shoulder bag at the tall Libyan, and followed it up with a roundhouse kick that landed just off target, to the right of el-Nouty's groin.

El-Nouty raised his hands to catch Nat's bag, and in doing so dropped the green, plastic-wrapped book. Though it had missed its intended target, Nat's kick landed in the sensitive inguinal region, momentarily stunning the Libyan, and hindering his leg movement.

Nat heard a woman shriek, and a chorus of voices calling for the police. Nat realized his temper had dragged him into a bad mistake. He should have followed el-Nouty and recovered the documents in private, where the police wouldn't intrude. Shit, he thought, if I'm arrested it's all over—the embassy will tell the Sûreté they never heard of me. "A rogue," he could see the grin on the blond man's face explaining to the Sûreté. "Certainly he was once an agent, but he retired. We know nothing of his business."

Then Nat made his second bad decision of the afternoon: he decided to grab his bag and the book and run.

The screams for the police came dimly to the aging ears of Gus Mersault who had only that moment seated himself in a straight-backed chair—against regulations, he knew, but then his legs weren't what they had been when he pounded the beat as a youngster. Children again, Mersault muttered to himself as he rose from the chair; the seat hadn't even had time to get warm.

Wearily Mersault adjusted his cap over the gray locks—"too long," the director had said three days before when they hired him—reactivated him after four years and eleven months of retirement. Then he remembered the smile on the man's face—the man, a captain now, who had been a raw patrolman when he, Mersault, had commanded the third precinct—the man smiled and said, "You're fortunate you *have* so much hair left at your age to be a problem," and he'd run a hand over his own thinning locks to emphasize the statement.

Yes, Mersault thought, he'd get a trim . . . tomorrow, or perhaps the next day. He did want to keep this job—it supplemented his pension, which had lost its fight with inflation, but even more it saved him from the tedium of retirement. Evalyn's death two years ago had ruined the enjoyment of not having to work.

But the teenagers—good kids really, he thought, but they put each other up to things, he remembered when he was . . . Anyway, he wondered if they would be the same bunch he'd talked with yesterday. He'd be disappointed if it were. They'd seemed so surprised and delighted that someone would take time to talk with them, rather than just scolding them. He felt they'd left

216

thinking him a friend. But nothing surprised him anymore. A lifetime as a policeman extinguished one's disbelief in almost anything people could do.

Louis Gold had witnessed this scene of unvanquished resolve, his own mind filling with a thunderous terror. Vaguely he now recognized el-Nouty. He'd been told about him during training in the Negev—so long ago, Gold thought, why can't I remember? But really all that mattered was the memory—the confirmation—that this tall dark man hated Jews.

Now Gold stood rooted in awe as he watched Nat's kick. The dark giant towered over Worthington by a head, but the blow clearly had stunned him. Gold's amazement dissolved into dismay when the Libyan recovered his balance and aimed a swift deadly kick at Nat's head.

Dark anger burned in the Libyan's otherwise dispassionate face as he aimed at the American's head, with a kick backed by the explosive sinew of his superbly muscular legs. Nat twisted agilely to avoid the impact he knew could snap his neck. Straightening up, he hurled himself away from the foot. But the tip of el-Nouty's shoe caught the bridge of his nose and sent him sprawling onto his back.

White-hot bolts of pain shot through Nat's head as it smacked onto the concrete platform. Nat continued to roll, trying to avoid further blows. His eyes watered from the shock of the kick, and momentarily he thanked his reflexes for sparing him the brunt of that kick. He tried to stand up, but before he could, el-Nouty attacked with a flurry of blows and kicks that came so swiftly Nat could hardly tell from which direction they flew. Nat rolled again and tumbled into a crouch, expertly blocking most of el-Nouty's punches with his forearms. But the Libyan used his steel claw like a switchblade; Nat could only dodge that.

217

His vision still blurred with tears and his head spinning, Nat continued to retreat. El-Nouty's superior size began to tell. His martial skills were also better rehearsed than Nat's, not rusted by a long period of inactivity. Nat began to tire. He backpedaled away from the Libyan, spun away, and repositioned himself, but el-Nouty pressed the attack and gave him no room to breathe.

Gasping raggedly, his right arm tingling and almost paralyzed from a massive blow to the upper arm, Nat spun away from el-Nouty once more and slammed into the platform guardrail with an impact that nearly knocked the breath out of him. A corner! Nat looked about him. He was jammed in the corner of the platform with nothing but space behind him and el-Nouty in front. A malevolent grin spread over the Libyan's face.

"Stop. Police!" the old policeman yelled with surprising volume and timbre as he ran toward the fight, fumbling with a revolver holster. "Halt!" Mersault yelled again as he managed to pull the revolver free of its holster.

Mustafa Salem el-Nouty whirled on his right foot and danced away from Nat, withdrawing, as he did, a stub-nosed revolver. By Allah, Mustafa thought, I hate to use this thing, I hate to lower myself to this level of killing—it has no class. He squeezed off three quick rounds.

Gus Mersault, reactivated policeman, grandfather to three and widower with too much gray hair barely heard the sound of the first shot, for it smashed through the left side of his face, and exited through the back, carrying a lock of gray hair with it. Redundantly, the next slug shattered his breast bone and macerated his heart. The third one missed. El-Nouty castigated himself for missing.

The platform reverberated with the terror of people screaming and diving for cover.

218

Nat saw his shoulder bag—and the MAC-11 inside it—some ten yards away. Too far. With his head cleared from the few seconds of relief, Nat sprang once more at el-Nouty, and landed a solid kick that catapulted the handgun from the Libyan's hand and sent it flying over the guardrail. By this time both Nat and el-Nouty heard whistles from below; other policemen on duty had been summoned by the gunshots.

El-Nouty threw a last kick—which Nat evaded—and sprinted toward the green *Guide Michelin*, which lay untouched on the platform. He plucked it from the concrete without breaking stride and made for the shopping bag, which still rested near the guard rail, halfway to the restaurant.

Nat pursued. They squared off again.

El-Nouty flew at Nat with a side kick followed by a roundhouse and two swift hand punches, but Nat ducked and spun; they landed harmlessly.

Nat kicked, but el-Nouty had anticipated the thrust, and responded with a block that caught Nat's leg and threw him on the pavement. With Nat down, el-Nouty gave him a swift kick to the head, and this time Nat remained motionless.

Time was critical: the police were coming. El-Nouty restrained himself from finishing off Nat. He'd leave that to the police.

Oh, God! Louis Gold thought, the Arab's killed him! And stoked by anger and indignation, he made his way toward el-Nouty, slowly at first, and then quickly, finally running, as he saw the tall bronzed man reach into the shopping bag, and pull out of it a coiled climbing rope and a brace of carabiners and hardware, which he slung bandolier-style over his shoulder. Gold was halfway there when el-Nouty reached into the bag and withdrew another coil, fixed one end to the guardrail, and hurled the rest over the side.

The Libyan leaned over to check his means of escape, then turned and looked down at Nat, who had begun to stir. With his left hand, he withdrew a glinting scalpellike device from a special scabbard sewn into his coat, and fixed it to the shiny stainless steel hook on his right hand.

Wide-eyed with mounting terror, Gold rushed toward el-Nouty with breathless speed, and ran headlong into the Libyan's hardened muscular body, just as the man bent low to slash Nat's throat.

The impact was much less than he would have liked it, Gold thought briefly. $E = \frac{1}{2} MV^2$, yes, he remembered the physics equation well. Kinetic energy is equal to one-half of a moving body's mass times the square of its velocity. Yet, he thought, even though he had been moving pretty damn fast, his slight body had hardly an impact on the Libyan's.

El-Nouty stumbled slightly, and then sprang away, startled. He looked first at Nat, who was on all fours by now, shaking his head to clear it, and then at this shrimpy kike with the bushy eyebrows. Jew! El-Nouty thought. Unclean filthy animal!

Daylight returned to Nat's eyes as if he were lying face down on the bottom of a murky swimming pool. The images above him bent and twisted before his vision found its balance and set them right.

(A train, that's what it feels like, doctor, a train running from my head, down into my belly and back again, and it hurts, doctor, it won't stop hurting! So they carried him back into surgery and cut some nerves.)

But the express was back again and Nat felt rent apart from the inside as a blinding fist pounded him from his head to his balls and back. He pushed himself up on one elbow and when he searched the wound on the side of his head, his fingers came away glistening red.

Through spinning eyes, Nat watched as el-Nouty approached the thin man with the bushy eyebrows. Regaining his balance but still too weak to rise, he watched as el-Nouty's fashionably clad foot slammed into the thin man's abdomen, doubled him over like a closed jackknife, and hurled him into the guardrail where he collapsed like a sack of gristle and assorted bones.

Nat rose unsteadily to his feet and nearly fell again before he gained his balance. His gun! He must get to his weapon. Though he was recovering quickly, he was in no shape to take on el-Nouty barehanded. Lurching toward his bag, Nat heard the increasing shrill reports of police whistles, but before he reached the bag, a shriller, spine-chilling shriek pierced the air overriding the whistles. Nat turned and watched el-Nouty shaking the thin man who'd lost consciousness for only an instant.

"Oh God! Oh God! It hurts, please God make him stop!" Gold screamed. El-Nouty's kick plunged deep into his belly and up into his chest until it sucked the very breath from him and made it impossible for him to refill his lungs.

Gold's screams became gurgles when el-Nouty grabbed him by the neck, but the frail little man's cry of horror cleared most of the mists from Nat's head, and he ran steadily, grabbed the shoulder bag, but before he could withdraw the Ingram, the thin man's screams crescendoed. Nat watched in horror as el-Nouty indifferently tossed him over the side of the platform. The shrieks of terror grew steadily fainter and then ceased abruptly.

The Ingram came freely out of the bag this time, and Nat loosed a volley at the top of el-Nouty's head as he disappeared over the edge.

Sprinting to the edge, Nat saw el-Nouty rappelling swiftly down the girders. Nat slung his bag diagonally over his shoulders and hesitated at the edge. But his doubts vanished with the arrival of two uniformed policemen at the elevator.

Ignoring their cries to halt, Nat painfully scampered over, clinging to the rope. His vision blurred, and then cleared as the ground swayed sickeningly beneath him. His arm ached from el-Nouty's powerful kick. Ignoring the pain from his arm, and the friction of the rope against his palms, Nat slid down the rubber-band-tight rope, made taut by el-Nouty's weight at the other end. Nat looked down and saw the Arab approaching the end of the rope. He himself was little more than halfway down. Below, the red stains spreading from Gold's crumpled body lying on the hard-packed earth of the Champs de Mars.

El-Nouty reached the end of the rope and attached himself to the girder. It took the tension off the nylon climbing rope, and Nat was jerked upward so quickly it tore his grip loose, and snapped him upward about ten feet. That act of timing saved his life, for el-Nouty's action took place at the same time the policemen on the platform loosed a series of shots from their service revolvers.

Ears buzzing with pain, Nat was vaguely aware of the explosions, and the dull metallic thudding of slugs against the tower's iron superstructure. All they have to do is sight down the rope and I'm gone, Nat thought, as he fumbled to regrip it with his weaker arm. The arm tingled and buzzed from the elbow up, and Nat realized gratefully it was recovering from the shock.

Another shot rang out, and Nat felt a slug rip through his shoulder bag. The ground and the splattered body of the thin man with the bushy eyebrows yawned up dizzily at him. Nat steeled himself for the next shot, which he expected to rip through the top of his skull unless he could climb onto the girders and out of sight of the policemen. He noted that el-Nouty had

222

moved to the interior of the leg, after tying the bottom of this rope to the exterior of a girder. How long would it take the cops to realize that cutting the rope was the surest way to get him?

As he leaned as far as he dare, stretching for a hold on the girders, Nat felt the rope begin to oscillate, and down below he saw el-Nouty's arm shaking it, trying to knock him off. The rope moved out from the girder and as it did, a slug whistled behind him, followed by the crack of the gun. Thanks, el-Nouty, Nat thought before he slammed back into the girder with a vengeance. His chest boomed like a bass drum when he collided with the tower, and his breath exited suddenly in a loud, involuntary sigh. Another slug zipped past, this one wide to his left. The bad guys don't have *all* the luck, Nat thought. And then remembered: "I'm the bad guy this time."

The rope drew away from the girder again. El-Nouty seemed determined to shake him off.

Oblivious now to the skin being scoured from his palms, Nat plunged the remaining thirty feet and landed squarely with both feet on el-Nouty's arm. The Libyan jumped back, and crouched in a vee of two girders. Nat ducked as one of el-Nouty's deadly kicks sailed at him and landed impotently against the girder. He crawled to the interior of the girder about five feet to el-Nouty's right and a couple of feet below him.

Nat wrapped his good right hand around the girder and with his left rummaged for the Ingram. Relief flooded over him at the secure feel of cool metal. Though it felt strange in his left hand, which was still shaking from the earlier trauma, Nat managed to pull it out and train it on his adversary.

"This is as far as it goes, el-Nouty," Nat said. "I want the documents, and I can either shoot you off that girder and take them from your dead body, or you can give them to me now."

El-Nouty glared at him. "I suppose you have me

223

where you want me, that's the American saying, isn't it?"

Nat's breath came in ragged gasps. He was infuriat-- ed by the Libyan's composure and grace, even now—clinging to a girder more than a hundred feet above the ground, staring down the muzzle of an automatic weapon.

"Of course," el-Nouty continued with maddening calm, "to be killed in battle with an infidel means I'll go straight to the arms of Allah."

"Then start praying," Nat said grimly. The three-shot burst chipped paint off the girder next to el-Nouty's arm. "I'm not going to kill you," Nat said. "I'll just shoot that arm you're holding onto the girder with. Then you can die like that little guy."

El-Nouty was silent.

"Do you think *you'd* scream all the way down?" Nat said, holding the gun firmly in place. Above them the police yelled and loosed an occasional shot. The sounds of sirens grew louder.

"It doesn't matter," Nat answered his own question. "We don't have much time before the police arrive. Give me the book!"

El-Nouty didn't move. His body stood stiff with tension. "All right," he said finally, and moved his hand to his coat pocket.

"Slowly," Nat commanded. "Unbutton your jacket." El-Nouty complied. "I don't want to see your hand near your right breast pocket. I saw you put the book in your left. If you make any other moves, you're dead."

The man nodded. Following Nat's instructions precisely, he withdrew the thin green book and offered it down to Nat.

"Closer," Nat commanded, reaching for the book with the same hand that held the Ingram, while the other hand gripped the girder, literally for dear life. The book inched closer to Nat's proffered hand, closer.

Nat put his middle finger on the trigger of the Ingram, so he could grasp the book between the pistol and his index finger. Stretching, reaching, Nat finally felt the book touch his fingertip and soon had the book clamped against the pistol. It rested uneasily, awkwardly. The plastic wrapping was slick between the smooth metal of the gun and his sweaty fingers. It started to slide.

El-Nouty sensed the movement, felt Nat's distraction, and in one swift motion grabbed a girder with both arms and, like a trapeze artist, swung both feet against Nat's arm, casting both the green book and the pistol into the air.

Simultaneously, Nat and el-Nouty leaped for the rope. Nat landed below el-Nouty by four or five feet, but quickly outdistanced him. El-Nouty, with only one hand, needed to rappel—but Nat's weight below him kept the rope too taut. The big man came down in jerks, using but one hand to stop the descent. Nat's hands were bleeding raw now; what would el-Nouty's one hand be like when he reached earth? They could hear the police wagons and an ambulance drawing near.

The rope grew slippery, lubricated by blood. The earth rushed lazily up to meet Nat, and he thudded solidly against it, a tiny cloud of dust rising around his ankles. Frantically, he scanned the area. He spotted first his Ingram, lying nose down, dirt clogging the barrel, and, about ten yards away, the green *Guide Michelin*. He stuffed both into his flight bag.

The underside of the tower was jammed with tourists, most of them too frightened to venture out where they might be struck by a stray bullet. A few people on the edge of the crowd looked at Nat curiously, but no one spoke to him. Their attention was riveted, instead, either on the battered, no longer bleeding body of Louis Gold or on Mustafa Salem el-Nouty who neared

225

the earth. Nat tucked the Ingram and the book in his shoulder bag.

The sirens wailed their rise-and-fall melody as they tried to push through the crowd. Already Nat could hear doors slam, and the gruff demanding voices of policemen pushing their way through the mob. El-Nouty reached the ground, as the police drew closer. The Arab looked first at Nat and then at the police. He fled. But against all his instincts, Nat did not follow el-Nouty. Instead he walked quickly over to where the thin man with the bushy eyebrows lay, his limbs bending in ways nature never intended them to, his head staring straight up.

He knelt beside Louis Gold's body.

"Thank you, whoever you are," Nat said. "Thank you. I owe you my life." And Nat almost felt tears well up in his eyes as he looked at Gold's face. It had remained unscathed through all the insults to the rest of his body, and now betrayed a presence of peace and— Nat looked at the face to make sure of what he saw— composure. Most violent deaths left their mask of horror on the victim's face. Nat knew, he'd seen many. But this man's face beamed upward, unfurrowed by worry or fear. And what Nat found most remarkable, and would never forget the rest of his life was the smile on Gold's face. It was a smile of victory, though Nat would never understand why.

"Mr. Worthington."

Nat leaped to his feet and whirled on the voice.

"It's all right," the man said. "I was his friend."

The voices of policemen grew louder as Nat regarded the man: his face was clearly Semitic, his skin dark, and his hair deep black. Nat examined the man's beefy physique, sizing him up for a battle.

"Come with me, won't you?" said the man. "I have a car nearby."

The following two hours were a blur. Nat and Gold's accomplice had shoved their way through the

226

crowds, police whistles blowing at them. Nat remembered asking about who would care for Gold's body but didn't remember an answer. Hands had pulled at him, and then he'd experienced a harrowing auto ride. Nat remembered asking the man who he was, and heard him say he worked for Mossad. When Nat asked him about New York, the man professed ignorance. Nat's head had begun to ache, and then came the competing pain in his arm, his hands, and finally the express that played through his ravaged insides. He remembered washing the blood from his hands and face and bandaging them during the auto ride, and changing into clothes he carried in his shoulder bag. He remembered being shoved down the escalator of a métro station with a ticket and directions for a rendezvous. He remembered thinking that he had to pack up and move out of the hotel, but his mind balked when he tried to decide where to go. And through it all, he remembered Tania, and he remembered the smile on Louis Gold's face.

Chapter Sixteen

||||||||||||||||||||||||||||||||||||||||||||||||||||||||||||||||||||||||||||

By the time he got back to his hotel, word of the massacre at the Eiffel Tower had made the radio news. On his way from the métro stop at St. Michel, Nat stopped at a newstand a couple of blocks from his hotel and managed to catch the news bulletin of the incident on the vendor's radio. Eyewitness reports conflicted—as all eyewitness reports do.

The radio announcer interviewed people who were on the scene: one said there were two men and no gunshots, others said there were four men who got away by helicopter. There were interviews with the maitre d', who said nothing, and with the ticket vendor, with the souvenir salesman—with anyone, it seemed, who'd been on the platform or anywhere near the Champs de Mars.

Nat's heart stopped when one person interviewed said that two men—one wearing a light-blue sweatshirt—ran from the scene and escaped by car. Then the interviewee, a woman, described the man in the sweatshirt as being close to seven feet tall and very dark complected and having but one hand.

What hurt Nat most was the identification of the elderly cop, and Louis Gold, although the radio didn't give either name because they hadn't notified their next of kin.

Smiling at the vendor and bidding him good evening, Nat trudged along the Seine, heading for his hotel room and another change of clothes and of his bandages. He kept his hands tucked into his pants to avoid drawing attention to himself.

Why did it always have to be the nice people who got hurt? Nat wondered as he walked. Evil people ran the world, and it seemed there was no lack of kind gentle people eager and willing to have their lives ruined by people like—like him, Nat thought, as he picked up his pace.

Nat stopped by a pharmacist's on the Rue St.-Jacques, and then went quickly to his hotel.

The hotel's ancient floor creaked with every step as he trudged slowly along the carpet runner. Nat lost himself in thoughts divided about equally between how good the hot bath would feel, and how long he had to clear out of here before the police caught up to him, and if they ever would.

He stopped at his door and inserted his key. A bar of warm yellow light glowed bright at the bottom of his door. He'd turned out the lights that morning, and the housekeepers never leave them on under penalty of immediate discharge by the energy—and franc-conscious—concierge.

Someone was in his room.

Writhing knots of fear squirmed once again in his stomach. Who was it? The police? El-Nouty? The KGB, CIA, another of those many people an agent crosses in the line of duty, any one of which could step out of a shadow at any time to settle a real or imagined score?

Nat quietly slipped his bag off his shoulder, wincing as the weight of the strap pressed into his palm. The pain had diminished. Perhaps he wasn't injured too badly after all.

The Ingram came easily out of the bag this time, and Nat checked the barrel to make sure it was clear of debris. Then, moving softly back to his door, walking next to the wall to minimize squeaks, Nat jammed the key in the door and burst in with the Ingram on full-auto, poised to fire.

"Good evening, Nat."

It was Everett Lowell.

For the first time in more than five years, Mustafa Salem el-Nouty found himself dealing with fear and failure. Now he stood motionless under the shower, steaming water beating on his head and neck as if he could boil away his problems.

He'd been seen, and he knew his appearance was memorable—and difficult to alter. The American, on the other hand, would blend in well with the local population and might never be positively identified. But as for himself, el-Nouty thought, it would be a matter of hours. Already alerts would be going out to airports and other transportation facilities. He must leave quickly, and by small plane. Like every good agent, el-Nouty had his contacts. An Algerian who occasionally passed along information to him would fly him under the radar tomorrow night and land him at a remote airfield in Northern Ireland. From there his IRA contacts would get him to London. El-Nouty gave thanks that Qaddafi had funded just about every terrorist organization in the world, including the IRA.

Once in London, he had his cover as an Indian spice vendor. That would allow him to move freely and accomplish his last mission there for Qaddafi. Then he, el-Nouty, would return to Libya a hero.

But anxiety nagged at the brown giant as the water

231

finally started to run cool, and he shut it off and reached outside for a towel.

It was the travel, he thought, he loved the freedom. That would be curtailed.

He stepped from the bathroom and gazed around him at the luxurious, elegant furnishings of his room. Would he forever say goodbye to them? Was he destined to spend the rest of his life in splendid isolation in Libya or risk death outside it, death in sordid little pensiones and hideouts?

Both alternatives depressed him. As he packed, he caught a glimpse of himself in the vanity mirror: he stopped, and for a short time regretted the handsome face, the stature that made him stand out in a crowd. For a moment, he wished for a genuinely anonymous appearance. But the feeling passed, and he smiled at himself: he was Mustafa Salem el-Nouty; favored of his Bedawi tribe, Qaddafi's most honored agent. He would prevail. Life could be a lot worse than living in luxury in Libya.

Nat suppressed a compelling urge to pull the trigger. Everett Lowell was sitting calmly in the easy chair by the bed, his fingers locked together over his ample, toadlike belly.

"Lowell."

"Excellent identification the first time." The man's voice, though tinged with sarcasm, sounded unusually soft. Suspecting a trap, Nat quickly scanned the room, keeping his Ingram trained steadily on Lowell the whole time.

But silence reigned, no noise of movement issued from the room, no cocking of bolts, releasing of safety catches, no hurriedly whispered orders. There were no agents in the room. Curiously, Lowell was alone.

Lowell hadn't changed either the expression on his face or his position in the chair during the entire time. That, too, puzzled Nat.

232

"What the fuck are you doing here?" Nat snapped. "And how—"

"That's not important now," Lowell answered, wearily dismissing the questions with a flick of his hand, like so many flies hovering about his abnormally pale face.

"It sure as hell *is* important," Nat rejoined angrily. "There are two people dead—and I could have been killed—and the entire fate of my mission here was jeopardized because you are a KGB mole, you self-righteous whore!"

Lowell's face registered total amazement, the whites of his eyes shining bright and prominent. Although Nat knew Lowell to be a good actor, he didn't think anyone was *this* good.

"A . . ." Lowell's voice squeaked and he cleared his voice and tried again. "A KGB mole?" he asked, his voice rising. "You think I—"

"Goddamned right," Nat said loudly, but with a sudden loss of conviction. "And I've got the proof." Silently, Nat leaned over and pulled out the *Guide Michelin* that at least two men had died for that morning.

"This," Nat said, waving the long thin green book at Lowell's nose, "was passed *not* from the Russians to us, but instead traveled from us to them. I was given to understand it was to be the other way around.

"*And,*" Nat continued, raising his voice to override Lowell's attempts to speak, "I had to use *my* man here to do it and that jeopardized a mission that was probably a helluva lot more important than whatever could be in here." Nat began tearing with his fingers at the plastic that encased the book.

"What you will find there," Lowell said, in a voice still fainter than it had been before, "is information that could swing the strategic balance in the world if the Russians got their hands on it."

233

Nat stopped fumbling with the plastic. "You knew . . . ?" he said, in angry disbelief.

"Yes." Lowell began. The words that followed seemed painful to utter. "That is why I sent the message that you were to use Niki as the neutral courier."

Dropping the book, Nat grabbed Lowell by the lapels. Despite the man's enormous bulk, he pulled him out of the chair to a standing position. "You *knew* all of that, and you let it happen?" Either Lowell was working for the KGB, or the man was even more incompetent than his reputation asserted.

But Lowell failed to answer. Instead, he closed his eyes and grimaced, as his face turned from white to waxen. Nat heard dripping liquid and looked down to see drops of blood splattering on the toes of his loafers, shining bright as they washed away the dust of the afternoon.

"Oh my God!" Nat exclaimed softly, and lowered the fat man back into the chair. "What happened? We've got to get you to a doctor; the embassy has a few 'safe' ones."

"No," groaned Lowell painfully. "There's no time . . . no time for that. Just listen to me." Slowly he replaced his hands in the position they had assumed when Nat arrived, and, watching him, Nat realized with a sudden, grim horror: Lowell was holding in his bowels with his hands. His clothes were soaked with blood and the room had the faint, warm moist smell of a freshly slaughtered calf. Lowell had been stabbed and cut up. Nat inhaled sharply.

"That's why I altered Rinehart's message to you," Lowell said, aware now that Nat would finally listen. "Because I knew that using Valente would ring the alarm bells in that weird head of yours, and that in spite of rules to the contrary, you'd tail him, and do exactly what you did."

Nat stared at Lowell as the wounded man inhaled a

234

ragged breath. Sweat ran down his face; the blue collar of his shirt darkened as the sweat soaked the fabric.

"I . . . I knew that if I contacted you directly and told you what I'd found out, you'd never have believed me, would not have followed my directions. You had to see for yourself."

"See?" Nat asked puzzled. "See what for myself?"

Lowell closed his eyes momentarily, and swallowed, slow and with difficulty. "Would you get me a glass of water? I'm very thirsty."

"Of course," Nat said, rising quickly to his feet and heading for the bathroom. Lowell looked as if he might die any second. Hastily, Nat filled a tumbler from the tap and returned. He tried to remember how many hours a man could live if he was disemboweled properly: it had happened in Vietnam all the time; it was a specialty of the Viet Cong. Nat recalled it sometimes took days for victims to die this particular brand of painful death.

Nat held the glass for Lowell while he drank. A trickle ran down the ashen jowls and joined the sweat at the front of Lowell's collar.

When Lowell had finished, Nat sat down again near him. He had to lean close to hear now.

"You were saying that I had to see something for myself," Nat said quietly. "What was it I had to see? Have I seen it?"

"Yes," Lowell began, after a pause. "Yes and no. You've seen parts of it, but not all. It started a couple of weeks ago when I—" He stopped. "No. I want you to tell me, first, why you thought I was working for the KGB."

"Okay," Nat said equably; after all, the man was dying. It didn't hurt to show him that measure of respect. The explanation was short, and when Nat finished, Lowell was shaking his head. Nat was puzzled.

"It's so silly," Lowell began. "That we let personal feelings color reality so thoroughly. As I sat here waiting for you, I realized how many times I slandered you and your work, just because I didn't like you. Distrusted you because of . . . because I couldn't rein you in. And now—" Lowell stopped as a grimace of pain passed across his face. "Now, you've let the same sort of emotional coloring change reality for you.

"No, Nat." Lowell's voice sounded almost relaxed now. "I am not a KGB agent. There were times I thought *you* were one, what with your inability to take orders and such. But no . . . no you can take the word of a dying man that—"

"You're not going to, sir. We'll get you to a good—"

"I have no more time to fool myself," Lowell interrupted quietly. "I know I'm dying. So listen, *listen*!" Lowell hissed. Nat settled into a stunned silence, oblivious to his own pain as Lowell recounted his story.

"You know how Rinehart likes to ride me," Lowell began in a strained monotone. "He always has, even before you came along to give him something to play with. Well, I've been able to handle all that for these years, but about two weeks ago, I took an intercepted cipher to him, involving the Mossad attack on you in New York. He—"

"Why did they attack me there?" Nat demanded. "And they—" he thought of Gold—"they saved my life here, just this afternoon."

But Lowell continued as if Nat had not spoken. "I brought the message to Rinehart and he attacked me for lax security aboard the yacht that day, accused me of having an unknown Mossad agent on board.

"He was right," Lowell conceded, "But the way he said it made me angrier than I'd ever been at him. And it also made me suspicious." Fire lit up Lowell's eyes for a moment. "So I put him under surveillance." Nat's mouth dropped open. Lowell went on, his voice bolstered by pride. "Yes," he gloated. "Yes, I did."

Lowell stuck out his jaw. "My agents are good. I know Rinehart didn't believe that and I know you

236

don't, but they are, and for two weeks we did a thorough job on him. We followed him and we tapped his messages and his telephones and raided his files—oh yes, Nat, those super-secret vaults—we did it all and we did it without him knowing it and without his god-damned elite security units finding out." Lowell finished, exhausted, and he couldn't go on for a few moments. The tirade had winded him.

For once in the entire time Nat had known Everett Lowell, he believed every word the man was saying.

When Lowell had caught his breath, he began again.

"I'd found enough by last week to be quite suspicious of our Mr. Rinehart. So, even though I couldn't find out then what your mission was, I *could* alter Rinehart's message to you. I couldn't change anything—there were too many other compartmentalized people involved for me to cancel things. But what I could do is arrange for an improbable courier—your Niki Valente—to raise the flags in your head."

"You certainly did that," Nat mumbled.

"Good, good," Lowell stopped and took a few painful breaths. "Well, if you'll open that handy little guide to Paris, Nat, I'll venture you'll find microfiche on which is recorded the plans for the American blue-green laser system, a system we've perfected, but with which the Russians are still at square one."

Nat was stunned. A powerful, satellite-mounted blue-green laser was the ultimate weapon against nuclear missile submarines. No, he remembered reading in the aviation weeklies, not that it would destroy either missile or sub, but it could penetrate the protective veil of the ocean's depths, and reveal the heretofore invisible subs. It would effectively neutralize the subs' main advantage—their concealability—and alter the strategic balance. Nat looked at the book on the floor as if it were radioactive, glowing green and dangerous. If el-Nouty had gotten it . . .

"If the Russians got their hands on that," Lowell

continued as if he'd been reading Nat's mind, "Then we'd be in real trouble, because we depend a lot more on our submarine-based missiles than the Russkies do."

Nat thought of the afternoon, of the cop who looked like Santa Claus, of Louis Gold, and he wished they knew how well they had died.

"But there's more." Lowell's head had begun to slump forward. With a great effort, he brought it upright once again. Below the chair, blood dripped silently into a widening pool soaking the carpet. "When I found out about the laser documents—that was two nights ago—I redoubled our efforts, because it was Rinehart who personally signed for the documents, and sent them on their way to the Russians."

The room began to whirl about Nat's head. No! It couldn't be! Rinehart was the father to him he never knew. It seemed impossible. Nat looked backward in his mind and gazed at visions of Rinehart: Rinehart as professor, carefully building a bridge of logic from one arena of arms control to another; Rinehart the National Security Adviser, calling Nat into his office to reprimand him for a breach of regulations and laughing at the same time, a little joke between them that regulations weren't really meant for people like them . . . people like them! Rinehart was him, he was Rinehart. It couldn't be, it couldn't—

"Please listen carefully to me now." Lowell's voice intruded on Nat's thoughts, dragged him back to the present, to face this dragon that couldn't be. "I've little—" his hands tightened again and a spasm twisted his shoulders and face, "—little time left.

"Then yesterday, I learned that the assassination of Pugachev was—" again pain interrupted Lowell's narrative. "Pugachev's assassination was ordered not in Washington but in Moscow. It . . . they . . . A faction of the politburo led by Kokh, the head of the KGB,

238

wants Pugachev out of the picture. Want to guess what faction of the politburo Rinehart is part of?"

"You mean what part he's siding with, don't you?" Nat asked, still unwilling to accept the impact of Lowell's words.

"No," Lowell disagreed. "I mean part of. We did some more checking . . . a long time into the past, Rinehart's past."

Nat had read the story a hundred times in civics texts and in briefings at Langley, how, embarrassed by his family's wealth in the midst of the poverty of the American Depression, Rinehart, like many other young, wealthy youths, attempted to join the Communist party. But Lowell told him the rest of the story. An alert recruiter discouraged Rinehart from actually signing anything, and turned him over to an expert from Moscow. They enlisted Rinehart in their cause by convincing him that he could do socialism more good by rising within the American government and feeding information back to them. Never in their wildest flights of fancy did they imagine the young zealot would attain the highest national security position in the United States. Rinehart was to become the ultimate mole.

Though the thought of a mole had obsessed the CIA for decades, they had never once suspected Rinehart.

And who was the talented expert from Moscow that Rinehart had been turned over to? Lowell asked rhetorically of Nat. Yes, Lowell said, none other than the dishonorable Mr. Kokh.

How many networks had been blown? Nat wondered in horror. How many people killed, how many . . . How many people had died because a Soviet agent was sitting at the right hand of the president?

"But that's not all," Lowell said.

It was enough, Nat thought to himself; it was too much! How could there be more?

"There's more," Lowell began, "and you can—uh! Shit, that hurts."

"Look, let's get you to a hospital, tell me the rest later," Nat said, starting to rise.

"You never did take orders well, and you still don't." A grimace resembling a smile made its way across Lowell's face. "Just listen." Nat sat down again obediently. Lowell went on.

"Your contract to sanction Pugachev is only half of the entire scheme. We—I, under Rinehart's orders—gave el-Nouty a contract to assassinate the president of Iraq. I didn't set any conditions, but I imagine he'll try when the prez gets to London for the oil import talks next week.

"It's all part of a one-two blow for Kokh's faction to take over the politburo, and through it the whole show."

"How—"

"It works like this," Lowell continued more slowly now, winding down like a music box. "Pugachev opposed the invasion of Afghanistan, said it spread things too thin, what with the rebellion among the satellites. But Kokh's faction overrode him, and presto, the Soviet Vietnam.

"What Pugachev didn't have," Lowell continued with an effort, "was Kokh's intelligence reports that Siberian oil and gas fields were running dry, production was dropping. Russia won't have enough oil for itself, much less export it like it does now. So, like everybody thinks, Kokh wants Afghanistan as a launching pad for the Persian Gulf. But with the world reaction over Afghanistan, even the politburo isn't buying it, particularly with Pugachev screaming 'I told you so!' over the mess in Kabul." Lowell closed his eyes slowly and Nat wondered for a moment if he had stopped breathing. But he soon stirred and determinedly resumed the soliloquy.

"What Kokh's done is arm an Iraqi liberation movement based on religious hatred."

Lowell didn't have to tell Nat that a majority of the

240

people in Iraq were Shiite Muslims, like those in Iran. But the government was Ba'athist. An uneasy truce existed.

"If you eliminate Pugachev, his very strong voice of moderation disappears from the politburo. And, with the simultaneous death of the Iraqi president and an uprising by this KGB-armed group, the Russians—personified now by Kokh—can tell the world they were invited in to keep the peace, and incidentally stay to keep the oil."

Lowell, visibly fatigued by this last recitation, once again closed his eyes.

The imperative was clear, Nat reflected: Pugachev must be saved. He attempted to shut out the vision of the dying man in front of him, to concentrate on what Lowell's information meant.

First, Nat thought, he *had* to abort the assassination.

Second, he ticked off in his mind, Tania could never defect, at least not to America, if the assassination aborted. Rinehart would see to that. Jesus! Nat's head spun. Loyalties, he reflected, where were the loyalties? Rinehart had failed him, deceived him—defrauded an entire nation, in fact. There was his country and there was—now—Tania.

Nat raged silently. Yet, he realized, in a way he'd done it to himself: Rinehart hadn't forced him to fall in love. Without Tania, the choice would be simple. The assassination could be stopped in a dozen ways. The voices in his head quarreled: your country demands your loyalty. To what, Nat answered, to another KGB agent somewhere? Don't I have a right to some personal happiness?

The seething anger nauseated Nat. The betrayal of Rinehart, worry for the safety of Tania, conflicting loyalties, the deaths this afternoon, his head, all roared through his entrails. Leaping from his seat, he lunged for the bathroom and barely made the toilet before the heaves gripped him. A tablespoon of clear yellow bitter

241

fluid reminded him that he'd not eaten since breakfast. Shivering, he stumbled back into the bedroom.

Before sitting down, he pressed his fingers into Lowell's neck; there was a faint pulse.

Nat again considered his options. He could carry on with the assassination, help Tania and Niki defect and worry about nailing Rinehart once they were all safely back in the United States. He could abort the defection and risk—his heart ached—losing Tania, ruining for all time her chances of becoming an American. Or . . . Nat thought, he could go now to the Intercontinental, slip into Tania's room, which would mean killing her escorts, and they could run away, vanish, go where no one could find them.

The last notion appealed to him. Like every intelligence agent of any experience, Nat had passports in a dozen identities, and substantial caches of currency to be used for expenses and paying informants, stashed in half a dozen banks around the world.

But beyond this Shangri-La image, Nat saw a lifetime of running, living as fugitives. He and Tania would never be safe. Nat watched as the dying Lowell's mouth moved tentatively, as if he were trying to force words into it. "Listen.

"You're on your own now," Lowell said. "Even if you don't stop Pugachev's killing, Rinehart will find out about this afternoon. And when he does, you'll be nothing but cold dogmeat if he catches you." Lowell's eyes glazed more and more, focusing ever less on the world of the living. "Build a case against him," Lowell warned. "You've got to stop him."

"Can I get help from your agents who covered him?" Nat asked, alert now.

"Yes." Lowell's lips hardly moved. His voice was fainter than a gentle breeze. "But the word will be out to kill you on sight. You'll have to be careful who you approach."

"Well, who should I approach?" Nat asked anxiously.

"Rinehart will try to pin my death on you."

"Who should I approach, Everett," Nat demanded insistently. Time was running out. "What are their names?"

"And the theft of the laser plans, they'll pin that on you, say you are KGB . . . Kokh will back it up. . . ."

"Everett, tell me the names of the agents I can get help from!" Nat was shouting now. He reached over, gently tapped Lowell's cheek to bring him back to the present, but Lowell's head just rolled to the left. He was dead.

Chapter Seventeen

‖‖

Daylight began to filter through the curtains before he'd finished cleaning up the last of the blood on the carpet.

Wearily, Nat stood upright, pressing his hands into the small of his back as he stretched and reviewed his handiwork. Just a faint damp spot remained on the brown carpeting, nothing to arouse suspicion. Upstairs in a storage area, Lowell sat rigid and dead, tied to the chair that had once rested here. In the pre-dawn moments of two and a half hours ago, Nat had frantically prowled about the sleeping inn, finally locating an attic with enough dust to indicate it hadn't been entered in months. The view left a lot to be desired, but then Lowell's eyes could no longer appreciate one.

Nat dragged another chair over to cover the damp spot, leaving the darkness submerged in a shadow, and then slumped, exhausted, onto the edge of his still-made bed. Why had Lowell done it? He'd certainly never seemed the altruistic type. He could have saved himself by going to a hospital—or was Rinehart after him too? Jesus! Nat cursed, suddenly aware that he'd neglected to ask Lowell one very basic question: Who stabbed him?

Despair flooded over Nat and pain throbbed in a concert of angry nerves. If only he'd died in Amsterdam; at least that would have been a nice clean divorce from life, instead of this ragged argument. As it was, his relationship with life dragged itself out interminably like some people's marriages do, replete with custody battles, recriminations, blame, guilt, anger and . . . and always the pain. And constantly the nagging question of how he would have done things if he could just go back and do them over again.

If he hadn't gotten emotional with Tania; if he'd followed regulations and let Niki operate unobserved; if. . . .

"Damnit, what's the difference," he said aloud. "You can't do it over: you're just going to have to make the best of it all."

The best of it all. His raison d'être: stiff upper lip, play the hand life deals you, whistle a happy tune, count your blessings, the power of positive thinking—

"Fuck it!" Nat said angrily and jumped up from the bed. It was six o'clock. There was time to pack up, settle his bill with the night clerk, and put some distance between him and Lowell's body. It might take a day, he calculated, for Rinehart's people to track him down—perhaps less if someone discovered Lowell's body.

Downstairs he found the night clerk snoring noisily, bowed like a supplicant before the graven image of a television test pattern that flickered erratically before him. Silently, Nat left enough travelers' checks to cover his tab plus a generous tip, and quietly let himself out the front door.

A cab, its driver grateful for a fare that early in the morning, picked him up on the Quai de Montebello. Nat talked with him casually, pressing him for information about the Eiffel Tower incidents. The police were still baffled, the cabbie related; radio news reports said the *flics* still had not issued a bulletin describing the culprits. Then the man launched into a tirade about crime and how the police were either corrupt or incompetent, and how they preyed on little people like him—giving him tickets, he said, brandishing a crumpled handful—and let the real criminals go free. Nat murmured sympathetically.

So they're still confused, Nat thought with relief. Either that or the KGB got to the Sûreté first and convinced them to leave investigation to them. Possible—but unlikely; the French were too proud to yield a public incident to foreigners. Unless . . . unless the pressure was irresistible.

The taxi dropped Nat off at the Gare du Nord, where he pressed aboard a bus with a crowd of workers heading for work. To throw off any possible tail, he changed buses several times. Finally, satisfied that no one was following him, Nat squeezed into a slot at the formica counter of a café in Montmartre serving quick meals to rushing breakfasters, and ordered coffee and a croissant. Shoulder to shoulder with his fellow diners, Nat mapped out his moves. Quickly he outlined the tactics of surviving, but his thoughts wouldn't gel into a plan he could trust. Anxiety ate at him. He had not yet decided whether or not to stop the assassination. He could still square things with Rinehart, he convinced himself. Call him, explain the tower incident, blame it all on Lowell, play the innocent—profess to be ignorant of the contents of the documents—and ingratiate himself back into the fold.

Plus . . . plus, he grasped for the possibility, maybe Lowell was wrong; maybe Rinehart was not a KGB mole.

That possibility seduced him. He had no trouble imagining life in the United States with Tania: life as . . . well, he'd manage. After all, a degree from *Har*-

247

vard must qualify him to do something more than just kill people.

Nat desultorily pushed a handful of change across the counter and left.

"And where did Worthington come from?" asked the disembodied voice on the telephone.

"You know as well as I do why he was in Paris."

"Yes, yes, of course, but why was he at the Eiffel Tower?"

Rinehart leaned back in the leather upholstered chair behind the desk in his study and sighed; it was nerely 2 A.M. To answer Kokh's question would reveal his own carelessness. Worthington had been at the tower, Rinehart knew now, because that greaseball Everett Lowell had placed *him*—the National Security Adviser—under surveillance.

That was bad enough, but the fat man had surpassed himself with treachery. It was hard to imagine, Rinehart thought now, 3,000 miles and nearly a day later, what could have prompted Nat to cooperate with Lowell. They were the bitterest of enemies. But somehow Lowell had reached Nat in Paris, and persuaded him to cooperate. And cooperate Nat did—by fouling up the drop at the Eiffel Tower.

By now, Rinehart speculated, Nat Worthington must be fully aware of the documents' contents. He must know that the U.S. National Security Adviser was connected directly with the KGB. But . . . Rinehart rubbed his eyes wearily. Nat couldn't know that Lowell was now dead. Surely Lowell would have contacted Nat early in the day—that would account for the quick action to thwart el-Nouty—and then split up to rendezvous later.

"Rinehart, are you still there?" Kokh's voice came in exasperated tones.

"Yes," Rinehart replied. "Yes, I am. Sorry about

that distraction, but the events of the past hours have been shocking."

"That's all well and good, but I think we'd better clear this up as soon as possible."

"Fine," Rinehart agreed equably. "To answer your question: I believe that Worthington was reached early in the day by the deputy director of the CIA—"

"What do you mean, you 'believe?' Do you know or don't you?"

"Of course," Rinehart apologized. "Yes, I know for a fact," he lied, "that Everett Lowell, head of clandestine services, reached Worthington and informed him of the drop."

Rinehart waited for a reply, but heard instead nothing more than a faint static and the sotto voce squeals of scrambled circuits in the background of this most secure of international calls.

A chill passed between Rinehart's shoulder blades momentarily, then vanished. "How?" came Kokh's voice finally.

"How?"

"Yes," Kokh repeated impatiently. "How did Lowell find out?"

"That's something that I have not yet determined. It's still ear—"

"You mean you don't know," Kokh interrupted. "Well, what do you intend to do about the situation?"

"I intend to find out how Lowell learned of the operation, and I intend to have every person who worked with him killed." Rinehart thought he heard a murmur of approval from the other end of the line. "Second, we will reach Worthington, coax the documents from him, and then kill him."

"How do you intend to accomplish this?"

"I know Worthington like a son," Rinehart said, nearly accurately. "I know how he thinks, how he operates; I understand his unorthodox methods. And I see no reason why he can't be located with dispatch and . . . sanctioned." Somehow Rinehart couldn't bring himself to use that harsher word when it came to Nat. He *did* like the boy so much . . . almost like a son . . . almost.

"You stick to cleaning up your end of this," Kokh said, "and let us take care of Worthington. I think it far better to use the Arab in this—you see, I understand him too. And I know he's burning to take revenge for the disgrace Worthington brought on him—typical Arab, but these little personality quirks are useful when you know how to use them.

"In any event," Kokh continued, "the Arab will give both our services the insulation we need, without greatly sacrificing efficiency. El-Nouty is a superb agent—"

"Yes, I'm familiar. We've used him many—"

"I know, Rinehart. Just listen, will you, please?" and without waiting for Rinehart's reply, the KGB head continued. "As I was saying, el-Nouty is a superb agent in normal operations, but with a blood feud to settle, he should be positively unstoppable."

"Yes," Rinehart agreed pensively. "Yes, you'll be right just as long as el-Nouty doesn't allow his emotions to cloud his judgment."

"That's reserved for your side," Kokh said enigmatically.

"What do you mean?"

"Your man Worthington," Kokh answered, "is messing around with Tania Valente."

Rinehart shot upright in his seat.

"What do you mean, 'messing around'?"

"Just that," Kokh replied evenly. "Seems that my head of security for the Kirov Company in Paris noted some odd goings on with Tania. Worthington, by the way, performed admirably with Niki; nothing, but nothing, was suspected. I have my people there on notice to inform me of any even tiny irregularities with the Valentes, and I received no call until yesterday,

250

when my head man there called to say that Tania had met in a hotel room with an unidentified elderly man."

"An old man . . . ," Rinehart said softly.

"I believe that's one of your boy's trademarks, isn't it?"

"Yes." Rinehart was stunned. "Yes, but how—"

"Mind you," Kokh continued, "we have no proof of this at all, but based on what players are where, I'd wager anything that the old gent my man observed was Worthington."

Unbelievable, Rinehart thought. He could swear Worthington was as emotional as a burnt-out match head. Could this be? He shook his head slowly.

"That's how we're going to find Worthington," Kokh boasted. "We have Tania; Worthington will come for her sooner or later, regardless of what happens at the opera house."

Rinehart made no reply, but stared unseeing at the papers on his desk. Too old for all this, he thought bewilderedly. I'm getting too old for all this. I'm not twenty-five anymore, and this is no longer 1934. But there was no question of backing out. There never had been, since that meeting with Kokh in the late fifties when the Russian made it clear that the KGB was going to call in its debts.

"It . . . it's late," Rinehart said. "I've had a long day, and you're going to have a long one yourself. I'll telephone you in the morning."

"All right," Kokh agreed, his anger apparently neutralized by the pleasure of springing the Worthington information. "Goodbye."

"Goodbye."

The acrid smoke of cheap cigarettes hung in stagnant layers and brought an occasional tear to el-Nouty's irritated and bloodshot eyes. The waves of competing, angry, and worried voices sloshed through the gray windowless room and washed meaninglessly

251

over his ears. Now their remarks were no longer aimed at him, but rather at each other.

Bored, el-Nouty peered at his wrist: it was nearly 11 A.M. Outside the sun would be high over the Paris skyline. He started to take a swig from his now-cold coffee and then reconsidered. Beyond this secure KGB sanctum in the bowels of the Soviet embassy, in Paris people were living out their normal lives—whatever normal meant.

For close to thirteen hours now he'd conferred with the KGB station chief and with a number of his agents, functionaries, and handmaidens. All seemed more intent on getting the goods on the others than in solving the issue at hand. Why had the American interfered? Where was he? Why had el-Nouty not been informed that this was more than a routine drop? On and on it went, with the same questions posed again and again.

When el-Nouty arrived at the scheduled rendezvous without the documents, Alexandr Popov had exploded, and swore to kill him if he didn't immediately hand them over. But the threats mattered less to el-Nouty than the blackening of his face. The American had humiliated him yesterday. He had honor to think of, his honor and the honor of Libya. Worthington had brought disgrace upon him, and for that Bedawi law had but one cure: revenge.

Now as Mustafa sat, bored, frustrated at the eternal bureaucratic in-fighting, his right hand ached as it did every time he met with disgrace, and he knew the pain would remain until he avenged the disgrace.

It was psychological, the doctors had told him. After all, he no longer had a right hand to ache. They called it "phantom limb" syndrome. He'd learned to live with it, learned to ignore it—until the day he killed his first Englishman. The pain vanished for nearly a month.

Waiting for a lull in the conversation so he could ask his leave and get on with hunting the American, el-Nouty massaged his right wrist the best he could, what

252

with the bandage covering the rope burns on his left hand. The telephone buzzed. Popov answered it.

In the dim light and haze, it was hard to tell, but el-Nouty thought that Popov's usually ruddy complexion faded by a dozen shades when the caller identified himself. Popov held the earpiece tight to his head so none of the room's other occupants could hear.

"Yes, comrade" and "No, comrade" Popov uttered with reverence. He flinched frequently and finally lowered the receiver to its base and turned to the gathering, now silent and expectant. He looked first at el-Nouty, a long hard look of confusion and distrust, and then finally at the rest of the retinue.

"Comrades," Popov began quietly, the color slowly returning to his face. "That was Comrade Kokh calling from Moscow." Popov's staff silently exchanged glances first among themselves and finally one by one at el-Nouty, who did not take his eyes off Popov. "It seems that Comrade Kokh has taken a personal interest in this . . . situation. Of course he has the preliminary reports we filed last night to Moscow Center, but he seems to have a great deal more information than we currently possess." Popov paused for effect and looked at each man one by one, accusing him with the regard. Who is the traitor, Popov asked silently. Who had bypassed him and sent information to Moscow Center without his knowledge?

It would be a long cold winter for someone, el-Nouty thought, and it's not going to be me.

"Regardless how he came by that information," Popov continued, "he has instructed me in a most unequivocal manner that the resolution of this situation and the ultimate recovery of the documents will be managed by Mr. el-Nouty here."

The silence was palpable. Kokh's instructions were the greatest insult he could pay to the Paris KGB office. Obviously Kokh wanted information concealed from Popov and the Paris office. But what?

253

"We are to give Mr. el-Nouty whatever logistical support we can offer," Popov went on. "But as of this moment, we have effectively been relieved of any responsibility for this situation." Again Popov's staff looked at each other with uncertainty and mistrust. "You may go now," Popov concluded.

The men rose uncertainly, silent. El-Nouty smiled at one of the men, who acknowledged it with an assassinating stare. El-Nouty raised himself from his chair and prepared to follow the last man out, when Popov spoke.

"Mustafa," Popov addressed him informally. "I . . ." the KGB chief hesitated. "Come here. Please."

El-Nouty shut the door and approached Popov, who still sat on the edge of his desk.

"Mustafa," Popov began again, "I . . ." Popov's voice stuck.

He must be sweating, poor devil, el-Nouty thought. He'd never seen the KGB station chief this intimidated. As el-Nouty faced him, Popov struggled with what he wanted to say. His eyes conveyed fear and uncertainty; suddenly, el-Nouty knew it was because the room was bugged.

"Never mind," Popov breathed quickly at last. "Here, let me give you the information Comrade Kokh wants you to have," and he hastily plucked a pen from its holder and started to scribble on a memo pad.

"I am your friend," Popov's note began. "I always have been since the time you performed your first mission for us. I've justified to Moscow Center your contracts with the Americans, I've sung your praises to every ear. Please remember that. Please."

El-Nouty felt embarrassed for the man. One of the most powerful men in the Russian government groveled now before him. Who, el-Nouty thought, was running whom now?

Mustafa smiled reassuringly at the man and continued reading.

254

"Thank you," ended the pathetic note.

For the benefit of the hidden microphones the men exchanged words suitably grave for the occasion and then said their goodbyes.

Nathaniel Worthington trudged through deepening late-afternoon shadows down the Rue St.-Rustique.

He had walked all day and still had reached no decision. His head, sticky with thought and lack of sleep, was spinning as he walked on toward the cemetery, not because he wanted to go there, but because it lay in his path. After taking precautions not to be followed that morning, he took taxis to the Gare du Nord, the Gare de l'Est, and the Gare St. Lazare. Traffic was light, and he struck up conversations with the ticket clerks—to make sure they remembered him—and then purchased tickets for Strasbourg, Copenhagen, and Madrid.

He repeated the ruse at both Orly—where he bought a ticket for Le Mans—and at de Gaulle, where he purchased a ticket to San Francisco. On the way back to town he thought to himself that a helluva lot of effort would be wasted tracking down all those leads.

Finished with this task, he had checked into a seedy suburban motel south of the freeway that encircled the city. Nat had avoided the usual anonymous haunts of criminals, for he knew that the code among thieves did not apply to espionage.

He spent the remainder of the morning at the hotel with cartons of hair bleach and makeup, lightening his hair to a sun-bleached blond color and experimenting with makeup to give himself the tanned California look. The effect, he knew, made him look younger. Rinehart knew—as he probably thought the KGB did—that his habit was to impersonate an elderly man. Nat would do the unexpected.

By noon he'd succeeded. Carrying his shoulder bag, he ventured back into central Paris, first to replace his American-looking clothes with those of a more continental cut, and finally to a branch of Crédit Suisse, where he removed from a safe deposit box a false passport, a wallet full of identification to match, and more than $5,000 worth of various European currencies. He left the Ingram in the box—he didn't need two—although he took the ammunition clips.

There was another box like this one in New York, another in London and yet a fourth in Amsterdam, all purchased without the knowledge of his intelligence service. He realized now what a good investment they had been.

He was now Herr Nikolas Wolfe, an independent sales representative for a number of German industrial chemical firms; that's what the business cards said. And the photograph in the German passport stared back at him—a blond, blue-eyed specimen of the Aryan race, age twenty-four. All the identities in his other life insurance policies were like this one, anonymous occupations, faces his could easily match with slight alterations.

Nikolas Wolfe, né Nat Worthington, then purchased a briefcase and transferred the contents of his shoulder bag into it. He buried the shoulder bag in a street waste bin.

Thus outfitted, Nat strolled about Paris, unconsciously winding up in the Montmartre section in the early afternoon.

There was Tania, he thought, as he wandered. And then there was Niki. And last of all there was the matter of the National Security Adviser of the United States working for the KGB.

Tania he loved. Niki he felt responsible for. The man was an annoying rogue and an egotistical bastard to boot, but there could be no denying he was a great artist. Pugachev's influence had boosted Niki's career and prevented the dancer's eccentric ways from getting him into trouble. Without Pugachev, Niki might well fade from the view of ballet.

256

Nat knew if he decided to flee with Tania, he'd have to somehow offer Niki the same option. But would Niki take it? A dancer must have his art, and his ego must have the applause. Neither could flourish as a fugitive.

Nat walked into the grounds of the museum next to the vineyards and sat slowly on a bench. There was, he thought for the thousandth time, the possibility that Lowell was wrong. The notion was seductive. In any event Nat knew he could convince Rinehart that he, Nat, *believed* Lowell was wrong. That would get Rinehart off his back.

Yes, he thought as he leaped off the bench, and made for the center of Montmartre, that was it! He could take care of everything by going now to the CIA station chief at the embassy with the microfiche and the story of what happened. He'd tell him that Lowell had fouled him up, misled him—as he always seemed to do—and send an urgent message to Rinehart asking for advice. Pugachev's assassination would take place as scheduled and Tania and Niki would accompany him home. He'd tip off the Mossad so they could stop the assassination in London, and then . . . then, after assessing as best he could Rinehart's strength in the government, he'd make a decision on whether or not to go after him and risk the wrath of the KGB and the CIA.

Nat stopped before he left the secluded park, and opened his briefcase. He relaxed when he saw the *Guide Michelin* with its documents resting securely under the Ingram. It was 6:27. At 6:33 he boarded the métro near the Place Pigalle, bound for the American Embassy.

The street number matched the address Popov had given him, so Mustafa opened the door and walked briskly inside. The cozy hotel lobby gave off a musty aroma of age and smelled like a museum.

The concierge stood up to greet him. He thought he

257

saw a momentary glance of disdain pass across her face when he stepped into the light. She probably takes me for an Algerian, he thought.

"Good afternoon," el-Nouty replied in faultless Parisian French. "I'd like to take a room here if you have one available." Her countenance grew in his favor as she listened to him speak. She looked over the edge of the counter, questioningly.

"My luggage will arrive shortly," he explained, smiling. "It was delayed by the airline—they probably shipped it to Crete or something."

She laughed at his joke. "It must have been the Communists," she said conspiratorially. "They've taken over all the unions, and they probably did it on purpose.

"In any case, monsieur," she added, "you are in luck. All our rooms were reserved for today, but a crazy American checked out without telling anyone, and left too much money to pay the bill to boot!"

El-Nouty's heart leapt. Was luck—was Allah—so firmly on his side that he'd be put in Nat's very room? He would have picked up Nat's trail in any event, but this would save time.

"That *is* good luck," Mustafa agreed out loud. "We can frequently be thankful for the inexplicable behavior of the Yankee, no?"

Mustafa paid the concierge in cash for one night's lodging and walked swiftly up the narrow old stairs to his room. He cursed silently when he opened the door and walked in to find the room had already been cleaned by the housekeepers. No matter, he thought as he slipped his shoes off and walked toward the armchair to rest a bit, he'd found Nat's trail, and it was hardly cold.

But the floor was. El-Nouty sat in the chair and closed his eyes, but a few seconds later, his socks grew wet and chilly. Someone's spilled a drink, he thought and rose to move the chair away from the area. He

258

wanted rest but didn't trust himself not to fall asleep in the bed. He moved the chair, and afterwards noticed the moist spot covered a large area, barely noticeable as a darker spot on the brown carpeting.

On impulse, el-Nouty poked at the spot with a finger and it came back faint red: someone had recently cleaned up fresh blood stains. Had the American killed someone or had he been killed? A dark shadow passed behind his eyes and his phantom hand throbbed. No one else must kill him, el-Nouty thought. Revenge is mine! I must erase this insult.

No, he thought, Nat *must* be alive, he had to assume that. Exhilarated by his find, el-Nouty put his shoes back on and decided to search the hallway for any signs of a struggle, an escape. Silently he opened the door and crept stealthfully into the hallway.

Down on his hand and knees now, el-Nouty scrutinized the carpeting and the walls minutely. It took him less than five minutes to spot the tiny light-chocolate-colored drops of recently dried blood. His heart raced. He had no trouble following the drops, first down the hall and then up the steps.

The trail led him to a locked door, which he presumed closed off the attic. The lock yielded immediately to a plastic shiv, and swiftly he opened the door and stepped inside.

Lowell's body had begun to bloat in the attic heat. The body sat tied to the chair like a kidnap victim, and a light scurrying of chitin-covered feet told him the insects had wasted no time. El-Nouty held his breath at first, but finally had to breathe in the loathsome air, filled with the stench of decaying death, and the contents of Lowell's bowels and bladder had emptied when he'd died.

Who had killed him, he wondered, and how? The latter questioned he answered after untying the man and watching the loops of his small intestines spill out on the dusty attic floor. A small battalion of roaches swarmed off and headed for the baseboards. El-Nouty suppressed an urge to vomit. He had to search the body, but he wanted only to leave the room and breathe some of the fresh exhaust and pollution-ridden air of Paris.

He set to work, swatting at the roaches and flies to drive them away, and then laying Lowell's body out on the floor as he imagined a mortician would do. He rapidly rifled through the dead man's pockets and was not surprised to find them all empty. Whatever Worthington was, he was thorough.

El-Nouty scrutinized the body and noted the dirt and scuffs on one knee of the dead man's suit pants: probably incurred during the scuffle with his assailant. He found little of value, and returned to his room.

Moments later, el-Nouty scrubbed and rescrubbed his hand and prosthesis, rinsing both with steaming water from the tap, feeling as he always did right after a kill, a little like Lady Macbeth. His deep concentration distracted him when the hot water scalded his good hand. After examining Lowell's wounds, he knew that the Americans had done it: knife techniques varied from service to service, and most were a trademark to the practiced eye. But why had the Americans killed their own man?

And the Russians—why had Kokh given an Arab contact agent the job of finding the American when it ought rightly to have gone to the KGB itself? The two events were connected, Mustafa told himself. Coincidence could not account for it. And Worthington—and the documents he'd filched from him yesterday—had to be at the root of the strange conduct. To find Worthington would be to solve the puzzle.

But, el-Nouty thought as he turned off the water and reached for a towel, he cared little for the satisfaction of solving the puzzle. That was overshadowed by the revenge he would take when he found Worthington. He looked at his watch: it was nearly seven o'clock. He had to get moving. Pugachev and his crew would already be in their reception now, rubbing elbows with the Kirov stars and members of the French elite. In a little more than an hour and a half, the ballet would begin. Mustafa smiled at himself in the mirror, flashing that smile that he loved to see, tonight would give new meanings to a danse macabre.

"Worthington killed Lowell."

"What!"

"You heard me."

A long low whistle echoed back to Washington from the CIA's station chief in Paris. He'd followed the two men's feud for years but he never thought it would come to this.

"Are you listening?" Rinehart asked.

"Yes," the CIA station chief said. "Yes, of course."

"Good, listen carefully now. Worthington is carrying some documents that must be recovered and returned to me immediately. Got that?"

"Yes."

"When you have those documents, kill him."

The man in Paris grunted his assent.

"And I want you to use Marvin Tavistock and Ray Merrill to find Worthington and recover the documents. When they do, I want both of them to deliver the documents to me personally. Is that understood?" Silence echoed over the satellite-linked line while the Paris station chief searched for a suitable reply. As the agent in the field, it was *his* prerogative to select personnel. "Is that understood?"

"Mr. Rinehart, I—"

"I asked you, is that understood? I want a yes answer and I want it now."

"Yes, Mr. Rinehart, but—"

"Those are your directions," Rinehart snapped. "If

261

you deviate from them, you'll be opening mail in Dubuque or Djibouti by next week. Goodbye!"

Slowly, the Paris chief of the CIA replaced the receiver. He'd never heard Rinehart sound so . . . what was it, angry? No, it was more like frightened. But why would one of the most powerful men in the world be frightened?

Niki Valente sweated and fidgeted, starting every time someone spoke to him.

"What's the matter, old friend?" The concerned voice came from the Kirov's chief choreographer.

"Matter?" Niki replied in a voice too high. "Nothing," he continued in a calmer tone. "Everything's all fine," he lied, as he fumbled with the little round purple death peas in his pocket. Fortunately, the company had vetoed the idea of coming to the reception in costume; otherwise he'd have had nowhere to conceal them.

Now he stood uneasily in a corner of the ornate room, overgilded and overstuffed with red velvet. Shifting from foot to foot, he pondered running to the toilet and flushing the damn peas down the loo. But he waited. The American had told him in unequivocal terms that should Niki disagree, he'd end up in a hospital with two nonfunctional legs. The thought made him shiver.

"Are you cold?" Another voice came from behind him.

"Huh?" Niki jumped.

"Cold." This time it was one of the corps members. "I saw you shiver and I thought you might be cold, though . . ." she hesitated and looked at his face, ". . . you're sweating."

"It's nothing," Niki lied. "It's just . . ." Just what, you damn fool? Do they all know? Why is she looking at you that way?

"It's just that I'm a little nervous," Niki said quickly.

"You?" She looked doubtfuly. "Ah-hah!" she said next, with a tone that chilled Niki. "I know what's wrong." Niki's heart thudded to a halt. She suspected he was going to defect! "You're—" No! he thought, don't say it. He looked for anyone else in earshot. "—sick."

He couldn't believe it. Yes, he thought. Cold chills, sweat. The flu. His heart resumed beating.

He smiled at her. "You've found my secret," he told her conspiratorially. "It's a touch of the flu, I think, but I don't want to tell them," he nodded his head at the Kirov officials, "because they might pull me tonight." He put his arm around her shoulder and leaned over to whisper in her ear. "You won't let out my little secret, will you?" She giggled. "Of course not."

At that moment Pugachev exploded into the room with his retinue of advisers, body guards, and sycophants. He shook hands with some of the French guests who had already arrived, all the while looking about the room. When he spotted Niki, Pugachev broke into a broad grin and he waved delightedly.

The black hole in Niki's gut deepened and broadened as he watched the huge man make his way across the room to him, stopping briefly to exchange hugs and kisses on both cheeks with the head of the French communist party.

The ballet dancer's fingers closed again around the capsules in his pocket. They were moist from his sweat.

"Niki!" Pugachev's bass voice boomed through the room and snuffed out much of the other conversation. Anxiously, Niki saw heads turn toward them. How could he put the capsules in the other man's clothes with all those people watching? And then Pugachev was all over him, hugging him, patting him on the back with bearlike arms, inadvertently lifting him an inch off the floor.

Now! a voice within Niki whispered urgently, and as he returned the Soviet leader's hugs, he secreted first two capsules in the side pocket of his coat, and another two in his left hip pocket.

Expecting any moment the cry of alarm from Pugachev's GRU bodyguards and the vise grip on his arm to drag him away, Niki somehow managed to slip one more capsule—this into the other side pocket of Pugachev's coat—before his resolve vanished.

"You don't look well, Comrade," Pugachev said, scrutinizing Niki's face. "Are they not feeding you well?"

"Just a touch of the flu, comrade," Niki explained and then as he had done with the ballerina, he leaned closer and whispered, "Don't let on. I'm all right, but they might try to pull me from the performance if they knew."

Pugachev laughed heartily, "Of course, of course," he said. "I won't tell anyone. Good luck with the performance."

And with that, the rotund Russian moved on through the gathering crowd.

Precisely a minute after 7 P.M., Nat Worthington bounded up out of the métro station, taking the steps two by two, weaving a broken field run among the clots of evening travelers. Silently he cursed the train malfunctions that made a nearly half-hour train ride out of what should have been no more than fifteen minutes.

Nat strode past the Hôtel Crillon, and less than five minutes later was arguing with a young, fuzzy-cheeked guard at the U.S. Embassy gates, trying to persuade him to contact the CIA station chief. The Marine insisted, naively but with some belligerence, that no one from the CIA worked there.

Finally Nat scribbled the name of the CIA's Paris head on a sheet of paper and proffered it. "Go on,"

Nat said. "Contact this guy. You can look him up in your embassy directory."

Reluctantly the young Marine did so, and then picked up the phone in the guardhouse and dialed, watching Nat suspiciously out of the corner of his eye. In a moment he stepped outside the guardhouse toward Nat, with the heel of his hand over the mouthpiece. "Your name," the Marine said. "He wants to know your name."

Nat told him, and after a brief conversation he was back.

"Sir . . ." The boy's voice conveyed a new respect. "The gentlemen said—I'm sorry, but he wouldn't tell me more—he said, that is his only reply was—here, I've written it down—'The Tiber in the Antique Manner.' Does that—"

"That's fine," Nat reassured him. "That's all I need to know. Thank you very much." And he turned and walked away, leaving the young Marine staring after him.

The statue of Tiber in the Antique Manner overlooked the octagonal pool in the northwest corner of the Tuileries gardens. Nat slipped the microfiche back into the green notebook, shoved it back in his briefcase, and left. He had a little over half an hour before his meeting with Tania in the little cafe in the Opera Quarter.

According to their plan, she was to feign sickness that afternoon and remain in the hotel while the rest of the company went to the opera house. Nat was sure she would be lightly guarded if at all since all the security would be needed at the ballet. After the security contingent left she was to slip out of the hotel, taking nothing more than her handbag, and go to the cafe he had reconnoitered earlier.

At 8 P.M. he would meet her there and see her to safety. He would then enter the opera house by means of the obsolete underground passages that honey-combed the ground underneath it.

If Niki had primed his capsules properly, they would explode at 8:30; using the confusion following Pugachev's death as cover, Niki would make his way to the sub-basement, where Nat would be waiting to lead him out of the building.

Now, as he walked among the darkened pathways in the garden, Nat mentally ticked off all the things that could go wrong. They might force Tania to go to the performance; they might leave a guard; Niki might not have primed the capsules correctly, or at the proper time; Niki might have forgotten how to reach the sub-basement, or he might have been so afraid of forgetting that he took the map Nat had given with him to the ballet and it had been discovered; there might—Oh, look, there's no use in dwelling on those things, Nat told himself. He'd done the best job he could, and now—well, all that really mattered was seeing Tania again.

Before Tania, he'd carried out his missions with the emotionless calm of a chess player with the only object to win the game, afraid not of dying, but only of losing. But she had touched him, touched him in boarded-up places in his heart where only Colleen's ghost had lived. And now he was afraid of dying. He wanted to see Tania again, to touch her, to see his reflection in her eyes, to hold her always.

Nat began to walk around the pool. Squinting in the dim light, he saw no one near the Tiber statue. What could be keeping the man? There had been plenty of time to arrive from the embassy. Nat climbed the short flight of stairs to the Terrasse by the Jeu de Paume gallery which overlooked the meeting point, and sat down on a bench to wait. Seven-thirty passed, and 7:40. Nat began to worry about making his rendezvous with Tania on time. He knew she'd wait. But he also knew that the longer she sat in that cafe, the greater the chance that some errant KGB agent going for coffee, or some balletomane with a mind for trivia, would recognize her. He had to get to her soon.

Finally, at 7:47, two men walked through the gate from the Place de la Concorde and made their way toward the statue, where they stopped and appeared to be deep in conversation. Nat recognized them as Ray Merrill and Marvin Tavistock, the same two who had given Rinehart's message to him earlier in the week.

Wearily, Nat stood up, his joints aching from fatigue. He hadn't slept in over thirty-six hours, and it was beginning to take its toll on him. Just to be on the safe side, he stopped and took his Ingram out of the briefcase and stuffed it into an inside coat pocket. Then he continued down the stairs.

At the crunching of his shoes on the gravel walk below, the two men interrupted their desultory conversation and turned to face him.

The fabric of Nat's coat bulged and sagged under the weight of the Ingram. Nat opened his mouth to greet the men, but they stared at him without recognition, apparently fooled by his disguise. The tall man's hand moved warily toward an inside coat pocket.

Quickly Nat spoke. "It's all right, guys. It's me. Worthington." He smiled, drawing closer.

The tall man looked closely at Nat, keeping his hand inside his coat. A look of recognition spread across his face, but he failed to return Nat's smile. Instead, he pulled his gun out of his coat and leveled it at Nat's head.

"You had to do it, didn't you?" he said.

Nat stared cross-eyed at the barrel Marvin Tavistock held steadily six inches from his face. "Do what?" he managed.

"You know, you cocksucker." Tavistock stepped forward. "You killed Everett Lowell."

Ice water shot through Nat's insides, and Lowell's dying words came flying back at him.

They'll blame my murder on you. Nat's stomach dropped into an abyss.

"No," Nat said. "It's not what you think."

"You fucking shitbird, don't try to deny it, you've always wanted to get him. Haven't you?" Tavistock yelled.

"Cool it, Marv," Merrill said in an undertone, looking nervously around. "Somebody might hear."

Ignoring his partner, Tavistock raised the handgun like a club toward Nat. As he did, Merrill reached for his revolver.

Nat knew the only chance he'd get was now. He stepped to the right, and armed the heel of his left hand into the tall man's jaw, stretching up on his tiptoes to give the blow all the force he could. Tavistock's front teeth flew out between his lips in a shower of white fragments as his lower jawbone rushed to meet the upper, leaving his throat exposed. Nat brought the edge of his right hand around and slammed it into Tavistock's Adam's apple.

Tavistock thudded to the pavement, and Nat wheeled around the edge of the statue. He'd die, Nat knew, asphyxiated, his windpipe obstructed by his crushed throat. As Nat dived behind the corner of the statue, Merrill loosed a shot from his revolver that added a contour the original sculptor had never intended. The report of the pistol shot echoed off the museum at either corner of the gardens.

Motionless in the shadows, Nat crouched, waiting for Merrill to move. He heard footsteps, slow, cautious, gritting against the gravel. A faint black-on-black shadow preceded Merrill's body. Nat pulled the Ingram from his coat and flicked the selector into full automatic.

The shadow crept slowly longer. Nat felt the tickle

of a drop of perspiration as it started an unsteady path down his forehead and soaked into his right eyebrow. He resisted the urge to wipe it away. The Ingram began to weigh heavily in his arm. His shoulder muscles ached and began to tremble.

Nat steeled his mind against the pain in his arm. After about four thousand years, Merrill's body floated into view, fluidly, silently. A good killer, Nat thought; but not good enough, he decided as he squeezed the trigger on the Ingram. The roar of slugs screaming at two thousand rounds per minute splattered through Merrill's body, lifted him up from his crouch, and dropped his lifeless form on the fine, round, hard-packed gravel at the base of the Tiber in the Antique Manner. Nat ran.

"She's there with you?"

"Yes, Comrade Kokh."

Holding the ornate phone in his good hand, el-Nouty leaned his elbow on the desk in the plush and tastefully done hotel suite overlooking the Place Vendôme. "Markov assisted me, as you told him to."

"Yes . . ." Kokh said absently. "Now you must get out of Paris, el-Nouty, as soon as possible. We've smoothed things over with the Sûreté, but they will begin to ask questions if you remain there much longer. Despite what many think, our power beyond our borders is not unlimited."

"Of course, I—"

"And the girl," Kokh interrupted. "She *is* all right, isn't she?"

"Fine—physically, that is. But she was very upset, very emotional. I had to give her a sedative to calm her down. She is asleep now in the other bedroom."

"I see. Well, just make sure no harm comes to her until you have him."

"Yes, Comrade Kokh." El-Nouty was exasperated. "I *know* that."

269

"Ah, I'm going over worn territory with you," Kokh said calmly. "Of course you have a right to be upset with me; after all, it was we who trained you and we know you are one of the most competent agents alive." There was an unnerving emphasis on the word "alive," but el-Nouty dismissed it quickly.

"Where will you go from here?" Kokh asked. "Not that it really matters. Now that you have the girl, I imagine with his resources he'd follow you anywhere in the world."

"I believe London, Comrade Kokh."

"London? Umm, yes, London," Kokh mused. "I can see distinct advantages to that. Familiar territory for you, not as familiar to the American. But you realize, of course, that once we help you exit from France, my branch will not assist you further . . . not until you have fulfilled the contract?"

"I don't believe I will *require* any assistance, comrade, thank you. And yes, I understand the terms of the contract."

"Well, then," Kokh said. "Good luck and happy hunting. I look forward to receiving the documents." They rang off.

El-Nouty stood up and walked to the open door of one of the bedrooms and peered in on the slumbering form of Tania Valente. It had all been so easy. If the rest was to be this simple, Nat Worthington was a dead man.

But not everything added up. El-Nouty went to the refrigerator in the kitchen and, pulling out a bottle of Russian vodka from the freezer compartment, poured himself a short measure. The murder of Lowell, there, the facts rang sour, he thought, settling into a comfortable armchair and sipping at the vodka. Popov had told him that Worthington had killed Lowell. But the evidence disputed that. There hadn't been enough blood in the hotel room to indicate that Lowell had been stabbed there. It had obviously happened some-

270

Chapter Eighteen

IIIIIIIIIIIIIIIIIIIIIIIIIIIIIIIIIIIIIIIIIIIIIIIIIIIIIIIIIIIIIIIIIIIIIIIIIIIIIIIII

Sprinting blindly, Nat shoved his way past pedestrians in the Place Vendôme and up the Rue de la Paix. At the Place de l'Opéra, crowds of limousines and taxis were delivering late arrivals to the front steps of the massive columned and arched structure, lit now by the intense beams of decorative spotlights.

Nat paused to let his ragged breath catch up with his legs. Tired, he was so tired. Perspiration ran down his back and covered his face. He knew he must look odd, dressed as he was in a fine suit, carrying a briefcase far beyond office hours and perspiring like a racehorse. He stepped into the shadow of a shop doorway where he wouldn't stand out.

Several minutes later, Nat left the shadows and walked calmly toward the small café and his reunion with Tania. There was no longer any question of what he had to do. Rinehart wanted him killed, and the only choice he had was to run away with Tania.

As he neared the café, Nat checked for a tail. He saw none, but his ears picked up the urgent wails of sirens coming from the direction of the Jardin des

273

Tuileries. They'd soon find the bodies of Rinehart's men. No matter, Nat thought. It no longer matters. He took a deep breath and walked into the café.

Waiters and busboys cleared a mass of cluttered but mostly empty tables among which a half dozen people remained. Tania was nowhere to be seen. Was there an upstairs room, or perhaps an annex used for overflow crowds on ballet nights like this? Anxiety gripped his chest when the maitre d' burst out of the swinging doors and strode toward him.

"You wish a table, *monsieur?*" he asked.

"No . . . I mean, yes," Nat replied. "I'm supposed to meet someone here for dinner."

"Did you have a reservation?"

"No, but we were supposed to meet at 8 P.M." Nat and the maitre d' checked their watches simultaneously: it was 8:17.

"Ah," said the maitre d' suddenly. "You must be the man . . ." He took a hard look at Nat. "But I expected—"

Anger and fear rose in Nat's throat. "You expected?"

"Yes, I expected a man with brown hair."

Nat almost laughed. Of course, Tania must have left a message with the maitre d'. Nat smiled. "You see, I'm an actor and," he ran his hands through the blond hair, "and we often have to . . ."

The man smiled broadly, but said no more. Instead he stood there, waiting expectantly.

After a few minutes, Nat realized the man was waiting for a tip. Shit, Nat thought, of course, nobody does things to be nice. He fished around in his pocket and pulled out a five franc note and passed it to the man.

"*Merci,*" said the man, pocketing the bill, and walking to his podium. "Madame instructed me to give you this," he said, as he pulled an envelope out of a drawer. "She left about ten minutes ago with a tall dark gentleman."

274

"A tall, dark man?" Nat repeated dumbly.

"Yes, *monsieur.*"

"Mediterranean in appearance?"

"Oui."

"Did he have a . . . a false hand?"

"Qui."

"Did he come in alone?"

"Oui, monsieur. . . . Monsieur?"

Nat's shoulders slumped and he looked down at his shoes. The envelope the maitre d' had given him slipped unnoticed from his hand.

The maitre d' bent over and retrieved the envelope. Nat made no move to take it.

Why? he asked himself. Isn't it enough I've spent all my life without someone to love? Isn't it enough I've nearly died defending my country? Isn't it enough that that country wants to kill me now in reward for my loyalty? Isn't it enough, God?

At that, a searing rush of anger warmed his cheeks and cleared his head. He saw the maitre d' standing awkwardly in front of him, his hand outstretched. "Thank you," Nat said as he accepted the envelope and walked out the door.

After he had turned the corner, Nat stopped in a doorway and angrily ripped open the envelope.

"I have Tania Valente," the typewritten note began. "She is quite safe and will remain so as long as you co-operate with my instructions. Beginning tomorrow, an advertisement will apear in the London *Daily Express* in the miscellaneous section of the classified advertise-ments." Nat read the text of the ad, his anger growing by the second. "Call the telephone number which will appear in the ad for further information," the note continued. "If within two weeks I do not have the documents now in your possession, or if you attempt in any way to interfere with my plans, I will kill Tania Valente, painfully and slowly."

Hands trembling, Nat shoved the note inside his

jacket. London. He'd get there somehow; he'd rescue Tania somehow. But for now, he told himself as he charged down the street toward the opera house, he somehow had to stop an assassination. He paused momentarily in a darkened office doorway to affix the huge tubular silencer to the Ingram. He must be silent; he had only the element of surprise on his side and he wanted to keep it as long as possible.

Systematically he emptied his briefcase, cramming its contents into every pocket of his suit, inside and outside. He had everything: the documents, passport, money, extra clips of ammunition for the Ingram, a small flashlight, and sundry other articles of his violent trade, including a piano wire garrotte and hacksaw wire.

Pockets bulging like a tramp, Nat walked in the shadows as far as he could, crossed the street to the opera house, and climbed the front steps. At the top, a Russian agent stepped out from the shadow of an archway. Nat shot him with a three-second burst and the man slumped silently to the pavement.

Nat quickly pushed his way through the front entrance into the ornate lobby. From behind the closed doors, orchestra music drifted into the room in muffled tones. Nat scanned the room. Four bored ushers chatted by the foot of the stairs, and two security guards lounged against the wall near each entrance to the orchestra-section seats. Most of Pugachev's other goons would be upstairs.

As he stood in the foyer, the ushers stopped talking and stared at him. Nat shot one guard and ran swiftly toward the other one.

"Don't move your hand!" Nat shouted in Russian, "and be quiet." The ushers looked first at the guard, then at Nat, then at the other guard; they were stunned and unable to move.

"Pugachev is in grave danger," Nat told the guard, who remained standing. "Assassins have placed nerve-

276

gas capsules in his clothing," Nat yelled at him, when the man failed to respond. "Pugachev's going to die if he doesn't get out of his suit before 8:30—20:30 hours—you got that?" The guard nodded.

"Now upstairs!"

The man again looked uncomprehending.

"Upstairs. I want you to go upstairs and warn Pugachev of the danger. You can be a hero, save his life. . . . Go, go!" Nat pointed up the stairs and the man went, hesitantly at first as if he expected Nat to shoot him once his back was turned, and then at a dead run.

There were only seven minutes left before the nerve gas was supposed to detonate. Would the guard be able to alert Pugachev in time? Nat wondered what else he could do. He wanted to run out of the lobby, but he couldn't leave Niki. He had a responsibility.

Suddenly something burned the top of his ear. Nat heard a pistol shot and slammed himself against the wall. Sticky warmth was trickling down the side of his head. He clicked the Ingram to full automatic as footfalls muffled by the carpeting grew louder. Nat leaned around the corner and emptied the ammo clip. An unseen man groaned in pain.

Nat heard more footsteps as he fumbled around in his coat for another ammunition clip. The steps grew louder. The clip wouldn't eject. Oh, holy fucking shit Nat thought. He turned the Ingram upside down and tugged at the long straight clip. It wouldn't budge.

Bending over he stuck the gun body between his knees and tugged, but it was futile. While he was doubled over, a hail of slugs beat out a tattoo of mushrooming spatter marks on the wall, turning the area only moments before occupied by his chest into a plaster replica of the moon's craters. Nat lunged from his squatting position as the craters tracked down toward him.

Desperately, he jerked open the heavy door to the

277

theater chamber and scrambled inside it on his hands and knees, while another shower of slugs rattled against the other side of the door.

At the same time, the orchestra dwindled off in mid-note, and a tumble of startled conversation swept over the audience. Onstage, Niki Valente unceremoniously dropped a hapless ballerina from a half-completed lift and ran screaming to the wings with the rest of the company.

Still immersed in darkness, Nat continued to struggle with the Ingram's jammed clip. He had to be gone when the lights came on, but without a weapon he'd never leave the opera house alive. A wedge of bright light knifed through the dark aisle: his assailants were pulling open the door.

Finally, the clip scraped out of the Ingram, and Nat slammed a fresh one home. Covering himself with fire from the Ingram, he dashed down the aisle.

"Pugachev is in danger!" he yelled in Russian and again in French. "Nerve gas, in his clothes, nerve gas!" Then his words were drowned in a tsunami of screams and shouts from the audience as it panicked.

Yells of pain shot out from every direction as people reverted to a primitive survival instinct and punched, gouged, and crushed each other to escape. Nat elbowed and shoved his way toward the side exit nearest the stage, staying low on his feet and submarining his way through the masses at waist level. The house lights came on and a new cry, an animal growl of fear and surprise, welled up from the crowd.

A shot rang out. A gray-haired man in a tuxedo standing next to Nat shrieked and collapsed, a red bleeding ragged rip in his neck showering blood on everyone near him. Someone in the balconies must have spotted Nat.

New shots rang out from the balcony as Nat neared the exit door, but the slugs came from handguns, too

278

inaccurate at that long range to score anything but an accidental hit.

Nat fired the Ingram in response. This time he changed clips easily and emptied the new clip into the balconies too. Nat turned to leave when a sub-human screech pierced the pandemonium and froze the crowd.

First one of Pugachev's guards, then the general himself stood up and danced a macabre jig, tearing at their clothes and eyes, wailing in tones that a human being should not have been capable of uttering. Patrons and security guards alike turned to watch the spectacle.

Nat stared with them, open-mouthed in wonder. The nerve gas, he knew, killed silently, calmly, painlessly. What could this be? What Nat didn't see was a tall one-handed dark-skinned man, his well-manicured index finger pressing on a small electronic device hidden in a package of cigarettes. Nat did see Pugachev stagger to the rail of his box and lean on it for balance. The Russian tottered unsteadily for a few seconds and then tumbled end over end, ass over head, out of the box and plunged into the crowd below.

A new guttural scream rose from the audience, and the mass surged forth once again. Nat scampered through the exit door. The calm silence of the corridor came as a shock after the chaos inside. Nat fed another ammunition clip into the Ingram.

After saying a silent prayer that Niki would have the good sense to slip away and meet him at their rendezvous point, he broke into a dead run, heading around behind the massive stage.

He turned right, slipped through the door leading to the far reaches of the backstage area, and then descended the staircase that led down. Down past the massive winches and pulleys and machinery that levitated and dropped gargantuan scenery and sets, down past the banks of rectifiers and huge rheostats and circuit breakers that controlled the lighting, down past the sub-basements full of enough little-used props and scenery and costumes and odds and ends to stock a fair-sized museum lay, and down finally to the very, very bottom level, a huge empty cavern, once an underground reservoir used to store water in the days when fire was the worst enemy of the theater.

Stopping in the gloom of dusty, grimy fifteen-watt light bulbs, Nat paused to catch his breath. He breathed deeply but quietly through his mouth, listening for sounds of others behind him. Footsteps sounded far above, but he figured them for stage hands and tech people wandering about, confused by the chaos and probably trying to find their union steward to see if they were getting paid for all this.

It took only a couple of minutes for Nat's breath to calm, and his heartbeat to return to the normal frightened gymnastics of a hunted man. He pushed open the ancient wooden door and its rusted, arthritic hinges complained. A shuffling could be heard in the darkness, the movements of a frightened person.

"Niki?" Nat called softly.

"Over here," answered a shaky voice from the gloom. Nat walked into the room, shut the door quickly, and turned his flashlight on and shone it on his face momentarily.

"Niki, it's me. Nat Worthington."

"Over here," Niki called again, his voice firmer this time. Nat sent the light in Niki's direction and swallowed hard. The light caught a swarm of cockroaches the size of Brazil nuts, tens of thousands of them massed like starlings in a corner. Nat quickly searched and found Niki. He was moving toward him when a third voice pierced the dark.

"Hold it right there!" Instantly, Nat flicked off the light and dropped to the floor. He felt something scurry away from under his face as a shot rang out from the direction of the voice.

"It's Markov!" Niki shouted. "He followed me. I

couldn't warn you!" Two more shots exploded from Markov's gun, aimed at Niki's position. Then another slug splattered its lead against the stone floor near Nat's foot and fragmented into a hundred pieces. Nat felt one of them thud against the bottom of his shoe, but its energy was too spent to do any harm. Nat rolled nevertheless and watched for the muzzle flash of Markov's gun. Markov? Markov, of course. KGB head of security for the Kirov company. When all hell broke loose, he must have been watching the company and spotted Niki when he tried to slip away. Another shot rang out and Nat raised the Ingram to return the fire at the flash of light from Markov's gun. Nat loosed a three-shot volley, unafraid of betraying his position; the huge silencer suppressed the muzzle flash as effectively as it did sound.

Nat heard the three shots scatter harmlessly on the stone walls. He flicked the selector to full auto and sprayed the area the flash had come from, and as he did, heard first one slug, then another slap home. Nat held his breath and froze motionless on the floor. Then the metallic clank of Markov's gun hitting the floor echoed reassuringly through the chamber, then a loud scraping sound grew faster and then plopped still.

Markov had hit the floor.

Wounded men, Nat knew from having once been one, are frequently capable of extraordinary acts even when the wounds are mortal. They can last minutes or—he remembered Lowell—even hours, and in that time they can make their killer's work all for naught. Nat waited. Five minutes. The bubbly breathing from Markov's direction told Nat he'd been wounded in his lung; he might last for hours. Impatient, and fearful that Markov had told someone where he was going, Nat decided to move. He stood up. Markov made no response to the noise. What if Markov had a spare weapon—he probably did—and had loudly dropped the first one as a ruse?

Nat took a step, and then another. The grime and soil of a hundred years gritted loudly under his shoes. Still Markov made no detectable response. Nat moved another step and jumped, startled, as he bumped into a solid, damp cold object. Again, unseen things moved from his touch. Nat felt the outlines of a pillar and tried as best he could to put it between him and the last sounds Markov had made, then he turned on the light. He shivered as roaches and centipedes and other unidentifiable hard-shelled and multi-legged creatures scrambled away from the light. Nat leaned around the pillar and pointed the light toward Markov. The KGB officer sat on the floor, his back propped against a pillar, and his legs splayed out in front of him, feet sticking straight up. He looked like a toddler at rest.

A massive automatic pistol lay in the dirt near his right arm. The man wasn't moving. Nat checked to see the Ingram was on full auto and pointed it at Markov, finger on the trigger as he walked over to him. Markov's head was slumped on his chest, but Nat couldn't tell where he'd been hit. As he drew near and looked down at the man, Nat saw the widening dark wet of blood against the black fabric of Markov's suit, and the telltale bloody red froth from a lung wound. Nat leaned close and saw two wounds. Markov was still alive but unconscious. Nat searched his body, found no other weapon and then called once again for Niki.

"Niki, are you all right?"

"Yes, yes," the grateful voice said.

"Well, then follow my flashlight and come here."

Nat heard shuffling from behind him, and turned to see Niki, still dressed in full costume, walking out of the shadows and into the bright cone of light cast by the flashlight.

"What has been going on?" Niki asked. "This was not to be this way. Has something gone wrong?"

"Something," Nat said, and saw Niki stiffen.

"What?" Niki asked. "What's gone wrong?"

"I'll tell you when we get out of here," Nat said, casting the flashlight about for the manhole cover leading from the underground reservoir to the Paris sewer system.

"No, you'll have to tell me now." Niki's voice was petulant, frightened, but resolved. "After all, I can always return to the company. Markov's dead, he'll not be around to dispute my absence; I can slip back in, you know."

Nat was exasperated. "Look, Niki, your job's done now, Pugachev's dead. I don't need you any more, goddamnit, and if you don't shut up and come with me, the only alternative you've got is returning to the Kirov and *hoping* no one noticed you gone and *hoping* no one remembers how close you were to Pugachev, and—"

"But why did you break in like that?" Niki asked, confused. "You were supposed—"

"Niki!" Nat interrupted sharply. "Let's go."

Voices came through the mists like echoes. Markov willed his body to remain still; as the mists cleared, an excruciating pain stabbed him above his left breast and drew colored stars of the universe each time he breathed. Shot. He'd been shot. Now he remembered. The American, the American Popov was searching for. And Niki Valente . . . now it came back to him as the fog cleared and the voices from across the chamber came to him more clearly.

"Niki, *Niki!*" The American's voice betrayed his frustration. "Come *on* . . . now or I'm going to leave you here."

"I want to know what went wrong or I'm not going."

When the shooting started, Markov had rushed with his men to herd the dancers out of danger. After all, they were his first charge; let Pugachev and his GRU

283

thugs take care of the rest. When they'd gotten them all out, Markov saw Niki slip away and decided to follow.

Markov had been puzzled when Niki eschewed all the obvious exits and headed down. After descending into the storage levels, Markov remembered the stories of the hidden passages beneath Paris, recalled dimly the time he'd been allowed to read that decadent book *Les Misérables* by Hugo, with Jean Valjean's escape from the soldiers through the sewers. Was Niki going to try this?

When he caught him, Niki had been hysterical, too frightened even to tell Markov exactly what was supposed to happen. He made no sense. No matter, Markov had decided, Niki had told him that someone was to meet him.

So it was the American, Markov thought now. He opened his eyes a crack, peering through slits at the two huddled figures by the flashlight. He heard the American talking to Niki as he lifted a gray piece of plywood from the floor. So that's it! He thought proudly, the American was going to help Niki defect. Slowly Markov felt about for his automatic. He might even survive, he thought, remembering his wounds from the Second World War. He stifled a cough.

Markov saw Niki and the American standing, arguing.

Oh, God, it hurt to lean over, Markov thought as he quietly swept the floor about him with his hand. Finally, a fingertip felt the cold security of the automatic's barrel. He stretched. But his head dimmed suddenly as he leaned over.

Markov managed to straighten up, the automatic dangling from his index and middle fingers by the trigger guard. So heavy, he thought, so very heavy. He was hurt worse than he'd imagined.

The automatic was leaden, but the familiar shape gave Markov strength as he raised the pistol and aimed at the two figures in the light. Which one? Kill Niki, and the American would escape, or maybe even come over and finish off the job. Markov lowered the pistol and thought for a moment. But kill the American, Markov figured, and—if he lived—he'd return to Moscow a hero who killed the American agent and brought back the traitor Valente. Yes, he thought, raising his arm again, it would be the American.

His arm was more unsteady than it had been even a few seconds before. He lined up the sights on the middle of the American's broad shoulders, silhouetted in the stark light, and then lowered the muzzle about eight inches. The .45 slug should pass through the American's spinal cord and rip his heart out. He was about to squeeze on the trigger when a tremor of pain shook him; he relaxed his grip until the pain passed.

Nat pulled the plywood off the manhole and tossed it aside. Antique dust fluttered. "All right, Niki, I'm going now," Markov heard Nat say. "I'm not going to argue any more."

Nat's ultimatum galvanized Markov into action, the fear of losing his quarry more compelling than his pain. In what he somehow knew would be his final mortal act, the Russian raised his unsteady arm, sighted as before, and squeezed the trigger.

The roar of the automatic in the cryptlike sub-basement deafened Nat and surprised him more than the ripping tug of the slug as it lacerated the bulging inside pocket of his coat. Niki exhaled audibly as if struck in the solar plexus, and then staggered back against the wall.

Then Nat saw Niki's face change from surprise to outrage, and back to surprise. A spreading red blotch appeared on Niki's leotard, centered symmetrically on his breast. While Nat stared in horror, Niki Valente slid to the floor and died.

Whirling, Nat dropped his light. He heard Markov's automatic clank against the floor. In the dim illumination cast by the fallen flashlight, Nat took careful aim from behind a pillar. He continued to empty the rest of the Ingram's clip into Markov's head until he was sure the man was dead.

The assassination he had sought to foil had taken place; the dancer he'd come to rescue lay dead at his feet, and the woman he loved was the hands of his enemy. Numb with failure, Nat climbed down the rungs set in the manhole.

Chapter Nineteen

||||||||||||||||||||||||||||||||||||||||||||||||||||||||||||||||||||||||||||||||||||

The ancient wood-grated escalator clanked and thumped loyally upward—working, but barely, a reflection of the London above the underground. Blankly, Nat read the advertisements (ad-*vert*-isements, they said here) adorning the walls: "The Shape of Toast to Come," "Abortion Advice," "Wren Bureau." He closed his eyes against the shabby squalor of the escalator shaft and imagined visiting the Wren Bureau to hire a bird.

At the top, he surrendered his ticket along with the rush of afternoon commuters at the exit gate, and then walked out into the unseasonably cool weather of London's East End.

The diesel-and-fetid-water scent common to all docks and wharves wafted by, clearing from his head some of the cobwebs that still remained despite a day and a half of straight sleep. Stopping to purchase a copy of the *Evening Express*, he continued on the trail of the evening dock smell.

SPIKE LOOKS SET FOR ROYAL WIN, said the appropriately huge tabloid headline above the picture of a grinning greyhound. They hadn't found Nat yet. He'd be a big front-page story when they did. He pretended to read the newspaper as he walked slowly along the sidewalk, furtively glancing about from underneath his downturned brow. It was unlikely that anyone would have followed him, but now . . . now nothing was impossible. Nothing.

As he trudged along, the pedestrian traffic gradually reversed itself until he was a lone figure pacing against the tide of dockworkers going home. Finally, he stopped at the door of a pub with an "IND Cooper" sign outside and milled about with a dozen or so other evening drinkers waiting for opening time. The accents that surrounded him were a melange of cockney and East End, blended with heavy foreign accents—mostly Greek and Corsican, he figured.

Two days, Nat thought. It seemed more like a year. The image of Niki's body etched into the stark cone of flashlight illumination continued to play through his mind.

Two days ago . . . yes, he had been in Paris two days ago. He had had no trouble finding his way out of the sewers. All he did was walk downhill and when confronted with a decision, he always followed the water— or whatever else ran in the center part of the tunnels, until he reached the main trunk sewers, which had the names of the streets below which they ran clearly marked. After three hours of wandering, he'd located a mob of vagrants camping near a steam line and bribed them to lead him out.

The door to the pub clicked and then swung open. Nat followed the crowd, which had doubled in size within the two minutes he'd been standing there, into the dimly lit pub. He ordered a pint of Bass and settled himself at the elbow of the bar where he could observe the patrons without being too prominent himself.

Taking a thirsty draught off the top, Nat leaned on

the bar and continued to review his odyssey. In Paris he had stolen a car and driven it to a small resort town on the English Channel near Calais. There he'd appropriated a 30-foot sloop, sailed across, and beached the boat in England. No customs, no police, and no questions. He'd slept in a seedy transient hotel near Earl's Court for a day and a half.

Nat drained his glass and motioned the bartender for a refill, and then he ran through things one more time:

—He had documents for a powerful blue-green laser capable of making our submarines easy prey for the Soviets.

—The National Security Adviser of the United States had tried to give those documents to the Russians.

—The National Security Adviser had sent him on a mission to kill a Russian politician, Pugachev, because an opposing Soviet faction in the politburo—the KGB —wanted him out of the way.

—Rinehart wanted him killed.

—All that stood between the Russians and an invasion of the Persian Gulf from their bases in Afghanistan was a suitable "invitation" from a suitable country. And that last obstacle was in the process of being hurdled: somewhere in London, somewhere out there with the woman he loved, was a Libyan assassin who had been hired to kill the Iraqi president so the Russian KGB would have their invitation.

Nat ordered another pint and checked his watch. A little after six; he had another half an hour to kill. Waiting, always waiting. He wished that even one of those thick-headed spy novel writers would write about how much of an agent's work consists of tedious hurry-up-and-wait, dig through the sand, find one particular grain. But, he supposed, that would never sell books. No one wanted to read about a man waiting.

Who else was in on it? Nat morosely pulled at his new glass of ale as he visualized the faces of the agents

289

he'd worked with. Was that bright kid from Mississippi who'd graduated from Princeton and won a Rhodes scholarship one of them? What about the quiet former political activist from the Berkeley area—was she really a covert KGB agent? Or even . . . he remembered the agents he'd supervised and he replayed every failure he'd had: had they been intentional? Had—oh, damn, it didn't matter anymore. He could never go back and he'd never know the answers. In the final tally, Nat knew he'd just try to survive. Maybe he'd never topple Rinehart, and maybe the new generation in Cambridge would be speaking Russian as a native language, but he couldn't just quit. No matter how seductive that giving up and letting the waves sweep over his head seemed, he knew he wouldn't give up.

Dumb, he thought, as he got up and made his way out of the jammed and smoky pub. Really dumb, Worthington.

They're never going to let me out. I've heard too much, they're talking too freely around me like it doesn't matter what I hear. Sounds of traffic from other side of building. I wonder where I am. London. I know that, but where? Think I'll sit in that chair by the window, at least I can see a patch of blue sky if I press my cheek against the window pane and look up. Lousy view, the back of some other building across the alleyway. Funny how they paint the drainpipes such funny colors. Somehow they ought to be black and rusty, not bright blue. Funny English.

Or perhaps they're not English. Certainly the people in this house aren't. They're all Libyan, that's what that ass el-Nouty told me. And look down there: I'm only two stories off the ground. I can tell by looking at the building across the alley. If only there were no bars on the window. If only the door wasn't locked and if only the house weren't filled with scruffy dark skinned men carrying guns. If only—No! I won't cry. That won't help Nat. That won't help either of us. I've *got* to do something. They're using me as bait to get Nat and I know they'll never let me go.

But why don't they get rid of me now? Of course, Nat will demand some proof I'm still alive. But what? And what can I do about it? Funny room, I wish it had something in it, something I could use to escape. They want me safe to trap Nat. I won't let them. I can always kill myself, then they wouldn't be able to use me. I could . . . smash the window pane and use the glass to cut my wrists. But I've heard that doesn't really work, and besides that huge man outside the door would be in here in a second before I could use the glass. But I could cut him good, yes I could . . . but what good would it do? The rest of them would just come in and tie me up and I would be even more trapped than I am now.

No . . . no, I shouldn't do that. But what have I got left? Does it matter? I don't even know where Nat is, and from listening to them talk they don't either. But they have their plan. If I could just overhear more of it, then I might be able to help Nat, warn him about el-Nouty. El-Nouty: what an odd man; bizarre with that hook. He thinks he's a real lady killer. The way he looks at me makes my skin crawl. And the way he tried to touch me on the airplane on the way over from Paris. The airplane. It was Soviet and the pilot spoke Russian. She didn't understand. Why were Russians helping this Arab? Why did they let her go with him rather than arresting her and turning her over to the KGB?

Oh God! I don't understand any of it! And Sarah. Who is Sarah? Must be someone special to el-Nouty, but I don't think he loves her. I don't think he's capable of loving anyone but himself. And why was he going to kill another Arab . . . the president of Iraq? I thought all the Arabs stuck together. And why did he talk as if the Americans were paying him to do it? What were Americans doing with Arabs and Russians and if the

Americans were involved why did they—everybody want to kill Nat?

The sky is so beautiful. I wish I could be outside seeing all the pink and purple and gold. Walking in that big park like Niki and I did two years ago when we performed in Covent Garden. That big park with the palace at the end. The sunsets then had been so warm and comfortable.

I love London. I wish I could see it. But Nat's out there somewhere. I want him. When did I start to love him? New York? Yes, then. When he was so kind and courteous, he treated me like I was really somebody, not just another woman, not like Niki did—as a convenient spittoon for his sperm.

I don't miss Niki. Should I be sad he's dead? I'm not. I'm glad to be free from him. The newspaper, perhaps I ought to read it again, maybe I could get some idea what Nat is planning. No. I've read that over and over and besides it's yesterday's paper. All so mysterious. Nat blamed for Niki's death. But I *know* Nat wouldn't kill Niki . . . not at least without a good reason. And Pugachev. At least they hadn't blamed Nat for that one, though I'm sure they'll try very hard. Mysterious, his death. Three others in that box dead too. What could have killed them? Maybe I'll ask el-Nouty. El-Nouty, el-Nouty, el-Nouty. Always it came down to el-Nouty. El-Nouty told me to do this, el-Nouty tells the men in the house to do that, el-Nouty commands even the Russians who got me here. I didn't realize how easy it was to get out of a country when you had power like they do. El-Nouty is the key. Somehow I've got to see him, talk to him. The man outside won't bring him. The last time I asked I think he wanted to hit me. El-Nouty comes when he feels like it but never when he's summoned. Perhaps if I unbutton my blouse a little and smile. That's really disgusting. The man outside the door is such a pig. I can smell him even when the door is closed. At least el-Nouty doesn't smell. The others kid him about it; they say he smells like a whore. A pimp. That's what he is, a pimp. But he's my key. Maybe if I . . . maybe then he'd let me out of this room. Not a bad room, plain but comfortable. I have my own bathroom and WC and they bring me my meals and set them on the table. It's clean, comfortable. Lonely. I could play dumb. El-Nouty probably thinks women have no brains anyway. Maybe I could . . . But I don't want him touching me. I'd rather die . . . or would I? Would I do that if it meant helping Nat? What would he say if I succeeded and found out that I. . . . There's no reason in going on that way, I'm not going to get out of here . . . or am I?

"Hello out there," Tania spoke to the door as she dropped her bra on the floor and replaced her thin silk blouse. "Hello?" She tapped daintily on the wood and finished buttoning the front, leaving the top three buttons loose. "Please? I want to talk to you. Hello?" She rapped again, louder. She swallowed hard and took a deep breath as she heard the bolt slide back and watched the door begin to open.

The street vanished into blackness beyond the faded yellow penumbras of streetlights. The light was as fatigued as the buildings it tried to illuminate. The dock area was a slum. No, Nat decided, it was worse than that. Most of the shipping had disappeared and the ghosts of warehouses and boarded-up businesses gave the section the air of the cemetery.

Cautiously looking about him, constantly scanning the shadows for an unpleasant surprise, Nat trod the worn pavement with its abstract patterns of patches and crackles, past dark sooty buildings decorated with dirt caked on dirt. It was 6:27 and he knew he had to time things or else the door would never open to him. He walked another two minutes and lingered at the entrance to a dead-end alley. He shivered, then wondered if the chill came from the wind, or from deeper inside himself.

The sweep second hand glided round toward twelve as he leaned across the entrance of the alley and washed its boundaries with the light from his flashlight. He saw a line of windows, protected by pitted and rusted iron bars, the glass panes either broken or painted over from inside and the sills sporting two centuries of dust over dust. Piles of rubbish leaned chaotically against the walls, an overturned oil drum vomited a fermented chum of rotted food and plastic, paper and the indestructible containers of fast food. A narrow path threaded its way among the various lumps and piles. Blending into the landscape was a lump of a drunk curled around a brown paper sack, his back against the only garbage can still standing upright in the alley.

Nat shined his light against the foot of the alley and fixed the position of a door, so grimy and sooty it faded evenly into the surrounding grit and grime, almost invisible. Nat stepped gingerly over the drunk—he couldn't tell whether the man was dead or passed out—and picked his way toward the door. Shards of broken glass bottles gritted under his boots and glittered like a pauper's diamonds in the light.

Nothing but the odd patter and slither of rats reached his ears. Nat raised his hand to rap on the door jamb when the interior door opened. Nat smiled, then noticed the scowl etched on the face of Colin Graham: ex-MI6, ex-Scotland Yard and from the looks of things, ex-friend of Nat Worthington's.

"You're in some deep shit, old boy," Graham said and then disappeared into the gloom of his office. Apparently this was all the invitation Nat would get. "Close that, willya?" Graham growled as Nat followed him through the door.

Colin must be in his sixties by now, Nat figured. World War II had drawn him into its net as it had the rest of England's young men. But unlike most of the others, Colin accidentally became a hero. He had been a smuggler, so MI9, the escape and evasion people, tapped him to develop underground communication links on the continent to help captured airmen and soldiers escape. After he personally led twenty-five captured officers from a camp in Belgium (he never told MI9 that he'd gone mainly to bring out contraband diamonds) they made him a hero.

"The respectability was stifling," Colin had told Nat during a mission in East Germany in 1978. "As hard as I tried, they still made me out an honest man."

Graham, a wiry man with a hatchet face who looked more like an accountant than a hero or a jewel thief, was hired after the war by Military Intelligence Section Six where he continued until he found himself trying to bribe one of Nat's agents in Amsterdam. The bribe, Nat determined, had nothing to do with his service for MI6, but was for one of Graham's own schemes where he was trying to smuggle Russian diamonds through Amsterdam and sell them on the Israeli diamond exchange. By the time Nat's agent reported this to him, Mossad had targeted Graham to an early retirement, and only Nat's good contacts within the Israeli intelligence agency prevented Graham's death. Nat then turned Graham into a CIA double, reporting to the U.S. what transpired within Her Majesty's government. He retired three years ago and ran a miniconglomerate of shady and outright illegal activities.

Grahm owed Nat his life; that was a big one and Nat was there to collect.

"You're in deep shit," Graham said again when they reached the landfilllike room used for an office.

"I know that," Nat said. "And I didn't need you to tell me that twice."

"I think maybe you do," Graham looked at him balefully. "There's an army out there and they're all looking for you." Nat was silent. "Do you have any idea that the Russians *and* your own CIA are after you? That they've called up every former agent you ever stood in line with or shared a taxi with? This very day, not twelve minutes after you called me this morning, his eminence the CIA chief himself sat right there and told me that if you came here and I didn't tell him, he'd kill me and he'd take three weeks to do it."

"Yeah," Nat said weakly, in reply. "Yeah, I figured that. I—"

"What in hell did you do, Nat? What in ever-loving hell could you have done?"

"It's over, Colin," Nat began shifting uneasily from foot to foot. "You don't want to know."

Colin Graham, middle-class quartermaster to the less-than-savory, stared at him.

"Mind if I sit down?" Nat asked, indicating the chair earlier sat in by the CIA chief in London.

"Yes, I mind," Graham replied softly. "I'm not sitting down either, because I might start listening to you and we might spend some time going over old times and how you saved my life, and I might just be tempted to do things that my better judgment tells me could get me killed."

"Like giving me help?"

Graham read the expression on Nat's face and broke the silence. "Oh, I'm going to pay off that debt, Nat. You see, my telephone isn't working well and I've got to go down to the corner to use the pay phone to call this special number that the CIA bigwig left me and while I'm gone, I guess I forgot to lock the armory— you know where it is—and I figure it'll take me about ten minutes to locate the telephone number and another fifteen minutes to walk down to the box. I'm giving you your life back right now, Nat, because I'm giving you twenty-five minutes to take what you need from back there and vanish. Oh, and I left my keys in the car out back. If it isn't back by midnight, I'll report it stolen."

"Thanks, Colin."

"Don't thank me," Graham said brusquely. "It's a business deal, that's all. My life for yours. I've repaid the principal by giving you time to run. Whatever weapons you find in the warehouse are the interest. No, Nat, don't thank me, because if I ever see you again, then I *will* call the spooks and I won't guarantee you time. *Comprende?*"

Nat nodded, stunned. Would it be like this everywhere he went? Would every person who owed him treat him the same way—or worse? Maybe there was no point in even going through the motions? Then he saw Graham check his watch.

"Time, old friend." Graham gave him one long, last look, then turned and walked out the door.

"All right, woman," el-Nouty said, annoyed, as he pushed open the door. The guard had been tripping over his own tongue when he burst into his study moments before. This time el-Nouty decided to answer the ballerina's summons.

"All right, I'm here. So what do you wa—" As he stepped into the room he caught sight of Tania Valente, her face made up like a courtesan, sultry, inviting, and her unbound breasts pressing against the thin fabric of her blouse. He felt himself begin to stiffen.

"I thought," she smiled coquettishly, "that we might be able to reach some kind of understanding."

Mustafa looked at her realized how much he wanted to do it to her right now. Then alarm bells rang through his quickening desire: she *had* to be trying to seduce him in order to escape . . . didn't she? Or perhaps she'd seen how superior he was to that wimp Worthington. Maybe she had had time to think about her situation, to realize Worthington was a dead end, while he, el-Nouty, carried a promise of a rich and glorious future. And perhaps, he thought, she had an indication of what his body might do for hers.

297

Waving the leering guard outside, el-Nouty closed the door and walked past Tania and sat down on the bed.

"An understanding?" El-Nouty finally said after seating himself. "What sort of understanding, my dear?"

"I've done a lot of thinking in the past few hours," she began. "I . . . I've been very . . . ah, impressed—grateful, really—about how well and, and courteously you've treated me in the hours since we left Paris." She looked carefully into his eyes. "I've come to the conclusion that you are not what I originally thought you were."

"Which was?"

"Well, I . . ." Tania hesitated. "Well, at first, I thought you were a real . . . a real brute. You see, I thought you were like all the KGB people I've met. I've discovered, much to my . . . my delight that you seem to be a man of culture and . . . upbringing. That throws a whole new light on a lot of things."

"A new light?" El-Nouty asked encouragingly. "What sort of new light?"

"This whole defection thing was the American's idea, and I went along with Niki and him because I wanted to leave Russia. I have no great love for America nor for the Americans. What I wanted was to use Worthington to free myself from Russia, and to rid myself of Niki.

"But you . . ." she fixed him with the sexiest stare she could muster, "You are a far different matter." She walked toward him and stood directly in front of him. "In the short time I've been associated with you, I've found you to be a man of intelligence, culture, strength, and . . ." she paused, taking a deep breath, "and, well . . . very . . . physically desirable." She reached down and ran her fingers through el-Nouty's hair.

298

El-Nouty disengaged himself from and stood up. "So what do you want?" he asked suspiciously.

"Nothing."

"Nothing?" Genuine puzzlement spread over his face.

"I want you to decide that for yourself," Tania began. "Certainly I'm comfortable right now. You've provided for me very well. But perhaps later, after . . ." She let the promise slide into insinuation. "Perhaps you'd think it appropriate for me to have a television or a bit more freedom, or even a walk in the park. But for now, I realize you are a brilliant man and are considering whether or not this is my ploy to escape. I want you to be convinced that those are not my intentions at all. I want you to learn to know me—a man like you has a mind for women. I can sense it. I want you to read me like a book and then treat me the way you want."

El-Nouty was silent. He stared lustfully at the creamy white of her breasts showing inside the unbuttoned blouse. The hint of one edge of her nipple sent a quiver to his groin. She would look very nice indeed in bed with Sarah—her white ballerina skin and Sarah's dark Arab skin. He could see them now.

"You've certainly given me much to consider," el-Nouty began as he walked toward her. "If what you say is genuine—and believe me I have enough intelligence to make sure it is—then we may indeed have an understanding that could be . . . ah, mutually beneficial." He stopped before her and drew her to him.

Tania pressed herself against his hard body and for just an instant felt excited by the feel of his muscular body and the hardening movement in his groin. She let him fondle her breasts then, but stopped him as his hands wandered lower.

"Uh . . ." she said pushing away slightly.

"What's wrong?"

"Well . . . uh," she stammered. "It's that time." She

looked at him as he pulled away in disgust. "I'm sorry," she said contritely. "I'm really, really very sorry."

"How long?" el-Nouty demanded gruffly.

"Well, it's passing. I don't think it should be more than a day or so. But we can . . . you know, fool around before then."

"No," el-Nouty said. "You're impure now."

Tania's face sagged.

"But that doesn't mean we can't work something out in the meantime," el-Nouty said suggestively. Her face brightened. "I'll give you some limited freedom to walk around the house. Hassan will follow you, and will let you know what is off limits. You must follow his instructions to the letter. Is that understood?" She nodded her assent.

"Good," el-Nouty said. "Then, in a few days, you can . . . show your gratitude; either that or, if I think for a second you're trying to deceive me, I'll kill you."

"Don't worry . . . please," Tania said earnestly. "I'll be anxious to show you my gratitude. You won't be disappointed."

Oh, Nat! she thought, after el-Nouty had left her alone in the room, Nat, if I ever see you again, will you forgive me? And, as she remembered el-Nouty fondling her breasts, she wondered if she would ever forgive herself.

Chapter Twenty

||||||||||||||||||||||||||||||||||||||||||||||||||||||||||||||||||||||||||||||||

Tuesday dawned electric. Sizzling torrents of sunlight poured through the nearly clean glass panes of Nat's room and puddled in warm pools by his feet. The heat made him sweat, and he woke up. He shook his head, disoriented, and then remembered where he was: a large bed-and-breakfast near the Earl's Court underground station in London.

At a quarter of eight the buzzer in the hallways sounded first call for breakfast, and Nat threw back the covers and headed for the showers before the hot water ran out. They'd spend a long time finding him, Nat told himself as he stood under the steaming water. Colin Graham's car was hidden in the farthest reaches of an underground carpark at Heathrow. They'd have a helluva time tracing him.

After dressing, Nat wolfed down eggs, bacon, and toast and stepped in to the bright warm sunshine of Tuesday and made straight for the bank of pay telephones in the Earl's Court station.

Despite the warm sun, Nat walked in a cloud as the

headlines in Monday's *Daily Express* came back to him. There had been a huge story about the upcoming visit of the president of Iraq, who would arrive Wednesday for talks with the prime minister. And there was the puzzling story about Pugachev's death. Nat was blamed for the Russian's death and for those of Lowell, Markov, and Niki Valente. That much wasn't at all surprising.

What puzzled Nat was three paragraphs describing Pugachev's death: prior to the Russian's spectacular fall from the balcony, people in adjoining booths swore they heard a loud sizzling noise and described an overwhelming odor of frying bacon, as if the Red Army general had actually been cooked.

Nat reached the telephones and dialed the number left in yesterday's *Daily Express*.

"Hello?" a voice answered, and Nat immediately plugged a two-pence piece into the telephone.

"El-Nouty," Nat demanded. The telephone thudded against a table.

"El-Nouty," Nat repeated to a different voice.

"I'm happy to learn you've arrived safely."

"Yeah," Nat replied, "I'll just bet you are. Let's cut through this bullshit. I'm not going to talk and drink sweet coffee for half a day like you people do. First of all, I want to know Tania is all right, or else we don't talk any more. Understand?"

"Very well, Mr. Worthington," el-Nouty sighed. "Though I wonder if you don't perhaps mistake me for some sort of barbarian."

"You're a fucking madman, that's what you are, el-Nouty."

"Perceptions can frequently be wrong. But we are not here to discuss manners. Mrs. Valente is in perfect health. She is comfortable and well fed, and I have no objections to proving that—provided, of course, we can agree on a method of doing so that assures her safety, as well as yours and mine."

302

"I want to see her."

"Good, good." And how do you propose to do that?"

Nat had thought about this all night. "I want you to take her for a walk in Hyde Park, all the way from Speakers' Corner to the Kensington Palace, and back. Do what you want to make sure she doesn't escape, but I want to see her walking under her own power, not drugged, not harassed in any way."

"And you?" El-Nouty's voice was polite, condescending.

"Don't worry about where I'll be. I might be a mile away with a telescope, but I'll see her. And regardless of where I am, I won't have the documents on me. So don't try to tell the authorities all about this; if you do, the deal's off. I want the walk to start at 1 P.M. today."

"I see."

"Yes, I think you do. I think you're intelligent enough for it all. If I'm satisfied with Mrs. Valente's condition, I'll give you another telephone call; then we can discuss the documents. Until I'm satisfied, we don't talk." Without waiting for a reply, Nat hung up. It was unlikely that el-Nouty could have traced the call, but Nat was taking no chances.

He returned to his hotel room, and carefully packed his clothes in an olive-green duffle bag, covering as he did the weapons he'd obtained the night before. Then, slinging the bag over his right shoulder, he set out on foot for Russell Square. The day was young, and he had plenty of time for the long walk, a walk he hoped would help organize his plans.

"We're taking a little outing this afternoon, my dear. I just spoke with the American, and he wants to make sure you are all right before he turns over the documents to me."

Nat was in London somewhere! Tania's hopes rose. But she dared not let her emotions betray her.

303

"That's . . . interesting," she replied coldly. "So what sort of demonstration should we give the man?"

El-Nouty looked at her suspiciously.

She went on, nervously, trying to convince him. "After all," she said, smiling coyly, "I perform very well on stage. Ballet is theater as well as dance. I project well—at least, according to the Kirov coaches. And, after all, this is a performance for an audience of one, isn't it?"

A broad smile broke out on el-Nouty's face. Had she passed the test, then?

"Yes," el-Nouty laughed. "Yes, you have a party of one. But I'm beginning to wonder now who the audience is—Worthington or me."

Tania's face fell.

"Don't worry, my dear," the Arab said reassuringly. "It really matters little for whom you are acting. You see, until I recover the documents and perform certain errands tomorrow, you will be watched very closely and very carefully by Hassan."

Tania's eyes flicked inadvertently to the hulking man who filled much of the doorway. He bowed slightly, and grinned at her.

"Afterwards," el-Nouty continued, "it will make no difference. I will have my documents in hand and my tasks completed. Your performance in the ensuing days in keeping to your end of our little . . . 'understanding,' as you call it, will tell me what side your heart is on and for whom you act. Then I shall decide whether you live, or whether you join the American in the early grave I am planning for him." He smiled benignly.

"Don't worry, my dear. We have time . . . much time. And, to tell the truth, I am inclined to believe your story. But in my profession one does not succeed by trusting people; they are all, including yourself, to be suspected until they have proven themselves worthy of trust."

El-Nouty moved toward the door. "Oh. And one

304

more thing," he said, stopping by Hassan in the doorway. "I've decided that since we're beginning to get so busy now, I must, unfortunately, renege on my offer to give you the run of the house. So Hassan here must, regretfully, restrict you to this room. But you have the afternoon walk to look forward to, and after that . . . well, we can discuss that later. For now I need to go meet my sister, Sarah, at the airport."

Without further words, he left. Tania heard Hassan slide the bolt into place on the closed door.

She fumbled through her luggage, and found nothing to write with. They had even taken her eyebrow pencil and her lipstick. Quietly, she rummaged through all the drawers in the room—nothing. Under the bed, in the bathroom, in the tiny closet: nothing, nothing, and nothing.

In despair, she sat down on the foot of the bed and started to cry, when she spotted her bra lying on the floor by the door. A strap had broken, and she'd pinned it up with a safety pin. Slowly, she rose and walked over and picked it up. A plan was forming.

"Hassan?" she knocked on the door, "Hassan, are you there?" she shouted. Only a few seconds passed this time before she heard the bolt slide back. Hassan was eager for any glance at her tits, she thought crudely. Oh, she thought, if it works. . . .

"Yes?" Hassan stuck his head through the doorway.

"Hassan, can you get me some cigarettes?" she asked. "I can pay you."

Grunting his assent, but cautioning that he would have to light them for her—lest she start a fire—Hassan dutifully bolted the door and clomped off down the hall to retrieve a pack from his room at the end of the hall.

By 11 A.M. Nat had checked into a large student hotel between the British Museum and Russell Square, and was on his way to a nearby convalescent-supply house.

No one took much notice of the man on the street shortly thereafter in a wheelchair with a black watch tartan blanket over his knees. Nat wheeled himself awkwardly down the sidewalk to a crosswalk and waved vigorously at the first empty cab that passed. It did not stop. The next one, though, swerved madly at him and lurched to a halt inches from his side. Homicidal, he thought; London cabbies are all frustrated Stuka pilots.

"Where to?"

"Kensington Gardens. Queen's Gate would be fine."

"Hope in. . . . Uh, wait just a moment," the cabbie stammered, embarrassed. "Let me give you a hand. And he got out to help Nat into the cab.

Ten minutes later, the driver dropped Nat off at Queen's Gate, helped him into the chair, and, after thanking him for a generous tip, sped off. It was nearly noon.

Nat covered his small knapsack carefully with the blanket, then pushed hard on the rims of the chair's wheels and started off on a wobbly and erratic course.

He followed the wide sidewalk up Kensington High Street toward the Palace Garden, growing more and more proficient with the chair. He *had* to get better, for his life and Tania's would depend on his becoming a wheelchair-ridden old man. Their lives depended on the acting, but there would be no reviews of the performance—just life or death.

By the time he reached the westernmost corner of Kensington Gardens, Nat had just about mastered the chair. He wheeled it through the park gate and rested for a moment. He looked down the slight incline, past the ponds and roads. They would be walking toward him—Tania and el-Nouty—if el-Nouty followed Nat's directions.

To his left the Kensington Palace walls belted the

grounds like a brick cinch, running among the trees, whose leaves had started to turn. A gaggle of adolescents battered a soccer ball around on the grass in front of him, while the main part of Kensington Gardens with its trees and ponds and latticework of paved tarmacadam paths stretched out to his right. From behind him, the notes and echoes of a church pealed the midday hour and he silently winced as he heard one of the notes distinctly off key.

As if on cue, a flight of ducks on the nearest pond took to the air, circled the opposite end of the water, and splashed down to resume their feeding, from a group of schoolchildren, toddlers, nannies, and elderly people bearing popcorn, peanuts, and bird grains. The sun beat down upon the entire scene with the warm bright hues of Cézanne and turned the blanket over his knees into an oven.

Kensington Gardens and Hyde Park are two contiguous parks, separated only by a busy street that winds its way in an arc from Hyde Park Gate back to Kensington High Street. Tania and el-Nouty would walk up a main diagonal footpath leading from Speakers' Corner to the Kensington Palace, starting—Nat checked his watch again—in fifty-three minutes. He'd wheel himself down to the road that separated the two parks, and wait by the large duck pond for Tania to show up. With luck, he would shoot el-Nouty through the blanket with his silenced Navy "Hushpuppy" pistol. The Ingram with its silencers was too bulky to use. With luck, el-Nouty would collapse like a man with a heart seizure, and he and Tania would flee. With luck—and a lot of help from his shooting arm, his acting skills, and his nerve. With luck. Balls, Nat thought as he released the brake on the chair and freewheeled down the slight incline toward the lake, If luck is all I have going for me, I might as well eat the barrel and pull the trigger right now.

At the opposite corner of the park, at Speakers' Corner, Hassan pulled a bicycle out of a cream-colored rental van and pedaled off through the park. He passed Nat near the small restaurant that fills the space between the large lake and the road dividing the two parks, but took no notice of him. When he passed again, Nat was throwing corn to a group of mallards being harassed by a hissing swan. Hassan pedaled a number of other parallel paths, and found nothing unusual. This he reported to el-Nouty.

At precisely 1 P.M., in accordance with Nat's instructions, el-Nouty and Tania stepped out of the van. Hassan followed by some twenty yards.

El-Nouty stretched and looked around him. "It is a nice day for a walk," he declared. "But I detest this effete English sun. Where I come from the sun is virile all year round."

Tania nodded, feigning interest. But her heart was pounding. Where would Nat be? Would she see him?

"Come, my dear," said her companion, interrupting her thoughts. "We're walking too slowly. I want to get this over with; I want you to meet Sarah tonight."

"Of course," Tania agreed, picking up her pace. "Besides, I'm getting hungry," she said, hoping this would convey her lack of concern for Nat.

"There's a restaurant about halfway through," el-Nouty said. "We can stop on our way back."

Was this consideration he was showing? Perhaps he wasn't such a total blackguard, maybe he did have his socially acceptable graces after all. At least he'd given her back her purse and her makeup in the panel truck so she could make herself up. And he must have a human side if he wanted her to meet his sister.

El-Nouty marched straight ahead, eyes scouring the trees, cars, oncoming faces for any sign of Nat Worthington. Tania watched him, fascinated. He looked like . . . she searched her memory . . . like a falcon; even his artificial hand had the air of a single talon.

He'd told her that he'd killed men by ripping them open with the sharp stainless steel prosthesis. A small shiver ran up her spine as she remembered the cold stare of his black eyes, a black that spoke of the chill of death. She believed him.

She looked around her, scanning the tall buildings that encircled the park. El-Nouty said Nat could be in any of them—or even farther away if he had a powerful telescope. Oh, Nat, I want to feel you're near. Even if I couldn't touch you, I want to feel that you're close. They walked on.

Nat saw them approach the restaurant at 1:27. He kept one hand resting on his lap on the automatic with its link-sausage silencer. The knot in his chest loosened when he saw that el-Nouty and Tania walked alone; Nat could never pull it off otherwise. They were still more than one hundred and fifty yards away. Trying to maintain the idle motions of an old man in a wheelchair feeding coty-domestic waterfowl, Nat strained his eyes for a look at her. Had she been hurt?

Hours seemed to pass as their bodies grew almost imperceptibly larger. Tension gripped Nat's chest again and pounded his heart against the back of his breastbone.

They grew closer and Nat spotted a backup, maintaining his distance about twenty yards behind Tania and el-Nouty. He was a big man—a big target, Nat noted—sporting a Castro beard and a disastrously bright red shirt. A good target.

Nat swallowed and emptied the last of his corn into the middle of the ducks who'd now surrounded his chair. They quacked and squawked greedily after the bonus as Nat wheeled himself slowly through them and up to the restaurant's main entrance where the path met the street. Two quick shots. Oh, God, let it work right. Dear God, I've never made deals with you before, but just let me pull this one off and I'll . . . Nat couldn't think of anything he could possibly do that would be a good exchange.

"The restaurant's just up ahead." El-Nouty pointed to the building as an old man slowly wheeled himself up the path. By Allah's goodness he was in one piece. He'd never confine himself to the indignities of a wheelchair: he'd decided long ago that he'd rather be dead, by his own hand if necessary. They were parasites, these cripples. Society treated them too softly.

Tania looked around and saw that for the first time, they were clear of the trees. Praying that Nat could see her from wherever he was hidden, she reached into her purse and pulled out the pack of cigarettes that Hassan had brought her that morning. She hoped he wouldn't wonder what had happened to the other thirty-nine cigarettes.

"Do you have a light?" she asked el-Nouty.

"Of course," he answered, pulling a silver engraved lighter from his pants pocket. "I've always wondered why ballet dancers all seem to be tobacco addicts. It is such a terrible habit for the physical conditioning you require."

"I don't know," Tania said as she grabbed his hand and guided the flame toward the cigarette tip as she'd seen her friends do.

To Nat's left a mother sat on a bench next to the restaurant and ate a take-away hot dog, while her older girl wheeled an infant's stroller around. Christ, he thought, looking over at the woman's half-eaten hotdog, please leave, please go away so you don't get hurt. He sat there staring at Tania and el-Nouty as they approached. Strange things came into his head as Nat watched them grow closer.

He smelled acutely the exhaust of the autos passing by, only feet behind him as they zoomed around the blind corner and faded down the road; the fragrance of changing seasons, the moist musk of decaying vegetation. His hands itched intolerably from contact with the new blanket, his buttocks ached from sitting so long and his leg muscles, tight and complaining from disuse, made him want to get up and stretch.

Tania and el-Nouty started up the short rise. Laying the pistol between his legs, Nat released the brake and started to wheel himself down the hill, when Tania stopped and performed a bewildering act: she smoked a cigarette. Nat gripped the brake again and watched. El-Nouty's backup man stopped as he waited for them to finish the little ritual of lighter, puff on the cigarette, exhale and continue.

Tania did not smoke. They'd talked about it, agreed it was a vile, revolting, disgusting habit and they would never tolerate the sour shit-tasting mouths in anyone close to them. He watched as she crumpled up the empty cigarette package and threw it in a waste bin.

You beautiful brilliant woman! Nat thought as he watched, transfixed.

As they resumed their walk up the hill, Nat again released the brake, when a shriek of horror pierced the back of his head. He whirled around, and saw the baby's stroller roll over the curb and into the traffic. From the direction of the blind corner, Nat heard the racing of an engine as it changed into higher gears.

No! Nat cried inside. No, this isn't fair. In nightmare freeze-frame motion, Nat saw the mother look up, annoyed at her child's scream, and then, catching sight of the stroller, throw her hot dog on the ground and jump to her feet.

The woman oozed through time but when he looked again at Tania and el-Nouty, they seemed to be running up the hill. She'll never make it, Nat decided.

The sound of the car grew louder. The mother seemed to have moved only inches.

In the end, he made no conscious decision. He didn't weigh the infant's life against Tania's. He would never

311

recall deciding, but he catapulted out of the wheel-chair, dumping his gun and pack on the ground wrapped up in the blanket. He remembered how the woman gawked, wide-eyed and stunned, as he shot past her and dashed into the street and snatched the handle of the stroller. He would remember the infant's squawk of alarm as he jerked the stroller—probably giving the kid a good case of whiplash, he thought—and he remembered the bright green Fiat as it burst around the corner and slammed on its brakes, skidding through the spot occupied only split seconds before by the stroller.

Nat vaguely heard shouts of surprise behind him as he scooped up his blanket on the run and dashed into the restaurant.

Quick! Nat shouted soundlessly to himself as he rushed into the men's toilet. Off with the wig. Suppose someone followed me? Reverse the jacket. What will the newspapers make of this one? Take off the glasses. Front page on the tabloids tomorrow; oh, how they love a good miracle. Wipe off the makeup. What would el-Nouty do? Stuff the gun in the knapsack. Would el-Nouty continue the walk? Cram the wig and glasses in a paper sack. Did he suspect him? Deposit the sack in the bottom of the pack. Surely someone would follow him in seconds. Fold up the blanket. That's all he needed, to be a hero—they'd find out about him for sure. Check to see if you have those damn documents. I could tell them I was an actor studying for a role. There they are! But they'd never let me be! Footsteps, running. Getting louder. Flush the toilet and walk out calmly.

"My God, man!" an agitated middle-aged man with a waiter's apron careened through the door. "Have you seen an old gent run in here?" and without waiting for an answer he pushed frantically past Nat headed for the far end of the washroom. Nat walked quickly outside.

Retracing his path, Nat joined the gathering crowd, though which he could hear the sobs of the mother and her two children. She was babbling hysterically about the old man. Nat swam along the fringe of the crowd, making his way around to catch sight of el-Nouty and Tania's position before the accident.

Calm heart! He futilely commanded. He saw them retreating in the distance, three little dots scurrying into smudges. He rejected the thought of following them. He'd be too obvious if he ran, and if he didn't, they'd lose him in minutes.

No! Goddamnit! he cried under his breath as he searched for a place to sit. She was *this* close and I let her go. This close! He unshouldered the knapsack and sat on the edge of a wooden park bench and stared at the top of his shoes. Get going, he thought, the police might question everybody around. And when he stood up to leave, the rubbish can with Tania's cigarette pack filled every inch of his vision.

He rushed to the bin, and his heart sank when he saw half a bale of waste paper. There was no time to rummage through it, so he gathered up the top of the plastic liner of the bin, hauled it out, and set off across the park with the pack on his back and the garbage slung over his shoulder like a Skid Row Santa Claus.

"What in *hell* was that!" El-Nouty exploded finally, as the van pulled away from the curb with Hassan at the wheel.

Tania winced. "You're hurting my arm! Please. How should I know what that was all about?"

"It was part of a trap," el-Nouty said, but there was doubt in his voice now. His grip on her arm relaxed slightly.

"How could it have been?" Tania asked. "Look— it's not helping for you to squeeze me like that."

El-Nouty dropped his hand, and Tania massaged the white fingerprints he'd left on her arm.

Yes, thought el-Nouty, staring blankly at the opposite wall. How could it have been? The van jounced and lurched through traffic, passing Grosvenor Square on a roundabout trip home. Tania stared at his trancelike gaze, afraid to say anything, lest she arouse another fit of anger. The van stopped, started, weaved in and out of traffic, throwing her from side to side, but el-Nouty seemed like cast metal bolted to his seat. Tania listened to Hassan wind up and down through the gears, muttering all the while under his breath in Arabic. Probably obscenities. Finally el-Nouty relaxed his rigored muscles and leaned back against the wall of the van and looked at her, searching her eyes, her face. She felt naked under his piercing glare. He's deciding whether to kill me now, she thought.

"You asked the right question," el-Nouty said enigmatically.

"The . . . right question?" Relief flooded through Tania like a hot flash.

"Yes," he replied. "Just a minute ago. You said 'How could it have been.'" He looked at her blank expression. "A trap," he explained and then watched her smile politely, but clearly not understanding.

"I accused you," el-Nouty said. "And I'm afraid I jumped to a conclusion, perhaps. At least I'm willing to believe that for now."

Tania watched as his face began to relax. The lines diminished and the mask of anger and bloodlust seemed to vanish, replaced by the usual one of arrogance.

"Slow down, Hassan," el-Nouty ordered, leaning toward the front. "We don't want to get picked up by the police."

Hassan obediently slowed, and began to drive smoothly and without the muttered curses.

It took Hassan twenty minutes to chauffeur them

back to the townhouse on Bayswater Road, very near Hyde Park. Hassan drove into the alley behind the house and el-Nouty took Tania in by the rear entrance and escorted her to her room.

"I want you to be ready by 5 P.M.," he told her. "We're to meet Sarah at the Dorchester at 5:30.

"What . . . what should I wear for tonight?" Tania asked.

El-Nouty leered at her. "Look through the clothes I bought you before we left Paris." And with that, he turned on his heel and left the room, bolting the door behind him.

It took Nat less than fifteen minutes to sort through the rubbish and pull out five cigarette packs. Only two were the right color; these he stuffed into his pocket and left the rest of the rubbish in the bag as he headed off for a corner of the park where he could find a little privacy and dissect the packs.

Settling down on a park bench across the street from the Dorchester, Nat carefully uncrumpled the cigarette packages, finding at the bottom of the last one a wad of neatly folded, tissue-thin paper, covered with smudgy writing. Nat pulled the papers out, holding them gingerly as he spread them flat in a tiny stack, being careful not to rip the fragile surfaces. Tania had unrolled each cigarette and used the paper to write on. The scratchy-looking Cyrillic letters had blurred slightly as the paper absorbed the ink—or was it ink? Nat held one paper up close to his eyes to read it. No, it was not ink at all, but the brown of dried blood. The letters of each word were a tiny matrix of dots, as if they had been laid on with a pin.

Nat began reading the paper marked "1."

"Dearest Nat,
    I am being held by el-Nouty in a house somewhere in London.

315

I am to be the bait to catch you. First of all, let me describe my surroundings as best as I can. My room faces an alleyway. From looking out, I know I am on the second floor. The window is barred with heavy metal. I opened the window just now and used the mirror in my compact to look to the sides. One end is a dead end, and the open end is covered with a high iron gate. I've never seen anyone in the alley, or I'd yell for help, although with the huge man Hassan just outside my door, I'm sure they'd be on me in a second. Beyond the iron gate, I can see the ruins of on old church, and part of a red neon sign. I can only see two letters of it: EL. Frequently taxis and buses go past the entrance and occasionally park in front of it. I hear traffic constantly, even through the night."

Terrific, Nat thought, that's just terrific. That eliminates all but about half of London. Except for the ruined church. Despair oozed through him like tar: heavy, paralyzing despair. The note continued:

"Besides el-Nouty and Hassan, I've heard different men's voices outside my room, and have overheard many of their conversations. But the," Nat flipped to the last slip of paper. "Running out of space, something about kill, tomorrow, some leader, London. I love you, Tania. P.S. Noon today heard very faint church bells, one not . . ." Nat held the paper up to try and make out the word crammed in the very last square millimeter of the paper, ". . . in tune."

One bell was not in tune! She was near!

A ruined church, lots of taxis and buses. Head down, absorbed in the riddle, Nat covered the ground between Hyde Park Corner and the restaurant where

316

the incident happened in less than half an hour. The crowds were gone. It was 4 P.M.

Waiting for the traffic to thin so he could cross, Nat watched as a taxi—this one painted dark brown instead of the usual black pulled up to the curb some ten yards to his left and disgorged a crowd of American tourists. Tourists—taxis and buses. Large numbers of taxis and buses mean rail stations or . . . he thought deeper, hotels.

Hotels! Shit, the fucker is falling into place! Nat stepped off the curb and jogged across the street, barely escaping the homicidal bent of another driver in his black beetle taxi. Somewhere near here—or somewhere near the off-key church bells he'd heard—there was a ruined church with a train station nearby, or . . .

("I can only see two letters of it: EL.") . . . or a hotel. Yes, that's got to be it! A hotel, a neon sign, a ruined church. Resisting the urge to run—he wanted to be as unobvious as possible—Nat boldly strode down the middle of Kensington Gardens, directly along the path he had traveled in the wheelchair earlier. When he got to Kensington High Street, he tried to remember the direction from which the church bells came. West, he decided, and walked up, past the private street on which the Russian embassy resided.

At the first major intersection, he saw a church. Winding his way through a forest of metal legs supporting a scaffold over the sidewalk, Nat loped across the street and looked at the church schedule. There were no bells due until six. Then he looked up and realized this was Church Street, Kensington. There were other churches up the way, toward Notting Hill Gate.

How far does the sound carry? he wondered. Could he have heard the bells of a church much farther away? And how much farther away from that was Tania?

"Pardon me, but can I help you?"

317

Nat turned around, and had to look down, and when he did, he fond a wizened old man with a clerical collar and a wreath of wispy white hair ringing his bald head.

"I didn't mean to startle you," the little man said. His gray eyes sparkled.

"Oh . . . ," Nat stammered. "I was just . . . it was just that I saw the . . ." he pointed inarticulately at the schedule of concerts. "I was, ah, in the park earlier and heard the bells of a church. But one of the bells was out of tune, and I wondered if this—"

"Yes," the man said, apology running through his voice. The English would apologize for an act of God, Nat thought. "The bell cracked late last week—don't know why exactly—but we've had so many people asking after it, I've spent half my time just explaining it to the residents of the neighborhood. People get used to the sound of things. They expect certain things, and when they change, well. . . ." He raised the palms of both hands and shrugged.

This was probably the most exciting thing that's happened in Kensington in months, Nat thought, and he smiled a little as he envisioned little old ladies with flowered tea sets cringing when the bells struck the cracked note.

Nat smiled. He said goodbye and started to walk away, when he stopped. "Ah, father?" The man stopped and turned around. "How far . . . how far does the sound of your bells carry?"

"Well," the man stopped. "Let's see . . . back in 1957 we had an interesting temperature pattern, and people in Chelsea said they heard it way down by the Thames."

Super, Nat thought. "No . . . I mean, usually?"

"About a mile, perhaps. Perhaps a mile."

Nat thanked him, again said goodbye and walked a dozen paces when he stopped again.

"Father?" Nat had to yell a bit this time. A faint

318

flash of impatience crossed the kindly man's face. Nat hurried back to him. "Is there a demolished church near here—an old one in ruins or something?"

The old man looked at him. "Yes," he said. "Yes there is. Why do you ask?"

"Well I . . . I remember visiting a friend at a hotel near one on my last visit here, and I remembered it had a pretty good restaurant."

"Indian one?" The old man asked.

"Uh . . . yes. Yes, a really good Indian restaurant."

"It closed." The old man said. "But there's a good one I like a lot of Leicester Square. They have the best puris and a lamb curry that—"

"But I'd like to go by that place again . . . you know just for remembrances?" Nat asked.

"It's a really good Indian restaurant, really. Just take the tube to Leicester Square, and it's just off the little street . . . let's see what's the name of the street?" He stared up at the darkening sky. Nat checked his watch: it was almost 4:30. "I can see the little restaurant right now," the old man continued, with his eyes closed, "just like I was standing in front. It's near the Swiss House—you know the one with all the stores and—"

"Father," Nat interrupted. "Could you just tell me where the old ruined church is?" The old man's eyes opened, wide. "I'm sorry, father," Nat apologized. "But I'd like to go by there and I haven't got much time."

"Nor have I."

"Sorry?"

"Time," the old man said. "But never mind. You can find the ruined church by walking up Church Street here," he pointed with an outstretched arm, "and turn right at Notting Hill Gate. Walk on the side opposite the park, and you'll see the old church on your left, as the street turns into Bayswater."

Nat thanked him profusely and set out up Church Street.

"Young man," the priest called after him. Nat stopped and turned around. "Ardmore Street. It's really a fine Indian restaurant."

"Can't you move any faster?" El-Nouty said from the other side of the closed door. "It's five o'clock now. I don't want to be late!"

"I'm almost ready!" Tania yelled back. "Some of the clothes don't fit right. I'm having to pin them." Damn, she thought. Are all men alike? If she ignored the sound of el-Nouty's voice, she'd swear it was Niki rushing her.

"All right, all right, but hurry," El-Nouty said and walked back downstairs.

Nat ran, heedless of the attention he drew to himself, knowing only that Tania was within earshot of the church. He pounded up Church Street, his breath coming in an easy, measured rhythm. Past the lines of antique shops, past the pubs, past the bookstores and the Thomas Cook Travel agency, his legs carried him swiftly to Notting Hill Gate, where he turned right, dashing among the pedestrians. As he ran, holding the straps of the knapsack taut against his chest with his hands, a plan emerged. I'm coming, Tania, I'm coming, he thought over and over, in rhythm with his legs.

When Notting Hill Gate turned into Bayswater Road, he slowed to a walk to catch his breath. The run had invigorated rather than tired him, quickened his thoughts and sharpened his mind. Walking along the Kensington Garden side of Bayswater Road, directly across the park from his earlier walk, he scanned the buildings on the opposite side. Several down-the-heels hotels stood near a small square. As Nat approached the street leading to the square, another building came into view—a brown-stained and soot-blackened old stone church! Looking around him, Nat continued past the street. A black limousine eased out of traffic and pulled to the curb across the street from him.

A long row of white-stone buildings ran from the corner down Bayswater Road as far as he could see. It had to be near here, he thought, reversing his path to cross the street and return to the square. The quiet rush of blood through his head drowned the gathering rush hour traffic as Nat focused on the square. Budget hotels lined its outer ring, and the ruined church dominated the green. A street paralleling Bayswater led off to his right and left along the front face of the square. A number of taxis and tour buses lined the square and the street in both directions.

Nat inhaled deeply. His life and Tania's hung on chilly, calculating ruthlessness. Then Nat turned right and paced slowly up the street running east off the square, looking first for the iron gate guarding a dead-end alley. He quickly found it.

El-Nouty pounded impatiently on Tania's door. "The limo is waiting for us. Aren't you ready yet?"

"Yes, nearly," Tania replied. She heard the bolt slide back from the door. Moments later, el-Nouty's tall, elegant frame appeared in the bathroom mirror where Tania was applying the final touches of makeup to her face.

"May I be of assistance?" he asked smiling at her image in the mirror and gazing pointedly at the still-open back of her dress.

Tania reddened. "No . . . I mean, yes, of course." She managed a quick smile, then steadied herself as el-Nouty hooked the dark green silk dress at the nape of her neck. "Thank you," she said, trying to suppress a shudder as el-Nouty's hands caressed her shoulders. Masking her reaction, she turned to face him. "We're in

321

a hurry," she said demurely. "I guess we'll have to be going."

But el-Nouty just smiled and pulled her to him.

After walking back and forth, Nat deduced that the Transnational Hotel was the only hotel visible from any of the blind alleys he'd found, and only one building—the first one he'd found—had any glimpse of the hotel's sign. As he stood, back to the iron gate, he found he could see the entire sign from the building on the left, but only the last part of "hotel" from the building on the right.

Nat looked up and down the street, and finding it clear he stood on the lower horizontal bar of the gate and carefully hauled himself up, holding on to the spear-blade points of the upright bars. Silently, he dropped to the dark weed-matted surface of the alley.

He followed the branching of a ludicrous bright blue drain pipe on the opposite wall, and then looked once more at the second-floor windows, behind one of which he hoped Tania waited. Toward the foot of the alley, he found he couldn't see the hotel sign at all, and at the open end he saw the last three letters. He satisfied himself that he had the correct room when he could see the last two letters of "hotel". He stood directly under the second window from the street, grabbed the drainpipe, and slowly began climbing up.

When he drew even with the window on the second floor, he heard faint voices carrying through a slot at the bottom of the window where it had been raised for ventilation. One was Tania's! Nat's heart leaped at the sound, and then raced with anger as el-Nouty's louder, arrogant voice followed it:

"Yes, she *is* waiting for us. But she will not mind." *Who* was waiting for them? And where? They were leaving!

Nat desperately examined the iron bars over each of the windows. They were half an inch thick and anchored to the building at four points. If Tania were in there alone, he'd be able to hacksaw the bars or use some C-4 to blow the supports away. But with el-Nouty there . . .

"But I thought you hated to be late." It was Tania's voice now, rising higher and edged with tension. "Now see what you've done," she said reproachfully, "I'll have to repair my makeup."

Repair her makeup? Anger and revulsion swept over Nat as he listened. That damn greasy bastard, I'll . . .

"You can do it in the car. It's waiting for us," el-Nouty commanded impatiently, and the voices faded from Nat's hearing.

He had to get around front as quickly as possible. Nat scrambled down the drainpipe, and scaled the iron gate with less caution than before. While he sprinted down the street, Nat unshouldered his knapsack and located the Ingram.

One, two, three, four he counted; el-Nouty's was the fourth building from the hotel. Nat's footstrikes clattered from the walls of the narrow street, the leather heels tap-tapping as he ran. Ahead at the corner, a taxi unloaded a matronly woman, and beyond it, a tour bus pulled up, preparing to disgorge its load of tourists. As he reached the corner he poured on more speed to avoid getting caught in the mob.

Nat flew past the matron, gained the corner of the hotel in another three steps, and planted his left foot to pivot around the corner and dash past the first of the tourists who'd just stepped from the bus. But his leather-soled shoes lost their grip in the marble pavement and like a baseball player trying to steal home, he slid, caroming into three Japanese businessmen who had just alighted from the bus. Nat caught their open-mouthed mask of surprise as he spun through them at ankle level knocking their feet out from under them, and coming to rest against the front wheel of the bus.

Quickly picking himself back up, Nat shook his

head, issued a hasty "Sorry" to the three businessmen, who still sprawled over each other like bowling pins, and continued his race for el-Nouty's house. He rounded the next corner with a dancing series of tiny steps to avoid slipping again, but as the street came into view, he saw first Tania and then el-Nouty step into the black limousine. A large Arab man shut the door behind el-Nouty and then walked back toward the house as the limo gracefully pulled away from the curb and into the eastbound traffic.

Nat barely had time to catch the license number of the limo before it disappeared into traffic.

Slinging the knapsack over one shoulder, Nat strolled past the house, casually scanning the front. There was no way to predict the reception he'd get if he rang the doorbell, or how many people would answer. But, he decided, as he turned and ascended the steps, there was one way to find out. He pushed the lighted doorbell, and heard a bell ring inside.

A pinpoint of light winked in the peephole of the varnished wood door, then vanished, followed by rattling sounds of unchaining and unbolting.

As soon as the door started to crack open, Nat lunged into it with his shoulder. In a cry of anger and surprise, an Arabic voice cursed his mother's diseased genitals, and a large, dark man crashed into a tiny entrance hall table behind the door, sending shards of a broken vase flying across the freshly waxed terra cotta tile floor.

The sudden lack of resistance sent Nat tumbling across the foyer, landing at the base of an ornate mahogany stair bannister. He sat up quickly and pulled the Ingram out of the knapsack and flicked off the safety, just as the large Arab stood up.

"Hold it!" Nat commanded, scrambling to his feet and training the automatic pistol's muzzle on the other man. At the sound of Nat's voice, Hassan froze in his crouch. When he saw the gun, he slowly straightened up and moved his hands above his head.

"*Parlez-vous français?*" Nat asked hopefully. The man nodded, and followed instructions to assume the position to be searched, spreading his legs and leaning against the wall.

Nat found a Ruger .357 magnum in his waistband and a razor-sharp Bedouin knife in a scabbard attached to his belt. Nat removed both.

"My grandfather's," the Arab said, with a worried look, as Nat took the knife.

"It'll be fine," Nat said. "And so will you—if you tell me where el-Nouty went with the ballerina, and who they are going to meet."

The Arab was silent. Nat looked at the broad back of the man and the massive shoulders that hunched against the wall.

"You can give me the information now," Nat said, "or you can give it to me in your dying breaths."

"You smell like a camel's ass, you little whore-son," the Arab replied.

"Nice," Nat replied. "All right, you want to play that way, look at this—" He threw the Arab's knife on the terra cotta floor. It clattered noisily and slid into the wall, across the foyer from the Arab. When it stopped, Nat fired. Three shots burst at it, mangling the blade and the magnificently crafted gold handle. If he wanted a reaction, he got one. Hassan whirled on Nat and flew at him with surprising speed, screaming the wounded cry of one who has seen a treasured heirloom gratiutously destroyed. Nat trained the pistol on Hassan, but fired only one three-shot burst at him before the ham-fisted hands plowed at Nat's face and body.

A sideswipe took the Ingram out of Nat's hands and another caught him in his ribs on the right side, and lifted him up and over the bannister. He hit the floor and rolled to his feet, amazed to see the bannister over

325

which he'd just flown disintegrate under a kick from a limb that looked more like a tree-trunk than a leg.

Hassan turned on Nat again, the tranced look of anger and pain transforming his face into a terrifying mask. Nat stepped back and avoided the next punch which came slower than the last and then stared as a hint of blood came to the man's lips. The hint became a flood as suddenly Hassan slipped noisily to one knee, the impact rattling glassware in a case somewhere in the next room. The initial three-shot burst had finally taken affect on this hulk.

Good work, Worthington. With your usual combination of subtle interrogation skills and restrained self-defense, you've successfully extracted the vital information you so dearly need at this critical point.

"Fuck!" he yelled to break the silence left by the dead man's last breath. He looked slowly around the room.

Then Nat ransacked what appeared to be el-Nouty's study, tossing books in random directions after flipping through their pages in search of hidden notes. There was a small gold mine here, Nat told himself as he went through files and notebooks, saving some to stuff into his knapsack, tossing others on the floor.

Nothing in the study told him where they might have gone. Neither did anything in the living room, or in el-Nouty's bedroom. Sweat poured down the sides of Nat's face as the initial adrenaline wore thin and fear began to creep in. How many people used this house? What if el-Nouty returned suddenly? What if a contingent of Libyans or KGB or—the thought sickened him—CIA happened by? Still, he pressed the search and walked upstairs.

He entered the first room on the second floor. As soon as he opened the door, the latest fragrance of Tania's perfume hit him like a brick.

He walked slowly in, looking at her belongings spread about on the bed, on chairs. He saw the blouse

326

she'd worn that night in Paris at the Intercontinental. He wondered what she'd worn when el-Nouty kidnapped her.

"You were here just a minute ago," he said aloud. Tears blurred his vision. "Just a few minutes ago I could have reached through the window and touched you."

Tania and el-Nouty alighted from the limo in front of the Dorchester, the Arab guiding her with a firm hand around her arm. "Say one word, or try to escape, and I'll kill you in an instant. Understand?"

She nodded. They walked quietly through the lobby.

"Do you really think that I have so little sense as to think I could escape from you?" Tania asked, in the most ingratiating manner she could manage, when they had stepped into the elevator.

El-Nouty looked straight into her eyes, searching. He was not sure. He smiled slyly.

"No." The smile grew broader. "No, I think you are smarter than that."

When they left the elevator, and began walking down the lushly carpeted hallway toward Sarah's room, Tania had begun to relax. I'm safe for now, she thought. I'm safe as long as we're with his sister. After all, what could happen when his family is around?

She got an inkling of the answer to that question when el-Nouty opened the door, and Tania saw Sarah lounging on the bed, naked.

Chapter Twenty-One

||||||||||||||||||||||||||||||||||||||||||||||||||||||||||||||||||||||||||||||||||||||

Nat found the next bedroom empty, but he struck pay dirt at the end of the hallway. The room stank with the rank odor of unwashed clothes and rancid cheap cigarettes. Nat figured it belonged to the man he had just killed; they both smelled alike.

It seemed hopeless at first: mounds of filthy clothing covered the rumpled bed, an overflowing wastebasket spilled papers on the floor, piles of papers and pornographic paperbacks covered the desk.

The man was truly a pig, Nat thought. Then he noticed a small piece of cream-colored memo paper tucked into the dial of the telephone, which sat amid the debris on the desk. Nat picked up the sheet of expensive-looking stationery and saw el-Nouty's initials at the top. In a florid handwriting was the notation: "Sarah—Dorchester—5:50. Call the limo at 5:15. MSeN." It was written in Arabic, but Nat's rudimentary knowledge of the language got him through. It was clearly a note from el-Nouty to his manservant. The Dorchester. *That* was where they'd gone. He'd bet on it. Nat stuffed the paper into his pocket and bounded down the stairs. He stopped in the foyer to recover the Ingram. He stuffed it into his knapsack, stepped over Hassan's lifeless body, and walked to the street to flag a taxi.

Cabs passed him in droves while he stood there waving his arms like a windmill. In the distance Nat heard the church with the off-key bells begin their six o'clock concert.

"Tania, I'd like you to meet my sister, Sarah," el-Nouty said, easing her into the room.

Tania's heart pounded like it would leap out of her throat, she felt her mouth drop open, powerless in her astonishment to prevent it. Sarah was naked. But she was beautiful, Tania thought as she stood there. She was young, she thought, very young . . . a teenager. But a woman in body nevertheless.

"Come." El-Nouty tried to take Tania's arm, but she shook free, startled. "She won't bite," el-Nouty said, but Tania hardly heard the words.

What had happened? Was this his sister? His sister? Tania thought, fascinated at the sight of one of the most beautiful woman/children she had ever seen, yet repulsed by the idea of her behaving in this way in front of her brother . . . her family! She looked at el-Nouty, waiting for him to act. Surely he'll slap her and demand that she dress, Tania thought. He'll chastise her for her brazen immodesty and she'll dress and we can get something to eat.

She watched with horror as el-Nouty left her side and went to Sarah's bed. Sarah sat up and put one arm around el-Nouty's neck and leaned up to kiss him deeply and passionately. Not like a sister kisses a brother. Then el-Nouty sat beside Sarah on the bed and cupped one of her ample breasts in his left hand, rolling the nipple between his fingers as it grew hard in response.

330

"Come on," he said, looking at Tania.

When Tania failed to move, he spoke again. "I said, don't just stand there. We came here for a reason.",

"A . . ." Tania's voice squeaked. She cleared her throat. "A reason? But . . . but I thought she was . . . I mean I came to meet your . . ."

"She *is* my sister," el-Nouty said. "We are . . ." he looked at Sarah coyly, ". . . closer than most brothers and sisters. We have been for—how long, Sarah?— three years now. Yes," he smiled. "It did my father's heart good for a worthless woman to serve me so well. His first-born was a female, and as was his right, he drowned the infant. I was the second and Sarah was the third."

Was she hearing this right? "Surely, this is a . . . a joke? This really isn't your sister." Tania smiled nervously.

"Are you shocked?" el-Nouty said, sitting upright on the edge of the bed. Sarah reached around with a long slender hand and massaged his groin. El-Nouty looked at Tania. "Of course you are." He laughed loudly. Tania started to turn for the door, but before she could reach the knob, el-Nouty was on her, pulling her away and throwing her on the bed beside Sarah.

"We have an . . . understanding, remember?" El-Nouty smiled as he looked down at her. "I think it's time we, ah . . . understood, what that means."

"But my . . . my—"

"I'll let Sarah find out about that for me," el-Nouty said. "She'll keep me from being contaminated if you are indeed afflicted with that nasty curse. Sarah?" Some silent communication passed between them, and then Sarah began caressing Tania's neck, her breasts, running her hands along her legs. Tania jerked away, and before she could stand up, a white-hot flash of pain obliterated the feeling on the left side of her face.

"Be nice to Sarah, Tania,' el-Nouty said, staring down at her supine body, "or I'll have to do more than

331

just slap you. Is that understood?" Tania remembered her mind shouting, "No! No!" but she felt her head nod up and down.

"Good," el-Nouty said in a schoolmaster voice. "Now, Sarah."

Cabs whizzed past as if he were a ghost. He'd just about resigned himself to running all the way to the Dorchester, when one pulled over to the curb and he heard the familiar "Where to, Guv?"

"The Dorchester," Nat told the driver and climbed in back with his knapsack. "And hurry, please."

The taxi weaved in and out of traffic. Nat reached inside the knapsack and made sure everything was there: the documents, the Ingram, and four baseball-sized blobs of C-4 plastic explosive with time fuses inserted.

Tania shivered under the rasp of Sarah's tongue on her breast. It tickled rather than excited; but, she thought, looking up at the ceiling, she'd been an actor with Niki all these years—she'd be one for just a little while longer. Tania had a plan and she knew it would work.

"Do you like that, Tania," el-Nouty asked as his voice grew nearer. "Do you like that? Huh? Or would you like this?" Tania turned her head and caught sight of a completely nude el-Nouty, standing over her head stroking his swollen penis with his left hand. "This is what you really want," he told her. "Admit it," he said. "Admit it, damn you!" He raised his voice and Tania flinched, ready for another slap when Sarah ceased her futile efforts to raise Tania's nipples to attention, and crawled over her to take el-Nouty's penis in her mouth.

"Now!" el-Nouty shouted. "Come here, you Russian bitch, and suck on this. Now, damn it!" he shouted.

Tania complied, pulling back her hair to keep it from getting tangled.

332

El-Nouty looked up and grinned lasciviously as Tania's open lips approached him. But his sigh quickly turned into a shriek of horror as Tania bit down as hard as she could, bit until she drew blood, for vengeance. El-Nouty jerked upright, smashing his head into Sarah's with the hollow, thumping sound of two unripe melons colliding. As Tania jumped up, she saw Sarah slump over, unconscious from the collision, and blood start to run from el-Nouty's nose where it smashed into Sarah's face.

Though still howling in pain, el-Nouty made a grab for her. Tania would remember for years the expression on his face when she sprang from the bed and kicked him in the Adam's apple. Only those familiar with ballet dancers might believe the tempered-steel muscles that dainty, svelte ballerinas develop. But her would-be lover would never forget.

As Tania grabbed her clothes and ran into the hall, she cast a last glance at the elegant assassin, gagging from the kick and clutching his penis as blood ran down his leg.

About half a mile from the Dorchester, the traffic lurched to a standstill and Nat decided to run the rest of the way. He paid the driver and set out, past Grosvenor Gate, past the spot where he'd left the sack of garbage earlier in the day.

One foot in front of the other, Nat urged himself on. The stress of the day and his lack of food was wearing on him. His legs ached.

At the Mount Street Gate, Nat crossed Carriage Road and then dashed for his life across the parallel and more frenetic Park Lane. At the pale-brick structure of the Grosvenor House Hotel, he stopped for a moment to catch his breath; he didn't want to attract too much attention when he entered the Dorchester. His knapsack and casual clothes were bad enough without walking through as if he'd just run a race.

The Dorchester was just a block away. His heart had quieted from the exercise, but it rattled against his ribs with anticipation. Just a few more moments, Tania. I'm coming. He touched the swollen spot where el-Nouty's henchman had hit him, but felt no pain. He would later, he thought; if there *is* a later.

Nat shoved his hands into his pockets, and walked on.

"Leave the luggage," el-Nouty growled at Sarah as they dressed in the clothes they had worn to the hotel. "Just leave them here and let's get out! We can send for it later." The pain in his groin made him surlier, if that was possible, and the swollen area of his throat hurt when he spoke. He grabbed Sarah by the arm and jerked her up off the bed. Pain shot through him.

By Allah's arm of vengeance he'd kill her, kill her as slowly and as painfully as he could. She'd suffer for this. A woman! It was bad enough for the American to blacken his face, but a woman! He'd never rest until he could squeeze the life out of her with his own hands.

Shivering with terror, Tania felt she could read el-Nouty's thoughts. The courage of action had faded, and she was back in a nightmare. Out there was a monster who knew where she was. It was only a matter of time before he found her. There was no way she could escape. She started to cry.

"There, there, dear," the bejeweled matron said, sitting beside her on the bed. "I'm sure he won't find you here, will he, William?"

The older gentleman, attired in a tuxedo, murmured, no, they wouldn't allow any harm to come to her, and wouldn't she tell them her name, and wouldn't she like them to phone the front desk or the house security man—they were very discreet about this sort of thing. The couple interpreted her reluctance to call anyone as a desire to avoid unnecessary publicity or to cause a

334

scene in public—two very upper-class motives they understood well.

Tania leaned on the older woman's shoulder and cried.

The matron's husband paced back and forth in the room, glancing at his watch frequently.

"William, stop that pacing this instant—"

"But—"

"The Smith-Bagleys can just wait."

"But . . . but—"

"If you *must* carry on like an outboard motor, please remove yourself to the lounge and wait for us."

He stared at her and then sat down.

Oh God! Tania thought, wiping at her tears with the back of her hand, if they only *knew*. They thought it was a marital spat. If they only knew the man out there was a killer.

She remembered the hatred that burned in el-Nouty's eyes as she ran from the room. Upstairs, she had run holding her clothes in front of her as modestly as she could as she approached the older couple coming out of their room.

"Please help me!" she had cried, tears streaming down her beautiful face. "He's going to kill me, I swear he is, please help."

"William, open the door." The woman's resolute words untied part of the knot of fear that squirmed in Tania's stomach. "Well, don't just stand there gawking at the young woman. Open the door!"

El-Nouty ignored the temptation to search the adjoining floors of the hotel, for as he stepped out of room 404 and closed the door behind him, the pain in his groin sent swirling mists of agony across his eyes. A doctor, he thought, I'll have to get a doctor quick. "Come," he commanded, and Sarah followed him submissively to the elevator. When she was sure he was

335

not looking, she smiled. She hoped the ballerina was somewhere safe.

Nat gained the southwest corner of the Dorchester and turned left into the grand semi-circular drive, just in time to see el-Nouty's chauffeur standing at the open door of the limousine, about 30 yards away, waiting for the approaching Libyan. At el-Nouty's side walked a striking Arab woman.

What had they done with Tania?

Nat broke into a run, unslinging the knapsack from his back as he watched el-Nouty shove Sarah into the back of the limo.

Nat unzipped the knapsack and pulled out the Ingram. The back door of the limo closed.

Twenty yards away, fifteen. The limo's engine caught, revved. Nat raised the Ingram and zeroed in on the driver's open window as well as he could at a dead-run. The limo shot forward with a screech, and Nat watched an acne trail of bullet pocks graze the passenger window into cobwebs and then trail off the rear fender, taking the paint and leaving blobs of gray primer showing. An armored limo. It pulled around the corner of the Dorchester and sped down South Audley Street with Nat in pursuit.

He emptied the Ingram's clip into the rear of the car. But it disappeared around the right-hand turn at Grosvenor Square and Nat slowed to a stop. Behind him, he heard shouts and in the distance, police sirens. Cursing, he ducked into an alley just off Aldford Street. He turned his reversible windbreaker inside out—it was now navy instead of khaki—pulled out a plastic Harrods shopping bag with handles, unfolded it, and dropped his pack inside. He propped a white Newport sailing cap on his head to hide his hair and stepped back into pedestrian traffic, just as a police Rover with its lights flashing pulled into the Dorchester parking circle.

336

They'd be looking for a blond man in a khaki windbreaker carrying a red knapsack. He no longer fit that description, but he decided to take the rear entrance of the Dorchester just the same. The workers might remember him later, but he wouldn't be here later. For now, finding Tania was all that mattered.

Only el-Nouty and some other woman had left. That meant either that Tania was still here in the hotel somewhere, or that she'd been dropped off before el-Nouty arrived. The first was a possibility he had to explore. The second depressed him to think about, so he didn't.

Taking the exit stairs two by two, Nat quickly arrived at the third-floor landing, where he stopped. Drops of blood on the concrete lead down the stairs to the door. There were footprints—too large to be Tania's—formed where the someone had walked barefooted through some of the blood. Kneeling, Nat discovered the blood had not fully clotted yet. He stood up and surveyed the scene.

Then Nat followed the blood up the stairs to the fourth floor and walked into the hallway. It was empty. Four doors from the stairwell, at the end of a trail of blood splatters, he found number 404. He knocked. In the silent wait of the corridor, he heard the gentle murmur of the ventilating fan, the sound of a television set somewhere farther down the hall, and another police car siren somewhere outside. But he heard nothing move in the room. He knocked again, then pulled a lock pick out of his pack. In less than twenty seconds, the tumblers yielded to his touch.

Nat pushed the door open slowly, standing to the side as he did. Cautiously, Nat peered around the bottom edge of the open door and, seeing no one, grabbed the Harrods bag and stepped inside. When he flicked on the overhead light, the drying blood stains on the sheets glistened red in the still-wet spots, and a milk chocolate brown in those that had finished clotting. He

337

shut the door and stood there, taking in the scene. There was too little blood for a major wound.

Looking around, he tried to make sense of what he saw. On the floor lay a skirt. He picked it up: it had Tania's faint scent about it. Other clothes hung in the closet and puffed out of a Gucci suitcase. Nat examined those and found they were a different size from those Tania wore—the woman who accompanied el-Nouty to the limo.

Tania's skirt left on the floor, a trail of blood that traveled to the staircase and returned, blood on the bed, the woman's clothes which indicated they'd left in a hurry, the large bare footprints in the blood. The blood had to be el-Nouty's.

El-Nouty was bleeding, walked out—or *did* he walk? Nat opened the door and went down the hall to look at the blood again. It was splattered on the wall, and the drops were far apart until they reached the stairwell door. El-Nouty had run to the stairwell, slowed to open it, thus the blood pattern.

All right, Nat thought as he returned to the room and sat down in the armchair facing the bed and its blood-stained sheets. It's el-Nouty's blood. It begins in bed. He runs out of the room. Why would he run out? Because he was chasing someone. Whom would he chase? Tania.

Nat assumed that Tania wounded el-Nouty and ran; he ran after her but didn't find her, so returned to the room and then left. There was no indication in the room that any of Tania's other clothes were here, so she must have left, grabbing up most of her clothes but not the skirt. Therefore she must still be in the hotel!

Cheered by the prospect, Nat picked up his bag and strode out of the room. "Tania!" he yelled up and down the corridor. Getting no answer, he walked up the stairs.

At the fifth-floor landing, Nat stepped into the corridor and walked half its length and shouted, "Tania?

Tania?" he didn't care whom he disturbed. He'd do it on every floor if he had to.

"Tania! Are you here? Can you hear me?"

Inside room 511, Tania's head snapped up as she heard Nat's voice. She squeaked something incomprehensible, which the old woman took as fear.

"Don't worry, dear, we'll hide you. We won't let him harm a hair on your beautiful head."

"No," she said, happiness flooding through her. "He's not the one—

"Oh, Nat!" She freed herself from the woman's kind embrace and jumped up, oblivious that she wore no skirt. She fumbled with the deadbolt in her frantic haste. "Oh, Nat, Nat I'm here!" She shouted at the door as she finally unlocked the bolt.

Nat heard her voice and dropped the shopping bag, forgotten in the corridor as he rushed toward the sound.

Tania threw open the door just as Nat got there; he stumbled and fell into the room, barely regaining his balance before he hit the bed.

"Oh Nat!" she cried and they embraced. "Don't ever, ever let me go again."

"I won't, I won't I promise." he said as they kissed, blind to the tears that had begun to smear the old woman's mascara.

Chapter Twenty-Two

||||||||||||||||||||||||||||||||||||||||||||||||||||||||||||||||||||||||||||||||

Raindrops the size of marbles pelted against their bedroom window, driven by cold gusts of wind. The sound of the rain and the gentle shoosh of cars passing on the street outside lulled Tania into early-morning consciousness.

She lay there in the interstices of dreams and remembered the night—the way Nat had held her, the way he made love to her, *with* her . . . It was as if they had known each other a long time.

She rolled over to drape her arm over his shoulder and found instead his knees. "Uhumm," she grumbled. She wanted his shoulder to put her head on, as she had when she fell asleep.

"Good morning, lady," she heard first in Russian; then, in English, "I hope you slept well."

"Nat?" she said dreamily.

"The same."

"What time is it?"

"Time to get up." He was sitting up in bed, reading something. Papers were strewn all over the bed, and

341

the lamp-shade was tilted to give him more light. Outside, it was dark.

"What are you doing in the middle of the night?" she asked, propping herself up on her left elbow.

"It's not the middle of the night. It's nearly 8 A.M. Coffee?" He gestured toward the night table at his left. It held a tray with a silver urn and a variety of pastry.

Tania stretched and sat up. The smell of coffee made her mouth water. "Where did you get that?"

Nat grinned at her. "Room service. Even in London you can get a continental breakfast if you know where to stay."

"And where is that?" she asked, laughing. "Last night seems a long time ago."

"Brown's."

"Oh," she said noncommittally, still half-asleep.

Nat leaned over to kiss her. Tania returned the kiss long and deeply. After a few seconds, he pulled away.

"I've been reading these," he said, showing her a handful of papers. "They're some documents I took from el-Nouty's house yesterday when I came for you."

Tania took one and held it stiffly as she read it.

"I can't make out any of it," she said after a moment. "It's all scientific. What is a maser?"

"A maser is what scientists invented when they were trying to invent the laser."

"That's not much help." Her eyes on the tray of food, she slid out from under the sheets. "Go ahead. I'm suddenly famished. . . . Go on, I'm listening."

"It's used mainly in observatories with radio telescopes that study faint signals from outer space. A sort of amplifier."

"So why were those papers in el-Nouty's house?"

"Because a scientist named George Elliot Cosgrove-Ames working at the University of London found another use for the maser: he designed and built a prototype which cast intense focused beams of microwaves, just like a laser can shoot beams of light—

342

the principles are well known, it was just a matter of applying them to an appropriate device."

"Still, I don't understand," Tania said as she sat on the bed.

"That's how el-Nouty killed Pugachev."

"How? They said that Pugachev danced about in his box and then fell into the audience."

"Yes, but some of the papers reported more," Nat leaned over. "Some quoted witnesses as saying they smelled cooking bacon around his body. Don't you see? Somehow el-Nouty positioned a maser somewhere in the opera house and cooked Comrade Pugachev to death."

In a room looking out the back of 58 Prince's Gate in the Knightsbridge section of London, the rain beating against the windows brought no relaxation or joy to Mustafa Salem el-Nouty. His body throbbed with pain and anger.

"The bitch," he cursed as he sat up and looked out the window. He could see the embassy guards walking back and forth in the rain, their caps glistening in the afternoon light. Number 58 Prince's Gate was the Libyan cultural office, and Mustafa hated to be here. He rarely used their services, although the colonel had repeatedly offered them. But last night after putting Sarah on a plane for Benghazi, he had no strength left to look for another place to stay.

The jackal Worthington had killed his trusted servant and ransacked his home. He couldn't stay there tonight. Perhaps he'd never be able to go back. His carefully constructed cover, developed over more than six years of painstaking work, was shot.

And the bitch—he groaned as even the thought of her made the stitches in his penis throb—the bitch sent him to the hospital. There were thirty-seven large stitches on the outside and Allah only knew how many others inside, sewn in little tiny loops by surgeons using

343

microscopes. She'd damaged him in an Arab's most treasured spot. He would probably have pain there for the rest of his life.

He'd kill the bitch and the American. He'd devote his life to it, for without that revenge, he'd never again regain his honor.

El-Nouty sat up slowly, steeling his mind against the pain. He *must* get up. He had a job to do that night, a prior commitment to keep before he could be free to pursue Worthington and his Russian whore. The president of Iraq would die tonight.

Then, he thought, as he slowly slipped his legs over the side of the bed, straining to avoid screaming, he'd be free to hunt Worthington and the ballerina. He'd call in favors from nearly every intelligence agency in the world and he'd have agents from all of them hunting for Worthington. And where he found Worthington, he'd find the woman. He smiled as he thought of the slow death he'd inflict on each of them, death totally without dignity, mutilation of each as the other watched. Maybe he could even figure out a way to make them kill each other. The thought alleviated his pain, and he got out of bed.

"Why?" Tania asked, "Why are you doing this? Why does it matter anymore? You said last night that you could hide us, that we could go somewhere they'd never find us."

"Because," Nat said slowly, replacing the receiver back on the phone base.

"Because why?" Tania's voice was angry, frightened.

"Because there are so many of them out there, they'll never leave us alone. Because I care what happens to the world—I know that sounds stupid after . . . after all this. And believe it or not, because I love you."

The rain had slacked off. It was after ten o'clock,

and he and Tania had argued for the past hour. He didn't like it. Her points were too good.

"And there's another because."

"Which is?" Tania asked.

"Cosgrove-Ames."

"What about him?"

"He's dead," Nat said. "I just talked to his secretary. She said they found him brutally murdered, and his prototype maser stolen. I'm convinced it was el-Nouty, and I worry what'll happen with that maser in his hands."

"I still don't see how you can save the world," Tania said. "There are evil men out there with worse devices than that. Are you going to try and stop them all?"

"No," Nat said. "But if I stop this one, I'll feel better."

Sitting on the bed at Brown's Hotel, a silent understanding passed between them. "I understand . . . I think," Tania said. She got up from the foot of the bed, replaced her cup and saucer on the tray, returned to the bed and sat down by Nat.

She took his cup of now-cool coffee from him and set it on the bedside table. "I want to remember times like this," she said as she hugged him, putting her head on his chest. "We've had too little time to stop running. I think I understand now. But I don't like it at all."

Nat leaned over and they kissed.

The first few steps were the hardest, el-Nouty found, pacing angrily back and forth in his room. The local anesthetic the physician had just given him helped the physical pain, which was bad enough, but did little to ease his wounded pride.

Damn Worthington, damn the Russian bitch. He couldn't get them off his mind. He slammed his fist into the wall, which brought an orderly to inquire if everything was okay. This personal guest of the colonel's, reflected the orderly as he scurried back down the hall, was certainly a strange bird, with odd demands. But he *was* a friend of the colonel's. . . .

His head clearer now that the anesthetic had blocked the pain from his privates, el-Nouty dressed. He'd function well tonight, he convinced himself. He had to. It would be his only chance at the Iraqi president. He walked out of his room and descended to the basement armory of the embassy.

The armory was a supermarket of weapons: plastic explosive, AK-47 machine guns, RPG-7 rockets, and even a couple of SAM-7 Russian ground-to-air missiles. Closing the armory door behind him, el-Nouty marveled at this cache of deadly weapons cradled in the soil of civilized London. As antiterrorist units around the world had known for years, Qaddafi's support of every terrorist group from Black September to the IRA included millions of dollars of direct financing, and the use of Libyan embassies around the world to smuggle large quantities of weapons under diplomatic seal.

But el-Nouty was not after garden-variety methods of death. He'd leave those to people less skilled in the art than he. He walked across the cramped space and knelt at a combination-locked cabinet to which only he had the combination. As he twirled the dial, he remembered the maser and the international coverage given to Pugachev's death. He wondered when the right time would be to let the right people know how it had been done and by whom. He, Mustafa Salem el-Nouty, had given world leaders a new danger to worry about. It was like dropping the first atomic bomb; everybody would remember this one.

The cabinet clicked open. El-Nouty pulled out his perfect weapon for this job.

Other assassins perfected their skills using a certain type of rifle or bomb, and therefore assassination opportunties tended to be limited and could be guarded against. El-Nouty, on the other hand, liked to fit his weapon to the assassination, taking the unexpected—and therefore undefendable—action. The maser was his best. This one, though, would work nearly as well.

Switching on the fluorescent light over a gunsmith's workbench, el-Nouty placed the crossbow and box of bolts on the table. This one was a beautiful piece of work. As accurate and as powerful as a rifle at ranges of up to a hundred yards, it was a totally silent weapon. The cross bow was an invention of the medieval necessity to pierce the armor worn by knights. It worked well, firing metal-tipped bolts shaped like tiny rockets through the armor, and sometimes, if the distance was right, through the knight.

The crossbow was soon replaced by the gun, and fell into general disuse. But this crossbow had advantages no gun could have. It was so silent it could be fired from beneath the noses of the best of guards. And since it was more silent than the most silent of silenced weapons, no one would know where it was shot from. And instead of a standard bolt, this one would fire a powerful shrapnel grenade that would shred the Iraqi president if it landed within ten yards of him. He attached the special block-and-tackle that was necessary to pull back and cock the tempered-steel bow parts, and then held the rifle stock butt to his shoulder and squinted down the optical sight. He pulled the trigger. An almost silent, soul-satisfying twang whispered through the armory.

It was time to go. El-Nouty packed the crossbow, extra bolts, and the cocking mechanism into a canvas duffel bag. He had to be in position before the security men made their checks. The idea of killing the president while one of the guards stood only feet away made him feel as warm as having an ejaculation.

"Think, *think*," Nat urged. He and Tania sat at opposite ends of the sofa in their room, surrounded by the debris of half a day's room-service meals, el-Nouty's scattered papers, and Nat's notes. Later afternoon light filtered through the curtains.

"I've told you everything I overheard," Tania said wearily. "We've been going over this for hours now; I don't see what good it will do. How can we possibly hope to find him?"

"Look at what we already know—" Nat replied patiently. "From the paper, we know the president will return to the Iraqi embassy after the summit meeting, sometime tonight. We know the meeting is scheduled for Whitehall. The assassination has to take place at one or the other location, since he'll be nearly invulnerable in his armored limo going to and from the meeting. The only thing that could get him in the car would be a rocket launcher, like the hit men used with Anastasio Somoza, and that requires a coordinated attack. But, el-Nouty wouldn't work that way. He's a loner. And, since I doubt he can get inside Whitehall, I'd say the embassy would be the place." He looked over at Tania for a reaction, but her eyes were closed. The strain had started to show in her face, Nat reflected guiltily. The tiny lines seemed more intense, her features sharper, older-looking. Nat sighed. How much longer was this going to go on? Would there ever be a time when the two of them would just be together, alone, at peace?

For the past eight hours Nat had tried to second-guess el-Nouty's plan. He'd read every daily newspaper available, brought up to the room by a bellman. From the newspapers Nat had learned the approximate itinerary of the Iraqi president; for security reasons, exact routes between stops were never announced. Good security, Nat knew, meant changing routes unexpectedly, so that even an insider could never be sure of the route. Thus he had ruled out el-Nouty's attack in transit.

Nat had also learned from the newspapers that his

presence in London had been reported; an inside page of the *Times* carried an old passport photo of him. Fortunately, it no longer resembled his current appearance.

"I have a headache again," Tania announced and got up to get more aspirin.

While she was gone, Nat ran through the details one more time, thinking out loud.

"He can't get him in transit," Nat muttered. "He can't get him inside Whitehall. The Whitehall area is so sterile, he'd have to set up his maser in a government building, and I don't think even el-Nouty can pull that one off."

Nat stopped to chew on a dried-out sandwich still lying on the tray on the coffee table.

"No," he said, shoving the rest of the sandwich into his mouth and swallowing, "it has to be in the embassy itself, or near it. Maybe he's bought someone inside the embassy . . . no, el-Nouty wouldn't trust anyone. But if he did it himself, he'd never get out of the embassy alive. Besides, he has to do it without anyone finding out or Qaddafi will have hell to pay."

Tania resumed her seat at the end of the sofa, and sat facing Nat with her feet tucked underneath her.

Nat looked up. "How are you?" he asked.

"I'll be all right," she said uncertainly, "as long as . . ."

"As long as what?"

"As long as we come out of it."

"Yeah." They looked at each other glumly in silence. Nat reached out and touched her hand. "Tania . . . are you up to going over things one more time?"

She grimaced. "One more time. No more."

"Okay," Nat said, making a neat pile of his notes. "I'll just focus on a couple of things. First: you said you heard el-Nouty tell someone—you assume Hassan—that the kill would be made at night. Correct?"

349

Tania nodded. "Good. That for sure narrows it down to the embassy. I'd almost forgotten you said that." He added a scribbled notation to one of his papers. "What else? Wait— A lot of what you said earlier didn't make sense so I didn't write it down. Let's do it this last time and I'll take more careful notes. Okay?"

As Tania took a deep breath to begin, Nat glanced at his watch. At 5:30, the Iraqi president was scheduled to meet with the prime minister of England. The meeting could last any length of time. Nat knew that the longer it lasted, the better chance he had of guessing where el-Nouty would strike. If the meeting ended abruptly—as these sorts of things did if one side or the other got miffed—then they had no chance of stopping the Libyan and . . . Nat drew on the thought— a lot less chance of getting out of this one alive.

"Okay," Tania exhaled, speaking rapidly. "I heard them talking about the kill set for tonight. I couldn't hear everything, you know. I think el-Nouty was walking back and forth in the hall or something. His voice would fade sometimes. One of those times—he might have gone into Hassan's room—he said something about hanging the queen."

"Hold on," Nat stopped her. "Hanging the queen. Were those his words? Were they going to hang the assassination on the queen or something?"

Tania kneaded her forehead with one hand. "Wait, let me think . . . It's possible el-Nouty said the words close together but in different sentences." She thought for a minute. "No! I remember now, I didn't hear him say they were going to *hang* the queen, but it was something about a scaffold, and then something about the queen."

"Something something, something." Nat flung his notes on the table. "Damn!"

Then he saw the dismay on her face. "Oh, Tania, I don't blame *you*. After all, it was your skill in describing el-Nouty's house that brought us together.

350

It's not your fault. Anyway, it's probably not important."

Wet puddles reflected the clouds that scudded across the fading light of the London sky. The rain tapered off to a light mist and then stopped entirely, leaving the trees to shake themselves dry in the gentle breezes. The beauty of the night was lost on el-Nouty.

He hurried along with the duffel slung over his shoulder, a fresh injection of anesthetic numbing the pain in his groin. The Iraqi pig would be meeting with the prime minister any minute. Surveillance on the street in front of the embassy would be lax until the guards got the alert that the meeting had ended and the president was on his way. He had to be in position by then.

From the Libyan embassy, el-Nouty walked down Exhibition Road, turned west on Prince Consort Road, then went along the semicircular drive between the Royal College of Music and Royal Albert Hall. There was little to distinguish the old building he now approached from the rear—just another old apartment building being refurbished. The back of the unoccupied six-story structure projected above the two-story buildings behind it—mostly garages that opened onto a tidy little alley called Jay Mews. A tarp covering a structure on the top floor was all that indicated that any construction at all was going on.

On the other side of the building, facing Queen's Gate, scaffolding ran from the ground to the top as workmen painted the bricks and installed new window frames; glass had not yet been installed.

Looking around to make sure no one saw him, he slung the duffel strap over his shoulder and scaled the wall of one of the two-story buildings, using the outdoor drainpipes as footholds. Darkness had started to fall as he crept across the rain-slicked roof, down the other side of the short building, and across a barren courtyard between it and the apartment building.

Stealthily he climbed up the slotted-steel fire escape that ran along the back of the tall apartment building. He made no sound louder than the water still dripping from the roof and gurgling in the downspouts. At the fourth floor, el-Nouty peeked through a window and scanned the room for a sentry. There was none. Slowly, steadily he climbed through the window. El-Nouty knew from experience that the security men—all attached to Scotland Yard—would stake out the roof and the top, fifth, floor and that they'd station a man on every other floor of an unoccupied building. He had no doubt that men were stationed on the first and third floors. But it mattered little. His silent kill would leave them in confusion, allowing him plenty of time to escape.

Padding silently through the empty room, his wet footprints in the plaster dust shone in light cast by streetlamps. The door into the corridor creaked once as he opened it. El-Nouty froze. One minute, then two passed. The noise went unnoticed. He followed the corridor to the front of the building and admitted himself to an apartment that faced Queen's Gate. Entering a large room facing the Iraqi embassy, el-Nouty stayed away from the windows and close to the wall to avoid detection by observers he knew would be posted on the rooftops across the street.

But el-Nouty also knew that sentries are human and they relax when they feel they can. The Iraqi president was nowhere near. El-Nouty figured the sentries would be talking among themselves now, drinking coffee and smoking to pass the time. Smoking required concentration, and it constricted the blood vessels in the eye, making them less efficient. El-Nouty was glad most Scotland Yard men had the habit. It made them sloppy guards and easy targets.

Crouching, he could see the sidewalk in front of the

houses across the street. He moved to the extreme north corner of the living room, and from which he had an unobstructed view of the Iraqi embassy and its military consulate about forty yards south of him at an acute angle.

From the duffel bag el-Nouty pulled a heavy-duty camera tripod and extended its collapsible legs. He screwed on the stock of the crossbow and attached the funel-shaped starlight scope to the bow, carefully matching the precision-machined alignment marks.

The starlight scope turned the murk of what had now become night into a surrealistic green-and-yellow world. But it mattered little what color people were as long as he could see them in the dark. The streetlights were on now, shining brightly; looking through the eyepiece, el-Nouty adjusted the screen to avoid washing out the image. This accomplished, he centered the crosshairs on the entrance to the Iraqi embassy.

It looked fine; in fact, it would be almost too easy. Pulling out the cocking mechanism el-Nouty cranked the bow string into place, set the trigger and latched the safety. It took only three seconds. Then he loaded the deadly hybrid weapon. He reached into his bag and removed an aluminum box the size of a shoebox. Inside, nestled among the gray foam cushioning plastic, were three explosive grenade bolts.

The custom-machined grenade fitted into its slot on the crossbow. It resembled a straightened banana, fat at the girth and tapering to a blunt nose. Four fins at the tail would stabilize it in flight. El-Nouty smiled. It was a masterpiece, he admitted to himself, and it was all his brain-child. The last item he retrieved from the duffel was a radio receiver, tuned to intercept the security squad's frequency. Making one final adjustment on the crossbow's arm, he plugged the radio earphone in his ear and sat down to wait.

"Christ!" Nat exclaimed as he slammed the telephone receiver down; it rattled out of the cradle and dropped on the floor. "Where? If I only could find el-Nouty."

Tania picked up the telephone and replaced it in its cradle, and then looked up at Nat as he paced the room. Pity filled her eyes; she wished she could help him in his struggle.

His contacts at Mossad had just told him they were sorry, but no, they couldn't help him, not after that . . . unfortunate incident in Paris. His good friend with the Israeli intelligence service said the biggest favor he could do for Nat was not to report their conversation and good luck, but goodbye.

"Those damned idiots!" Nat cursed. Oh, word would get back . . . sooner or later. But to late to do anything. The Russians would have their foothold in the Persian gulf and instead of the ill-trained Arab fuckups who tend to shoot themselves in the foot, Israel will be looking at a couple of hundred thousand crack Soviet troops and tanks who'll be able to do anything they want. The pitiful state of the U.S. forces prevented them from doing anything even if the army got its way with the KGB-run National Security Adviser.

Shouldn't he and Tania get out of the country now before Rinehart and Kokh consolidated their power, before they set the armies in motion that had to mean either the capitulation of the United States and the abolition of Israel, or nuclear war?

Over and over again, Nat had run the information through his head, stared numbly at his notes. At some point, his mind drifted and he was startled to find himself thinking about sailing, and the good taste of a cold beer along with it. He had no idea how long he had been daydreaming when it hit him. Perhaps, he thought later, what he'd needed most was to take the pressure off his mind and let it idle a bit. It was so obvious! He stared out of the window at a tinker-toy construction of pipes and boards that ran its way up the face of a building down the street—a scaffold. A scaffold is used for hangings, but also for construction work. And the queen . . . well, it wasn't the queen at all but—the road on which the Iraqi embassy was located, Queen's Gate.

"I've got it!" Nat told a startled Tania. "I know where el-Nouty's going to be. You told me yourself. You gave me the answer and we had it all along." He explained, showed her the map of South Kensington and the road called Queen's Gate.

"It's a perfect ploy . . . come here." He motioned her to come to the window. "See," he pointed toward the construction work. "All of the boards and tarpaulins break the front of the building into a series of cubicles. There's no way to keep a complete watch on the whole building without stationing an army directly across the street with nothing to do but observe. Because look up at the upper floors . . . you can't see the windows for the scaffold walkways, and over at the end of the building, it's totally obscured. It's perfect. Perfect!"

Nat turned from the window. "Get dressed," he told her excitedly.

"What are we doing?"

"I don't know. But I'll figure out something by the time we get there." He zipped up the knapsack with the Ingram and the explosive devices to take it along.

"Let's go!" he said, and turned the knob of the door.

Before they could reach the elevator, a bulky man stepped out of an adjoining corridor.

"Hold it right there, Worthington." The man said in English laced with a Russian accent. Nat looked at the pistol the man held pointed at them as he walked forward out of the shadow of the corridor. Nat watched the gun sway slightly from side to side as the man approached them, and with the closest swing slightly away from him, Nat dropped to the floor, kicking up

355

with his feet as he did, catching the gun hand with his foot.

The silenced Makarott sneezed softly in the silent hallway. "Run, Tania," Nat yelled as he sprang to his feet and chop-blocked the gun hand as it started to swing around. "Back to the room!"

Before the gunman could bring the pistol to bear, Nat swiftly grabbed the gunhand with his left hand and the wrist with his right and snapped it viciously backward until the bones in the man's wrist cracked with an audible pop. His short scream ended when Nat slammed his fist into the assailant's throat. The man gurgled and slumped to the floor, writhing in pain.

"Very good, Mr. Worthington." Nat spun to face the familiar voice, and as he did, saw the KGB's Paris station chief, Popov, standing about five yards away, holding a silenced automatic machine pistol to Tania's head. "That was an excellent performance," Popov told a panting Nat Worthington.

"Popov," Nat said flatly.

"Well, I'm glad to see you can still talk," the Russian replied.

"How did you—"

"El-Nouty," Popov said without hesitation. "You don't think we'd let a filthy Arab out of our sight, now do you?"

Dully, Nat remembered the previous day. Popov's men could have picked him up at el-Nouty's house in Bayswater, or at the Dorchester. His heart sank and the dull blade of defeat combined with the sour taste left in his mouth by the excitement. "I see," Nat replied.

"Any more questions?" Nat shook his head. "All right, let's have the documents."

"I don't have them," Nat replied. Of course, they needed him to recover the documents. He and Tania would live long enough for that to happen.

"You don't have them?"

Nat smiled, "I just don't have them here." Popov looked at him suspiciously.

"If you don't have them here," the Russian said slowly, "where are they?"

"I'd be awfully dumb if I told you that, now wouldn't I?" Nat asked.

"You'd be awfully dumb if you didn't," Popov said, looking at Tania.

"How about a deal?" Nat offered.

"Such as?"

"You can figure it out," Nat began. "An exchange. Us for your documents. And I think I can help you with some other information that might make you a hero."

"Of course," Popov agreed. "Yes, I think we can do business."

Nat smiled broadly. "The documents are in the safe at the hotel I stayed in last night. It's over by Russell Square." Nat started for the stairs. "I presume you have a car outside?" Popov nodded and followed.

"Worthington?" Popov called after him. "Don't get any ideas." The Russian made a show of slinging his raincoat over his gun and forearm, which remained pointed at Tania. "You don't want her hurt."

They passed through the lobby without incident.

While Nat slid into the driver's seat of Popov's embassy Mercedes with Tania next to him and Popov by the door, the limo carrying the president of Iraq pulled away from the foreign office in Whitehall and headed northeast along Parliament Street toward Trafalgar Square. Several reports of possible violence had been telephoned to Scotland Yard in the past hours, and the president's entourage would take a circuitous path home to foil any such attempts.

Unfamiliar with the back streets of Mayfair, Nat pulled out of the parking space and headed for Piccadilly where he turned east, heading for Piccadilly Circus. But when he got to lower Regent Street, a police car barricaded the road and a bobby informed him that he'd have to detour.

"What's the blockade for?" Nat asked politely, dreading the answer.

"Some foreign dignitary . . . an Arab of some sort."

"The president of Iraq?" Nat asked.

"Yes, yes, I believe that's the bloke," the bobby replied. "Well, get on with you, please, we don't want to tie up traffic."

Nat said good night, wheeled the Mercedes through a U-turn and headed back toward Hyde Park Corner.

"What was that all about, Worthington?" Popov demanded angrily. "I don't like that kind of foolishness with police. Do you understand?"

"What did you think I was going to do?" Nat responded, matching Popov's anger. "Scream that I had a Russian spy holding me hostage? The cop'd be rolling in the street with laughter. You know, for a supposedly cool spy, you're awfully jumpy. Christ, I'm afraid you'd blow Tania's head off if I blew the horn. Calm down, Popov. Enjoy the ride. After all, we're going to make you a hero."

Popov glared at him, squirmed in his seat as he placed his back at the door so he could watch them better. He opened his mouth to speak, but thought better of it, and settled down to watch Nat drive.

Nat relaxed only slightly when he heard the safety on Popov's Burya-Graz click into the safety position. At least nothing would happen if they hit a bump.

Oncoming traffic flashed past Nat in a blaze of white and red, but he drove mechanically, trying, praying for a way out. Nat turned up New Bond Street and met another barricade at Oxford Circus. They were making a broad sweep from Whitehall that would take them in a long arc around what terrorists might consider their most likely route. The policeman told Nat it would be about ten minutes before they could cross.

El-Nouty was waiting out there. Waiting; and Nat could do nothing.

Nat drove on. They worked their way west, but were turned back three times before Nat announced that he was going back down Piccadilly since the motorcade must have passed there by now.

Traffic was jammed on side streets and people cursed silently all around Nat for this untimely traffic jam; it was 9:17, according to Nat's watch. Where would el-Nouty strike? Nat drove south now along Berkeley Street in Mayfair. The president would arrive in the next ten minutes or so.

Traffic started and stopped at the light on Piccadilly. They drew close to the intersection. A couple more light changes and they'd be through. Cars in front of him were accelerating through the yellow caution lights, and a couple narrowly missed collisions with cars on Piccadilly that had started too soon. The light changed and a few more cars passed. Popov glared at Nat and frequently glanced at his watch, but as yet he'd said nothing. Sweat trickled down Nat's scalp and ran down his face.

Finally the light changed again. Five or six minutes, and el-Nouty would strike. Nat accelerated, following closely on the rear bumper of the car in front of him. The light turned yellow and the car in front of him accelerated as the light turned red. Nat pressed the accelerator to the floor and prayed.

The police report filed by the owner of the battered Land Rover, reported that at approximately 9:20 P.M., a Mercedes sedan with three passengers shot out from a side street, identified as Berkeley Street, and ran a red light in front of him. The elderly Land Rover driver was shaken up—he told police—when his car smashed into the side of the Mercedes, seriously damaging the door on its passenger side.

With his back to the passenger door, Popov thought nothing amiss when Nat accelerated closely behind the

359

car in front of him. But the blinding collision behind him hammered the door handle into his right kidney and slammed the back of his head into the window. Dazed but still conscious, he flicked the safey off his gun and jerked the trigger.

But the impact propelled his shooting arm outward and the bullet blew out his side of the windshield.

"Grab the gun, Tania!" Nat shouted as he used his fist to clear away the remainder of the shattered windshield so he could see. Tania grabbed for the gun, but it slid out of Popov's grasp as he lost consciousness from the blood spilling from his punctured right kidney and the blow on the back of his head.

"Hang on, sweet one," Nat shouted as he weaved the crippled Mercedes through traffic and away from the shouts of horns and angry drivers. "We've got a helluva ride ahead of us!" It was now 9:21. Nat had five minutes to stop el-Nouty.

But he was going the wrong way, east on Piccadilly; the shortest route was west, but the accident scene blocked that avenue.

"Well, fuck it, so they'll give me another ticket," Nat said out loud into the air that streamed through the open windshield. Tania cried out in alarm as Nat wrenched the wheel to the right, careened over the curb onto the sidewalk, and barreled through the gate into Green Park.

Trees rushed by on either side as Nat quickly accelerated rapidly. The broad tarmacadam path was plenty wide enough for the sedan. Evening strollers leaped out of the way, or froze wide-eyed in their path as the Mercedes bore down on them. The left front tire thumped erratically, the result of the collision with the curb, as the speedometer passed seventy. Still, Nat pressed the accelerator. The trees whipped by with frightening speed and the wind rushing through the windshield tore at their hair and brought tears to Nat's eyes which blurred his view of the path.

Nat hazarded a glance at his watch, another minute had passed. 9:22. Where would el-Nouty be now? Where would the Iraqi president be now?

Nat eased off the accelerator as they approached Wellington Arch and raced off the curb and into traffic amid a cacaphony of angry horns. Disregarding the horns, Nat rounded the Arch and merged into traffic on Knightsbridge, paralleling Hyde Park. A mile, Nat thought. Maybe a bit more. 9:23.

The earpiece in el-Nouty's ear whispered and buzzed frantically now. The entourage was approaching. His heart beat stronger; it would be an easy kill.

Leaving nothing to chance, the Libyan slowly raised himself from his sitting position to check the aim of the crossbow. He stretched as he got up, and winced as he felt the tug of the stitches; the anesthetic was beginning to wear off. No matter, he thought; when the grenade explodes, they'll think the attack came from near the car. Absent any sound of a grenade launcher, they won't look in my direction. I'll just wait for the building's security people to clear and then I'm out the same way I came, and back to the embassy—to the doctor and another dose of anesthetic.

The green-and-yellow image in the starlight scope was perfect. A three-foot-long flexible cable release, like the kind photographers use, ran from the trigger guard of the cross bow to minimize vibration when it was time to fire.

The radio crackled with security personnel checking in. Just a couple of minutes, and it would be all over.

Lurching through traffic, cutting off drivers, and speeding up the wrong side of the street, Nat felt the bad wheel on the front start to go flat. The soft tire made maneuvering the car difficult, but not impossible. The air streaming over the hood and through the windshield cooled the nervous perspiration that had soaked

361

him since Popov's ambush, and the chill brought his thoughts to a fine edge. He would try to warn the security people who would undoubtedly be blocking the entrance to Queen's Gate. If they did not heed his warnings, he'd have to crash the barricade and ram the Iraqi president's car.

Up ahead, where Knightsbridge turned into Kensington Road, Nat saw a parade of cars with flashing lights turn out of what must have been Kensington Palace Gardens and then turn left.

Nat pressed the accelerator to the floor. The nearly flat tire threatened to wrench his hands off the steering wheel, but he hung on with a death grip. By Exhibition Road he ran a stop light and swerved to the right to narrowly miss a taxi which had just turned out. That set him into a head-on collision course with traffic stopped for the light. Tania crouched low on the front seat, wedged between Nat and Popov's lifeless body. Her face was white with fear.

Desperately, Nat tugged at the unresponding wheel as the car hurtled toward three sets of headlights. Finally, like a headstrong horse, the car yielded at the last split-second and they plunged between the traffic signal post and a Rolls Silver Shadow. Nat braced for the impact, but he succeeded only in shaving the door handle and a bit of paint off the Rolls, and putting the traffic signal out of commission for the night.

Nat wrestled the Mercedes back into his lane, ramming a low island in the road, which catapulted them into the air. The engine raced for an instant as the rear wheels left the ground.

The Mercedes groaned and rattled from its war wounds. For an instant Nat imagined what the Soviet embassy's reaction would be on finding their car in such a state, complete with an agent who was in even worse condition.

"Get in the back seat, Tania," Nat said, using his

brakes for the first time since they had left the park. "Quick, quick!" he shouted.

Tania climbed over Popov's body and scrambled into the back, where she sat huddled in silence. Dear God! she thought. Please let us be all right. As she lay down behind the seat she wondered if the dull, dead ache she felt now in her soul was what condemned people feel right before they die.

Approaching Queen's Gate, Nat flashed his headlights and leaned on the horn. A guard rushed across the barricade to meet him. As the Mercedes skidded to a halt, Popov's dead body slid from the front seat and wedged itself beneath the dash.

The guard, carrying an assault rifle and wearing a flak jacket, jogged toward the Mercedes, his face twisted with anger. Beyond him, Nat saw the lead vehicle in the president's motorcade pull to a stop in front of the Iraqi embassy.

Four stories up in an empty room, el-Nouty leaned to his right, trying to catch a glimpse of the motorcade, when he heard the screech of tires and a long, incessant auto horn. Briefly glancing at the corner, el-Nouty saw a battered Mercedes and its driver, a man in his middle thirties. A sentry approached the Mercedes.

El-Nouty had turned his attention back to the presidential motorcade when the face in the Mercedes registered in his mind. Worthington! The Libyan's insides went black with rage. He jumped up and swiveled the crossbow toward the auto. Yes, the scope confirmed it. It was Worthington.

"Listen," Nat told the guard breathlessly as the man approached the car. "There's a man trying to kill the president of Iraq! He's . . ." Nat scanned the street and spied a five-story building with its front shrouded with scaffolding. "He's in there." Nat pointed at the building.

363

The soldier held his rifle at the ready, suspicious of the auspicious arrival of this battered car and panicked man. He walked closer.

Can't let them see Popov, Nat thought and started to open the door and get out. The door wouldn't open; it was jammed from the sideswipe at the Rolls. The man drew closer.

El-Nouty started to swing the crossbow back to the embassy—he'd get the president first, then the American bastard—when he saw the Mercedes start to move. For a moment el-Nouty was unsure of which target to take.

"Look, if you don't believe me," Nat yelled, shifting the Mercedes into reverse, "have your men search the building."

"You'd best just stay right there, mate," the sentry said and raised his rifle.

Damn you to hell, Worthington, el-Nouty cursed under his breath. Nothing, nothing was more important to a Bedawi than erasing the blackening of his face. Men he could betray, but he couldn't appear before Allah in disgrace. He swiveled the crossbow back toward the Mercedes.

The assassin swiftly aimed the crossbow at the slowly moving car. Wondering briefly where the ballerina slut was, he squeezed the trigger release.

The Libyan himself barely heard the musical twang of the bow as it launched the grenade. But he paid it no attention, for even as it flew silently through the night air, he was already turning the weapon around for his second target. The president stepped out of his limo, and el-Nouty reached for another grenade bolt.

As the soldier approached the car, Nat stretched over for Popov's gun. To his left, he was horrified to see the president of Iraq get out of the limo. It was the last thing he saw for several minutes. As he leaned his head over the seat, a blinding white light turned the night into a supernova and lifted the Mercedes into the air.

Through the starlight scope, el-Nouty cursed at his missing hand. While he fumbled to reload in time, he watched helplessly as the security men, spooked by the exploding grenade at the end of the street, shoved the president back into the limo. He fired as the large auto sped off, but the grenade exploded impotently under the car's trunk, rocking it slightly and excavating a small hole in the street and several large ones in a nearby embassy clerk.

All around him he heard the frantic steps of men descending the staircase. In seconds the building would be empty and he'd be free to leave. At least, he thought, I got the American.

Chapter Twenty-Three

||||||||||||||||||||||||||||||||||||||||||||||||||||||||||||||||||||||||||||||||||||||||

Multicolored pin pricks of light burned through Nat's vision as the Mercedes lurched over on its side, turned over by the explosive grenade that had landed just beneath it. Saved, he thought; someone—el-Nouty?—missed by inches. Then, seconds later, he felt the concussion of another explosion, this one farther away.

"Tania!" he shouted, but his ears heard nothing; the sound of the concussion had deafened him. A salty taste filled his mouth. It was his own blood. Dizzy, he scrambled into the back seat and saw Tania speaking to him. In the dim shadows left by streetlights, he read her lips: she was all right.

Nat stood up and peered cautiously through the window of the overturned Mercedes. The sentry who had been talking to him lay face down in his own blood, bleeding from gaping wounds. The scene had become Fellini chaos. Well-wishers who had been waiting for the president ran and screamed in every direction, and mobbed the street.

"Come on, quick," Nat told Tania. Grabbing Popov's

gun, he pulled himself out of the car, and helped Tania out. His hearing was starting to return.

They ran with the mob, losing themselves in it. When they entered a shadow, they left the crowd and ducked into an alley next to the Royal Geographic Society.

It had to have been el-Nouty. The Libyan embassy was just a few hundred yards from here. Nat hoped the Bedawi assassin would go there.

They soon found themselves crossing the open space by the Victoria and Albert Museums. There was a flash of movement to their right; some thirty yards away the fleeting shadow of a man passed back into the darkness of the night.

"This way," Nat whispered. "Come on."

They sprinted down the narrow curving street, toward the shadow. When they reached the corner, they caught a better look at the figure—a tall man running awkwardly, as if injured.

"El-Nouty!" Nat shouted. The black-on-black shadow figure hesitated and then picked up his pace.

"It's him. Wait here." Nat pointed to a small entranceway with stone columns and then bolted after the Arab.

The corner approached, and with it the brighter lights of Exhibition Road. Then Nat heard the sound of footsteps behind him. He stopped and looked over his shoulder. Tania was following him. You headstrong fool, he thought for a split-second, and then poured on all his reserves as el-Nouty disappeared around the corner. The Libyan embassy was now no more than a hundred yards away.

Seconds later, Nat skidded around the corner and blinked at the bright street illumination. El-Nouty was nowhere in sight. Nat stopped, flicked the safety off Popov's gun, and walked more slowly now. A rustle in the bushes behind him gave a half second's warning; Nat whirled and ducked as el-Nouty's sharpened hook swiped through the air where his throat had just been. Taking advantage of Nat's loss of balance, el-Nouty kicked with his right leg and knocked Nat's weapon to the ground.

They stood there, warily facing each other, the sound of their breathing rasping against a backdrop of distant sirens. El-Nouty chopped; Nat parried and stepped back into position.

Where the hell is the traffic? Nat wondered as he and el-Nouty circled each other. Where are the guards who usually hang out behind the embassies? The explosions must have something to do with—Nat ducked as el-Nouty struck again, again missing his target. Trying to maneuver into position, Nat tripped on a crack in the sidewalk and went down heavily, knocking the wind out of him.

El-Nouty kicked, and Nat rolled out of the way and back to his feet, but not before the tall, powerful Libyan slammed a stinging left into Nat's right arm, rendering it momentarily useless. Nat spun out of the way as el-Nouty moved in. But el-Nouty was favoring his right side, moving stiffly.

Nat took advantage of a slight hesitation and kicked the Libyan squarely in the lump protruding from the right side of his groin. El-Nouty howled a scream that reverberated from the windows of the street. Tania grimaced. She'd heard that same scream the day before.

Nat scrambled for his gun, managing to grab it up with his left hand as el-Nouty ran, limping raggedly, across the street. Concentrating hard, Nat aimed and fired. The shots splattered off the pavement behind the Arab.

Nat pursued el-Nouty, hoping to close the gap until he could aim more accurately. Feeling was slowly returning to his right arm, but it swung almost like dead meat as he ran, throwing him off stride. Still, he closed the gap.

Then el-Nouty turned right up Prince's Gate, and the building blocked his line of fire. Nat rounded the corner, took his stance, and fired at el-Nouty's receding figure as the other man gained the Libyan embassy's white marble portico.

The slugs followed el-Nouty up the steps. As the clip ran out, Nat saw the tall man stumble and fall noisily. The front door opened, and a pair of hands pulled el-Nouty inside and slammed the door.

Nat turned and ran. Tania had followed him part of the way, and now he took her arm and pulled her quickly toward him and hugged her. "Now," he said, "we've got to get out of here."

"Is he dead?" Tania asked as they crossed the street toward Hyde Park.

"I don't know," Nat answered, putting an arm around her. "Does it matter?"

"Yes. Does it matter to you?"

Nat nodded, and then picked up the pace. "Yes," he said. "It matters . . . for the future. But let's get out of here. We can't forget that el-Nouty's just one of a hundred people who would like to kill us."

She looked up at him as they walked through the gate into Hyde Park. They stopped and kissed, longer this time. The sirens grew louder while they disappeared, arm in arm, into the thick darkness of the night.

Epilogue

||||||||||||||||||||||||||||||||||||||||||||||||||||||||||||||||||||||||||||||||

"Anything new in the papers?" Nat asked as he stamped his feet in the entrance hall to clear them of snow. "Not that three-week-old papers have a right to be called new any more." He unlaced his boots and left them in a tray inside kitchen door and stepped inside. The humid heat from the gas stove wrapped him in a comfortable warmth.

"Nothing more than before," Tania said offhand as she got up from the table to kiss him. "How'd it go today?"

"Not too bad," he said, sliding into a chair by the kitchen table and unzipping the down parka that made him look like the Michelin man. "I got the heat regulated so they won't freeze to death, and I fed them both. I think the calf isn't too far off." He said.

"Coffee?" Tania asked.

"Sure."

He listened as the hot coffee gurgled in his cup, the sound melding with the whistles of the wind as it stormed down off Mount Aspiring, and tugged at the shingles on the roof. "Sounds like we're going to get a bad one this time," he said matter of factly.

"Did you give them some extra feed in case the snow's bad enough to keep you from getting to the barn?" Tania asked. Nat nodded as he sipped the black coffee from a mug cupped between both hands.

How long had it been, though? Six . . . no, it was going on seven months now since they'd left London. The Mossad had been so grateful at the outcome of the incident on Queen's Gate, that they'd have done anything Nat asked even if he hadn't thrown in the blue-green laser blueprints.

What they had done was to arrange his passage out of England; faked his death and Tania's in a remote region of Zaire, sent them through minor—but effective plastic surgery in Tel Aviv, and then shipped them off to New Zealand with new identities and documents which would stand up under the closest scrutiny.

"Anything more on Rinehart?" Nat asked her. Since their arrival, Tania had become the expert in world affairs. Most of the shipments the helicopter brought in during the winter were her books and newspapers. Nat had been content to settle into the life of trying to run a farm. It took all his energy. A degree from Harvard was not the best preparation.

But the little farm had been a success. Located below the slopes of Mount Aspiring, a 3,035 foot peak in the Southern Alps of New Zealand between Queenstown and Haast, which is to say nowhere at all, the farm was in picturesque fiord country with a viking climate, thanks to its relative proximity to Antarctica.

It looked like the Swiss Alps—although the mountains were not so grand. But most of all, it was theirs, and theirs alone. And they were alone. As best as they could figure, their nearest neighbor was thirty-five miles away, and most of the land between them belonged to Tania and Nat.

"No," Tania answered. "Rinehart's still reported in

372

critical condition in the intensive care unit of Georgetown Medical Center."

Figures, Nat thought. Two months after Queen's Gate, both Kokh and Rinehart had heart attacks. The Soviets were experts at inducing them—it was how they eased people out of office. Rinehart and Kokh had had everything riding on the invasion. Now Russia was still stalled in Afghanistan, they were running out of oil, and the new U.S. President had all but invaded the Middle East with new bases: in Egypt, Saudi Arabia, Oman and even in Israel. But he'd never go back, Nat thought. He wanted to live, live without fear of being hunted by other men. And that dream would come true as long as he didn't lead those other men back here. And . . . he thought of el-Nouty. Was he dead? It didn't matter, Nat thought. He'd never find us here.

Tania shuffled through the pages of the *New York Times*, set it down and glanced at the headlines of the *Times* of London. "The politburo elected a president," Tania said with interest.

"Who?"

"I never heard of him," she said. In fact, the death of Pugachev and Kokh's rapid illness had left such a gap in the politburo that new names no one ever heard of were popping up constantly.

"Well," Nat said when an answer wasn't forthcoming. "Who's the new head?"

"Aleksandr Basov," Tania said. "He was head of the heavy industry commission."

"They must be in real trouble," Nat said. "But who cares?"

Tania looked at him. *She* cared, Nat knew. "Want to go back?" he asked.

"Not on your—our—lives," she said seriously. She was always serious about that.

Nat had been amazed how easily they'd adapted to the isolation. In fact, he thought, the worst part had been getting used to the seasonal reversal. It was April, and here that signalled the beginning of fall, and the first snowstorm of the year.

And there was a lack of entertainment: only the radio. He knew he could rig a dish antenna to pick up television signals from satellites, but he'd resisted. It was a pleasure not having the intrusion. Besides, it didn't matter any more if he got the world news three months late.

The evenings were filled with conversation with Tania, refreshing after a day's hard work. He'd begun a book, and he daydreamed often, thankful he could let his mind rove without wondering if there was a killer around the corner. And the pains from his scars had vanished as if by conquering his fears and doubts, he'd beaten the pain. In the back of his mind, he worried about the pain returning. And he liked to speculate: Where was el-Nouty? He just felt it in his bones that the man was alive. Was the Libyan hunting for him and Tania? And the Israelis? He'd bet they had already built the blue-green laser and were using it to pressure both the Americans and the Soviets.

And he wondered—less sadly as the months went by—about Rinehart and the trust he'd betrayed, of Nat's and that of millions of other Americans. And about Rinehart's people? Were they still working their dirty deals with the KGB?

"Fuck 'em all," Nat said as he got up to get another cup of coffee. Tania didn't reply. She was used to his verbal comments on his nonverbal thoughts. "Fuck 'em all. Nothing they can do will ever effect us again." He put his coffee cup down on the counter and walked over to Tania and kissed her.

"I love you," he said.

"I love you too."

#1 THE 1 THRILLER OF THE YEAR!

THE DELPHI BETRAYAL

LEWIS PERDUE

From the depths of a small, windowless room in the bowels of the White House...orchestrated by the finest minds and most powerful political forces of our time...spearheaded by a vast consortium of the world's richest multinational corporations—an awesome conspiracy that would create economic chaos and bring the entire universe to its knees.

A riveting international thriller in the tradition of Robert Ludlum and Ken Follett.

☐ 41-728-4 **THE DELPHI BETRAYAL** $2.95